AN UNSUITABLE ALLIANCE

DUTIFUL WIVES ~ BOOK 2

BEVERLEY OAKLEY

SANI PUBLISHING

ABOUT THE AUTHOR

Beverley Oakley has written more than thirty sweet to sizzling historical romances, laced with mystery and intrigue.

She also writes Africa-set aviation romantic suspense, with a dashing pilot hero (based on her husband) as B G Nettelton.

Visit Beverley's website - www.beverleyoakley.com - to sign up for her newsletter and receive a free Ebook.

CHAPTER 1

I t was not the name by which she knew him. Since inheriting the title, he'd won celebrity as a poet and become the darling of the gossip columnists. Adelaide's mother couldn't keep those snippets of the real world from her, though she tried.

James. Fifth Viscount Dewhurst. Adelaide closed her eyes against the afternoon sun and tried to block her last memory of him: desperate, pleading. Not the James she knew – the irrepressible charmer who knew no woman could resist him, least of all Adelaide.

Tristan must have misinterpreted her shocked silence for memory failure, for he squeezed her hand and repeated, 'Lord Dewhurst. I'm talking about my old friend, James.' Very gently he added, 'He and his wife were very good to you, if you remember.'

If you remember...

Her husband's reference to her previous life was almost more painful than the reference to James, though panic quickly succeeded shock at his next remark.

'James is coming to visit us? *Here?*' She gripped Tristan's arm tighter and concentrated on the path. One foot in front of the other, head down so she didn't stumble on the stones that bordered the hydrangeas from the neat gravel walkway. Tristan continued to talk in the measured, comforting tone he used when her equilibrium was unsettled. In the past he'd sought her reassurances that she was comfortable with his plans; that there was nothing he'd neglected to facilitate her comfort. Always Tristan put Adelaide's feelings first.

Not today.

Tristan was too excited at the prospect of seeing his boyhood friend to recognise her horror, assuming Adelaide would be delighted to play hostess since she'd foolishly voiced the desire just last week to entertain more often.

She remained silent as she walked at his side, contemplating her own strategy if this visit was a *fait accompli*. She just needed to know when, so she could prepare.

'At the end of the week!' She repeated Tristan's calmly delivered answer to her question in the tone Black Jack, the South American parrot she'd owned in Vienna, used to mimic the death throes of a man at the end of the gallows. A good thing her husband considered Adelaide an invalid, that he'd misconstrue the flare in her eyes, the gasp as she pressed against the pain in her side – her heart?

'Adelaide, you are discomposed. Perhaps I should not have invited James without consulting you, but I thought since...' Concern clouded his kind blue eyes as he trailed off.

'He was very good to me.' She whispered the old litany.

It's what Tristan liked to believe.

'He was. Shall we go back to the house?' He stooped to cup her face in his hands, as tender with her as if she were another of his rare hothouse blooms. As if she might wilt at the suggestion of anything beyond the ordinary, the mind-numbingly mundane.

And yet today she more than wilted as she stumbled on the smooth, carefully raked gravel path. Her heart was in danger of tearing in half. *James. Here, at Deer Park ...?*

She pushed away the fear, straightening of her own accord. Adelaide could be a good deal stronger than Tristan believed her. Than her mother painted her.

'So silly of me,' she murmured, smiling as she tucked her hand once more into the crook of her husband's arm, firming her step, indicating with a nod that they continue their usual morning walk. Minutely managed and predictable. Around the path that bordered the maze, over the little bridge and across the lawn, skirting the deer park beyond the iron gated border to the dower house where her mother would be waiting. Keeping up the pretence of recovery in response to his troubled gaze, she added, 'Really, I'm perfectly fine.'

How many times had she made similar reassurances? Of course, she hadn't been fine when Tristan had made her mistress of Deer Park three years before; a marriage offer she'd only accepted because she believed she'd be dead of grief within the twelvemonth. And if not dead, then at least free of her mother. Neither had happened.

'So James has left Milan.' She forced herself to say his name. It came out as a faint thread of sound.

James. He needed to stay far across sea and land if she were to have any peace in this life.

'James's father died three months ago so of course he must return from the Continent and take up his responsibilities at Dingley Hall.' Tristan stopped and put his hands on her shoulders to study her more closely. 'Darling, you're very pale. Perhaps we should call Dr Stanhope—'

'No!' She truncated the hysteria in her response, adding with commendable calm, 'Please, let us carry on.'

Tristan was clearly not convinced by her assurances, but

he returned to his commentary as they walked sedately through Deer Park's beautiful gardens. 'James's standing has changed with his father's death, and now that his book has become a sensation so have his fortunes. He'll be able to put to rights all that his father almost destroyed through his love of gaming.' He gave a half laugh. 'I'm told my old friend is nearly as famous as those fellows up in the Lakes. I daresay I should read *The Maid of Milan* before he arrives. Perhaps you'd enjoy it, Addy.'

The Maid of Milan. Dear God! An image of herself and James, naked limbs entwined upon a vast expanse of white linen tablecloth in the Villa Cosi after the guests had gone, seared her brain.

No, she was getting beyond herself. James had continued living in Milan with Hortense, the wife he despised. Of course there'd have been other women after Adelaide had been dragged, screaming, from James's arms. Adelaide could not be James's *Maid of Milan*. Not after the terrible finale to their affair. In three years Adelaide had heard nothing from him. Nothing, except that one terrible, terrible letter …

She nodded weakly, forcing herself back to the here and now, noticing Tristan's limp was more pronounced than usual. He hated his disability while embracing Adelaide's weakness. She clenched her gloved hands, breathing away the panic, about to quiz him on his health when he forestalled her, the normal resolve of his firm mouth sweetened by reminiscence. 'I haven't seen James since his marriage to Hortense, and they were newlyweds, just like Cassandra and I.'

Trying to calm her breathing, Adelaide studied her husband's strong, handsome profile for some sign that he was testing her. The fear of losing Tristan's high regard was always with her now. How much easier it had been when she'd felt only indifference towards her husband.

But he was not testing her. Of course not, for he believed Adelaide as pure as the driven snow and as delicate as a porcelain vase. Why would he question her when she'd been so very careful with the truth?

Her mother had seen to that.

But this was not about her, she could see that as she studied the uncharacteristic excitement that roiled in his eyes and the agitation with which he mused upon the past.

'The happy foursome,' Adelaide said, smiling weakly, recalling Tristan's tales of the convivial friendship shared by Tristan and James, and the neighbouring young women they'd married: Tristan's first wife, Cassandra, his childhood sweetheart, who'd died five years before he'd married Adelaide, and James's first wife, Hortense, Tristan's cousin, who'd died three years ago.

For so long Adelaide had felt no jealousy and little curiosity. Lord, she'd felt almost nothing for two years.

The fact that James and Tristan had been boyhood friends had seemed of no importance when she and her mother had arrived at Deer Park for what was to be a one- week stay while they looked for other lodgings. Hortense had asked the favour of her cousin Tristan on behalf of Adelaide's mother, Hortense's mentor. Naturally Hortense wanted Adelaide as far away as possible from James.

An irony, then, that Adelaide had married Tristan.

Hortense must have railed at that.

Now James was coming and Adelaide had no idea where his loyalties lay.

'Do you miss Cassandra? Am I anything like her?' Swallowing down her anxiety, she slanted an enquiring look up at him. He'd given her an avenue to change the subject.

Tristan raked his hand through his buff-coloured curls, fashionably long about the forehead, then touched her face. She'd not thought him as handsome as James until recently.

Now his chiselled features and air of studied calm appealed so much more to her than James's careless passion.

She was moved by the thickening of his voice. 'Cassandra has her place in my heart but, Addy, I swear, until I met you I knew nothing about *true* love.'

She could not meet his eye and hoped he'd not misinterpret her lack of response. In the early days of their marriage she'd not troubled to hide her disinclination for his attentions, but now, the truth was she was too choked by emotion to know what to say.

She continued to walk, silent, gaze focused on the middle distance, her expression betraying nothing. Nothing of the terror that James's visit would disrupt the peace she'd finally found in her life, or of her admiration of her husband's fine character, his handsome looks, his noble aspirations which to her surprise, she who was so shallow, was beginning to share. Tristan had presence though he was not one to worry about his appearance beyond ensuring he was in line with fashionable trends. He was comfortable in his own skin, decided in his views.

Determined as to what was morally correct.

'You seem preoccupied, Addy. I shouldn't have mentioned your departure from ...'

He trailed off and Adelaide waited, her breath coming faster, fear replaced inexplicably by the desire for him to touch upon the *forbidden topic*. Suddenly she felt infused with the strength to tackle the lie her mother had concocted to explain Adelaide's invalidism. Perhaps it was the danger posed by James's return that crystallised how much more Tristan deserved than Adelaide had given him.

Not that she could ever give Tristan the whole truth – his love for her would never survive that – but she could at least begin to assert herself. Transcend the lie her mother had fabricated that had made Adelaide acceptable to Tristan but which had shackled her to a life of deception.

Tristan left his sentence unfinished as he slid his gaze across to her mother coming across the bridge to fetch her.

She fought to steady her voice. 'I'm glad you're so happy, Tristan.'

'More than I can say. James and Hortense were very fond of you, you know. But you seem anxious.' The concern in his blue eyes was genuine. How many women were lucky enough to be granted a second chance with a man of Tristan's calibre? Not only had he fallen immediately in love with her, but his fortune – which her mother had found so irresistible – came with an unexpected title, to boot. Not that any of that had mattered back when Adelaide had wished for death rather than marriage.

'A slight megrim, that's all.' The familiar lie tripped off her tongue. She couldn't remember when she'd last had a megrim. Her robust body continued to betray her, yet the pretence of delicacy was ingrained in her.

The flare of disappointment that clouded Tristan's expression reminded her it was Thursday.

'I'm sure it'll be quite gone by this evening,' she reassured him, bolstering her own smile while a flare of feeling shot through her heart. Thursdays were becoming increasingly fraught as she welcomed her husband to her bedchamber for the weekly duty visit. In the first two years of marriage that's all it had been; a duty as she lay in the dark and let Tristan do to her what a husband did. She didn't even think of James, for it would have sent her mad – more than she already was – to dwell on what she'd lost, knowing she'd never feel love and passion in her life again.

She slid another glance up at Tristan and was surprised at the little thrill she felt to see how affected he was by her reassurance she would be well enough for him to bed her. He wanted her, desired her.

And she was starting to desire him. No, she very definitely *did* desire him.

Maybe she could respond tonight, though he must never discover her true nature. Her lustful impulses would only shock him and threaten the security for which she had traded everything else in her life. It was what her mother always said, though lately Adelaide's feelings for her husband were giving her the strength to challenge her mother's strictures. Surely Tristan could only be delighted at some spark of feeling from her?

His soft kiss upon her brow made her restless for more. Tonight she would meet Tristan halfway. Her mother need never know.

'Mrs Henley is here,' he whispered, giving her shoulders a squeeze and smiling a guileless smile, for how could he know how dangerously he had tilted her world by his invitation to a man she'd hoped never to see again? 'And I must go, for I have an important paper to write.'

She gripped his wrist to stay him. 'You take your responsibilities as the local MP seriously, Tristan.' She bit her lip, wanting to convey something of what she felt when the avenues open to her were so limited. 'I'm proud of you.' He looked taken aback, as well he might. Adelaide had not voiced such a sentiment, before. She tilted her head, warming to her theme: her admiration for her worthy husband. 'You are firm in your convictions, even when all is lost.'

Smiling at his unconcealed amazement, she released his wrist as she prepared to meet her mother. She wanted Tristan to know how much she'd started to take an interest in the events which concerned him, that she was preoccupied with more than her own supposed frailty. She might wait a little, though, to tell him she'd begun reading, with growing interest, the pamphlets and news-sheets he discarded. Her mother declared he'd dislike Adelaide voicing strong opinions, and as much as Adelaide believed her mother mistaken, she had the power to make Adelaide's life a misery if she overreached herself. 'Public sentiment is that the ringleaders of this latest agitation should hang. You preach moderation, Tristan, and *I* would not hang them, either, but those in power are not so tolerant – are they?'

'Tolerant?' He seemed to look at her with new interest. 'I should like to hear your views, Addy. The law believes that men who seek to overturn society should definitely hang.'

Adelaide smiled her first easy smile. 'I care more than you think. And I follow the issues that interest you, though we might not have discussed politics together in the past. I'm starting to feel well again, Tristan.' A glorious inner glow was permeating her body, infusing her with the strength and moral courage needed to acknowledge the past sufficiently to embrace the future. With Tristan by her side, it could be a good one. She took his hand, bringing it to her lips. 'You ask me my views on what is tolerant? I believe nothing is black and white. When people are judged they should be judged on what is in their hearts as much as by their deeds, for sometimes unintended consequences are the result of passionate beliefs ... or naiveté.' She brought it back to the men standing trial though she could have been speaking of herself. 'Men who cannot feed their families have no choice but to resort to desperate acts.'

There was appraisal in his eyes, and she wished her mother wasn't nearly upon them. 'Perhaps this evening you might expand your views, Addy. I'm a lucky man to have married a woman whose intelligence matches her beauty.'

❄

'JAMES, now Lord Dewhurst, is coming to stay.' Adelaide made sure she said the words while Tristan was still within hearing in as conversational a manner as possible.

Adelaide was almost amused by the horror on her mother's face and the stricken look she sent Tristan's retreating back before she gripped Adelaide's arm and hurried her down the path towards the dower house, well out of earshot. They passed the lychgate and continued down the drive. This was no conversation to be had presiding over the seed cake that awaited them in her little drawing room where they could be overheard by servants.

'Dear God, Adelaide, *when?*'

The only time Adelaide's *ennui* was unfeigned in her mother's presence was in response to her mother's overreaction. She shrugged as if the matter were of little concern to her. 'The end of the week, I think Tristan said.'

'Then you must go away! You can't possibly remain at Deer Park with James in the same house.'

Adelaide slanted her mother a pitying look. 'Where do you suggest I go, Mama?' she asked. 'Since we returned to England you have cut off all contact with any of the old society we once enjoyed.'

'Don't blame me for what I did only for your sake, Adelaide! Stop this!' Mrs Henley breathed deeply though she did not slow her rapid footsteps. '*Why* is James coming here?' Her voice held suspicion. 'Tristan knows nothing—?' 'It's perfectly reasonable James should visit and just surprising he didn't do so earlier. Tristan and James were boyhood friends, Mama, and James was married to Hortense. You accepted her assistance—'

'I didn't expect you'd marry Tristan or that James would visit.'

Adelaide lengthened her stride, enjoying the less languid pace and a rather grim satisfaction at her mother's disordered wits.

Her mother rounded on her. 'You cannot see James. Dear God, you must know that.'

If it wasn't so tragic Adelaide might have laughed at the way her mother's mouth twitched, her anger at being unable to engineer this matter to her satisfaction so obvious.

She was not surprised by the older woman's solution to the conundrum, though she was quick to knock it on the head. 'No, Mama. I refuse to succumb to some dreadful malady the entire time he is here. Besides, what does it matter? What happened is well in the past. I have had no contact with James in more than three years and I am Tristan's loving, loyal wife and'—she gave emphasis to the words —'always will be.'

'It's not *just* you I worry about,' her mother muttered.

They were at the gates. The driveway swung out from manicured gardens through the deer park, a dense two miles of ancient elms, to the main road which connected London with three hours of indifferent travelling. James had written from London. James was three hours away.

Very firmly, hoping desperately it was true, she told her mother, 'I am no longer the easily led child James knew.'

Mrs Henley clenched her jaw and closed her eyes as she paused on the path leading to the front door of the dower house she occupied by the entrance to the park. She appeared not to have heard. 'James swore to me after the—' She cut short the words, opening her eyes to her daughter's trained upon her.

After the child, Adelaide wanted to scream. The child that had died within the hour of being born and which she'd never held. But the topic was forbidden. Her mother had taken control of her life and shut her out of it the moment

11

she'd learned the ghastly truth. Her mother – and James – had organised everything.

Now James was acting alone and her mother was not happy.

'I'm sure he meant every word of his reassurances, Mama,' Adelaide muttered, forcing a faster pace towards the dower house. 'But for whatever reason, and it may even be that Tristan insisted upon it, James is coming to stay. Now please, stop making more of this than need be. I'm a happily married woman and I shall do my husband the courtesy of ensuring that the hospitality his friend enjoys reflects well on a man of Tristan's station. That is *all* that is required of me.'

ADELAIDE OFTEN WONDERED if the Thursday night ritual had been different when Tristan was married to Cassandra.

Perhaps it hadn't been a ritual. Probably not. And certainly not as restrained.

Who had set the agenda?

Tristan certainly had in this marriage between them. The intimate dinner for two, the most elaborate meal of the week unless there were visitors, which was rare though Adelaide enjoyed entertaining. Tristan feared it exhausted her strength.

After the servants cleared the dishes from the grand mahogany dinner table Adelaide would rise gracefully, leaving Tristan to his port and coffee. On every night but Thursday she would retire to the drawing room where Tristan would join her and they'd read companionably or discuss the safest of the local and newsworthy events while she sewed or embroidered until bedtime whereupon a kiss at the top of the stairs before they repaired to their respective apartments signalled the end of the day.

On Thursdays, however, Adelaide would make her way to her apartments to prepare herself.

Milly would brush out her rippling titian tresses – red-gold, thick and the envy of her former schoolmates – while Adelaide would support her chin on her clasped hands, enjoying the sensation as she gazed unseeingly at the looking glass, ears attuned to the sound of Tristan's soft tread. Sometimes he was so stealthy he'd catch her by surprise and mistake her intake of breath for something else. Fear.

Tonight, the routine was no different.

'Thank you, Milly, that'll be all.' He was here, and Adelaide was holding out her hand so he could raise her and settle her comfortably on the *chaise longue* by the fire.

'Are you sure you're warm enough? Perhaps another cushion?'

'Mama's been telling you I'm in a decline again.' She dressed up the censorious tone with a smile. 'I don't know what I need do to convince you I'm as robust as'—she grinned—'that opera dancer who's taken London by storm. What's her name? Kitty Carew.'

'Kitty who?'

She was surprised at his apparent shock.

'Miss Carew, famous for her titian tresses and singing voice, has been enjoying enormous popularity since taking the lead role in Covent Garden. I'm not a complete recluse. Surely you've heard of her?'

Adelaide hoped Tristan's frown didn't stem from any particular disdain for actresses in general, since that's what she'd always wanted to be.

And was, she reflected painfully.

But he smiled as he drew her across his lap so her head was tucked up beneath his chin. 'Miss Carew may be famed for her lovely hair but it cannot compare with yours, Addy.' Adelaide stretched languidly and snuggled against him as he went on, 'Your mother says I must take extra care for you're still not fully recovered from your chest inflammation—'

She put her finger to his lips, surprised at the shiver it sent through her. 'It's all in Mama's imagination. I'm perfectly well.' Reaching up, she tried to wind her arms about his neck and draw down his head level with hers, but he would not give her access. Resigned, she relaxed back in his gentle embrace, acknowledging the brush of his lips upon her temple with a sigh. Her husband set the standard between them. Affectionate, controlled. Unvarying.

'I thought the chive and butter sauce that accompanied tonight's fillet of sole was particularly good.' Idly he stroked the length of her arm as they both gazed into the dancing flames.

'Has James confirmed his arrival?' There. She'd said it. Much better to get it out in the open. No doubt her Mama had said something to Tristan about her health in the hopes of at least postponing the impending visit. 'I'll need to prepare.'

'Sunday. Three days. I've assured your mother you are keen to do more entertaining. Are you sure you're not cold, my love?'

Was it not obvious that the accumulated longing created by his ministrations had to have an outlet somewhere? Her body was his – he might as well use it as a source of pleasure. Adelaide suppressed her sigh of frustration. Her ideas on pleasure and duty were so at odds with those of her mother's, yet, until recently, she'd never considered testing her mother's convictions. She shivered again, this time from both fear and anticipation.

'Three days,' she repeated, enjoying the warmth of his embrace while she could. In the meantime she played the game, spouting banalities when all she wanted to do was slip between the sheets and feel her husband's warm, naked body against hers. God knew, she could act a charade with the best of them.

Not that she intended putting her acting skills to the test when James arrived. It would be far too dangerous. James was a wild card and Adelaide was not about to jeopardise the new-found love she'd discovered with her husband. She'd thought on it all day and realised that her mother was right: she couldn't see James.

Tristan held her tighter. 'Not too short notice? You will be marvellous, as always.'

It was time. Rising, he scooped her up and carried her to the bed, closing the door between her private sitting room to block out the light before blowing out the candle beside her bed as he pulled back the covers and laid her on the soft feather mattress.

She trembled as the cool air brushed her exposed skin, and she closed her eyes in pleasurable anticipation of soon feeling the warmth and weight of her husband bearing down on it.

Extraordinary how the delicate balance had shifted in the past few months. In the early days of her marriage, when Adelaide had railed against a marriage of her mother's choosing, she'd always appreciated that Tristan was kind and considerate. It was not so hard when she could switch her mind off and inhabit a different plane while Tristan made love to her.

But how much harder it was now, to suppress the desire that consumed her in the marital bed.

Now, as Tristan moved above her, Adelaide had to tense against succumbing to the waves of pleasure which started at the tips of her toes and radiated upwards. If she released the demons of lust prowling the depths of her depraved soul, would Tristan start questioning every fiction her mother had invented? Would the opening of her heart have unintended consequences and instead sound the death knell to the tiny shoots of happiness just beginning to sprout within her heart? Despite the courage she'd built up earlier to reveal something of what she felt inside, Adelaide knew she couldn't take the risk. She must continue to let Tristan, who regarded these weekly nocturnal episodes as a necessary function in their quest for a longed-for child, simply do

what a husband did.

She tensed as he finished and squeezed her eyes shut, conscious of the tear that slid down her cheek, hating herself for not being everything Tristan believed of her, wishing at least that her soul was not black with sin.

Usually, Tristan's swift withdrawal was followed by a kiss on the cheek, signalling he was ready to leave her to her rest. Tonight, to her surprise, he continued to cradle her in his arms. His warm breath tickled her ear. 'Do you mind if I stay a little longer?'

'Of course I don't.' How wonderful if he stayed the entire night. Dangerous, though. She'd wrap her legs around him, bury his head in her breasts and use every feminine wile she'd ever learned to coax him into gasping raptures. If her mother's prophecies came true, she'd be risking the comfortable security of both of them if Adelaide gave any hint of the shocking, wanton creature that lurked dangerously close to the brittle exterior she cultivated with increasing difficulty.

'Tristan?'

He raised himself on one elbow to regard her through the gloom and Adelaide summoned her courage to ask what had been occupying her mind for some weeks now. It was only when she opened her mouth to speak that she realised how greatly her hopes rested on his answer. 'If we are unable to have a child, could we perhaps adopt a baby girl from the Foundling Home?'

He touched her cheek and the regret in his tone sent her hopes plunging. 'I know how you long for a child, my darling, but it would be unfair to the child.'

'We'd be giving it a home when it might otherwise die in the workhouse, Tristan. How is that unfair?'

'Likely as not the infant would have been born in sin, Addy.' He looked regretful. 'We live in a judgemental society. Imagine the life of pain to which we would subject this child? While this little girl would grow up with every material comfort, she would never be fully accepted by society.' His arms tightened around her. 'You're trembling, Addy. I know you're disappointed and I'm sorry.'

With difficulty, Addy forced out the words? 'Do *you* think like this, Tristan?'

There was a degree of comfort to be gained by his robust response. 'You know I don't. I'm just reminding you that society is harsh.'

She wished he hadn't elaborated when he went on, 'Reputations count for everything. Imagine if we had then a natural born child who became her sister? How would our adopted daughter feel when she was overlooked by suitors who courted our natural daughter, purely because,' he hesitated, 'of her tainted birth. Such things count for too much, I agree. But a woman's reputation – and that naturally includes the assurance she was born in wedlock – is the most precious of commodities.'

For ten minutes her husband held her, silent and unmoving. Then, with a soft kiss on the cheek, Tristan slipped silently out of her bed and, doubtless imagining she was enjoying sweet and dreamless slumbers, left her to return to his own apartments.

※

THE FOLLOWING afternoon Tristan was working in his study when he was disturbed by a series of determined raps upon his door. With a frown, he put down his pen. He knew it wasn't Adelaide's knock. The two parlourmaids, Daisy and Kate, rapped softly and discreetly. Mrs Henley's was loud and demanding. Adelaide's, he thought, smiling, was just perfect.

Perfect, just like her.

Not for the first time he wondered how she could have a mother like Mrs Henley. In response to his call, the woman sailed into his study like a Spanish galleon waging war on a British sloop. He had no defences.

Except the veneer of good manners. He'd cultivated inscrutability to a fine art, for he was a man of politics now. He needed to be inscrutable in Mrs Henley's presence if he wasn't to give offence. The truth was, he couldn't stand the woman. Yet she was the unofficial weather vane in his marriage to her daughter, regulating the delicate balance that prevented Adelaide from slipping into the emotional abyss.

As a result, Tristan had had to exorcise a little part of himself. The exuberant passion he'd enjoyed with Cassandra must forever kept in check so as to regulate the calm relations required to prevent Adelaide from potentially fatal overexcitement. The fiery impulses of his youth must never override good judgment, though Mrs Henley was a perpetual challenge, as was her ally, Dr Stanhope.

At least Mrs Henley got to the point as she took the seat closest to the fire and began without preamble. 'Do you consider it wise to have James Treloar here as your guest?'

Nevertheless, the question surprised him. Crossing one leg over the other, he corrected her. 'You mean Lord Dewhurst? I thought James and Hortense were your friends?'

His smile was pleasant but he was seething. Was there no satisfying this woman? She stipulated the strict rules he must adhere to in his dealings with his wife to prevent her spiralling into nervous hysteria. Did she intend to vet his choice of friends, too?

'Hortense was an angel.' Mrs Henley dropped her eyes. 'Sadly, she is now *with* the angels, but I have no doubt she, too, would agree that it is far too great a risk to Adelaide's delicate sensibilities to be confronted by James, such a potent reminder of a terrible episode in her life.'

He was at a loss. 'Really, Mrs Henley, I had thought that an old acquaintance – one to whom you both owe a great debt – would be a positive influence. The horrors Adelaide endured occurred *subsequent* to her departure from James and Hortense, do not forget. I worry about Adelaide's lack of society. I cannot shield her from everything simply because it *may* bring back memories and besides, her health is improving. She needs stimulation.'

Mrs Henley made no attempt to match his patient tone. The pause before she spoke was the calm before the storm. Lord, he might wish Adelaide was more responsive during their mild discussions, but he quickly sent up a prayer of thanks she'd not inherited her mother's obduracy in protesting the single-minded rightness of her views. Mind you, he reflected, lately Adelaide seemed a good deal more responsive in all matters. He was prevented dwelling on this by Mrs Henley's anger.

'At the time that you made clear to me your interest in Adelaide you swore you would abide by my recommendations to ensure her continued mental and physical well-being should she consent to be your wife.' Mrs Henley leant forward. Her hard green eyes, so different from Adelaide's calm, endlessly patient moss-green ones, flashed fire.

He felt trapped. 'The fact I have not seen James in ten

years does not alter the fact that he is one of my dearest friends. Your fears are groundless, Mrs Henley. James and his wife were good friends to you and Adelaide in Vienna and Milan. I do not believe Adelaide's health will be compromised by his visit and unless Adelaide herself requests it, I stand by my invitation.'

'Do not even bring up the subject again with Adelaide!' With an effort to rein in his irritation – vast – he managed, crisply, 'I have lived intimately with your daughter for three years, madam, and I believe that not once have I acted in a manner either thoughtless or counter to her delicate constitution.' He rose, not caring it was the height of rudeness; he was inflamed by her insinuation that he fell short in his duty of care towards his wife.

'If you will not write and put it to Lord Dewhurst's conscience as to whether his visit is advisable, Lord Leeson, then I will!' Furiously, Mrs Henley rose, whisking aside her skirts as she brushed past him. 'Adelaide has made great gains during the past year. Bringing back the past has the potential to make a complete invalid of her.'

'I WANTED to elicit your feelings on the matter, sweetheart.' Tristan's unexpected presence in Adelaide's private sitting room was a welcome surprise. He looked so troubled her heart melted as she put down her pen, then hardened as he went on, 'Your mother maintains even mentioning the subject is detrimental to your health, but Addy'—he bent down and put his hands on her shoulders, and the light friction of his thumbs stroking the bare skin of her collarbones created wicked sensations, though she managed not to squirm—'for once I want to be the judge of what's good for you.'

'A liberating idea.' The irony of her tone made him raise his eyebrows as she went on with what she knew was uncharacteristic briskness. 'Mama believes she is the only qualified judge when it comes to my wellbeing. I wish you would allow me more say as to what is good for me. But you ask whether I object to James's visit? No, Tristan. James is your friend and any friend of yours is welcome here.'

Her heart warmed at his thankful smile yet she had no intention of being at Deer Park when James came. She'd already sent a letter to her Great-Aunt Gwendolyn with details of their hasty visit. Adelaide knew her mother and her aunt did not get along, and in fact Adelaide hadn't seen Aunt Gwendolyn since she'd been a young girl, so it gave her a little thrill to set a plan in motion that her mother would dislike but could hardly object to. Adelaide didn't care where she went, so long as she went somewhere.

James and Tristan could catch up on the past ten years without her.

Glancing at the piece she'd written for anonymous inclusion in the local newspaper, she conjured up her most disarming smile for the man whose patience and moral fibre were the antithesis of everything she'd known prior to coming to Deer Park. Tristan was her future. Maybe she should tell him about the article she'd been asked to pen after her first opinion piece had been so well received, though she'd never tell him about the poems she'd written, back in her wild days. Nevertheless, she wanted him to know she was so much more than he thought her.

When she returned from visiting her aunt, Adelaide intended being the architect of her dealings with her husband. Her mother could no longer dictate everything that happened between them, though she would try. No, Mrs Henley would find that Adelaide was not as biddable as she had been the past three years. For when Adelaide was in love, she was not biddable at all.

As for James – well, she and James had nothing to say to one another.

CHAPTER 2

Adelaide was not surprised by her mother's visit the next afternoon, for they'd not taken their customary morning walk together. She received her in her private sitting room, rang for tea and cake and faced her coolly across the richly carpeted expanse of flooring.

'Before you say a word, Mama,' she began, not moving from her semi recumbent position on the chaise longue. 'James's visit will go ahead, but I have decided the best course is to tell Tristan after tea that you have received a letter requiring us to pay an urgent visit to Great-Aunt Gwendolyn.' It felt good to do the dictating, even if she was only arranging a course of action that would be more preferable to her mother than remaining at Deer Park.

'I'm glad to hear it.' Mrs Henley took a seat and poured herself tea. 'Let us say no more on the subject. The past is the past and you must concentrate on proving yourself a good wife to Tristan.' Her gaze took in the plush surroundings, the many small touches Tristan had overseen in the hopes it might please Adelaide. He'd commissioned her favourite artist to paint the friezes and the room was often filled with flowers he'd ordered.

'I am a good wife.' Adelaide focused on her tea and hoped her mother would drop the subject. 'I always will be.'

'A good wife provides her husband with an heir, if not a nursery—'

'I do my duty, mother,' Adelaide ground out, trying to block out thoughts of what it cost her these days to ensure she appeared *only* to regard it as a duty.

'As long as you strike the right note. Yes, you must do your duty, Adelaide, but you must never hint that it is an act you welcome.' The gimlet stare made her shudder.

'You've told me all this, mother, and I swear, Tristan would never guess—'

'He'd better not, Adelaide, because you've been given a chance most women in your situation have not.' Again, her mother's eyes roamed over the room's lavish appointments. 'Tristan loves you, Adelaide, but he will not – I promise you – if he so much as suspects the weakness and depravity of your character. You have ever been a disappointment but you are all I have and I am all you can rely upon. I thought I'd trained you well, that you were of my mould. How wrong I was.'

Familiar though this litany was, Adelaide once again fought the familiar shame which threatened to swamp her, though she refused to succumb to the tears that had sprung so readily to her eyes in the early days. In the six months after she and James had been parted and she'd been dragged from Milan back to Vienna before being shipped off to England, all she'd done was cry.

'Nevertheless, as your mother, I have stood by you and I remain determined that you shall not squander this God-given opportunity. Tristan's continued high regard is our only salvation, Adelaide. Remember that. Now come.'

Draining her tea cup, Mrs Henley rose. 'Let us go downstairs and find Tristan so we can tell him of Aunt Gwendolyn's letter.'

With helpless frustration Adelaide trailed after her mother. Once again Mrs Henley had taken charge and Adelaide's ideas of independence seemed suddenly hopeless, for if they ran counter to her mother's she knew who held the power.

At the moment, it wasn't Adelaide.

Mrs Henley knocked and they entered as Tristan rose, his forced smile replaced by one of pleasure when he saw Adelaide. He took a step forward, extending his hand for hers, the flare in his eyes as intense as the day she consented to be his wife, and Adelaide felt an unexpected jolt somewhere in the region of her heart, her determination bolstered to bridge the distance between them, despite the oppressive presence of her mother, always a footfall away, it seemed.

'Tristan, I—'

She stopped, pulling back as a warm, fragrant breeze stirred the papers on his desk.

The French doors from the garden had been thrown open, and the heavy tread of Hessian boots upon the wooden floor pulled their attention towards the muslin curtains which swirled in eddies, silhouetting the shape of a man: a slender man of middle height – the only ordinary thing about him – dressed in a black cutaway coat and buff breeches, who materialised before them like a young demigod, smouldering with an enthusiasm he did nothing to inhibit, for good manners were always in abeyance to the passion that ruled James's life.

'Tristan!' Tossing his low-crowned beaver upon the ottoman, James strode forward, arms outstretched, his voice taut with emotion.

Nearly four years, it had been, and from first impressions

it was as if nothing had changed. Inky curls framed his delicately boned face and his eyes were like coals burning the fire within. No, nothing had changed, she could see, for James was still like a coiled spring, eager for love, eager for life, as ready to give as he was to take ... without discernment.

Adelaide froze with nowhere to go, tense with premonition while shafts of sensation, painful and familiar, tore through her.

Could this really be happening? Unwillingly, her gaze was fixed upon James's profile, dusted with dark stubble, tapering up to angular cheekbones delineated with the slivers of sideburns sported by the fashionable Corinthians of the day.

In four years he could not be so unchanged whereas she ...

She touched her face, her heart. She was a mere husk of what she'd once been. Tristan knew nothing of the passions that burned within her when her heart was engaged – and she didn't know if he ever would, for suddenly she felt reduced to nothingness by the force of James's personality. She'd been his equal once – a woman of fire and vitality – and she'd loved him with a savagery that her mother claimed bordered on insanity. She'd been a child, thrust into adulthood by this charismatic older man. *Married* older man. But as she looked between the two men before her it was Tristan who made her heart beat faster, as much with longing as with fear of what he would think of her if he knew the truth.

James had not seen her; his gaze was focused entirely upon Tristan, and Adelaide was astonished to see a different kind of pleasure light up Tristan's face as he was enveloped in a welcoming embrace far less restrained than her husband was used to.

'Forgive me for coming early, Tristan. I had no choice.'

'Nonsense!' The pleasure in Tristan's voice was like

nothing Adelaide had ever heard. 'You'd be welcome if you climbed through the window at midnight for no better reason than you needed a bed. So good to see you, James. It's been far too long.'

She had been forgotten. Rooted to the spot, Adelaide could only wait to be acknowledged, but how she wished she could melt between the floorboards.

'When I heard the weather promised rain and worse, tomorrow, I admit I acted with my usual thoughtless spontaneity—'

James halted, perhaps alerted by movement just beyond his peripheral vision, and Adelaide caught her breath, wiping her sweating palms nervously on her skirts as he turned his head to peer into the gloomy recesses beyond Tristan's shoulder.

And as her glance met the familiar grey eyes of the one skeleton in her closet she'd hoped to consign forever to her past life, she felt the thread of happiness she'd found with Tristan pull dangerously taut.

The fire in James's eyes changed to something different at the sight of her; the telling stillness of his normally active, healthy body indicated that his senses were fully alerted, and Adelaide felt hers answer with a sensation akin to having her steady world ripped from beneath her feet, leaving her to spiral into orbit until her mother's icy tones ripped through the silence.

'James, I trust you are well.'

'Mrs Henley. I did not see you.'

They greeted each other with courtesy, concealing the brittle antipathy Adelaide knew lay just below the surface.

Her mother took a step as if to shield Adelaide from his dangerous influence. 'We had not expected to see you, either, James, as you were due tomorrow and Adelaide and I'—she feigned regret—'have been summoned on an urgent visit to my aunt in Lincolnshire.'

Tristan swung round to face Adelaide who dropped her gaze and blushed. Leave the explanation to her mother. How she wished she could be incinerated to a little pile of ashes with no more of the worries and charades that were her lot. Instead, she had to remain stoic, keep steady, pull taut that wayward trembling mouth and corroborate her mother's lie.

'So lovely to see you again, James. Unfortunately, yes, Mama and I must leave immediately.'

Tristan looked more disappointed than she'd expected. 'Why, Addy, this is news to me. An indisposition of your aunt's? Surely you must have heard it after the post arrived?'

Yes, decidedly havey-cavey, Adelaide silently agreed.

Leave answering that one to dear Mama. It was all too much effort to abide by the falsely polite drawing room responses required of her in this hothouse hellhole.

Her mother drew herself up. 'Adelaide was very fond of her great-aunt. The news was a shock and my poor girl is feeling not quite the thing and needs to lie down. Don't you, my dear?'

Tristan bowed to Mrs Henley as Adelaide took a step to follow her. 'My commiserations, ma'am. I shall arrange for an early departure tomorrow morning once I learn more of your requirements, for of course you cannot leave today. No doubt you'd be so kind as to pass onto Mabel the changed circumstances?' He nodded, smiling.

It was a clear dismissal. Even her mother had to concede that by the time they were packed it would be too late to begin their journey today and that accommodation for James had to be made.

Adelaide darted a glance at James, wishing *she'd* volunteered to arrange an extra setting at dinner and have the Blue

Room made up for their unexpected visitor. Then she could hasten away now, leaving them *all* behind.

Instead she was trapped, unable to dwell on what she read in James's face for the brief second her gaze unwittingly returned there.

No, she couldn't do this. She turned to follow her mother out of the room.

'Addy, don't fret over your great-aunt alone in your chamber. I'm sure James wants to see you before you leave tomorrow.'

Oh God, Tristan. Don't do this to me. With a firm, sweet smile plastered onto her face, Adelaide turned back. *Another megrim perhaps? Yes, she was always having them, wasn't she? It was plausible.*

'James and Hortense were so good to you and your mother—'

'Indeed they were, but I'm very tired, Tristan.'

'As is James, for he has ridden all the way from London, but a glass of Madeira will help you both sleep better.' Tristan was already at her side, taking her elbow and leading her into the drawing room, settling her on the small two-seater Egyptian sofa in front of the fire. With his back to them as he organised the drinks, Adelaide followed his movements. No, she had nothing to say to James. Instead, she nodded and smiled as Tristan carried on a cheerful monologue amidst the chinking of glass and pouring of the wine.

'Lord, I can't tell you how good it was to see you striding into my study when I was expecting you tomorrow, James. Ten years it's been, d'you know that?'

'Too long.' James looked at Adelaide and the corners of his mouth turned up in that secretive smile he used only for her. 'Forgive me for bursting in on you like that.'

'You haven't changed, James.' Bearing drinks, Tristan

could not contain his boyish pleasure. 'Impulsive as ever. Hortense thought she could change that, poor girl.'

The silence was suddenly heavy as Tristan took a seat beside Adelaide. She wanted to curl right into him for protection. Instead, she took a small sip of her wine as James replied, 'Hortense wanted to change the world and together with Mrs Henley, she tried. I admired their dedication to the unfortunates who swelled the prison ranks, but I felt I was better placed trying to effect change through words rather than actions.' He took a measured sip of his wine. 'Unfortunately, Hortense didn't see it that way.'

Tristan shook his head. 'Poor Hortense. How greatly disappointment changed her when once she'd been so lively.'

James's laugh rang hollow. 'We made our peace in the end.'

Adelaide squeezed shut her eyes. How bitterly Hortense had hated her and with good reason. Yet Hortense had never loved James as Adelaide had.

'What a joy she finally was blessed with the child she longed for,' said Tristan, trying to lighten the tone. 'Charlotte is her name, isn't it? But what a tragedy Hortense did not live long enough to see her child grow up. I take it that is why you've been looking for a wife.'

Adelaide stifled her gasp as she moved closer to her husband. Right now she needed the security of Tristan's proximity but, as ever, he seemed to be just out of reach.

She curled her toes inside her dainty green slippers, aware of James's furtive glance as she stared at her hands. Oh God, what could she possibly contribute to this conversation?

James stretched out his legs as he'd only do amongst friends. 'As I mentioned in my letter, Miss Wells and I were due to wed at the end of the month but the death of her father has delayed our nuptials until late August.'

'Tell me more about this Miss Wells.' Tristan rose to refresh their wine, leaving Adelaide feeling exposed and vulnerable.

'She grew up in London, like Adelaide'—he nodded in her direction—'and also joined her parents in Vienna when she'd finished her schooling. Miss Wells and I met last year at a military ball after I'd returned to Vienna. Her father was a friend of General Waldenberg.'

An interesting similarity, Adelaide thought vaguely, wondering if Miss Wells's mother were as violently opposed to gaiety as Adelaide's, until James said, 'Alas, her mother died several years ago, leaving Miss Wells entirely alone but for an elderly aunt who has reluctantly agreed to chaperone Beatrice on occasion during the season.'

Adelaide murmured, 'How sad,' but Tristan was more robust. 'We look forward to meeting Miss Wells, don't we, Adelaide? How is she bearing up under this double loss?'

Adelaide darted a look when James did not immediately answer. She was surprised by his response.

'Miss Wells,' said James, not looking at Adelaide, 'is one of the most remarkably self-contained young women I've met.'

'Then she is your ideal mate,' Tristan laughed. 'The sobriety to your passion, the cool head to your unfettered brilliance.'

Adelaide focused her gaze on him, admiring the mobility of his face. He knew what response was required in any situation. Well, if one discounted the intimacies of their marriage. He wasn't like James who somehow was equally passionate in joy and love as he was in sorrow.

'So, other than you and an apparently indifferent aunt,' Tristan went on, 'Miss Wells has no one.'

Adelaide pushed aside the emotion that threatened to engulf her. For so long she'd felt she had no one and didn't wish it upon anyone. She touched her husband's shoulder as she rose, then turned to their guest.

'Congratulations, James. I'm so sorry I'll not see you again as Mama is determined on an early start.'

'And as Mrs Henley is as determined as her former protégée, Hortense, you'll be seeing dust as dawn breaks.' Tristan's response was humourless. 'Unless the weather moves in tonight.'

'I don't think that'd be enough to stop her,' James murmured.

Adelaide heard the men laugh and raise their voices in more lively conversation as she took the stairs to her bedchamber. She paused at the top. Not for the first time she wanted to turn right and head for Tristan's apartments so that he would find her curled into his feather mattress when he retired later.

Instead she turned left, heading for her own. Alone. Alone and sick from the churning in her stomach.

Almost dragging her feet she turned the door knob and entered her room where Milly had stoked up the fire and was waiting for her with a welcoming smile and a warm mug of sweetened milk.

'I've a nice supper for you, miss, as the master said you were feeling poorly after your walk and I wondered if you'd be up to dining with them this evening.' She pushed Adelaide down onto her dressing table stool and began to rub her shoulders. 'Poor miss, the megrim's bad tonight? Master were that worried about you. Said he hoped you'd see out a whole evening but was afraid your nerves weren't up to it—'

'He *said* that?' When had this been? No doubt after her mother had cornered him, she thought bitterly.

Milly began removing Adelaide's hair pins. 'Well, it were Mrs Henley what used the words "nerves", miss. 'Parrently Mrs Henley told the master all about how delicate you was feelin' and said to make sure you drank your warm milk.' The girl continued to chatter while Adelaide stared stonily into the looking glass and wondered if Tristan, himself, had ever used the word 'nerves' to describe her moods. The idea filled her with horror. Hortense had succumbed to nerves and Adelaide had witnessed her slow and steady decline. In three years her mother's protégée was transformed from an intense, passionate and clever young woman into quite simply a bag of nerves. One who jumped at the slightest movement and saw conspiracies everywhere.

'And now you must eat your supper, miss, and have a good night's rest, for Mrs Henley has organised for a dawn start and is quite determined the weather will hold until you're well on your way.'

Grimly, Adelaide echoed James's earlier sentiment. 'If Mama is determined upon it then I'm quite sure the weather will hold.' Moving to the fire, she settled herself in front of her supper tray. But she had no appetite and after several mouthfuls pushed away her plate and put her hands to her head.

'You really are poorly, miss,' sighed Milly as she turned back the bed covers and picked up Adelaide's night rail which had been warming over the fire screen. 'The master will fret. How about a nice drink of your milk, then? Or just one more bite?'

'One more bite for the master,' Adelaide agreed, obediently taking a mouthful. 'I'd do anything to please the master, don't you know?' Exhaling on a sigh, she turned so Milly could undress her, adding under her breath, 'if he'd only ask.'

CHAPTER 3

Tristan tended to the hissing fire, filled with pleasure at the unexpected company of his oldest and dearest friend, and aware that James was watching him with quiet intensity.

A log at the back of the fireplace exploded in a shower of coals, breaking the silence.

'Come on, James, out with it. You're here to ask me something, aren't you?' Tristan resumed his seat, reaching for his drink and raking back his hair, tinged now with silver at the temples, wondering how his friend could appear so unchanged.

James was hunched forward, eyes fixed on him in that familiar, intense fashion he remembered so well. Not a grey hair peppered his dark locks nor did a suggestion of life's disappointments dim his striking poetic looks. James would be into his thirties but he looked as bright and eager as he had when he'd been the university student and daydreaming poet Tristan remembered.

James shrugged. 'A small matter, in its way, though Lord knows, I hate being a supplicant—'

Tristan cut him off with a mixture of embarrassment and irritation. 'I am forever in your debt and nothing you ask me is too much. Besides'—he knew he was in danger of sounding mawkish but said it anyway—'I owe you twofold. First for saving my life when you leapt into the river and fished me out all those years ago, and then when you sent me Adelaide. I only wish I knew how to repay you.' He cleared his throat, embarrassed that he was allowing his finer feelings to get the better of him. 'Not only do I owe you my life, but because of you I enjoy the most profound happiness with the best wife a man could have.'

James looked at him oddly as he relaxed back in his seat. 'I'm glad Adelaide suits you. You and Cassandra were so happy.'

Tristan felt a curious surge of feeling he was not prepared to identify, for it cut too deep. Adelaide was very different from Cassandra who'd taken life by the reins and galloped hell for leather, laughing all the way to her shocking, untimely death while negotiating a hazardous jump just beyond the park.

'Adelaide is my greatest joy. She never ceases to surprise me.'

At James's look of enquiry, he went on. 'When she first arrived here with her mother she barely said a word and kept to her room. It was after a week that I witnessed her transformation. Some young relatives of mine came to visit and they wanted to put on a play. Adelaide took it upon herself to organise the production.'

'Adelaide would have made a fine actress had society permitted it.' James grinned. 'Don't mention to Mrs Henley I said that, though.'

'I avoid discourse with Mrs Henley on anything but the most crucial matters.'

The men laughed and Tristan was reminded of the

companionable times of long ago that they'd spent in each other's company. He felt a warm inner glow as he went on with his story. 'The children adored Addy. She organised costumes and stage sets and played multiple parts, herself. I had not given a thought to remarrying until then. Nor, I believe, had Adelaide considered marriage.'

He swirled the liquid in the bottom of his glass, aware that James had noticed his abrupt change of mood. Should he go on? James had always been able to prize more information from him than Tristan intended to divulge so it would perhaps be preferable to reveal it on Tristan's terms.

James was his best friend and best friends invited – and were owed – confidences, weren't they?

'How did you change Adelaide's mind if you believed she was not inclined towards marriage?' James looked genuinely interested so Tristan plunged in, acknowledging that the combination of brandy and a willing listener was a potent one.

'When Adelaide and her mother arrived here after leaving you on the Continent it was clear that Adelaide was in a highly emotional state. I assumed she was fragile by nature.' He chose his words carefully, for he would not betray Adelaide, and yet James was the least censorious of anyone he knew. 'It was only later,' he said, slowly, 'that I learned from Mrs Henley the true cause of Adelaide's suffering.'

Tristan was gratified by the flare in James's eye which surely signified his friend had grown fond of Adelaide during the three years they'd known one another abroad.

He wondered if he should go on. Had he any right to divulge the demons that plagued his wife? Yet Adelaide's welfare was his greatest responsibility and James would want to know why she was so changed from the apparently lively young woman he and Hortense had known.

His hesitation lasted but a second. James might be impulsive and, on occasion, fiery, but he was fiercely loyal. And Tristan had his full attention.

'Adelaide is scarred by the events which occurred just after she left you—'

'*After*—?'

Tristan raised his hand. 'Please, say nothing to Adelaide for she may see it as a betrayal of her secret.' He hesitated before pressing on. 'I would trust you with my life, James, and it would ease my burden to share it with you.'

James inclined his head, warily.

'Learning the truth precipitated my marriage proposal though no doubt Adelaide might have supposed the opposite would be a more expected reaction. Of course, had she not been so damaged, she could have had her pick of any eligible blade around town. I was a third son at the time, merely renting Deer Park, though I'd lived here all my life. I expected William, when he inherited, would choose to remain at Marlow Hall and sell this place to cover his debts. Since he died I've salvaged most of what our great- grandfather built up, but that's another story—'

'Indeed, it is,' James interrupted him, his intense look willing him to get to the point.

Tristan stared into his glass. It was not in his nature to deviate like this, but he felt he was venturing into dangerous territory. Territory representing the charred no man's land that separated Adelaide and himself, preventing them from finding what he believed each craved.

'I'd not have presumed Adelaide would consider a dry old widower ten years older and with a leg that plays up in bad weather, were it not for her aversion towards men—'

'Aversion towards men?'

'Adelaide is a damaged soul. She'd think anyone good enough if he had only a kind word and placed no demands upon her.'

James's expression was a study to behold. Haltingly, he said, 'You do not speak of the Adelaide I know. When I knew her, she was bold and beautiful, brimming with life and wit —' He looked as if he ought not ask the question that resonated silently between them.

For three years Tristan had told no one of the great raging sorrow that ate away at him every time he gazed upon his wife.

God, he'd never wanted anyone so much and yet, he'd made a promise.

He might despise Mrs Henley, but she'd lived with Adelaide her whole life. She knew, more than anyone, the effects of the torments her daughter had lived through and she'd sworn Tristan to uphold her strictures regarding the delicacy with which he must treat Adelaide.

Yes, restraining himself in the bedroom was the greatest burden Tristan had ever carried, and it was a relief to share the reasons for it with his dearest friend. Someone whose integrity he could trust.

Cupping his cut-glass snifter between his hands, he began his difficult story, aware by the intensity of James's expression that he shared Tristan's concern for Adelaide. 'Their party ran into a ragtag bunch of French deserters. The women were held hostage overnight.' He glanced at the door. Lowering his voice, he went on, 'Adelaide was violated. A brutal, unspeakable act. Her mother says she didn't speak for weeks'—he hesitated, adding in a rush— 'and begged me never to do anything that might remind her of what she suffered.'

He felt drained but relieved, too. James would not judge Adelaide harshly for what had been beyond her control. Unlike some.

He rose to attend the fire, more to occupy himself than because it needed it.

Turning at James's uncharacteristic silence, noting his grey pallor, Tristan began to feel uncomfortable. Had he misjudged his friend? He cleared his throat as he replaced the poker and returned to his seat. 'Perhaps I ought to have said nothing, but knowing that Hortense and you were so thick with the Henleys just prior to this I felt I ought to explain why Adelaide might be different from the way you remembered. I didn't want you probing for answers.'

It was rare to see James struggle with words. His fingers clenched and unclenched and his mouth was drawn tight. 'My God, Tristan,' he muttered. 'I'm glad you told me. Christ!' He raked a hand through his hair. 'I cannot believe this.' Finally, he promised, 'I swear I shall never mention anything to Adelaide that could possibly remind her.'

At the sideboard, Tristan refilled their glasses, pausing to place a grateful hand briefly upon James's shoulder before forcing a change of subject. 'Tell me, James, when do we meet the lucky bride?'

With an obvious effort, James answered, 'We are just three hours away and you are welcome at a moment's notice. I'll be spending the season in London squiring Beatrice to various events while Dingley Hall is renovated.' He seemed to have trouble focusing on his train of thought. Staring into the flames, he muttered, 'I was horrified by the disrepair last visit and despaired that Papa's fondness for the gaming table would leave sufficient for the necessary building work, but my book has done enormously well. I didn't expect that.'

'I'm glad your literary ambitions have been realised, James, but you have been to England in the past without seeing me? That was too bad of you.'

James looked abashed. 'You and Adelaide were newly married.' As he stared now at his shoes, his expression grim, Tristan felt a great welling-up of affection for the fact his friend cared so much about Tristan and Adelaide's wellbeing.

James exhaled on a sigh. 'I didn't want to intrude on your newfound happiness.'

An ironic statement. Tristan tapped the side of his glass, thinking. 'Perhaps you'd have been the tonic she needed.' Mention of his wedding night recalled his wife's haunted eyes, her patent terror. Not a pleasant memory and very different from the wedding night he'd shared with Cassandra, as eager as he to consummate their union, both of them brimming with curiosity and hearts full of love.

He tried to sound more cheerful as he went on, 'Adelaide's demons are not such regular visitors these past few months. She's made great progress. Now she takes an interest in the things around her. Increasingly, I see glimpses of the vibrant creature she must have been.' He thought back to their recent surprising exchange when she'd shown a knowledge of his political interests and a desire to learn more. The signs that she was on the road to recovery were indeed hopeful. He eased himself back into his seat, contemplating the amber liquid that had been the ruin of James's father and Tristan's half-brothers, crystalising the idea which had been forming in his head for months. James was watching him with that look he'd once found so unsettling before they'd forged such a deep friendship as young lads, so different in character, forced together by proximity and the lack of alternative playmates.

Tristan met his gaze. 'I've said nothing of this to the ladies, James, nor hinted at it, but I am determined to see Adelaide realise her potential. I believe a change of air will do her no end of good and that a season in London would be a marvellous distraction.' He studied James's face for signs that he understood where this was leading. 'The truth is, I'd like to take up my seat in the House of Lords and I think Adelaide is up to a few months away from Deer Park. I'd never have considered it, otherwise.'

'Good for you, Tristan.'

James's response, however, was more lacklustre than Tristan had expected and in the lengthening silence he expanded on his theme. 'At last Adelaide is emerging from her shell. She's more lively... more responsive, and she's interested in matters which concern me. Politics, even! I think with nurturing she could become a fine political hostess.' He could go on with his eulogies but could not expect James to listen.

James nodded.

'Six months ago such a proposition would have been unthinkable but it is my hope Adelaide can be coaxed into going to London, for I fear there will be resistance. She is afraid. However, were it on the basis of being needed rather than for pleasure alone, I think it could be done.'

James's earlier talk had unleashed an idea that he was eager to put before his friend. Now Tristan gathered his thoughts before launching into his proposition, surprised at how much he wanted James's endorsement that his notion was a good one. 'Perhaps Adelaide could chaperone Miss Wells when Miss Wells's aunt requires a rest from the constant gaiety?'

James appeared not to have been attending. Tristan frowned. 'Well, James, have you nothing to say?'

James stirred as though it took great effort. He seemed uncharacteristically drained of vitality, his face ashen as he replied, 'My God, Tristan. I'm sorry but I can't get over what you've told me. It puts a whole different complexion on things. Poor Addy. I had no idea.'

Tristan cleared his throat. 'Of course she will never forget.' Nor would he. 'But time is a great healer and it has been more than three years now. It is my hope that a little gaiety in the city will divert her and stop her brooding, which is inevitable given the quiet life we lead – but I am loathe to push her.' Tristan twirled the amber liquid in the bottom of his glass. 'For three years we've remained at Deer Park with an annual visit to Bath to take the waters to relieve the tedium. Now I'm fired up to shoulder the political responsibilities my brothers considered burdens. Take my seat in the Lords and make a difference, this time for my fellow countrymen. Before I inherited, I was content to remain at Deer Park, serving the community at a local level and providing the safety and sanctuary Adelaide needed. But lately'—it was almost painful to give voice to something so important to him—'I've been wanting to do more. Robert's death was a shock. He was groomed for this role, though he would have bankrupted the estate, but no one expected *William* to die so soon afterwards.' He gave a short laugh. 'You know my father said his first marriage was for expediency, his second for love, so it was unfortunate my elder half-brothers inherited their mother's love of gaming and drinking and, like her, went early to their graves.'

James looked earnest. '*Your* mother was wonderful. But Tristan, I do not think Addy will take to the idea of being thrust into the role of chaperone and enduring endless balls and parties with Beatrice and me.'

'Hortense and Mrs Henley did their prison work for two years, traipsing through those stinking hellholes in Vienna. You must have come to know Adelaide well. Who better to help guide Adelaide through this next, perhaps difficult phase, than someone who knows what she is capable of?'

He was surprised at James's reluctance, disappointed when his friend said with a decided lack of enthusiasm, 'Put it to Adelaide, by all means, Tristan, but I do not think she will agree. Nor do I think it advisable. Not after what you've told me.'

Tristan nodded and sat back, contemplating the fire. He had to accept this, of course, though he thought it an odd response from someone who embraced every madcap idea and who'd clearly been fond of Adelaide.

Finally he said, 'Well, James, you've not told me what urgent request had you riding hell for leather to Deer Park so you could set Beatrice's mind at rest.'

James rubbed the stubble on his chin. He took a long time answering. 'I found Beatrice was in tears yesterday – though trying hard to hide it, for she is a stoic young woman which is partly what attracts me. Well, her very well-founded fear is that her Aunt Wells is such a gorgon she'll not be allowed a minute alone with me. I reassured her that the old termagant can't possibly keep up the pace we intend to set, so I promised I'd find her the perfect chaperone.' Obvious amusement vied with embarrassment as he added, 'I told Beatrice that I was the man for brilliant madcap ideas that either crashed to earth or soared to the heavens; that she could dry her tears and I'd have all her worries solved by the time I returned to her side tomorrow afternoon.'

Tristan shook his head. 'Well, James'—he raised his shoulders and presented his hands, palms upwards—'have I not provided the perfect solution?'

James looked doubtful. 'In truth, the very reason I dashed here so impulsively was to prevail upon Addy's good heart and beg her to chaperone Beatrice. I thought it the ideal plan. But the moment I saw Addy in the library I realised it was not. Now you've told me this and it makes the whole proposal unthinkable.' He shook his head. 'I've no doubt Beatrice would be delighted to have Adelaide as a chaperone, however, in view of what I've seen and what you've told me, I rather suspect Adelaide will be none too receptive.'

There was both regret and gratitude in his expression as he continued. 'Perhaps you are right that a London season will bring back the spark that was such a feature of Adelaide's vibrant character, but I do not think'—James studied his boots —'that it is a good idea, after all, to burden her with much more than accompanying you to the amusements you feel will benefit her.'

Leaning forward, Tristan fixed his old friend with a penetrating look. This was not the James he knew. The bold and irrepressible young man whose passions inspired those around him.

'Let me be the judge of what is good for Addy,' he said softly, 'and do me the great favour of assisting me where I think you may be of help, whether it's requesting her as chaperone to Beatrice, or simply stepping in when I'm unavailable.' Taking in James's startled look over his steepled fingers, he went on, his voice thickening, 'I love Adelaide more than I believed it was possible to love anyone. I want to see her shine; to reclaim the delight she clearly once found in life and the lightness of spirit you have been fortunate enough to have witnessed, James. If I can persuade Adelaide to come to London with me, then I would consider it an enormous personal favour. Can I do that? Can I count on your help in restoring Adelaide to the woman she was'—he shut his eyes against the pain that accompanied his words—'before her terrible ordeal at the hands of those savages?'

CHAPTER 4

A week in her great-aunt's tiny cottage in Licolnshire was enough to try the nerves of a saint – and Adelaide didn't need her mother to remind her she was no saint.

'That was the worst week of my life, Mama!' she declared as they crested the final hill and saw majestic Deer Park in the distance. 'Aunt Gwendolyn wanted me to be her slave. She'd have had me stay forever to mash her food for her, if she could.'

'A more dutiful girl might have done it, too, Adelaide.' The censure in her mother's tone should not have hurt as much as it did. 'You were never cut out for hard work, my dear. Thank the Lord Tristan treats you like a porcelain doll for I don't know where else in the world you'd be looked after so well.'

She might have added 'for so undeserving a girl'. Adelaide had heard it before but then she was now three years into her marriage and the term had perhaps grown stale.

'I was a dutiful daughter, Mama, when I visited all those prisoners with you in Vienna,' she reminded her. 'For years I was at your beck and call, making notes on their conditions, asking them—'

'You can act a part, Adelaide, and for that we should both be grateful.' Her mother sniffed. 'Sadly, the desire to make a difference in the world did not spring naturally from your passionate and selfish nature. At least you've managed to hide the truth of what you are from your husband or I can't think where we'd be.'

It was impossible to conceal the bitterness engendered by her mother's damning character appraisal. Adelaide leaned into the squabs and turned her head. 'You should have had Hortense for a daughter,' she muttered.

'We cannot change our lot in life, Adelaide. It was God's Will I make you a better person, for clearly you were born in sin. I tried to curb your wilful ways from childhood. Lord knows, you were the worst behaved girl at Miss Wilkins' Seminary.' She barely paused before driving the blade deeper. 'When we make rash and foolish decisions we live with the consequences and that is the lesson you are still learning. Hortense was passionate about furthering the opportunities and consequently happiness of the wretched souls we sought to help—'

'And distinctly dispassionate towards her own husband who spent years trying to wring some feeling from her cold, cold heart, Mama, after she turned out to be so completely different from the woman James thought he married!'

'Don't you raise your voice at me, girl! You are in no position to criticise Hortense. What you did to her—'

'She brought it upon herself, Mama!' Blessed relief it was to answer back. Strange how Adelaide felt so much stronger in the face of a confrontation she'd imagined would sap her of all she had. 'If Hortense had offered a little kindness James would have responded like the good man he was. His finely tuned sensibilities required—'

'Too rich by half, Adelaide! Finely tuned sensibilities, indeed! He was a grubby adulterer and your vanity was aroused by his poems of love and longing. Where were *your* finer feelings of loyalty towards your mother? Towards *Hortense* who laboured at my side while you thought of nothing more important than the impact of your copper locks on potential suitors or whether your dress was in the first stare? You destroyed everything good in Hortense's life'—her mother sucked in a heaving breath—'and in mine, too.' She was close to tears. 'But you speak the truth, Adelaide. Hortense was the daughter I should have had, but you poisoned the love between us and destroyed her marriage. And who salvaged a future for you?'

Adelaide was still trembling from this violently passionate exchange when they drew up in front of the house. Tristan was there to help her out of the carriage, clearly shocked when he held her.

'You're not well, Adelaide. Why, you're trembling all over. I'll take you to your room.' Scooping her into his arms while one of the servants tended to his mother-in-law, he carried her up the stairs.

'I'm perfectly alright,' Adelaide protested, nevertheless enjoying the close proximity. She was pleased that Tristan's limp was not so much in evidence today, so she simply rested her head on his shoulder and allowed herself to enjoy feeling safe and protected. She breathed in the comforting familiar smell of him: horses and nutmeg and fine port. He was an Englishman through and through. Solid and dependable. Just what a flighty girl like herself needed, she told herself firmly as she pushed all thoughts of James from her mind.

When she brushed her hand over Tristan's cheek he looked down and returned her smile.

Just what she *wanted* now that maturity had softened the

excesses of her wild youth. No, she never wanted to see James again.

'Don't go,' she protested after he'd removed her shoes and dress and pulled the bed covers over her. He'd been as efficient as her maid – and as resistant to her charms, she reflected, with a longing look at his lean, muscular physique. The boyish, almost sheepish smile undid her. Yes, there were creases about his eyes and silver at his temples, but a depth of experience stared out at her from his sea-blue eyes. So different from the single-minded passion of James's roiling grey stare.

'Stay with me, Tristan,' she begged, tugging his arm. He yielded and sat on the bed, crossing his long, lean legs at the ankle. She noticed the mud that clung to the cuff of his trouser legs and imagined he'd just returned from one of his long rambles. Tomorrow, she decided, she would join him. 'Don't you want to hear about my ghastly five days away?'

'I thought you were fond of your great-aunt. Not that I've heard you mention her.'

'Mother felt I should accompany her.' Adelaide slanted a disgusted look up at him. It had the desired result for he laughed and took both her hands in his.

'You're a dutiful daughter, Adelaide—'

'Mother doesn't think so. Besides, I'm much more interested in being a dutiful wife.'

She saw puzzlement turn to shock as he interpreted the look in her eye. For surely there could be no misunderstanding her meaning; she'd been told her whole life her eyes were dangerously full of expression. Every fibre of her being cried out for him. Perhaps it was James's visit that had cemented the change in her; made her realise finally that James belonged to her past and that Tristan was her future. Whatever it was, she felt charged with energy and the determination to make something of her life. Of her marriage. She would be an invalid no longer.

'You're overwrought, my dear.' He kissed her brow, preparing to rise, but she pulled him down.

'Will you see me later?' She could hardly beg him. She needed to be careful.

'Would I squander any opportunity, my love?'

'You could stay longer now—'

'It wouldn't be good for you.'

She curled an arm about his neck and pulled him down to place a kiss upon his lips, drawing back to enjoy the shock upon his face.

'Addy—?'

Tossing aside the bed covers, she shifted to make room for him, snuggling against his chest when he yielded slightly, nevertheless terrified of his reaction. She was blatantly seducing – no, trying to seduce – her husband for the first time in her life and she had no idea whether he'd be horrified or delighted. She just knew she had to convey to him her receptiveness for taking intimacy to a higher level.

So far so good. He was breathing more rapidly, she noticed, as he carefully removed his boots. She willed him to hurry. She was on fire. She closed her eyes in anticipation, her mind whirling with all the possibilities of what she might say, but the words with which she'd intended to unburden her heart were lost in the passion of his kiss.

Scorching. It shocked her, as did the speed with which he moved now as he caged her body with his, his hands roaming over her as he trailed hot kisses along her jawline, down her neck, across her décolletage. Adelaide arched with impatience, resisting the urge to be the one to unbutton his trousers.

'God, Addy, I love you,' he muttered as he gripped the

hem of her shift to raise it, nuzzling her neck. 'I've never loved any woman as I love you. Are you sure you want—?'

Her reassurance that she'd never wanted anything so much was truncated by a sharp rap on the door and her mother's nasal whine on the other side. 'Addy? I've brought you something to help you sleep. Can I come in?'

Horrified, she and Tristan sat up quickly bolted as the door knob turned.

'Wait, mother!' Addy pulled the covers up to her chin as Tristan leapt to the floor, straightening his cravat and pulling on his boots with lightning speed.

'Why, Tristan …?' Mrs Henley's cloying smile didn't fool Adelaide. 'I didn't know you were here. I'm so sorry to interrupt.'

Adelaide felt like seizing the mug her mother carried with such false solicitude and hurling it at the wall. Instead, she hurled herself back down onto her bed with a sob as her husband bowed before leaving the room.

Breathing heavily, Tristan strode to his study, his wife's final devastated look scorched upon his consciousness. Had he got carried away, making too much of her suggestive look when they'd only ever enjoyed the most restrained of intimacies? Yet he'd been certain she welcomed – no, had sought – his advances. He was sure he'd not mistaken her ardour, for she'd explored his body with an urgency that matched his.

A familiar rap on the door several minutes later, followed by the arrival of Mrs Henley, only intensified his turmoil.

'Adelaide is suffering a dangerous excess of emotion and needs to be kept quiet if her nervous malady is not to result in uncontrollable hysteria.' Mrs Henley's bony frame shook with anger as she lowered herself into the chair closest to the fire. Even the heavy pouches beneath her eyes seemed to tremble. She smoothed her puce skirts. 'Lord knows what brought it on. I made the mistake of making what I thought an entirely innocent remark about the past during the last leg of our journey and she flew up into the boughs. I'm glad you tried to comfort her'—she sent him a warning look that suggested she knew exactly what form his comfort took—'however, I found Adelaide highly agitated and in tears after you'd gone.'

Tristan had never experienced his wife's temper, but he'd been warned often enough of Adelaide's excitability by Mrs Henley. But Addy in tears? Lord, he never intended to upset her. He really had thought— He regarded his mother- in-law with undisguised scepticism.

Mrs Henley sniffed. 'James has gone, I take it?'

He was surprised at her tone but put it down to the fact she was distracted by Adelaide's latest turn.

'James and his betrothed will return next week for an extended visit while their new home is being renovated. Are you well, Mrs Henley?'

She was staring as if he'd invited the devil himself, fanning her flushed cheeks. 'You've invited them *here?*'

Tristan hoped the slight raising of his brows was sufficient to remind her that this was his house.

'James is under pressure to finish his third canto for his publisher before the marriage, and the plasterers are still busy at Dingley Hall.' He spoke in clipped tones and wished with all his might he could simply evict the dreadful woman. 'I'm sorry, Mrs Henley, I'd thought James a good friend to you.'

'*Hortense* was a good friend. And Tristan, I am grieved that Adelaide will have no choice but to endure what can only be a reminder of a time she would rather forget. Indeed I am very sorry you did not consult me.'

'And I am very sorry you feel that way, Mrs Henley, and admit I am perplexed you have such an aversion to James.

James and I grew up together, went to Eton and Trinity together. He is like a brother.'

Mrs Henley rose. 'I hope you will reconsider, Tristan.'

He was fuming. Did her stubbornness stem from the simple fact that he had not consulted her? 'I will not, Mrs Henley. In more than three years I do not believe you've had cause to fault my judgment regarding what is best for Adelaide. Why not let James be a reminder of happier times when you and Adelaide and Hortense threw your energy into improving the plight of the prison wretches in Vienna during your late husband's diplomatic tenure there'—he paused heavily—'rather than making *James* the incarnation of Adelaide's unhappy past?'

He followed her to the door. 'Good afternoon, Mrs Henley. I shall now return to check on Addy. I will ask her directly what she thinks.'

Mrs Henley inclined her head, her expression cold. 'I think it inadvisable in view of her emotional state but by all means, Tristan.'

He would not be dictated to. 'Then as her husband I must do what I can to calm her.'

With a grim smile Mrs Henley gave a languid wave in the direction of Adelaide's chamber. 'Perhaps it's not such a bad thing for you to see the ill effects of such dangerous overexcitement. I believe Adelaide will be in no state to attend to you, Tristan. Don't say I didn't warn you.'

He entered the room upon the lightest of knocks and took a seat by Adelaide's side, taking her hand in his and whispering, 'My love, your mother tells me I've upset you, but I'd rather hear that from your own lips.'

The look she sent him as she turned her head to gaze into his eyes filled him with panic. It was like the early days when she'd stare right through him, as if yearning for something as far removed as possible from her new husband.

'Addy?' He squeezed her hand but there was no response. 'Addy, my love. Listen to me.' He said it with more urgency this time, desperate for something, anything from her, that didn't confirm how ill prepared she was to take their relationship to a higher level.

Her hand remained limp in his and her look was vacant. Horrified at what he'd done, what he perhaps was guilty of precipitating, Tristan tucked the blankets around her. In the early days of their marriage Adelaide had often been like this. In fact, it had only been six months ago, when he'd insisted that Dr Stanhope limit the laudanum Adelaide took so regularly, that his wife had begun to emerge brighter and more clear-headed.

Had Adelaide been so emotionally vulnerable after their encounter she'd felt the need to dull her senses? Was the unaccustomed passion of his lovemaking too horrifying a reminder of what she'd endured at the hands of the soldier rapists who'd devastated her life?

The glands in his neck prickled and he swallowed with difficulty. Perhaps Adelaide was not yet ready to accompany him to London.

ADELAIDE BATTLED to hold at bay her inevitable anxiety in the lead-up to James's visit and that of his bride-to-be. When they arrived a week later, together with Beatrice's Aunt Wells, Tristan's comforting presence was just the antidote she needed. She was relieved that James seemed satisfied with his lot and sufficiently attentive to his betrothed. The intensity of the feelings they had once shared were well in the past.

And that was where they were going to stay.

By contrast, Adelaide did not intend the recently ignited

passion she felt for her husband to remain in abeyance due to her mother's strictures for long. She wasn't sure how she might go about matters without appearing the jezebel her mother continually told her she was, but little by little she was gaining confidence that greater boldness on the intimacy front would not demean her in Tristan's eyes.

There'd been no reference to their interrupted love-making the previous week. She'd woken the following day feeling heavy headed and lethargic but her mother had denied putting anything in her milk to make her sleep so deeply.

For months after the dramatic end of her affair with James, Adelaide had welcomed the oblivion offered by the laudanum Dr Stanhope had supplied her. She'd objected strongly when Tristan insisted she limit her dependence upon it, but he'd been right. She now relished the clear-headed feeling she enjoyed every day upon waking. And, more lately, the increasingly wonderful prospects the future held.

Yet she felt confused. Had her highly emotional state and desire for Tristan's love accounted for how strange she'd felt all that next day? It had been so long since she'd allowed herself licence to behave as she truly felt. Was it really so dangerous?

To be safe, she'd decided to let Tristan set the tone between them during his weekly Thursday night visit and when he'd conducted proceedings just as he always had, she'd been too frightened to encourage him as she had previously. Her heart was so heavy and she was so afraid of pouring out an excess of emotion which would make him think her unhinged, she'd merely smiled at him and nodded when he'd kissed her brow and told her he loved her, before retiring to his own apartments.

Now, on this fine sunny afternoon, Mrs Henley was

indoors entertaining the elder Miss Wells – who did indeed resemble some fearful beast with her penchant for the high hair of her youth coupled with a girth of similar dimensions – while Adelaide prepared to play the good hostess.

Taking a deep breath, she smoothed her spotted muslin skirts and forced a spring into her step as she covered the expanse of lawn to where Tristan, James and Beatrice were ensconced in chairs beneath a canopy erected by the lake. The grass was emerald green, and fluffy clouds scudded across the sky. It was a day to feel buoyed by hope.

Although still smarting from her interview with her mother earlier that morning on what she must and must not do when in the company of Tristan and James, Adelaide managed to inject liveliness into her tone as she sank into a chair beside James's betrothed.

'How are you enjoying our lovely spring weather, Miss Wells? I trust your husband-to-be has shown you the attention you would hope for.' She nodded at James and Tristan who were lounging on cushions laid upon the grass, deep in discussion a few feet away.

'He has. And I must confess that on beautiful days like this I wish we were going to live permanently in the south.' Miss Wells shifted on the comfortable chair that had been set up for her, dropping her dark brown eyes, as if it were wrong to voice a negative sentiment. 'Of course, I can't complain since I'll be living not far from where I grew up and that's what I most desired.'

'Your father was a diplomat, I believe.'

'Yes.' She played with the tassel of her cushion, adding proudly, 'He assisted General Waldenberg when he was conducting negotiations in London a few years ago. I'm told you lived some years in both Vienna and Milan.'

Adelaide turned her head away in case Miss Wells might see there was more behind the guileless lie she must formulate quickly. 'I visited Milan only briefly at the end of my sojourn. Its warmth attracted me,' she said. Not: *'I went to Milan to be with James who had removed there at Hortense's instigation in the hopes of the weather improving her chances of carrying her fifth pregnancy to full term after four still births and miscarriages.'* Adelaide slid her eyes across to the two men who were in the midst of animated discussion. The sight made her heart lift. Life at Deer Park seemed so oppressive sometimes.

James intercepted her look, holding it for a second so that her heart pounded with fear. What had she read there? Anger? Disappointment? Intent? She pretended studied indifference.

Beatrice reclaimed her attention, asking, 'But you went to school in England?'

'Yes, until I was seventeen when I rejoined Mama, who at the time was very involved in prison reform.'

'Prison reform?'

'Mama tried to improve the condition of women prisoners.' Adelaide didn't mean her answer to sound so clipped. She'd witnessed sights in the name of altruism she'd never get over.

'Are their conditions bad?'

'Shall we walk?' Adelaide rose. She needed to get away. 'You've obviously not visited a prison and I hope you never do. James is unlikely to take you.'

Beatrice reached for her shawl, smiling as she responded ingenuously, 'I don't mind if he does. I'd follow him anywhere, even back to Vienna, which I hated.'

'James is a lucky man to find such loyalty in a wife. Let's take a turn around the lake, shall we?'

Beatrice took Adelaide's arm, signalling to James her intention as she and Adelaide began to walk. 'Loyalty is everything.' She lowered her voice. 'Aunt Wells says I will need it.' When they were well out earshot she added, 'She tells me men are the weaker sex when it comes to ... their impulses, and it was impulse that led James to propose.' She pressed her lips together. 'I must make sure he does not regret it. James is everything to me now that my parents are dead. Even though I am out of mourning I still miss them dreadfully.' She glanced in Adelaide's direction as if fearing her meaning might be misunderstood. 'Of course it's more than that. I love James for his impulsiveness. He is so different from me. He's what I need, for he makes me laugh ... and my parents always told me I should marry a man who could make me laugh.'

Adelaide shot her an appraising look. The young girl was pretty though she seemed to take little trouble with her appearance. And she was certainly determined. Curious, she asked, 'Where did you meet James? I believe it was at a ball in Vienna.'

'We were acquainted but James had paid me no special attention until he picked me up in the middle of a snowstorm—'

'What!'

Beatrice laughed. It was a pretty, tinkling unaffected sound. 'Yes, outrageous, I know, but I was used to my papa's fits of temper. We would argue about ... politics mostly, and on this occasion he put me out of the carriage and I was standing in the snow, waiting for him to do a turn-around within the next few minutes, only James arrived in his carriage and, despite my protests, insisted on being chivalrous. He was furious with Papa!'

Adelaide shook her head at Beatrice's amusement. 'How irregular,' she murmured. 'On your papa's part, I mean, though I can well understand James being motivated by honour to tell your papa exactly what he thought.'

'Oh, he did, and there was lots of shouting, then one thing

led to another and suddenly we were to be married.' She shrugged. 'I think James sometimes wonders, like I do, how we got to this point.'

Adelaide changed the subject. James had no choice but to marry Beatrice now unless he were to cause a scandal.

'What other warnings has your aunt given you?' Adelaide asked, wondering if Beatrice had any inkling of what was meant by the formidable Miss Wells's caution regarding men's impulses.

Beatrice's hesitation and obvious puzzlement made Adelaide realise the girl had pretended greater knowledge and sophistication than she possessed. 'She says men like James are rarely loyal to their wives but that I must not plague James with questions or quiz him on what he does when he is not with me, otherwise he will hate me for it.'

'Disloyalty is not the hallmark of most married men.' She sent Beatrice a sympathetic look. 'My husband and James are both good, loyal and decent. I would expect my husband to make a full accounting to me without hating me for it.'

Beatrice was clearly not expecting such frankness. 'Aunt Wells says above all I must not demand the identity of the woman who inspired James to write his poems.'

The corroboration she'd clearly been expecting from Adelaide was not forthcoming. Uncertainly, she went on, 'The success of *The Maid of Milan* means it's inevitable people will ask me, but Aunt Wells says that my ignorance will be my protection. Do you think he *should* tell me?'

Adelaide faltered. Unable to meet Beatrice's look, she hoped the girl didn't see her discomposure.

The Maid of Milan. The very title seared her to the tips of her toes.

How could James have been so blatant when he'd named the piece that had won him such acclaim?

Or was it only Adelaide who could read between the lines?

They had just returned to the others but fortunately the men were too involved in their own discussions to notice Adelaide's loss of countenance.

'No, he should not,' she whispered as fresh understanding of the implications of James's new notoriety ripped through the carefully orchestrated fiction she had created for herself. For three years she'd taken little interest in society gossip other than what appeared in the news-sheets and political pamphlets Tristan left lying about. She'd known nothing about James's so-called literary success until Tristan had told her. Even as Adelaide had chatted with Beatrice, hoping to reassure herself that James's affections would be thoroughly engaged by the pretty young innocent, Adelaide had imagined the past was just that.

Now it sounded like James's book was more of a sensation than she'd realised.

'Let us take another turn about the rose bushes,' she said, hoping her urgency would not be remarked upon. She started to traverse the lawn, not looking behind to see if Beatrice followed, for she could not just stand there two feet from Tristan with her face blanched of all colour. Tristan would notice and start quizzing her on her health, and Adelaide didn't know if she could stand up to the scrutiny.

Beatrice matched her steps to Adelaide's, blinking rapidly as she twisted her primrose-gloved hands. Dear God, and she was *still* talking about it. 'Aunt Wells says James wrote many of the poems in *The Maid of Milan* years before he met me. Of course, James never expected the book would create such a sensation or that people would be so interested to learn the identity of the red-haired woman – titian-haired, I think he describes it. That was when I told Aunt Wells I was going to ask him about it, but she said that wives should not seek to know about their husband's pasts.' Shamefaced she added, as she drew level and slightly out of breath, 'But I disobeyed her and ... I asked James, and Aunt Wells was right. James was angry and seemed to think I was quizzing him.'

Adelaide couldn't look at her. 'So you asked him about ... the woman? Have you read the book?'

'No. Aunt Wells tells me it's not a proper book for a young lady. I'm just afraid James is still angry with me. You see, it was only yesterday I asked him and we've not been alone since.'

Adelaide forced a reassuring smile as she slowed her pace by the reed-fringed lake. 'I'm sure it will all be forgotten by tomorrow, for James, as you might have noticed, is ruled by his passions and he is rarely in the same mood for long.' She patted Beatrice's arm. 'Everything,' she added firmly, 'is forgotten in time.'

Platitudes. If only they were true.

As the two couples formed a walking party along the river bank a little later, Adelaide was determined to put on a good show.

'Miss Wells will make James happy, Tristan, I'm sure of it,' she declared with forced conviction.

The path was narrow and Adelaide and Tristan went ahead while the other two lingered to look at nesting birds. 'She's not the shrinking violet she appears and James needs a strong wife.'

Tristan squeezed her hand before releasing it. 'I'm glad to hear you speak of my friend as if you were concerned for his happiness. I was afraid you shared your mother's antipathy towards James, though I can't imagine what he's done except injure your mother's vanity.'

'James mocked Mother's obsession for lost causes.'

Tristan looked surprised and then immediately satisfied,

for the answer was plausible – and true as a part explanation. 'Prison reform?'

Adelaide shrugged. 'All our efforts yielded nothing except the scorn of the authorities and the occasional *thank you* from a wretched soul who had a shovelful of hay for a bed rather than the cold stone floor.' She glanced at her husband. 'You'd effect more change with your passionate rhetoric in parliament during one sitting than I would toiling beside my mother for a whole lifetime.' Dropping her eyes, she added, 'I'm sorry if you think it reflects badly on me that I do not share Mother's obsession with "doing good works". Certainly, I was just as horrified as she by the conditions suffered by the wretched souls we saw languishing in prisons, but truly, Tristan, I can think of more effective ways of forcing change than Mother's.'

Tristan nodded. 'It sounds like you should be the politician, darling.' He stopped by a willow tree that sent its branches trailing into the waters below and turned to take both her hands lightly in his, but before he could speak Adelaide took the initiative.

Fear made her breathless but she tried to slow her words. She wanted Tristan to see that she was not being ruled by her passions.

'Tristan, take me to London. I know how much you want to assume your political responsibilities. You may not think it now but I can become the political hostess you need.'

The ideas which had been roiling in her head crystallised as she spoke. She needed to leave Deer Park. She'd rusticated too long in the country, allowing herself to live her mother's lie as if she were no better than the invalid her mother would likely as not paint her for the rest of her life. Her desperation increased as she saw his uncertainty. 'Please, Tristan. I've read all the political pamphlets you have. I've educated myself on these terrible uprisings in the north and I support your views for moderation. I know you think me weak in body and sometimes, perhaps, weak in mind. If that were so it's only because of ... of the past. But the past is over. Please, Tristan, give me this chance so I can prove that I've now managed to put a line under what has gone before ... and that I'm committed to my future ... with *you*.'

She saw surprise, then admiration flit across his features. It radiated hope and joy and echoed every sentiment in her heart. The sound of the others approaching was like an advancing menace.

The spell was broken. Tristan closed his mouth on whatever he was about to say and turned, for James and Beatrice were upon their heels now.

'Miss Wells?' Tristan bowed, his smile ready as ever the consummate gentleman, though she sensed his disappointment at the timing of the interruption. 'Shall you and I walk ahead, perhaps? I would like to become better acquainted with the young lady who has won the heart of my dearest friend?'

They swapped companions, Tristan and Beatrice taking the lead along the path that dipped and meandered beside the sluggish river. There were tree roots and overhanging branches to negotiate, which Adelaide normally didn't mind, but when James had to grip her arm to save her from tumbling into the murky depths, her senses leapt into awareness.

She gasped, wrenching herself free of his clasped fingers, and he spoke for the first time, his words careful as he faced her on the path. 'I'm sorry if this makes you uncomfortable, Adelaide. Tristan was so insistent I visit and that I bring Beatrice and her aunt along.'

'Of course you had to accept!' Adelaide managed a brittle laugh, one eye on the disappearing backs of the others. 'You and Tristan have been friends forever.' Forcing to mind a neutral subject as they resumed walking, she tried to steady her voice. 'But it must be strange to be at Deer Park and see me presiding as mistress, not Cassandra. She was close to both you and Tristan. Her portrait still hangs in the drawing room. She was very beautiful.'

'Cassandra made a fine hostess, but she had an advantage since she already knew the house and servants and tenants, having grown up on the neighbouring estate.' The words were banal, a polite rendition of what each already knew, but it was a safe subject, and would have remained so had James not added, 'Cassandra was considered a fine-looking girl but she wasn't beautiful. Not like you, Addy. I've never met anyone as beautiful as you.' He spoke as if he had no notion of the effect his words must have on her. 'Everyone in Vienna thought it. There was a brightness about you and people wanted to bask in your glow.' He slowed his step, glancing at the growing distance between the others.

The hard knot in Adelaide's stomach rose to her throat. *Not here, James*, she thought. *Don't make any of your passionate declarations here.*

'I had to come and see how you fared, Addy.' Longing resonated in his every word, matched by Adelaide's longing for her husband to look over his shoulder and perhaps wait for them to catch up.

Her fear eased slightly when James added, 'I rushed here, bursting with the idea of asking you to chaperone Beatrice this season for it gave me the excuse I needed to see with my own eyes that you were happy. Tristan is my dearest friend and a noble man – so much nobler than I – but I had to be reassured you'd found a future you could live with.'

'I'm happier than I believed possible.' She spoke the words with more conviction than truth. But she was on the right path. She would go to London with Tristan. She would shine, make her husband proud, and in such a metropolis she need hardly ever see James.

'Everything that happened between us'—he broke off, choking on the words and rubbing his hand across his forehead as if it really took everything he had to utter them— 'was magic. I'd have faced any challenge, cut off my right arm, even, if *I* could have been your future, Addy. The only thing I couldn't do was ruin you.' She did not doubt his sincerity when he added, 'I mean, more than I already had.'

He stopped walking, and his voice dropped to a thin thread of sound. 'You know that, don't you?'

Adelaide steadied herself on the trunk of a willow, hating the fact that his words elicited such a depth of feeling. She'd lived without feeling for so long. But it was returning – it had returned – and all her feelings were for Tristan. How could she ever have been attracted by James? By the danger he posed?

It could never happen again. She'd grown up.

'I know I am quick to act on my emotions, and I'm undisciplined. I know my faults. But believe me, Addy, for the first time in my life I put *your* happiness ahead of mine when I knew that to indulge my heart's desire would destroy you. You wanted to run away with me but I could not let you. A lost reputation can never be salvaged, and you'd have come to hate me for damning you in society's eyes, though at the time, if you recall, you said you hated me more for allowing your mother to take you away.'

Breathing through the pain, she whispered, 'Please don't remind me of what a foolish child I once was. The past is the past, James.'

'It is.' His acknowledgement was contemplative, as if he truly believed it, and she was glad. Passion still lit up his eyes and his movements were still animated like they'd been in his youth, but perhaps his idealised notions really had been tempered by experience.

'We must rejoin the others,' she murmured, but he stayed her with an abrupt hand upon her bare wrist and she leapt back as if stung.

'I'm sorry, Addy. Sorry for what you went through. Not just in Vienna, or when you followed me to Milan but … but afterwards.' He struggled with the words. 'Tristan told me.'

She frowned, her confusion apparent, until he replied, awkwardly, 'About the … the attack on your return to England.' He dropped his voice though the others were ahead and well out of earshot. 'My God, Addy … when you'd been through so much already.'

She gasped, her hand to her mouth. 'Tristan *told* you that?'

James nodded as he hastened to assure her, 'Tristan needed to unburden himself. He adores you – it's plain to see – but it'll go no further, I swear. Please understand that it was the kind of confidence made by only the most loyal of friends. He wanted me to know so I would understand why you are so changed … so I wouldn't probe, and yet here I have only dredged up the past. I'm sorry,' he finished, clearly wretched.

Adelaide swayed, pushing away his hands when he tried to steady her. 'What Tristan told you is a lie, James … a complete fabrication my mother invented as a means of effecting my marriage to Tristan.'

At his well-warranted shock she forced herself to continue. She was now the wretched one. 'Tristan spoke to my mother as he wanted to ask for my hand and she told him the story you heard. I was not in love with Tristan – then – but my mother persuaded me to accept, saying I'd never have another chance'— Addy traced the trunk of the tree with her forefinger as she remembered her tearful reluctance to her mother's stricture that she accept Tristan—'which was no doubt very true. She explained she'd already provided Tristan with all the excuses needed as to why I wasn't ... pure ... and why I had an aversion to ... to being intimate with a man. Despite all that, Tristan went ahead and—' She shrugged. 'As I felt nothing but dull resignation ... about anything in my life at that time ... I accepted.'

No point in elaborating to James how that lie had made her life a living hell, the more so as she tried to forge a proper, intimate union with the husband she'd grown to love.

James digested her words in silence as Addy watched the emotions flit across his mobile face, once so familiar and beloved. Turning her head away, she took a step forward, but he stopped her.

'Just one question before we rejoin the others.'

She halted. Her skin prickled and her insides churned with all the hurt and emotion that accompanied her answer to his inevitable question. She'd known it would be coming. Just not when.

'Three years ago ... Did you get my letter?'

She half turned but was unable to face him. With difficulty she whispered, 'It arrived the day after Tristan and I were married.'

'My God, Addy!' he muttered, closing the distance to grip her wrists, forcing her to raise her eyes to his. 'When I learned of your marriage I suspected my timing might have been less than wonderful.' Bitterly, he added, 'Or should I say, Hortense's timing. Her illness was so sudden. She died within a day of my calling the doctor. I made the funeral arrangements and the very moment I'd done my duty, before she was even in the ground, Addy, I wrote to you.' He put his face in his hands, his voice choked as he went on, 'You sent me no reply and then I heard you were married. Married to my dearest friend. I did not expect *that*. But would you have come, Addy?' He dropped his hands and waited, tensely, his eyes clouded with anguish. 'If you'd not already been married?'

Adelaide tried to speak past the terrible lump in her throat, but her words came out on a sob. So much for her determination not to revisit what he'd once been to her. 'I'd have hurled myself into the first post chaise, taken the first packet across the channel and ridden, bareback, the rest of the way to Milan if I'd not been married.' *Say it all and then it's in the past*, she told herself, clenching her fists at her sides as she tried to cast aside the agony of the start of her marriage to Tristan.

James shook his head, his voice barely recognisable. 'I paced my chamber for days, Addy, waiting for word from you. Hoping against hope you might even come in person.' Angrily, he added, 'My agitation was misconstrued as grief.'

'And mine as the terrors of an uninitiated wife. Or rather, a wife who'd been brutally violated and was not of sound mind as a consequence. A wife who loathed and feared the intimate touch of a man. My mother's curse.' She sagged against the tree trunk. 'Tristan was very understanding. He always has been. I've grown to love my husband very much.'

'I'm glad, Addy.'

He sounded both pleased and regretful.

'Just as I believe you can be happy with Beatrice if you commit to her with all your heart and soul. As I have to Tristan.'

James nodded. 'I intend to try. Now that I have reassured myself that you have found happiness, I expect you and I will have little reason to see one another again. I understand the difficulties it would pose.'

They resumed walking and were nearly upon Beatrice and Tristan when James said, in an altered tone for their benefit, 'Tristan, have I not secured myself a gem for my future wife?'

'You have and she's been telling me how clever you are. I shall put in an order for your latest literary marvel, *The Maid of Milan*. Find out what the stir is about.'

Adelaide hoped he was not aware of her stiffening as the litany *Don't read that book* chased itself round her head. But then calm was restored as she reminded herself that soon James would leave and their quiet, ordered lives would resume.

And Tristan would forget about the book. She would make sure of it.

'I'll drop into Hatchards for a copy.'

Hatchards? In London? Adelaide jerked her head up to find him smiling indulgently down at her.

He raised her hand to his lips and pressed a brief kiss upon her fingertips. 'In view of what you said earlier, I've been talking to Miss Wells about London revels. How would you like a trip to the metropolis … to enjoy the season, Addy? I think a bit of gaiety would do you the world of good.'

Excitement warred with fear. Yes, she wanted gaiety and to throw herself once more into the thick of life. She had told him so. But what if turned out to be one terrible mistake? She no longer trusted her judgement.

'We'll send an army of servants ahead to whip off the dustsheets and have the townhouse in Bruton Street in perfect order for our arrival in a few weeks. You could have as much or as little say in the organisation as you wished. Come on, Addy, what do you say to a few months in London?'

She glanced at the expectant expressions around her and her shaky resolve firmed as she thought of her mother.

Yes, she would immerse herself in the frivolity of a London season and her mother would hate it. Mrs Henley was happy doing her good works in the local village where she was venerated, if not, Adelaide suspected, entirely liked. She would never follow.

Adelaide would be free. Free to make something of her marriage.

She nodded slowly as she felt her mouth stretch into a smile. 'I would love to go.'

CHAPTER 5

Adelaide had three happy hours to dwell on these liberating thoughts until dinner when it became clear Mrs Henley considered the idea of a London diversion a tonic for them all.

'I've been corresponding with a woman called Elizabeth Fry and now I intend to meet her.' Mrs Henley sounded more animated than Adelaide had seen her in years. 'Mrs Fry is, like me, deeply interested in the conditions of those unfortunates who are confined within prison walls,' she explained to Beatrice. With a thin smile at James, she added, 'Your Hortense gave her life for such people and we cannot see her work go unrecognised. Perhaps, Miss Wells, you might be interested in accompanying me on occasion.'

James tightened the grip on his steak knife bearing its load mid-way to his mouth as he directed the older woman a combative look. 'Hortense died of something she contracted visiting those filthy cells. I will not have my future wife putting herself in similar danger.'

To Adelaide's horror Beatrice chose this moment to exercise the determination she'd suggested lurked beneath her passive exterior. 'I'm sure Mrs Henley wouldn't expose me to danger, James,' she said, smiling at James before telling Mrs Henley, 'I'd be most interested to accompany you.'

'I would rather you didn't go, Beatrice.'

Adelaide was jolted by the menace that lurked behind James's words. Perhaps they all were, for every face was trained upon his as if he'd uttered blasphemy. Which, of course, in Mrs Henley's eyes it was.

'But James, I—'

'In a few months I shall be your husband and it is my desire that you do not involve yourself with felons or otherwise expose yourself to danger.' He spoke under his breath as he faced Beatrice before returning his attention to his food.

Adelaide glanced at Tristan and registered the flicker of concern as she met his eye.

Just as relief poured through her that Beatrice looked about to make some tacit indication she accepted his dictates, the girl went on, ingenuously, 'But James, I want to prove that I care for more than just the dizzy pleasures of London—'

'More than you want to prove yourself a loyal wife?'

It wasn't only Beatrice's jaw that dropped at his clipped tone, though her shock at his patent displeasure was palpable in the trembling of her lip as she rose, dropping her napkin upon her plate and running a hand across her brow. 'Please excuse me, everyone … James. I fear I don't know what has come over me. A terrible megrim. Thank you for a lovely dinner but I'm afraid I shall have to retire to bed early.'

Her aunt Wells had already pleaded fatigue. Adelaide stared as Beatrice left the room, alone, only realising her abrogation of her hostess duties when Tristan said, mildly, as he rose, 'If you'll excuse me, I'll see that Miss Wells does not lose her way.'

He found her in the Long Gallery, crying quietly by the juncture in the passage which led to the two bedroom wings. 'Are your tears on account of your confusion as to whether to turn left or right,' he asked, offering her his clean handkerchief, 'or because of the harshness of James's words? Because if it's the latter,' he said as he led her to the window seat so she could sit down while he stared out into the darkness to enable her to discreetly dry her tears, 'you mustn't misconstrue his sharpness as anything other than concern for your wellbeing. His first wife died of prison fever. He doesn't want the same to happen to you.'

Beatrice sniffed and gulped, then raised her blotchy face to his. 'I thought he was just angry with me for crossing him in public.'

'If that were true your tears would be justified, but I know my friend better than that.' Tristan patted her hand. She seemed a child compared with Adelaide, though Adelaide was only a few years older. And most definitely not a child, but a fascinating woman, he thought with a charge of feeling.

He smiled at Beatrice. 'Granted, it's been a long time since I last saw James, but I know he's not a petty tyrant. Just as I know that his loyalty to you, now that he's pledged you his heart, will be unshakeable.'

Miss Wells continued to look miserable and it was only after he pressed her gently that she revealed, 'I'm not sure that offering marriage and pledging his heart are the same thing, for I fear James's heart belongs elsewhere.'

This was news to Tristan. The girl looked utterly forlorn, as would be expected, and he'd just determined that he'd tackle his friend about it when Miss Wells asked softly, 'Please, Lord Leeson, will you find out and tell me the truth? For I would not wish to wed a man who did not love me.'

Though Tristan promised he would, he felt full of misgivings. How could he relay potentially devastating news to a bride-to-be whose happiness depended upon it?

She rose, offering him a shaky smile. 'Thank you. I just need to know that the woman James writes about in his poems does not occupy the place in his heart that should be reserved for me.'

'Ah, Beatrice.' He touched her cheek, as if she were a child. 'James would have staked his claim by now if that were the case. You know he's one to follow his passions and clearly that was you. Besides, you say you have not read *The Maid of Milan*, and, I must confess, neither have I. You must be satisfied when he claims he has no single muse, only an amalgamation of all the women he has admired.'

Beatrice nodded but she did not look satisfied. 'You will ask him, though?'

Tristan nodded, hoping Beatrice did not parade such insecurity in front of James. He took one of her hands and raised it to his lips in a formal farewell, feeling a little like an elderly uncle.

'Goodnight, Beatrice, and try not to concern yourself. Fond though we are of James, I think we both know he is easily bored. Clearly there is good reason as to why he has chosen to make *you* his wife.'

As he watched her disappear at the end of the corridor he recalled the concern he'd read in the last glance he'd shared with his wife. After a difficult start to their marriage it was both comforting and, strangely, exciting that they seemed so often attuned to each other's moods and wishes.

He hoped James and Beatrice would enjoy similar camaraderie after a few years of marriage.

He also hoped that, soon, camaraderie would be augmented by something deeper.

CHAPTER 6

Outside Adelaide's window the London traffic sounded a cacophony of wheels on cobblestones interspersed with shouts and the occasional curse.

Adelaide paced the length of her private sitting room, did a twirl, and sashayed back towards the window, turning in surprise at the sound of clapping.

'You look perfectly delectable in that creation, my love.' Tristan strode forward, his arms outstretched. 'I see you've made the most of your shopping expeditions. No, no, don't look abashed. In three years we've not come up to town. It's about time you were presented, and you need to reflect honour upon me now that I've taken up the important business of politics.'

Adelaide stared at his boots as she listened. The idea of mixing in society both excited and terrified her, though her mother had poured scorn on her supposed fears, telling her pleasure-seeking was all she'd ever been interested in.

'Your friends will have to wage conversational battle with a country dormouse.'

'London's most beautiful country dormouse,' he said, tucking a tendril of hair behind her ear. 'But too modest by half. I saw you'd been reading the speech I'm drafting in opposition to what I feel is a particularly harsh Act and not to the benefit of the English people who struggle in these times of high food prices that have followed the end of the war.'

Adelaide raised herself on tiptoe to put her hands on his shoulders as she studied the set of his chin. The idea of supporting Tristan's political career was almost more exciting than being presented.

'The Whigs fiercely oppose legislation which labels any meeting for radical reform as "an overt act of treasonable conspiracy", don't they?' she asked. 'I'm glad you are as horrified as I am about what happened in Manchester. People should be allowed to protest when harsh laws push the price of food to unaffordable levels. I might not have enjoyed trailing after Mama through the prisons, but that wasn't because I didn't feel for the inmates. Most of the women, and a good many of the men, are there because the lack of food and work have pushed them into criminal acts.'

'Good Lord, Addy but you surprise me sometimes. A politician's wife in the making. You will do me proud.'

His admiration was balm to her soul and Adelaide was conscious of the delicious roiling in her lower belly for the fact that it was Thursday. Their first Thursday in a new environment. Tristan had not deviated from the old pattern since the truncated and somewhat unfortunate episode four weeks earlier but she was determined that in his arms tonight she would transport herself to heaven and take him with her.

Only last week she had tried to express what was in her heart by using her body to convey the subtle language of the feelings she could not put into words, but Tristan seemed immune. His soft groan and the convulsive banding of his arms around her had suggested his feelings were in accord with her own, but as her ardour had grown so had his concern. He'd put her away from him, suggested they read poetry together while they waited for the sweetened warm milk he called for, before the lights had gone out and proceedings had gone on as usual. Embarrassment had prevented her from discussing the matter.

Perhaps tonight, in their new London townhouse – new to her, at least – everything would be different.

Running her hands down the sleeves of Tristan's fine wool coat, Adelaide told him proudly, 'My husband will be the most eloquent speaker in the Lords.'

'No one can confuse your motives in marrying me.' He looked pleased. 'Two years ago I was the third son with no prospect of a title and minimal fortune, and now—'

'I am a viscountess and still my mother is not satisfied.'

Tristan laughed. 'She's happier in London than she was in the country.'

'So many more places to poke her reforming nose, I expect. Well, I hope she doesn't expect to drag me along.' Trying for somewhere between her usual demeanour and the natural exuberance she felt with increasing force as each day passed, Adelaide warned playfully, 'Beware, Tristan, for you are opening up a world of frivolous delights to me. Who knows how I may react? I'm sure Mama has voiced her doubts to you. She has little faith in my character.'

Tristan whirled her around the room in his arms. 'London will be good for both of us,' he declared, setting her down and kissing her before heading for the door. 'I thought myself happy enough a farmer in the country, but Robert and William's deaths have opened up a new world for me and I believe I can make a valuable contribution.'

'Oh, dear, I married a reformer and never knew it.'

Adelaide pretended concern. 'Now Mama will think me even less worthy of you.'

'Don't say that!' He swung round, crossing the room quickly to grip her elbows. His expression alarmed her and she felt her mouth drop open as his eyes bored into hers. 'You can never do ill in my eyes, Addy. Whatever happened in the past means nothing to me. I love you just as your are – and I always will!'

He stepped backwards after releasing her. 'Buy yourself as many dresses as you think you need, my darling. I trust your judgment. I certainly shan't lose my temper over a few unexpected dressmakers' bills.'

Tristan's words of love and trust thrilled her. Running after him, she said, 'Mama is accompanying me to Madame Claudette's this afternoon for the final fitting of my new gown. Please come with us.'

Adelaide's disappointment was swift and intense when, clearly in two minds, Tristan said finally, 'There's a debate I'm keen to hear this afternoon, Addy—'

'I'll postpone the fitting, then.' Other women's husbands attended them to the mantua-makers. 'Please, Tristan.' She affected her most appealing expression. 'I'd really love your opinion.'

Smiling, he cupped her chin. 'When you look at me like that, Adelaide, I can refuse you nothing.'

M<small>RS</small> H<small>ENLEY</small>'<small>S</small> sniff was a barometer of her opinion. Adelaide had learned to distinguish disgust from indifference and reluctant admiration. She thought, as she did a turn in a Pomona green lustring gown that her mother's sniff indicated the latter. However, since her mother's opinion had grown less important while her husband's had assumed vital proportions, it was the pride she saw in Tristan's eyes that delighted her.

'Madame is radiant, but with the right accoutrements she will draw gasps of admiration,' the dressmaker predicted, no doubt with an eye to embellishing the stakes for future business, thought Adelaide.

As she glanced at her husband she amended her cynicism. Tristan was looking at her as if she were the most glorious creature ever to cross his orbit. Every fibre of her being sprang to life. If the right gown could do this to him, what couldn't her animated and eager desire achieve when it came to being more of a wife to him?

'She will have the right accoutrements,' Tristan promised, still staring at her, and she knew he meant the family jewels which passed from his eldest brother, dead two years, to his next brother, barely cold in the ground, to himself.

Forgetting the French assistant and Madame Claudette herself, who fussed around her making small adjustments to the roulades at her hem, Adelaide gazed back at Tristan. He cut a fine figure in his dark cutaway coat of navy superfine and his tan breeches. Her mother, hunched on a small gilt chair wearing an expression of grim dissatisfaction, looked dowdy and out of place amidst these plush surroundings. Clearly, her daughter's unexpected elevation to the peerage did not delight her in the same way it would most. Rank meant nothing to Prunella Henley, but the money that might be channelled into her good causes was a different matter.

'What do you think, Mama?' Adelaide swept a low curtsy and fluttered her lashes in her mother's direction. It had the calculated effect. Her mother's brows joined in the middle and her mouth grew thinner.

'You look very fine, if it's compliments you're after, Adelaide.' Smoothing her skirts, she added, 'It seems an obscene amount of money to pay when it could be channelled into doing good where it matters.'

'I think it matters.' Tristan did not hesitate to jump to his wife's defence. 'Adelaide has never asked for fine clothes and until now I'd never thought to push them upon her. When I see how she blooms in a confection such as this I realise how remiss I've been.'

'Lady Leeson will be the most beautiful woman in the room,' gushed the little French assistant. 'While the most beautiful debutante will be'—she halted, then turned, simpering as she registered a new arrival to her salon— 'Miss Emmeline Hawkins.'

'You flatter my daughter too much,' said the small, thin woman being ushered through the curtained doorway. 'Emmeline will never be a beauty like Lady Leeson.' Nodding briefly at Tristan and Mrs Henley, the newcomer cast a critical eye over Adelaide. The woman's wiry grey hair had been dressed in the latest fashion, with ringlets from a centre parting, and a bonnet adorned with an elaborate floral confection. In contrast to the bright colours of her plumage, the even thinner, plainer creature she ushered before her, looked decidedly dowdy. 'My commiserations on the death of your brother, Lord Leeson,' she addressed Tristan. 'I do not believe I've had the pleasure of meeting your wife.'

'We've not been up to London since I married,' Tristan said after introducing the ladies. 'How is Miss Emmeline? I cannot believe she is out of the schoolroom.'

'With four sisters to follow during the next four years.' Lady Hawkins looked grim. 'And none of them beauties like your wife, Lord Leeson, more's the pity. I do not relish what is ahead of me.' She spoke like one with a terrible cross to bear. 'Indeed, Lady Leeson, you will make a far more favourable impression when you are launched upon society than my Emmeline, and the dress alone does not account for that.'

Adelaide didn't know what to reply to such backhanded praise. She pitied Emmeline as Lady Hawkins proceeded to elaborate on the girl's deficiencies once they were all seated at a small round table and given tea and sugar biscuits. Adelaide had only to wait for some small adjustment to be made to the trimmings of her gown while Lady Hawkins, it seemed, was more than happy to pass the time waxing lyrical on the trials of a mother with five seemingly unmarriageable daughters and a season to be endured rather than enjoyed.

'I think I shall take my wife to Gunter's for an ice,' Tristan announced once Adelaide's alterations were complete. He bowed to Lady Hawkins and Miss Emmeline. 'Everything is very new for her.'

'I lived here as a child, you forget.' Adelaide glanced at her mother. 'But I think the London you show me, Tristan, will be more to my liking than the old.'

Mrs Henley sniffed. 'Entirely in keeping with what I might have expected, Adelaide. You have an indulgent husband, indeed. Court presentation, gowns for all occasions, opera and theatre expeditions. You will become patroness of the arts rather than of the prisons.'

'If you enjoy paintings, Lady Leeson, you may care to view my nephew's studio.' Lady Hawkins rummaged in her reticule and produced a card which she handed to Tristan. 'The boy fancies himself a society painter though I will admit he's accomplished.' Adelaide glanced at his name – David Gilchrist – as Lady Hawkins went on, 'Though he's not found George Romney's fame, he's on his way to becoming a portraitist of some note. I think he might fancy his future assured if he could paint a beauty like you, Lady Leeson.'

❄

AFTER ICE at Gunter's Tristan seemed reluctant to leave his wife for the work he'd said earlier was so pressing.

'Mr Gilchrist's studio is around the corner, shall we step in?' he suggested, after they'd dropped Mrs Henley at Bruton Street. She'd complained of fatigue, though Adelaide thought boredom was more likely. She can't have enjoyed seeing Adelaide have such a splendid time.

At the paint-chipped door to Mr Gilchrist's dubious looking premises, they were greeted by a young boy who led them up a rickety staircase to a light-filled attic filled with canvases propped against the walls and, not surprisingly, a pervasive smell of paint and spirits.

Adelaide wanted to turn back when they found they were the only visitors, but Tristan pressed her forward. The artist, a tall, wild-haired young man, wearing a paint-stained cutaway coat over equally paint-stained breeches, was touching up a study of an insipid young lady sitting on a swing holding a pug in her lap.

Rather distractedly, and without looking up, he ordered the boy to procure refreshments. 'Look where you will,' he muttered, swinging round suddenly as Adelaide stepped into his peripheral vision.

His face was a study of surprise.

'You are new to town, Lady Leeson?' he enquired after Tristan had introduced them. 'Very new and not yet present-ed?' The blue eyes beneath his pale eyebrows narrowed as if he were assessing an object of great value. His mouth stretched into a slow smile. 'You say my aunt urged you to step in, and small wonder, for your beauty is above the ordi-nary, Lady Leeson, and my aunt is a shrewd woman. She'd know my star would be in the ascendant and perhaps my career cemented if you did me the great honour of allowing me to commit your loveliness to canvas.' He began to circle her like a predator sizing up his prey. Adelaide was conscious of Tristan's growing concern, but she put her hand on his wrist to stay any objection.

'We came merely to look, Mr Gilchrist,' Adelaide demurred, 'though I am flattered.'

His scrutiny which had begun at her ankles was fixed somewhere between her chest and her chin. At her words he straightened, tossing back an errant curl that flopped over one eye. 'Surely we can come to some arrangement?' he pleaded as he raked both hands through his wild hair, still grasping the paintbrush which deposited its load of burnt umber somewhere over his shoulder.

Tristan looked amused. 'A magnificent rendition of my wife in oils *is* a requirement for a man in my position, I do agree,' he said drily. 'May we look at your work?'

'Of course, of course!' Mr Gilchrist was at their heels as they stopped by each painting, many half finished, that lined the walls. His study of the young lady with the dog had been painted in a light which made his subject's very plainness interesting and her youthful absorption in her pug an endearing quality.

Adelaide could feel his breath on her neck as she studied the work. Uncomfortable, she stepped back as Mr Gilchrist addressed her husband in tones that rose from carefully controlled to deeply passionate. 'Lord Leeson, I swear I'd do justice to your wife's exquisite green eyes, catch the exact tone of her tresses – honey-gold or titian. What shall I call it? Please, madam, I implore you to remove your bonnet. Why, such a glorious hue and such lustrous thickness! Your skin – it glows, Lady Leeson. If I could render that on canvas … I could do it, you know! Do justice to your beauty.' He spoke so rapidly and with such enthusiasm that Adelaide and Tristan raised their faces at the same time to exchange smiles. Ignoring the painter who had now launched into a monologue detailing each step of how he intended to approach the work, Tristan murmured, 'Well, Lady Leeson, are you up to hours of inactivity while your beauty is committed to canvas for posterity? Such a painting would indeed add to my consequence.'

'As it would pander to my vanity.' The little glow that warmed her heart with each encounter with her husband, increased. 'I think it an excellent idea.'

CHAPTER 7

Lady Middleton's rout was Adelaide's entry into London society as a married woman and a surprisingly painful reminder of her wayward youth.

No sooner had she and Tristan been announced than Lady Middleton's daughter, Octavia, swooped upon her, brimming with excitement and ready to trade memories of the years they had both been students at Miss Wilkins' Seminary for Young Ladies in Kensington.

'You probably don't even remember me, Lady Leeson, for I was four years younger, but when you left the Seminary to go to Vienna we all knew you'd be the most marvellous success.' Miss Octavia's eyes shone. This was her second season but she seemed unconcerned. 'I knew I wouldn't receive a suitable offer in my first season, unlike you who were sure to be snapped up by a Russian prince or a fabulously rich nobleman. That's what we used to say, you know. Indeed, we had wagers on how magnificent a marriage you would make and you've not disappointed.' This remark was accompanied by a lasciviously undebutante-like glance at Tristan, who was in conversation a few feet away.

Adelaide's relief when Tristan reclaimed her, was short-lived, for almost immediately she was facing Beatrice. And that meant James was not far away.

'Lady Leeson, what a pleasure to see you again. James and I enjoyed our stay with you very much.'

Adelaide returned the greeting as she wondered who had chosen the young girl's gown with its three rows of bulky roulades at the hem; so unbecoming to one who lacked height. A glimpse at Beatrice's Aunt Wells with her old fashioned upswept hair and unfashionable rig-out confirmed her unsuitability as an arbiter of good taste. Or as anyone who should have any say over Beatrice's wardrobe.

'As did we. You must join me in an afternoon round of visiting dressmakers and glovers,' she offered, and was surprised when Beatrice shook her head. 'I should be terribly poor company. I'm afraid I don't know the first thing about being modish.'

'Then you must learn.' Though Adelaide said it with levity she was deadly serious. 'James was entranced by a young woman who knew her own mind, but you know how much he loves beauty. You are beautiful, Beatrice, and would be more so if you tried. I'll send you an invitation when I'm next visiting my dressmaker, Madame Claudette.'

Locking eyes with Tristan across the room, Adelaide excused herself and threaded her way through the crowd.

'I've not had a chance to greet you properly since you returned from parliament. How was your speech received?' She touched his hand briefly, aware that it would be vulgar to show her affection publicly, but she felt so very proud of her handsome husband.

Excitement blazed in his eyes as he lowered his head to her ear. 'I wish you could have heard it, Addy, and though I don't mean to boast, I was told I constructed a compelling and persuasive argument. I must say, my new secretary, Mr

Finch, has exceeded my expectations. What a turn of phrase he has.' He tapped his chest. 'Transferring passion to the page is a fine art and I'll admit that without him I don't think I'd have received the response I did.'

Resisting the impulse to embrace him or tell him of her secret part in polishing Mr Finch's more clumsy sentences, Adelaide smiled. 'Then we made the right decision in coming to London. I'm glad you're where you feel you can make a difference.'

'For all of us, Adelaide. Including our children.'

She turned her head away at his last words, but taking his arm, led him through the room. 'Come and congratulate James on the fact he is society's darling, today.' As it was inevitable she'd run into James she'd prefer to do so at her husband's side. 'Have you read *The Spectator*?'

'I have and I believe I was the first to congratulate James on such a fulsome opinion piece.'

'Beatrice suits him well. I'm sure he must have said so a thousand times.'

'She's a sweet child but, Addy, I'll be honest, a surprising choice. I expected James to marry a beauty like you but with a passion to match his own. I say, James!'

Afraid that the blanching of her skin might elicit a concern she could do without, she was glad James swung round to claim his attention.

'Even more accolades since I saw you this morning,' Tristan went on. 'Has it gone to your head, yet?'

The crowd pulsed round them and Adelaide was aware of the interest they created: the new Lady Leeson, flanked by the handsome MP and the passionate poet. She felt a surge of pride, knowing they made a handsome trio, though it was not how she'd envisaged making her debut into fashionable society. Her ballgown of gold netting encrusted with oyster beads over a cream under-gown was supposed to distinguish her – not her association with these two such different men who were best friends.

'You know me, Tristan. I couldn't live without adulation.' James nodded a restrained greeting at Adelaide before his irrepressible spirits rose to the fore. Soon his eyes were dancing with the excitement Adelaide remembered so well as he raked both hands through his inky curls. 'It has, however, exceeded my wildest expectations.'

'You've taken London by storm and because you're being so coy about it, everyone is crying out to know the identity of your mystery muse.' Tristan's smile was enquiring. 'Surely Beatrice has a right to know?'

'There is no mystery muse.' James's good humour soured abruptly. 'I told you, she is an amalgamation of all the beauties who entertained me during my misspent Grand Tour. I don't know who has been spreading rumours. No doubt my nemesis over there,' he added, pointing.

'Oh my goodness, how does he arrange his hair in such a manner?' gasped Adelaide. James's so-called nemesis was a young man of middling height, wearing the exaggerated clothing of the dandy and sporting a mass of unruly curls.

Her shock defused the tension and James laughed, his good humour restored. 'The use of wax combined with not washing his locks for some months. It's called the "frightened owl".'

'Not a hairstyle for the fainthearted,' suggested Tristan. 'But what is your quarrel with this man? I've not heard of him.'

'Not likely to, either, although he aspires to eclipse me and surpass the notoriety I've achieved with my book.'

'Do I detect professional jealousy?'

James gave a dismissive wave. 'I cannot be jealous of someone who has no talent.'

'It's a fine thing to have such a high opinion of oneself,

James. Just so long as Beatrice is not concerned by your antics.' Adelaide glanced at the young girl who was speaking to an elderly duchess a few feet away, and once again James dismissed the remark.

'Oh, Beatrice doesn't worry about things like that. She'll stand by me. She knows what I'm like.'

Tristan laughed. 'I do, but does Addy? She'll think you a puffed up popinjay if you go on.'

James sobered. With his gaze trained on Adelaide's face he affected a look of mock seriousness. 'In that case I shall crave pardon for anything I have done in the past, or may do in the future, likely to tarnish your high regard for me, Lady Leeson.'

Adelaide was unable to smile. It was too close to the bone. Tristan clapped his friend on the back. 'You're incorrigible, James, but I already know the worst of you so rest assured you could never tarnish my high regard of you. And I'll go so far as to speak on Addy's behalf, also.'

As the orchestra tuned up for a waltz, Tristan prepared to make his excuses. 'You must find your betrothed. No doubt Miss Beatrice has claimed the first waltz from you.'

James grinned. 'A distant cousin asked her for this one. He's afraid of stepping on some other unfortunate miss's toes.' He pointed to Beatrice who was being led onto the dance floor by a gangly youth in high shirt points and a mop of sandy curls.

Tristan followed Adelaide's look. 'You're longing to dance, aren't you, my love? I'd hoped my ankle would be up to it this evening, but I'm going to have to ask James to be my proxy.'

Before Adelaide could object, James was offering her his arm with no sign of reserve. 'Lady Leeson, it would be an honour.'

Adelaide's helpless fury was not eased when Tristan said mildly, 'Make sure you don't step on *Adelaide's* toes. I want her first dance in four years to be one she remembers fondly.' Furtively he skimmed Adelaide's bare arm with his finger tips and she felt frustrated desire ripple through her. It was quickly extinguished by fear. Oh, why was Tristan so trusting? She wanted him to sense something was amiss – though ask no questions – and whisk her out of James's arms to claim her for his own. That, and make sure she never laid eyes on his friend again.

'I wish you hadn't done that,' Adelaide whispered as James rested his hand on her waist and clasped her shoulder. 'Goodness, Adelaide, don't look so angry or someone will remark upon it.' He seemed surprised by her response. 'A harmless waltz? Don't you know I've ached to hold you in my arms for the past four years?'

'You've been drinking.' She was shocked. 'Promise you'll never say such a thing in public.' With Tristan so close it was easy to be immune to James's embrace. The feel of his strong body and his familiar woody scent was like a reproach for her wicked past and she couldn't wait for the waltz to end.

He put his head closer to hers. 'The last time we met you admitted you'd have crossed mountains and forded rivers to be in my arms.'

'If it had been possible *at the time.*' She would not look at him as he swept her round the room. He was a wonderful dancer. In Vienna, where the waltz had been danced long before being accepted in England, she used to feel he was dancing her to the moon. She'd imagined the two of them lifting off gently from the dance floor and floating to a place where they could be together. Angry with herself, she blanked her mind to all but the present. 'But it was not possible. I made one mistake in my life, James. We both did. Now we must take what we've got and make something wonderful out of it.' She raised her chin. 'The happiness I have found is too precious to risk. For three long years my husband has been the most considerate and patient of men. He helped me through the dark times I spent exorcising you from my system. I love him.' A lump rose in her throat and she glanced with longing at Tristan, who was watching her from the other side of the dance floor. He caught her eye and smiled: warm, loving and sincere.

So trusting.

'Do you, Adelaide?' he murmured. 'Gratitude and love are two different things. Your happiness means more to me than my own. You know that – don't you?'

She jerked her head up. 'Then do not persist with talk like this, James. I have every confidence you will discover with the very worthy Miss Beatrice the same loving contentment I have discovered with—'

'—your worthy husband.' He clenched his jaw as he swung her adeptly out of the way of a less coordinated couple. 'Is loving contentment to be elevated above searing passion?' He looked almost angry. 'Is cosy domesticity more important than feeling every sense on fire? Because we had that, Addy. Don't you remember—?'

'How could I forget?' she hissed. 'Stop! Tristan is looking at us but yes, the cosy domesticity you deride *is* more important to me. I am no longer the impulsive, wayward child I was when your charms blinded me to … everything but you. I allowed my youthful impulses to carry me away, thinking I could have what I craved and not pay a price. Well, we both know the price I paid, James, but as my mother continually reminds me, I got off lightly.' Plastering a smile upon her face as she saw Tristan approach the edge of the dance floor to receive her as the music drifted away, she added, 'My husband's political star is rising. The Miss Adelaide Henley you knew is no more. In your arms is Lady Leeson, wife of a respected member of parliament. A loyal, dutiful and *loving* wife who values her position and the trust of her husband too much to even *want* to engage in talk like this. Do you understand? Now ask Beatrice for the next dance. It's not hard to see from the look in her eyes how much she adores you.'

'What were you and James discussing so earnestly, my love?' Tristan's question was put innocently enough but Adelaide was unable to look at him.

'That I was the most fortunate of wives and that I wished James and Beatrice similar happiness.'

'London agrees with you, Adelaide. You looked so vital and glowing in Mr Gilchrist's studio – and in James's arms – I only wished I had Mr Gilchrist's talent so I could paint you myself; or James's agility so I could dance with you.' He handed her a glass of champagne and raised his own. 'To the toast of the town. But perhaps we should not be late home since you have your first sitting at noon.'

'You'll stay with me tomorrow, won't you?'

Tristan hesitated, obviously sensing she was distressed, and she rushed on, 'I'll need a chaperone. Please stay.'

The urge to spend time alone with her husband was suddenly a pressing need.

'Of course I won't leave you alone with Gilchrist, my dear. However, it is difficult tomorrow. Ah, James, I'd hoped I could prevail upon you to help.' Tristan waved his friend over. 'Adelaide needs a chaperone while Mr Gilchrist is painting her portrait tomorrow morning. Would you oblige?'

Adelaide gasped. 'No, if you can't be there, Tristan, then I'm sure I—'

'It would be a pleasure.' James inclined his head as he spoke over Adelaide's objections. 'Beatrice won't mind. She's promised to accompany her aunt to the tooth-drawer. I'm sure I know where I'd rather be.' He slanted Tristan a conspiratorial look. 'You'll no doubt want a full accounting of Mr Gilchrist's conduct on an occasion of such importance.'

S o Mr Gilchrist was going to turn Adelaide into a sensation and cement his reputation in the process.

James made the pronouncement shortly before Tristan left the studio while the painter prepared his palette and adjusted his easel beneath the skylight.

Adelaide plucked at her new fur-edged spencer and tried to settle herself in the armchair where Mr Gilchrist had arranged her, but she felt ill at ease.

'Smile,' James murmured. He was leaning against the arm of the chair. Very close. 'Lower your book and reveal those pretty pearls so Mr Gilchrist can do justice to London's most alluring mouth.'

'Don't talk like that, James!' Adelaide wondered if he was still in his cups from the night before.

It was a relief when they were interrupted by loud giggles on the stairs before the door burst open and a woman with striking hair and pretty, if sharp features, entered the room, followed by Phineas Donegal.

'Good lord, Dewhurst, you're the last person I expected!'

Donegal raked his hand though his 'frightened owl' as he surveyed the scene. 'See who I met on the first floor? None other than our esteemed songbird, Miss Kitty Carew, who tells me she's a friend of yours, Gilchrist.'

'We're artists, the both of us, ain't we?' Kitty said, after formal introductions had been made. She draped an arm about Mr Gilchrist's shoulders and simpered up at him, but the painter was absorbed in his work and did not respond.

His attention was focussed on Adelaide, though he seemed none too pleased with his subject. A deep furrow creased his brow as he tried a different arrangement with her hair, and then her hands.

James studiously ignored Donegal's banter. Even Adelaide could see Donegal's boasts about his publisher's high expectations of the book he was working on were designed to impress Miss Carew. Indeed, she appeared much struck, though Adelaide wondered how much of it was play-acting. Mr Donegal was, after all, a man of means and someone worth cultivating. The simpering creature was far too conscious of her good looks and decidedly out to profit where she might.

Adelaide observed her covertly as Mr Gilchrist worked on arranging Adelaide as he would like to paint her.

Miss Carew's alabaster skin and thick hair, similar to Adelaide's, were her best features. Her exaggerated facial expressions, no doubt honed for stage performances, were being amply employed as she responded to James's literary rival. When he asked what had brought her to Mr Gilchrist's studio, her rosebud mouth puckered and her smile was knowing as she replied, 'Why, to see for meself if Lady Leeson were all she were made out to be, if you'll pardon me expression, ma'am.'

Adelaide stiffened, but Donegal cut in before she could speak.

'And ain't she just?' he declared with ingenuous admiration. 'News travels fast, eh?'

Miss Carew touched the side of her nose. 'Not much gets past us theatre folk wot knows all about the gentry wot takes an interest in us. I knew Lord Leeson when he lived in London. A grand gent, he were, wot always came to the theatre ...' She put her hand to her chest and her expression became bleak. 'Then all of a sudden I hears he's to be married. Ain't seen him since, but I 'ad to gaze on the vision of loveliness wot caught 'is fancy, for Lord Leeson 'as 'igh standards, so I knew 'er Ladyship'd be a beauty. And now I see what all the fuss is about. Mr Gilchrist is going to paint the lovely Lady Leeson and make her famous. I'm sure you'll do yer 'usband great credit, m'lady. You got lovely red-gold 'air like mine, ain't yer? I can't tell yer how often I get asked to sell it, but I need me crowning glory to make a quid. 'Is Lordship allus did admire it'—she patted the cluster of tight little curls about her forehead and ears with a self-satisfied smile—'when I were on stage, o' course.'

Adelaide felt her chest swell with the air she was unable to breathe evenly. None of the others seemed to take Kitty's words amiss, they were delivered so artfully, but she was well aware the compliments hid a deeper meaning. And that Kitty Carew was definitely not admiring her.

Perversely, she wanted to burst into tears.

'Ain't Lord Leeson supposed to be chaperoning his wife?' Kitty turned to James. 'It were as much my reason for coming here. Not that *you're* disappointing, m'lord.' She sent James a brazen look and he grinned.

'Lord Leeson entrusted his wife to my care. She's like a sister to me. Knew her years before she married his lordship.'

'And you are to treat me with respect, James,' Adelaide responded, forcing lightness into her tone as she sought to dispel the troubling undercurrents she sensed whenever Miss Carew opened her mouth.

'It's very hard to treat you with respect in that frightful puce spencer which is not a colour that does you justice, my dear.' James turned. 'Surely you concur, Gilchrist? Do you not see the lovely Lady Leeson as a Circe or a Penelope, sheathed in peach gauze with a white veil partly covering her hair, released to cascade over her naked shoulders?'

'James!' Adelaide's cry of outrage was drowned by the painter's enthusiastic response. Donegal clapped but Adelaide noticed the narrowing of Miss Carew's eyes before she announced she was required at a dress rehearsal.

Relieved, Adelaide watched them leave after Donegal offered to escort her there. Meanwhile Mr Gilchrist had been fired by new enthusiasm. 'Why Dewhurst, I *had* thought along those lines, myself. The book—' He snatched the novel out of Adelaide's hands. 'Why, you're right! Lady Leeson's natural assets'—he looked appraisingly at Adelaide's bust— 'must be more in evidence if I am to transform her into the toast of the town.'

Adelaide half rose, her protests drowned by the two gentlemen's collective enthusiasm which, she acknowledged guiltily, was balm to her love of admiration. After all, James spoke only the truth when he reminded her she'd be doing nothing that the famous beauty Lady Hamilton had not done to wide acclaim.

By the end of the first sitting Mr Gilchrist had completed a preliminary sketch and painting of Adelaide reclining on a bed, clothed in white and pastel gauze with a fillet of gold upon her flowing tresses.

'My dear, your mother will love it!' cried James, looking over Mr Gilchrist's shoulder at the portrait as Adelaide sat up, clasping her flimsy coverings to her chest and feeling very exposed.

'I trust your husband will, too.' The artist's tone was dry.

Lord Leeson, after all, was the man paying him.

Mr Gilchrist went to the far end of the room to clean his brushes while James moved to help Adelaide untangle the layers of soft fabric caught around her ankles. The gesture, once so welcome, sent horror and remorse rippling through her, and at the touch of his hand upon her knee she recoiled, as if he were a spider.

'I cannot bear it, Addy,' he muttered. 'To be so close but—'

She was as angry as she was fearful. 'James! Tristan trusted you to chaperone me, not to—'

'I know, I know.' He looked miserable before he turned away. 'Tristan might be my dearest friend, but God knows it was the cruellest day he married the only woman I could ever love.'

'Stop it, James!' With a glance, Adelaide satisfied herself that Mr Gilchrist was out of hearing. 'You live in Fool's Paradise if you believe you can gain anything from this type of behaviour. I can never see you again, James, knowing how you feel. Do you understand that? I shall ensure that Tristan never throws us together again, for I can't have you threatening everything I hold dear.'

Mr Gilchrist's soft tread startled them and in dignified fashion Adelaide withdrew behind the screen to change.

She was unimpressed by James's stormy expression when she reappeared wearing her puce-coloured spencer over her muslin afternoon dress, though she was acutely aware of the way his eyes raked over her. Adelaide flicked a nervous look at Gilchrist who, fortunately, appeared preoccupied with the portrait.

Reluctantly, she slid her hand into the crook of the arm James offered her to escort her out onto the street.

Studiously avoiding James's eye, Adelaide addressed Mr Gilchrist. 'Depending upon my husband's schedule I'll let you know when I'm next able to sit.' She inclined her head at James, adding, 'And now I think you have neglected your bride-to-be for far too long. Let us call on Beatrice.'

CHAPTER 9

Tristan reclined in his wingback chair and gazed at the passing street traffic through the bay windows of his club. It had been a long time since he'd enjoyed the comfortable companionship of his old friend. Now, between sessions, he enquired after James and how things were going with his book, though soon he'd approach the topic that most interested him: how Adelaide's sitting earlier that day had gone.

'White's is not a place you frequent, I presume,' he remarked to James, indicating their surroundings. 'The Pater would be pleased, though.'

'I like to keep a foot in both camps.' James replied. Tristan noted that James had seemed troubled from the moment he'd walked in. He was still clearly distracted as he ran his hands through his carefully tousled hair and glanced around him before attending to Tristan. 'In the months before father died I often accompanied him here.' Relaxing a little, James added with a grin, 'Though I'd be off by midnight to raise hell behind the red baize door at Bennet Street.'

'I'm not surprised.' Tristan rained an eyebrow. James

seemed sometimes more like an errant younger brother than a poet making his mark. 'Had I been more in town I've no doubt the old man would have been forever at my door begging me to take you in hand.' He took a sip of his claret. 'Not that you'd have listened.'

'Your opinion's always held more sway than anyone's.' James sent him a level look over his glass. 'I value your unwarranted high regard for me too much, Tristan, to risk damaging it.' He smiled. 'Though back in our wild days – or rather, my wild days – I don't think anyone could have tempered my ingrained vices like the cards—'

'Or women!' Tristan laughed. 'No need to look at me like that. You always had an eye for beauty so, with all due respect to Hortense, I was astonished when you married my cousin.'

He thought James looked surprisingly uncomfortable at the topic and was about to move on when James asked with unsettling intensity, 'On the subject of women, I met an actress who spoke fondly of you. Kitty Carew.'

Warily, Tristan answered, 'It's been more than four years since I've seen her, but yes, I saw Kitty sometimes when I was in London.' He paused, adding with heavy emphasis, '*Before* I married Adelaide.' He disliked the way James looked almost smug. As if Tristan were somehow admitting to something that diminished him.

'We all need our diversions. Kitty is a splendid-looking female.'

'You misunderstand,' Tristan shot back. 'You know my feelings, James. There's no excuse for adultery – for either husband or wife. Yes, I was Kitty's protector, if you like to call it that, for six months. Cassandra had been dead four years and I had not met a candidate who came close to filling her place as my wife.'

'So you've never sought diversions during marriage?'

'Lord, no! Why would I when I'm married to a woman like Adelaide?' The mere thought of her sent tendrils of desire snaking through his loins. He just wished he could have more of her.

James twisted his glass between his hands. 'A desirable wife does not prevent a man from seeking additional pleasures. Especially if the wife considers her husband's advances taxing.'

At James's assessing look Tristan shifted, suddenly uncomfortable. Had Adelaide hinted publicly at disliking physical intimacy? Carefully he asked, 'Are you trying to tell me something?'

'Not at all, Tristan. You're a lucky man. You have everything I could ever want and I bear you not the slightest ill will, for God knows you deserve it more than I.'

Tristan drained his glass. He disliked the path this conversation had taken. 'You have a child, James. Soon you will have a young, eager-to-please wife who hangs on every word you say. Make the most of your good fortune and celebrate Beatrice in your next volume as you have the mystery muse of this collection which has turned you into an overnight sensation.'

James's curiosity made it incumbent upon him to honour his promise to Beatrice, though he wondered how to frame his question as he indicated to the powdered waiter for more drinks. His friend's words had also dispelled his good spirits. He searched his mind for anything to suggest Addy was unhappy or out of her depth. She had, he thought, seemed in better spirits than he'd seen her. Tristan was always conscious of taxing her emotional reserves.

Yet he'd misinterpreted her desire for greater intimacy considering she'd felt the need to dull her senses with laudanum immediately after pretending that physical intimacy was what she wanted those weeks ago.

Pretending?

No, he suspected she'd made a supreme effort in order to please her husband, only to discover that it was too much for her.

Tristan had been particularly cautious ever since.

He cast the reflection from his mind. 'Seriously, James, if Beatrice can't inspire you to greatness like this other wonderful creature then do not marry her, for you'll be no happier than you were with Hortense.'

Like himself, he noticed James was gaining nothing by their exchange. His friend drained his glass in one gulp. 'I'll give her babies and she'll be happy enough.' He sounded morose. 'If Hortense had only brought to term just one when she lost so many perhaps her misery would not have been such a millstone round my neck.'

'You got your child in the end.'

James looked up sharply. 'Yes, of course, a little girl whom Hortense kept away from me when we could no longer live together.'

Tristan clenched his glass and closed his eyes briefly. 'I'm sorry to hear it but Adelaide has not even that.' In the silence he continued, 'Cassandra and I were married for three years without issue. Adelaide and I have been married three.' He shrugged and opened his eyes to find James staring at him with obvious compassion.

'Perhaps having a child doesn't mean as much to Adelaide as you think,' his friend said, awkwardly. 'You could always adopt a little girl. I mean—'

Tristan tapped his glass, thinking. 'If I have no son the estate will go to my second cousin. I barely know the man and what I know I like little enough.' He broke off. 'It's not even that so much. Adelaide begged me the other evening to come to her more often because she so desperately wants a child. Do you know what torture it is to be in her arms and exercise the restraint needed so as not to repulse her or frighten her—'

'God, Tristan, I can't imagine what you're saying,' James mumbled as he brandished his empty whisky glass for a refill.

'Restraint becomes an art form when a wife is emotionally delicate. The doctor is forever reminding me to have a care. Meanwhile Mrs Henley is forever exhorting me to curtail Adelaide's pleasures so as not to overexcite her and perhaps precipitate an otherwise unavoidable emotional collapse such as the one she was recovering from when I met her.'

'Mrs Henley is a cow. I'd not put too much store by what she advises.'

They laughed, clearly in accord on this point.

'God knows,' said Tristan, 'I wish I could give Adelaide what she needs. I wish I could be with her more often, too, but I'm glad I have you to fill the breach.' His mouth twisted. 'Especially when I feel I can't trust myself with my own wife.'

James was clearly shaken and Tristan was moved. 'You're good for her, James. You remind Adelaide of her carefree youth, perhaps, before French barbarians stole her innocence.' Catching his friend's discomfited gaze, he felt suddenly very close to him. 'I'm glad you're here, James. Glad you're doing all you can for Addy. I can see how much of a paternal interest you must have taken in her when she arrived straight out of school and went to work with Hortense and Mrs Henley.' He finished his drink and rose. 'I must go. I trust you still find yourself free to accompany Adelaide to Mr Gilchrist's studio tomorrow. She was not overwhelmed?'

'Overwhelmed? No, she was superb. Mr Gilchrist found her the ideal model. But Tristan, I'm afraid that tomorrow—'

Tristan cut off his friend as he turned. 'Please, James, just this one favour? Adelaide begged me to come but I simply cannot. Not tomorrow or in fact for the next few days at least, due to my very heavy work commitments, but clearly she does not wish to be left alone with Gilchrist.'

He was relieved when James raised his hands in mock surrender. 'Adelaide will be disappointed, but you know I'd do anything to help you out.'

THE PAINTING, after two sittings, was now nearly finished. Adelaide, posing on the artist's chaise longue, smiled when she saw the difficulty with which Beatrice tried to put into words her ... admiration? She was relieved that James had brought his betrothed along with him today.

Absorbed in his work, Mr Gilchrist muttered as he mixed paints while James grinned as he put his arm about Beatrice's waist.

'You seem rather ... shocked, dear heart,' he whispered in her ear.

'Please raise your chin a fraction, Lady Leeson.' Mr Gilchrist was insensible to anyone other than his subject. Adelaide, catching James's eye, was suddenly speared by a frisson of uncertainty. Beatrice looked like a drowning schoolgirl. Was Adelaide really overstepping the mark with the semi-revealed bare ankle? Yes, she immediately thought, discreetly rearranging her gown.

'Perhaps I'll commission Mr Gilchrist to paint the next Lady Dewhurst,' James said, obviously enjoying Beatrice's fiery blush. 'Venus? Circe? Although I'll always think of you as the ever faithful Penelope ... How do you wish to be regarded? I need a new muse if I'm to pen another volume and keep you in the style to which you'd like to be accustomed.'

Adelaide's amusement turned to concern. James had gone too far. Beatrice was young and too out of her depth to deport herself with the required finesse in the face of such talk.

'I should rather not be painted,' she said. Clumsily. Woodenly.

James sighed and dropped his arm from her waist. 'As you wish.' The boredom in his tone was more cutting than any outright slight could have been and Adelaide winced at the girl's confusion.

Compared with Hortense, Beatrice was no zealot. Her beliefs were as unformed and malleable as any moderately well-educated young woman brought up to believe the pinnacle of success was a good marriage. From conversations with her, Adelaide saw she was idealistic and optimistic enough to believe love was part of the bargain.

But Beatrice's hurt look would only inflame James. He would say she'd snubbed him; sucked the pleasure from the exchange.

Beneath lowered lids, Adelaide studied him with growing anger. He was playing with Beatrice's feelings like a violinist.

The session was over. Mr Gilchrist put down his brushes, bending to attend to a question from Beatrice while James was quickly at Adelaide's side, sliding his hand up her arm in order to help her off the bed. She shook him off. 'Pay your future wife the attention she deserves,' she hissed, adding in a more gracious tone, 'Beatrice, it would be delightful if you could spare the afternoon to offer your opinion on what I should wear to Lady Glenton's rout next week.' She paused halfway towards the screen to change.

'Really?' The girl looked flustered as she glanced between her betrothed and Adelaide. 'James plans to work this afternoon on his poems ... so that's very kind of you.'

'Did I really propose to neglect you all afternoon, my beautiful Beatrice?'

He was too smooth, Adelaide thought as he smiled his charming smile, bringing a blush to the girl's cheek as he tucked her hand into the crook of his arm.

'Why, I had planned to surprise you with a trip to Gunter's, but if you want to admire Lady Leeson's finery then by all means we shall do so.'

'That was a charming thought, James, and if you'd rather—'

'I agree, we must advise Lady Leeson upon her wardrobe if only to have the satisfaction of telling the mob at Lady Glenton's rout that we garbed the toast of London Town.'

Adelaide rolled her eyes. 'You're too much, James,' she said, striving for a mocking tone as she slipped behind the screen and Mr Gilchrist's young maid, who'd been summoned by James, helped her with her fastenings.

'Beatrice won't know what to make of you if you must dress everything up as a joke.'

She emerged, plastering on a smile as she detached Beatrice firmly from her fiancé's grip. 'I think, Beatrice, we need to spend some time together so I can teach you a thing or two about how to keep your husband-to-be in check.'

IT HAD BEEN a long time since Adelaide had been clothed so sumptuously.

Coquelicot red it was called, and it really did accentuate the russet tones of her rippling hair, she decided, as she considered her appearance in the cheval mirror at Madame Claudette's Salon. Sunlight streamed through the large windows, enriching the sheen on the silks and lustrings arranged in higgledy-piggledy bolts amidst swathes of sumptuous trimmings.

Adelaide was delighted at how well she looked, and the warmth in James's assessing look told her he echoed the sentiment. She only wished it was Tristan smiling at her, but other than at Lady Middleton's rout, for four days he'd been involved with his work. Nervous Mr Finch had called with some paperwork he'd prepared for her husband, but it seemed Tristan was always out these days.

Guiltily she saw that Beatrice looked withdrawn and spiritless, her pale complexion gaining nothing from the primrose trimmings on her simple muslin gown. Though fashionable and, as required for a debutante, chaste, it was unbecoming.

'Who chooses your gowns for you?' Adelaide asked the girl, casting subtlety to the wind. Beatrice's potential for becoming a beauty had become an imperative, considering the way James was ignoring his fiancée. By contrast, the searing glances Adelaide intercepted as James gazed upon her reclining for her portrait were clearly calculated to make her fling herself into his embrace and damn the rest of the world – and any potential for lasting happiness.

James's obvious attraction needed to be channelled in worthier directions – like sweet Beatrice.

'Miss Maple, my governess, and Aunt Wells chose my London wardrobe.' The girl sounded doubtful.

'I think they could have been more ... perceptive in finding colours to enhance your colouring and those lovely brown eyes of yours.'

'I'm not terribly interested in clothes.'

As if sensing something gallant were required of him, James declared, as he ushered the ladies into the early summer sunshine, 'Beatrice refuses to see herself as the shining star she's destined to become, nor can she understand the new standard by which she will be judged. Hers has been a disciplined and restrained upbringing.'

'As was mine,' Adelaide replied, forcing gaiety into her tone as she took Beatrice's other arm. 'Only look at me now. The despair of my mother.'

'And London's brightest star.'

Adelaide did not miss the glance Beatrice darted towards her betrothed, as if uncertain how to interpret this. Nor did she miss the confusing cocktail of emotions that churned within her own breast. James was as in thrall to her as he had ever been. Meanwhile Tristan palmed her off onto his old friend though she begged for his company. When she'd been vulnerable and needy Tristan had always been there, but the more she blossomed the more he seemed willing to relinquish his role of quiet stalwart. He said his parliamentary duties required him, but Adelaide told him she required him more. The truth was, she found it increasingly difficult being alone with James, though she could hardly say that to Tristan.

'You'll have much more fun with James and Beatrice than an exhausted husband,' he'd said that afternoon, kissing the tip of her nose before sending her away with a brief caress.

Now, forcing aside her frustration, Adelaide said brightly, 'Shining Star? You flatter me, James. Well, Beatrice must be the vanguard. My glory days are nearly behind me as I approach my dotage.'

'A beauty you will always be, Lady Leeson – don't you think?' James appealed to Beatrice as if she must surely share his admiration. 'Come to the opera with us tonight, Addy? Beatrice and I have been invited to use her uncle's box. We can make silly faces at everyone across the gallery.'

'I'm sure Beatrice can think of nothing better,' Adelaide said drily, squeezing the girl's arm. 'You and I are old friends, James, who might take pleasure in such childish pursuits, but remember, Beatrice is soon to be your *wife*.' She sent him a meaningful look when Beatrice's head was turned. 'And now, if you would kindly escort me home, James. I'm afraid I shall have to decline your kind offer as I've barely seen my husband.'

James insisted on depositing Beatrice with her aunt before walking Adelaide the rest of the way home, but nonetheless, she was poised for a calm farewell in the late-afternoon gloom of the downstairs lobby of their townhouse.

'Ah, James!' Tristan appeared from an adjoining annexe. Though conversation with James had been general and unexceptional, Adelaide nearly jumped out of her skin as her husband's voice penetrated their cloistered leave-taking. 'Stay and have a drink with us. I'm exhausted and can think of nothing better than the company of an old friend.' He sounded in unusually robust spirits.

Taking his arm, she said, 'I'm afraid James must get ready for the opera tonight.' Heady satisfaction swept through her as she basked in the warmth of her husband's expression. Her mother had accepted a dinner invitation, meaning Adelaide would be alone with Tristan for the first time since they'd been in London.

'I invited Addy to join us in Beatrice's uncle's box, but sadly she has declined.'

'Declined? Why is that, Addy? Surely you'd enjoy a night's entertainment?'

'Please, no, Tristan,' she protested. 'I don't want to be the gooseberry between James and Beatrice.'

'Gooseberry, indeed,' scoffed James. 'Beatrice hangs off every word you utter. I'm the one who needs Tristan for company. Won't you join us?'

Tristan met Adelaide's look with an apologetic glance.

'Much as I would love to, I'm afraid my work is more important.'

Adelaide gripped his wrist. Desperately, she whispered, 'I shan't go without you, Tristan.'

'You'll have to on this occasion, I'm afraid,' he said, but Adelaide would not be fobbed off. She drew her shoulders back, declaring so that James could hear, 'Then I'm afraid I must definitely decline your kind invitation, James. I won't go if Tristan won't accompany me.'

'You'd prefer to spend the evening gossiping with your mother?' Tristan's mouth quirked. 'Her plans have changed, in case you didn't know, and she will be in this evening. I would not thrust that upon you. No, James, I insist that you play Adelaide's gallant escort this evening. I entrust her to you entirely. No doubt you'll do a far better job of introducing her to the city's pleasures than I will.'

He'd turned his head before Adelaide could focus her entreating look upon him.

'Splendid!' James clapped Tristan on the back, saying over his shoulder, 'I'll make it an evening to remember, Addy. I promise.'

CHAPTER 10

In her youth, Adelaide was used to prevailing, so it was a satisfying feeling to brush her lips across Tristan's hand as he stood behind her, securing her pale blue silk Witzchoura Mantle lined with white fur, and know that once again he'd been unable to refuse her.

'I'm so glad you changed your mind, darling,' she murmured, taking the opportunity to nestle against him before the butler turned to open the doors onto the portico.

At the bottom of the stairs the carriage was waiting for them.

'There's a certain way you look at me, Addy, that renders me completely unable to refuse any request.' Fleetingly, he kissed the top of her head.

His smile, when she turned, filled her with happiness, and when Barking wasn't looking she hugged him quickly. 'Show me exactly what this look is,' she began, 'so I know which one to use for future reference?'

Ushering Adelaide over the threshold he said softly, 'That one.' Then he laughed, more carefree than Adelaide had ever seen him. 'Like a wood sprite, my darling? Has no ever told you that you have the sweetest rosebud lips and the wickedest pair of eyes?'

'Tristan!' He had never spoken to her quite like this. Certainly, he'd never spoken of the effect she had on him. Little bursts of pleasure seemed to explode inside her. She giggled and clung to him as the postilion let down the steps and Tristan helped her in.

Tristan had his own box and Adelaide was glad of the privacy. She preferred sitting beside her husband without being covertly observed by James, at any rate.

'The painting is almost done and will be displayed in Mr Gilchrist's rooms on Wednesday,' Adelaide told him. 'You'll come to the unveiling? Mr Gilchrist is hoping to secure a great deal of patronage and is enormously grateful to you, Tristan, for honouring him with the commission.'

'Are you pleased with it? That's all I'm concerned with.'

'I think it's a flattering likeness.' Adelaide hugged the secret that it was undeniably a masterpiece. 'Most portraits manage that, though, don't they? James wants to commission Mr Gilchrist to paint Beatrice after they are wed but she refuses. She says she's not interested in showy things like clothes and portraits, but I think she should agree, if James wishes it.'

'I hope James does not repeat the mistakes of the past.'

'Hortense?'

'My cousin was a most unsuitable match.' Tristan leaned down to retrieve the opera glasses she had dropped. 'I've said it before, but James should have married someone like you, my dear.'

Adelaide was afraid she was going to drop the opera glasses again.

When she did not reply Tristan went on, 'However, if Hortense were still alive I'd like to spend the evening in conversation with her on the idea of prison reform. It is, once again, the subject with which my next speech is concerned.'

'You'll have to engage Mama's thoughts on the matter instead.'

'She's offered them willingly.' Tristan reached for her hand. 'I'd far rather spend the evening in discussion with her daughter who does not share the righteous passions of the mother.'

'You're doing a much more effective job of it than my mother is, trudging through filthy cells. I've had a lifetime of it, Tristan, and I don't ever intend being Mama's drudge again. You saved me from that.' With a hint of apology, she added, 'You know, of course, Mama was in favour of our marriage only because she thought she could prevail upon you to fund her causes.'

'I'm not interested in why your mother accepted me for you.' He tilted his head. 'I'm interested in why *you* accepted me when I know you'd have been happy enough with no husband had your pecuniary situation allowed it.'

A heavy silence punctuated their conversation. The opera was about to begin. The curtain rose and the audience clapped.

'Why did I accept you?' Adelaide's throat became dry. His interested gaze in the gloom seemed so much more than that. Could he suspect? Of course not. There had been no indication that he thought her anything other than a beautiful, delicate, damaged creature with a blameless past. He'd made it clear, lately, that he was more in love with her than ever. She closed her eyes and whispered, angling closer towards him, 'It's true that I needed a husband if I were not to become an old maid, and Mama was pressing me to accept your suit.' She tried to go on. Tried to tell him that he had become so much to her during the past three years; that when she'd married him she'd felt nothing but that her heart was now fully his. But the words wouldn't come.

'Ah, well, Addy.' Though he still clasped her hand he did not stroke it as she might have hoped. 'As long as you don't actively rail against your lot as you did all that time ago.'

She thought he was finished but obviously it weighed heavy on his heart for he said in the softest of whispers, 'I only wish I could give you a child.'

Galvanised into speech, she whipped back her hand and held it to her heart. 'Yes, I want a child. Desperately. But I want *you*, Tristan ... even more than I want a child. You know I am happy with my lot, as you call it. I have always appreciated what you've done for me. You were so patient when we married, Tristan, when I know I was not a pleasing wife.' She gripped his hands tighter and forced him to look at her. 'Tell me, have you ever regretted—?'

'Hush, let's not talk of it.' He leaned across and laid a finger across her lips. 'The music has begun.'

An aria was in progress though there were many in the audience who talked through the performance. It was not an excuse for choosing not to answer her question.

Once, Adelaide would have been relieved to cut off their uncomfortable conversation at such a point. Once, she'd have felt little concern that her question, so vital to a woman in love, received such an unsatisfactory answer. She told herself that all that was important was that he loved her now. She'd been truly well since she'd come to London. Right now she pulsed with vitality; but what about the occasions when woolly-headed listlessness plagued her? Though that had not happened for a long time, she had no idea when these lapses of focus might descend upon her, and the fear of being unaccountably overcome by inertia once again terrified her. She wanted to forge a greater bond with her husband now that she was more confident of her good health.

It took her a moment to school her voice into the controlled, lightly interested tone for which she strove but though she was trembling like she had the ague, she would have his reply.

'*Have* you ever regretted asking, Tristan? Please tell me the truth.'

He raised his eyebrows, and though he did not at first look at her, she could tell he was caught off guard by the intensity of her question. She did not usually traverse these paths with him.

'Very well.' He gave her his attention and the music seemed to fade into the background as Adelaide waited breathlessly.

'You must know I fell in love with you the moment I laid eyes on you. By the end of that week when you and your mother were guests in my house I was completely smitten. I'd have walked barefoot to Timbuktu to secure your consent, even if I knew it wouldn't win me your heart.' He stroked her cheek and Adelaide moved into him as feeling surged through her. She wished they were home together. Alone.

'I know how painful it is for you to talk about, but you must know that however you felt … about yourself … was not echoed by me. Whatever happened in your past makes no difference to how I feel about you. How I ever felt about you.'

These final words should have relieved the general anxiety she felt on the subject but they only served to heighten her fear that the truth would disgust him. The *real* truth. Yet again he was reassuring her he felt no repugnance for her sins of which he believed her innocent.

She drew back, straightening. What of his repugnance at having been taken for a fool by a lie which she'd perpetuated for three long years?

A lie which she'd guard to the death for she could not bear to lose him now.

Quiet finally descended as the opera dancer's thin but pretty voice struggled to reach the outer limits of the gallery. Adelaide leaned forward and held her opera glasses to her eyes, conscious of Tristan's nearness, desperate but so unsure as to how to forge a greater intimacy with that choking lie between them.

'She's a lovely creature,' she remarked. 'She looks such a child.'

'Kitty Carew is no child,' said Tristan.

'My Goodness, is that Kitty Carew?' Adelaide swung round to look at her husband as jealousy speared her. 'I met her briefly at Mr Gilchrist's studio during my first sitting.' She hoped he didn't notice the strained way she forced out the words.

Miss Carew, she saw with shock, was dressed as a boy. Adelaide's mouth dropped open as she watched the young woman cavorting upon the stage. No doubt in a few moments she'd reveal her real gender and her thick, beautiful hair would come tumbling out of her cap. But for the moment, all eyes must surely be on her shapely, outrageously revealed limbs.

She took a trembling breath, overcome suddenly by the all-consuming desire to whisk Tristan home and assert her wifely rights over him.

'I'd have taken you to London and you'd no doubt have seen her at the theatre had you ever shown the desire, Addy.' It was true. She'd had no desire for anything, back then.

Nothing except James.

But what of the friendship Miss Carew intimated she'd shared with Tristan? What form had that taken? She longed to ask him.

When Tristan rose, stating he intended furthering his

acquaintance with his friend's wife and intimating James would join her in his stead for the next act, Adelaide tried to stop him from leaving.

James, alone with her in their box?

'I'll come with you,' she said quickly, rising, she hoped with dignity rather than the scramble she felt it, but he patted her back into her seat saying, 'I'm curious to see how young Beatrice deports herself in public when she has neither James nor her patroness by her side. James told me you've taken it upon yourself to groom Beatrice into her new role as the wife of a flamboyant poet and public personage. I want to observe her for myself.' He chuckled.

'From what I know of James, he does not usually favour raw potential but rather the fully rounded product, ripe for the plucking.'

It was fortunate he did not observe the effect of his words.

James, however, always an astute observer of Adelaide's moods, did not miss her disordered state, remarking as he took her hand in greeting as he lowered himself onto the seat beside her, 'You and Tristan have not quarrelled, I hope?'

Fanning herself rapidly, Adelaide disengaged her hand as she shook her head. 'Never once and we're not about to start now. He wants to talk to Beatrice and satisfy himself you're not making the same mistake twice.'

He did not share the levity of her remark, judging by the tensing of his jaw in profile and the careful way he pushed back the curl that flopped over his eye.

'Are you referring to my marrying Hortense or letting you go?'

If there'd been more light he'd have seen her blanche whiter than her bones.

'How many times must I tell you—'

'If it is between us only, then surely the past is a place we are obliged to visit?' He swung round on his seat and the passionate edge to his tone resonated in the small place. 'When it has made us so profoundly what we have become? How can you pretend like this, Addy?'

'What do you mean?'

'You present to the world the face of the most dutiful wife. In a week – after the unveiling – all London will be abuzz over the exquisite Lady Leeson and your world will never be the same. Spare a thought for me, the man who loved you first.' He breathed out slowly before he spoke again, his voice taut. 'When your picture goes on display you will be invited to every fashionable event, your patronage will be desired, you will be feted, fawned over—'

'Apart from the fact you are speaking nonsense if you think the unveiling of my portrait will turn me into an overnight sensation, you clearly have little faith in my constancy.' She faced him squarely, glad to be able to take the moral high ground. 'Which is towards my *husband.*'

Swallowing past the lump in her throat, she added, 'To whom both you and I owe a great deal.'

He clasped his hands and regarded her steadily. Dismayed, Addy blinked as she caught sight of the small silver ring he wore on the little finger of his right hand. She'd given it to him when they'd pledged their troth, unable to do it legally. She'd been barely eighteen. Such a child. Such a child in love.

After a silence that seemed to stretch to eternity, he let out his breath slowly.

'I sometimes wish I'd drowned in the swirling river that carried me away the day I jumped in to rescue Tristan.' His face was pallid, eyes deepset and shadowed. 'When I met you … when I loved you, I often thought of that day I nearly died … saving your future husband as cruel irony would have it. I thought how much sweeter as a result was the experience of

holding you in my arms. Now'—he dragged in a breath—
'living has become a torment.'

'Hush and stop such nonsense,' Adelaide hissed. 'You were
not in love with me a week ago, if you recall. You were sorry
for this kind of talk and you acknowledged nothing could
come of it. If you didn't say it in so many words you
concurred with me that our world as we knew it has changed
and we have forged new happiness; me with Tristan and you
with Beatrice. She is young and unformed. She is in awe of
you and you, who like to be feted, will have the pleasure of
moulding her to your taste. Take consolation in that!'

'Do you never think of our child?'

He spoke the words low, almost inaudibly, and Adelaide
exhaled on a sob that took her by surprise. Closing her eyes,
she tried to swallow past her swollen tongue, to gaze her
hatred at him through her stinging eyes; for how could he be
so cruel when he knew there was no turning back?

'What do you want from me?' She thought she was going
to be ill. Faint. Lurching forward she found herself in his
arms and it was scant salvation that they were obscured by a
half-drawn curtain.

'Do you hate *me* for what was inevitable, if we'd only
considered the consequences of our madness?' she asked,
pushing his hands away. 'You were a married man. I was a
child. I knew nothing.'

'I'm sorry,' he muttered, clearly aware that his behaviour
was unforgivable given the abject cast of his shoulders, his
face averted as he stared with glazed eyes at the stage. 'I only
wish I did hate you. How much easier it would be.'

The act was coming to an end. The audience clapped
their appreciation and James leaned forwards so as to be
heard.

'So you'd rather go to your grave after countless decades
of unremarkable harmony.' He looked as if he were angry –

no, disappointed in her. 'Whereas I would rather wring the last drop of honey from life and collapse exhausted and satiated when my time had come, satisfied that for all the deficiencies of my character I had enjoyed life to the fullest.'

Adelaide could hear the approaching voices of her husband and Beatrice.

In a rush of angry disgust, she bit back. 'Then you'll either destroy Beatrice or if she has the backbone I think she may possess, she'll be the making of you. For this I do know, James'—unconsciously she counted the seconds before Tristan returned—'and that is that together, we would have destroyed each other.'

CHAPTER 11

The day of the unveiling had arrived.

Mr Gilchrist's studio was at the top of three flights of stairs in an unfashionable part of town, so Adelaide was taken aback to find it thronged with fashionably dressed strangers as she made her entrance on Tristan's arm with her mother on her other side.

She hesitated on the threshold and a hush fell upon the gathering, immediately followed by a great deal of chatter.

It was Mrs Henley who gripped Adelaide's arm when she faltered and propelled her forward, saying grimly, 'You wished this upon yourself, my girl.'

A beaming Mr Gilchrist rushed forward to usher them into the room and, feeling as if she were two people – the proud and confident beauty she once had been warring with the reclusive good wife who must be immune to admiration – Adelaide smiled and nodded in response to the various congratulations.

The painting was a decided masterpiece: lush, bold and true to life, depicting Lady Leeson as an innocent temptress in her Classical robes, the fall of her rippling hair ensuring modesty yet revealing sufficient creamy flesh to excite the imagination.

Tristan remained close by, as she had made him promise not to leave her side, while James was caught up in the throng, looking fevered as he mixed with poets and artists and the haut *ton*, a curious combination.

'You have made my nephew's name as I predicted.' Lady Hawkins appeared, eyes glittering with a look Adelaide wasn't entirely sure was approval. Poor, plain Miss Emmeline, trailing in her wake, may well have been the reason. The girl was decked out in splendour but her jonquil yellow pelisse couldn't mitigate her poor complexion or the lankness of her dun-coloured hair. Nevertheless, she had the grace to pay Adelaide a very pretty compliment before Adelaide paired her up with James's neglected betrothed.

During one rare moment alone Adelaide glanced up at Tristan and whispered, 'This is quite remarkable.'

'Remarkable that you look so radiant in the midst of such a hullabaloo,' he said, shielding her from the pressing throng. 'The painting itself is unremarkable for you will be considered a beauty from any perspective. Are you sure you're up to all this?'

Adelaide grinned, about to admit to just how much, when James lurched up to them. Relieved to have Tristan by her side, she gave him a playful tap on the arm. 'You've drunk too much, James. I think you were already foxed when you came here from St James, though I'm flattered you attended my modest little showing when the craze for you and your poems exceeds all else.'

'By tomorrow we'll both be London's darlings.' He twined his arm about her waist and pulled her to him, kissing her untidily upon her ear. 'Aren't you proud of us, Tristan? Why waste your time speechifying on slaves and sanitation and prison conditions when you could have engineered

Adelaide's rise to national heroine status years ago? You'd have been far better suited to Hortense than this magnificent creature.'

Adelaide sidestepped his clumsy embrace, seeking sanctuary within Tristan's orbit. 'Your friend is embarrassing himself,' she said coolly. 'Though perhaps James's poor behaviour is eclipsed by his friend over there.'

She indicated with a nod of her head Phineas Donegal who was swaying on his feet, one arm around a red-haired woman who looked as if she had no objection.

'Pah! He's a hanger-on,' James slurred. 'He's never written a thing to excite the public. He'll die in obscurity, a wretched, talentless—'

'That's enough, James,' Tristan said sharply, angling himself to act as a support to his friend who lurched precariously. 'You do yourself no credit with this talk. Remember, you're the one who has everything to crow about.'

James fixed his large, dark eyes on Tristan and his mouth opened though no words came. He touched his chest with his fist and his face crumpled. Finally he whispered brokenly, 'But it's empty in here, Tristan.'

'You have Beatrice.' This time it was Adelaide who spoke sharply, though whether that was wise or not she had immediate cause to wonder for James swung round, lurched into her, then stumbled back and assessed her with his lovelorn gaze. 'Yes, I have Beatrice,' he repeated, his tone low, his look intense. He hiccupped and his mouth trembled. 'And Tristan has you.' He looked blearily at his friend. 'You're a lucky man, Tristan,' he mumbled as he shambled away, repeating over his shoulder, 'A lucky man, I say.'

Shaken, Adelaide tried to smile. 'Yes, well, this is far more than I expected but I can't deny that I'm not enjoying it, vain creature that I am,' she babbled.

'As you're entitled to do. Nor is it vanity. I'd not want you to be anything other than you are, Addy.' He caressed her cheek.

She was tongue-tied, spoiling the moment with an embarrassed, 'A pea goose, that's what I am? Isn't that what you've always called me, mother?' Adelaide couldn't resist the remark as her parent closed in upon them. Mrs Henley had been gazing with undisguised censure at the vulgar red-headed woman talking to Mr Donegal.

'You've certainly not embraced your opportunity to make good when the chance has presented itself.'

'You're so right, Mama, my husband deserves a wife far more serious minded and intelligent than me … and yet, I do believe that when I've savoured this rare moment of gaiety, I shall be ready to move on to graver matters.' She opened her fan with an expert flick of the wrist and flashed a beatific smile. 'Perhaps I'll surprise you all, yet.'

Mrs Henley looked down her hooked nose at the daughter who bore so little resemblance to her and muttered, 'Develop a conscience, Adelaide? You? I don't think that will ever happen.'

Tristan had never felt more proud of his wife. Like a glorious mythical creature who'd emerged from the depths of enchanted obscurity, she navigated her way through the throng with her peculiar grace as if she had been born to it. When he made some remark to that effect she raised an eyebrow, her lips pursed in that beguiling, secretive smile that tugged at his baser desires. 'You did not know me in my misspent youth or you'd not be surprised. Don't worry, my love,' she reassured him with an impish look over the top of her fan, 'when I've made up for my lost years of gaiety, I promise to once again become the sober creature you and Mama both dream of.'

'You don't need to change on my account, Addy.'

But she'd already moved on and for a moment, alone, he watched her caught up in conversation with her painter. The awareness in Mr Gilchrist's attitude as he lowered his head to speak to her – closer than necessary? – made him draw breath, though it should hardly be a surprising observation that Adelaide must be an object of desire to all men.

Tonight he saw the protective bindings in which he'd encased her for three years unravel. The glint in her eye as she exchanged pleasantries with Gilchrist was confident and knowing. They did not belong to the Addy with which he was familiar. He caught himself up. He was behaving like a vigilant papa watching his daughter on the cusp of woman-hood make her tentative steps into society. These were not feelings that were becoming.

In any normal courtship he would have been long familiar with the protective if not combative instincts that would make him want to fight for his woman. Jealousy was unfamiliar to him and he quickly subdued it, acknowledging her right to speak to Gilchrist as a woman confident of her charms might speak to any man whom she sensed admired her.

But by God he wished he could take her home this moment and have her all to himself.

'Lord Leeson, I saw you the other night in your box. Did you get the kisses I blew in your direction?'

He turned, a strange new emotion flooding him.

Discomfort. 'Kitty. How nice to see you again.'

'You, too, m'lord.' She sidled up to him. 'An' your wife who sat beside you … Mr Gilchrist's protégée 'oo 'e would insist on referring to as "The Beauty", which got me hackles up, I can tell you. That's why I went and saw her meself when she were 'aving the painting done. Reckon she looks a bit like me, wiv that hair an' all.' She tossed her head as she skimmed her hands down her shapely body.

Tristan, aware of the curious glances in their direction, tried to steer the conversation towards safer waters. 'Are you well, Kitty?' he asked. As soon as he could, he'd move on.

She shrugged. 'Freddy gave me my congé. My boy, Thomas, and I manage well enough.'

'I did not know you had a son.'

She looked at him squarely. 'Aye, I do, m'lord. A lovely lad with blue eyes and fair hair. Same colour as yours, m'lord. Thomas is four.'

Dry-mouthed, he nodded. 'I'm sure you're very proud of him.'

'You're very welcome to come and see my boy. And me too, for that matter, if yer's feeling lonely, m'lord.' She thrust out her bosom. 'Fine ladies might think their beauty is enough to keep a man happy and there's no denying your wife is a cut above the rest when it comes to looks, but I reckon I got pretty good at knowing how to make yer feel happy when you were out o' sorts, m'lord.' Her voice was low and there was more longing than impudence in her tone, though her words shocked him to the core. 'We live above Mendelssohn's Apothecary in Culpepper Lane, not far from the theatre where I work.'

Before he could respond she'd melted back into the crowd and he looked round to see Adelaide at his side, Kitty's words still resonating. Her boy was *four*?

He tried to shake off the panic occasioned by Kitty's news as he forced levity into his tone. 'Have you had your fill of celebrity, my dear, or do you feel you were born to it?' He hoped Adelaide didn't notice that his hands were clammy as she gripped them for the briefest moment.

Forcing aside his disquiet, he went on, 'A politician's wife might find herself in the public eye. I was afraid you'd be overwhelmed but don't be afraid to tell me if you enjoy this as much as your smile suggests. I am just amazed.'

A shadow crossed her face. 'Amazed that you are discovering more and more with each passing day that you do not know the wife you married?' Discreetly she brought her face closer to his, her sweet breath teasing his heated cheek. 'I am tired, Tristan, and I want to go home – with you. Alone.' For a moment they were in a cocoon of intimacy, her words conveying a subtext he'd be a fool to misinterpret. 'Mama has met someone who shares her views. They've not stopped talking. We can go home alone, Tristan. Without her. Just you and me.'

The air left his lungs in a rush and he felt himself harden. Adelaide's confidence clothed her like a mantle of allure. Four o'clock in the afternoon and the sharp awareness of desire he'd constantly subdued since she'd become his wife ripped through his defences like a rapier.

There was no misinterpreting her meaning. With each passing day in London Addy was becoming less and less like the woman he'd married … and more like the incarnation of his desire.

Unfortunately marital intimacy was not to be realised. Mrs Henley seemed alert to any signs her daughter might wish to be rid of her, for she was quickly at their side, declaring her inclination to return home.

The moment the three of them were ensconced in the carriage, Mrs Henley professed irritation at the dangling feather of her daughter's headdress, though Tristan suspected it went deeper than that.

'Such vanity, Adelaide,' she muttered. 'When have you ever worn feathers before? You're nearly twenty-four with your youth fast disappearing.'

Tristan bristled. 'Adelaide is at the height of her beauty. She'd be as beautiful wearing feathers or a burlap sack.'

A radiant smile from Addy was his reward. Mrs Henley

gave a disdainful sniff. When he glanced back at his wife her smile remained fixed upon him: clear, confident and full of promise.

Staring out at the passing traffic as their carriage waited for a lumbering cart to negotiate a rut in the street in front of him, Tristan digested the new landscape. How many other men had been in the same position as he? Marrying wives who epitomised purity and innocence when they took their vows; wives who suddenly crossed the threshold into womanhood seemingly overnight and before their eyes?

Adelaide's eyes appeared very green today, her hair burnished with a golden sheen from the afternoon sun. Her lips were parted to reveal her white, perfectly formed teeth and her gloved hands were clasped demurely in her lap. The Pomona green pelisse she wore was modest but seemed to hug her womanly curves with a suggestiveness that spoke to a schoolboy's frustrated desire rather than that of a long married husband. Or was it the look in Adelaide's eye that provoked that response?

Whatever it was, the carriage crackled with unspoken meaning.

He nearly groaned with frustration when Mrs Henley, rather than retire to her own apartments as she generally did upon arriving home from an outing, professed the determined desire to work at her needlework and for some inexplicable reason, to require her daughter's company.

He was glad to note the dismay in Addy's voice when she complained, 'You never work at your Bayeux Tapestry at this time of day, Mama, when it is overcast and the light so poor.'

The response she received at this hedging brooked no further argument, and half an hour later Tristan was reluctantly changing into riding clothes to accompany James for a canter in the park while Adelaide was sorting threads for her mother.

It seemed Mrs Henley wished to discuss Adelaide's success from a more sober perspective.

'Your painting has been well received, Adelaide,' she remarked, drawing her needle through the taut linen, 'and as I've heard Tristan and every gentleman in the room declare, you shall have achieved your desire for notoriety by tomorrow's news-sheet.'

Adelaide knelt amidst a riot of colour upon the patterned carpet at her mother's feet, obediently untangling a skein of sky blue. The criticism in both her mother's tone and the unkindness of her phraseology ought not to have had the ability to hurt her when she should be so used to it. This afternoon, coming as it did after she'd felt floating on a cloud of goodwill and admiration, it was like a lance to her happiness.

She took a deep breath, determined not to allow herself to be crushed by her mother's latest criticism. 'I never sought notoriety, and every young girl embarking on her first season seeks admiration,' she muttered, not looking up.

'How would you know when you never had a season? Your behaviour made sure of that.'

Despite having so recently self-congratulated herself on her adult poise, Adelaide nearly leapt to her feet and flounced from the room. But the woman she had become valued dignity above a show of childish indignation.

'Tristan's speech was as well received as Mr Gilchrist's painting, I am told. I'm as proud of my husband as he is of me.' With trembling fingers she replaced the fully wound up blue and picked up an untidy skein of gold. She could not look at her mother. 'I have always wanted Tristan to think well of me, Mama. For three years you have forced me to act a part and to be someone I am not, thinking Tristan could never love me if he knew my true nature.' Tears stung her eyes as she recalled the numerous times she'd subdued her feelings. 'Do you not think Tristan is as indulgent a husband now that I am well, as he was before? Do you not think he is *happier*, now that he sees me blooming? Do you not want to see *me* happy?'

Her mother's hiss took her by surprise. Adelaide jerked her head up and stared up at the trembling jaw, the dark green eyes glowing in her mother's sallow face as she received the reply, 'Are you so stupid, daughter, that you do not understand your happiness – nay, your very survival – motivates my every utterance, my every action?' She patted the lappets of her bonnet with sinewy fingers which shook as much as Adelaide's. 'Do you not realise how you teeter on the edge of ruin and damnation every time you flutter your eyelashes at any man, and I don't just refer to one in particular though the Lord above knows you court a fiery hell every moment you spend with James. But you never were one to listen, Adelaide, were you? You never had the kindness or understanding that would see your mother's survival and happiness as bound to your own behaviour. I watch you with fear and trepidation, knowing that if you fall, you bring us all with you.'

Adelaide stared. Is this truly what her mother felt?

Shakily she tossed the skein of gold wool into the basket and rose to her knees to face her mother. 'Do not forget, mother, that it is because of me that we enjoy the comforts we do. No, you care nothing for comfort, do you? You're only concerned with your soul; but I don't hear you complain that you sleep on featherdown and are served dishes of your choice.'

Mrs Henley looked about to raise an objection but Adelaide forged ahead. 'Papa loved me a great deal more than you ever have and when he wished to have me at school near you in Vienna you insisted I go to England. When I came to you as a seventeen-year-old I felt I didn't know you, yet you offered me no guiding hand unless it was to drag me through every stinking alleyway and cell Vienna could produce to temper my natural exuberance. You wanted to crush me, Mama, while you loved Hortense. Like a daughter. Like you should have loved me.'

She swallowed around the lump in her throat. 'Papa died so suddenly and you didn't even care. You just went on with your saintly works as if that was all that mattered and the only person who showed me the tiniest bit of affection was James.'

She'd forgotten herself, sending a furtive glance towards the door before she continued, 'James became my friend because Hortense was just like you: more concerned with her soul and achieving sainthood than making her husband happy.'

She squeezed her trembling hands together and looked searchingly at her mother. 'Now I am married to a man I love and yet you have cursed my marriage with the terrible lies you've forced me to live every day. Please, Mama,' she begged, 'give me my freedom. Allow me to conduct my marriage the way I see fit. If you care one little jot about my happiness, will you let me do that?'

CHAPTER 12

Down the incline and across the field, foam flying from Major's mouth, Tristan felt like a lad again, exhilarated beyond measure, by the success of his dreams and projects.

He hadn't realised until now what it meant to exercise a social duty and find that he'd widened the avenue just a little by his own efforts, letting the light in for others. Until his speech the other night he'd thought he had little talent to sway others to his way of thinking.

'You'll be a philanthropist to make Mrs Henley proud,' James remarked as they drew their mounts level and proceeded at a leisurely pace across the common. He had sobered up remarkably since the showing.

'And you a poet who will take the world by storm,' Tristan responded. 'We, both of us, are fulfilling our destinies. Perhaps that was why the Henleys crossed my path when they did. I thought it was my destiny to bring the lovely Miss Henley a life worth living. Now I see she always had the capacity to do that herself. She has been remarkable since we came to London, do you not think?'

'Remarkable,' came the predicable reply, but Tristan noticed his friend was staring into the middle distance as if his mind were engaged elsewhere.

'You are thinking of Beatrice?' Tristan asked. 'And how you might enable her to fulfil her potential?'

James jerked his head around. 'Beatrice. Yes, of course. But Adelaide is trying to do that. Not that she's made inroads, as you'd have noticed of course. Still, Beatrice is very young … Perhaps too young.'

Concerned, Tristan asked, 'You are regretting this marriage?'

'It's too late to do that, besides. Apparently Beatrice is just what I need. Addy tells me so, at any rate.'

'And I'll add my voice to hers,' said Tristan, though he wondered if Beatrice's self-containment constituted insipidness in James's mind. It was not a trait James would admire; and if James did not admire, he tended to dismiss.

Turning in the saddle to look out over the stream, James added in a tone that suggested he should be glad for small mercies. 'She's not Hortense, at any rate.'

Seeming to decide a new tack was needed, he sighed deeply and turned his flushed countenance toward Tristan. 'This Mrs Elizabeth Fry you've been consorting with can only have taken her cue from Hortense who devoted her life to lessening the worst abuses visited on those who had no voice or champion.'

Instead of tending to her husband, Tristan might have added, but did not. Every husband required that his wife's first duty was towards his comfort but James, more than most, needed domestic felicity and admiration to feed the fires of his vanity.

'I thought you chose Beatrice as your special project.' Tristan tried to inject enthusiasm into his tone. He knew a disillusioned or dejected James spelt danger – both to himself and to those who loved him. Thank God James's career seemed in the ascendant. An admiring public would bolster him like nothing else. 'She's an unformed bud of the rose she will become, if I may attempt a poor imitation of your stylish prose.'

'Yes, yes, and now let us go back and see our collective rose garden'—James traded his gloomy spirits for a wicked grin—'for I believe Addy has invited Beatrice around this afternoon to help her choose which gown she shall wear for the Buckling's ball.'

'She made no such mention to me.' Tristan raised an eyebrow, pretending pique. 'A good thing you know so much about my wife and can keep me informed.'

He found the three women in the drawing room in the midst of an argument as to who would engage Beatrice for the afternoon. When Tristan heard the conflicting proposals he had no hesitation in voicing his opinion. 'Beatrice is already promised to my wife.'

His mother in law fixed him with a fulminating look. 'With all due respect, Tristan, Beatrice wishes to meet Mrs Fry. She has chosen to accompany me to the prison rather than pander to Adelaide's vanity.'

'In the absence of sisters and an interested mother,' Tristan replied coolly, 'Adelaide accepted with great pleasure Beatrice's offer of her company so that she might offer a second opinion regarding what gown she should wear tomorrow night and to the dinner we will be hosting after I address the House of Lords on Thursday.'

'Adelaide is looking for compliments. I am looking for a helpmate who is willing to assist me to effect change in the prison system which, might I remind you, Tristan, you claim to revile.'

'And which is the very subject that concerns my speech

on Thursday after which Adelaide will have her opinion sought by the politicians we'll entertain at dinner; politicians whose sympathies we are trying to engage.' Tristan clenched his fists as he tried to exercise calm. 'Adelaide will be far more effective as a gracious, intelligent *well-dressed* hostess than she could ever be dishing out blankets and alms to the filthy wretches already imprisoned.'

Beatrice stared at the ground while Mrs Henley looked as if steam were about to issue from her ears.

James looked angry. 'You know my stance on the matter, Beatrice, but I'll leave the final decision to you.'

Adelaide, gazing at Tristan with shining eyes, was the first to break the silence. 'So what will it be, Beatrice?' she asked with forced bravado, though Tristan was certain he could see a sparkle of delight – a rare thing in the old days. She clasped Beatrice's wrist in a show of sisterly camaraderie. 'Tristan says you'll be far more help assisting me to gain the interest and the ear of the men in power that matter. Let Mama venture off alone on her trail through the muck and filth. You'd hate it – believe me!'

At the end of the afternoon when Beatrice had gone, Adelaide threw herself onto the chaise longue in her dressing room and tossed off her bonnet.

'I've never seen you so forceful with Mother, Tristan,' she remarked, still smiling at the memory. 'But your boldness may come at a price. I should warn you.'

'No need.'

To her surprise he pushed aside her legs to sit down before whisking her onto his lap and patting her head onto his shoulder. Such easy familiarity was a delightful novelty. Still, it was an hour before dinner. She didn't expect much more in the way of intimacy.

'I've lived with your mother as long as I've been married

to you. Don't think I'm unaware of what I'm in for.' He tugged her tighter against him and his words tickled her ear. 'But I'm willing to take the risk.'

Closing her eyes Adelaide burrowed her cheek into the hollow beneath his collarbone and wrapped her arm around his shoulder. She could hear the servants in the corridor busying themselves and the aroma of dinner but she didn't care. She slipped her hand inside Tristan's shirt just as he said, 'You're fond of James, aren't you?'

She froze.

'Of course you are which is why you've taken an interest in Beatrice. You don't want him to make the same mistake he did with Hortense and be as unhappy in his second marriage, which he will be if he finds he's married a do-gooding little piece who'd be more suited to being a missionary's wife.' He put his hand over hers and sent her a questioning look. 'Don't know he's made the right decision but it's too late to cry off.'

'I know,' Adelaide said miserably. 'Still, there's hope, I believe, for Beatrice is genuinely in love with him and with a little direction she may blossom into the vibrant creature he needs.'

'Vibrant being the operative word,' Tristan agreed, leaning over her to kiss the tip of her nose. 'Someone like you. Vibrant. Exquisite. Loyal.' He laboured each word, kissing her mouth, her cheek her throat, before leaning back to give her exploring hand access to the rest of his bare chest. His eyes closed for a moment, as if in rapture and Adelaide's senses went into wild alert, overpowering the effect of the lead-in to his speech which had momentarily stunned her.

James should have married someone like her... but how deeply she'd be regretting such a marriage now she was older. Tristan was forgiving of the follies of youth. Perhaps he'd be as forgiving of hers?

'Oh, Tristan,' she murmured, nuzzling his neck and holding him tightly as a spasm of despair passed through her. She was glad he mistook the emotion which beset her, for with a searching look he began to undo the buttons at her décolletage, leaving her bodice gaping to reveal a further row of buttons which secured her front-fastening stays and then the ribbon which tied her chemise. Fortuitous indeed for Tristan needed all the encouragement he could get, she thought, her rapturous sigh surely leaving him in no doubt that this was exactly what she wanted. Twining her fingers in the short hair at the nape of his neck, she pulled down his head to deepen the kiss, arching into him as his free hand explored her now wildly sensitive breasts.

Shifting so they lay full length upon the chaise, Tristan cupped Adelaide's face.

With a soft moan, she ran her hands down the lean, muscular length of him, exploring the contours of his hard chest, lean waist and thighs in a way she'd never done before. Lord, in all their marriage she'd never even seen him naked.

The weight of him was sinfully exquisite and she was terrified he'd come to his senses and beat a hasty retreat for fear of terrifying her.

'I love you, Tristan,' she whispered, covering his face with hot kisses while she fumbled at his clothing.

His response was all she could have asked for: a low, primal growl as if the passion of a lifetime was waging battle with the restraint which characterised him. 'I'll always love you, Addy.' Then he said it again as he carried her to the bedroom where he began to show her just how much.

Languorous. Loved. That was how Adelaide felt as she rested her hand on the warm mattress beside her. Tristan had regretfully risen to make an appearance at dinner, for the sake of Mrs Henley, as much as anyone.

'Come in,' Adelaide now called in answer to the knock on the door, assuming it was Tristan checking on her after dinner. She wondered if he could hear the purr in her voice.

Her mother swept into the room, brandishing a paper.

'Your ambitions appear to have been achieved,' Mrs Henley announced, taking a chair at her daughter's side and slapping the news-sheet onto the counterpane in front of her nose.

'Read that, or are you too addled from the day's excesses? I'm not surprised you hadn't the energy to come down to dinner.' She stabbed at a bold headline proclaiming Adelaide: 'Society Beauty New Toast of the Town.'

'Me?' gasped Adelaide, sitting up, surprised and gratified. Her mother snatched back the news-sheet. 'Allow me to read it. Hopefully that will restore a more sober temperament, for the Lord only knows, Addy, sobriety is called for if you're not to be brought down for your airs and graces, taking us all with you.'

With a decided lack of enthusiasm, Mrs Henley outlined the success of both artist and sitter in taking the town by storm followed by gushing eulogies over the painting which the author declared would be gazed upon by half the country before long.

Adelaide refused to allow her mother's disgust to dampen her spirits.

'Oh, but it's too exciting! Why can I not enjoy my late blooming, mother? Tristan will be proud of me. I want to reflect well on him. He's making the kind of speeches that should make you happy. Why can't you be satisfied with that and accept I'm not the daughter you wished for?' Again the irrepressible smile that would not be kept at bay curled her mouth while she stretched.

Mrs Henley shifted in her seat and cast her a suspicious look. 'What's got into you, girl? You've looked like the cat that's swallowed the cream from the moment I entered this room. Tristan said you were unwell.' Her eyes narrowed and she clasped her hands in her lap as she twisted, straight backed, to glare at her daughter.

'Watch yourself, my girl,' she said in a low voice. 'Pride comes before a fall. Look at you! Preening over your success and now back to your old tricks, using your wiles to crook your little finger and make your husband your slave. He's a *man*, Adelaide—'

'A wonderful, loving man who is so happy his wife is not the sad, dispirited creature *you've* forced me to be all these years,' Adelaide defended herself. 'My *husband*, mother!'

'No man respects a woman like you, Adelaide.' Mrs Henley rose, snatching up the news-sheet and stabbing a finger in Adelaide's direction. 'A woman ruled by the wanton impulses of her body. It's disgusting! If Tristan should find out the truth—'

'God only knows I wish he knew it and I could be free of *your* lie.' Adelaide refused to be cowed. 'Why, it was … wonderful. For the first time I felt a true wife.'

'You threw yourself at him like a common lightskirt, Addy, and when he's sitting in the House of Lords, being slapped on the back by everyone who's read today's news-sheet, the doubts will be creeping into his mind as to how he can trust such a shameless creature.' Mrs Henley retreated a few steps but did not let up her attack. 'Let me tell you, I understand the ways of the world and the workings of men's minds far better than you. Unless you curb your interest in *that* aspect of marriage you won't keep your husband. I would advise a very protracted and severe megrim after your antics!'

Scrambling out of bed, Adelaide ran across the room and gripped her mother's wrist to stop her leaving. Hours ago she'd unleashed her passion for her husband but she burned with a different passion, now.

'You will not tell me how to conduct my life, mother!' she shouted as her mother unclasped her fingers. 'I love my husband and he loves me! What is unnatural in that?'

Mrs Henley regarded her with disgust from beneath her reptilian eyelids. 'You are no better than a wanton from the gutter, Adelaide,' she muttered, her hand on the door knob.

'No, mother! I'm a good wife.'

But her mother had already slammed the door.

CHAPTER 13

'Adelaide?' Beatrice's tentative voice on the other side of the door made Adelaide jump as she awoke, spilling the warm milk Milly must have brought up earlier.

'Your mother said you were unwell but James insisted I come up and see you. He's anxious to know your thoughts on today's news. I said I'd rather not disturb you if—'

Snatching up her shawl, Adelaide hurried to the door and opened it, shoulders back and head high. 'Unwell? Why, I just slept a little later than usual. Did you read yesterday's news-sheet, Beatrice? Isn't it too marvellous?'

Whisking a surprised and diffident Beatrice into her bedroom, Adelaide closed the door behind them and indicated her friend take a seat while she moved to her dressing table.

'You're famous, Addy. Everybody's talking about you.' Adelaide smiled. 'Do you envy me?'

Beatrice shuddered as she lowered herself onto the window seat and Adelaide began to brush her hair. 'Not a bit. I mean, I think it's wonderful for you to be a celebrated beauty because that's what you are, and I'm pleased about it. But it's not in my nature to want such things.'

Adelaide paused and turned. 'What *do* you want, Beatrice?'

The blush deepened. 'I want James to be glad he offered for me.'

'Well, he'd not have offered if he'd not wanted you for his wife, would he?'

Adelaide noticed the nervous twisting of the girl's hands in her lap. Beatrice was unable to hold her gaze as she went on, 'Sometimes I fear he deeply regrets it—'

'Oh, Beatrice …' Adelaide rose quickly and took a seat by her young friend. 'You mustn't cry.' She put a comforting arm around about her shoulders. 'Of course he doesn't regret it. He loves you very much.'

'Has he *told* you that?' came the muffled response. 'You're such old friends, he seems to tell you everything. He certainly hasn't mentioned it to me.'

Unable to lie, Adelaide said, 'He's told me how much he admires you. You're the perfect foil: the sensible young wife a mad and wildly unpractical poet like him needs.'

Gently she pushed back the girl's tumbled locks but her smile faltered at Beatrice's next remark.

'You don't think he'd be better suited to someone like you? Lively and beautiful? He seems to have far more fun in your company than mine.'

'Why, what a thing to say!' Adelaide could manage no better but she was saved from anything further by Beatrice's emphatic, 'He *does* need someone sensible, even boring, like me, to temper his wild impulses, doesn't he? I shall be *good* for him, Addy. Your mother says it and now you say it too.'

'Just not too good that James thinks you're censuring him,' Adelaide warned. 'That was the mistake his first wife made.'

Beatrice rose with a shaky smile and took Adelaide's hand. 'Do come down when you're ready. James is dying to congratulate you. You'd almost think he was the one who painted your portrait, not Mr Gilchrist. Thank you, Adelaide.' She smiled. 'Were it not for your wise counsel, I would have given James his freedom this afternoon.'

Dressed in a morning gown of sea-green with a matching toque adorned with a waving ostrich feather, Adelaide made her entrance in the drawing room, her eyes scanning the surprisingly large number of visitors as she searched for her husband, her heart fluttering with nervous anticipation as she recalled last night. To her disappointment Tristan was not among their guests.

A dozen other swains, though, thronged to convey their congratulations, James at the forefront having clearly brought a sizeable contingent from his club. He looked as if he'd not slept for two days.

'You're a rogue,' she murmured in his ear for the benefit of those nearby as he presumed upon his friendship to congratulate her with more warmth that might otherwise be seemly. 'Why is my husband not here when you've picked up every other stray, it would appear?'

'He is a conscientious man, Addy, and his work comes first.'

'He was the most conscientious of husbands last night, so I'd have expected to see him here,' Adelaide replied archly. 'I see you have made up with your arch rival. Good morning, Mr Donegal.' She inclined her head at the tall, lean man whose piratical leer and studied affectation suggested even more of the poet's self-absorption than James's.

'Yes, he says he won't stay away, despite our public aversion to one another, because you are always on my arm.

Expect to be feted, Addy, for you are the new Emma Hamilton.'

Addy shuddered. 'Look what happened to her. No, I shall tread the virtuous path and no hint of scandal shall be associated with my name.' She tapped James's shoulder with her fan and stepped backwards, adding, 'You must take care, also. I recently enjoyed a productive conversation with your loyal and incomparable affianced which convinced me she is your ideal mate. Don't you dare put a foot wrong.'

'You must come with us to the theatre tonight, Addy,' James pressed, but Adelaide just laughed. 'I've no intention of going anywhere with a crowd of artistic reprobates unless my husband is with me.'

So much for good intentions. When James and Beatrice, together with Mr Donegal and, to her surprise, Mr Gilchrist, once again crowded her drawing room later that afternoon, begging her to come and see *Personification* with them, Adelaide only acceded because her mother made her disapproval so plain. In truth, Adelaide had no desire to spend an evening out after receiving Tristan's note proffering his apologies for being detained by his work.

'James will protect me, mother,' she almost simpered, for it gave her a powerful rush to see her mother so out of countenance. 'Tristan would want me to have fun.'

Beatrice went upstairs with Adelaide to wait as Milly dressed her in a gown of palest green silk with the tiniest of bodices highly ornamented with a rich profusion of embroidered roses to match the small puffed sleeves and hem. Adelaide could see little real improvement in the girl's spirits despite their talk yesterday.

Hiding her concern, she slanted a look at her as Beatrice idly twisted a chocolate coloured curl around one finger, her expression distant.

'A sober temperament may be a good foil for your more spontaneous husband, but try to dress it up with a little mystique, my dear,' she advised, holding still as Milly used the hot tongs to create a mass of ringlets to frame her face. 'And don't look at me like I'm your gorgon of a great-aunt Wells.' Smiling through her admonishment, Adelaide pointed at Beatrice's plain dress and lack of coiffure before indicating her own selection of discarded gowns which draped the chaise longue with a sweep of her arm.

'See how much care and attention I've taken to ensure I cut just the right figure. It's not that I'm vain, Beatrice. Well, not *entirely.*' She smiled. 'I've just recognised that painting myself in a good light sets the right tone. Other good things follow. It's easier to engage one's husband's mind if you engage him on a baser level. There! I've shocked you. But please allow me to supervise your toilette so that your serious chocolate brown eyes and enigmatic twist of your mouth become eulogies to your quiet allure rather than dull reminders of the first wife with whom James was trapped for so many years. Yes, I speak plainly,' she went on at Beatrice's gasp, 'but only because I am filled with dread at the prospect of observing my dear friends – both of you! – chafing against the bonds of an unsuitable alliance.'

'But you said—'

'I said nothing I didn't mean, but you recall the proviso that you must expend some effort if you want to keep his heart. If you cannot do even that, then I advise you, quite seriously, Beatrice, that yes, you should then give James his freedom.' Sobriety replaced the bantering tone.

Beatrice's already pale complexion blanched further, her large brown eyes smouldering with a combination of hurt and outrage and Adelaide leapt to her feet, pushing aside Milly who'd been weaving pearls through her hair, to grip her friend by the shoulders.

'Passion!' cried Adelaide. 'I see it in your eyes, but has James seen it? You are very young but if you can *feel* things the way James does ... if you can empathise even a little with what drives him, you'll do well together. Come.' Brooking no argument, she hustled Beatrice to her dressing table stool and sat her down. 'Milly, you're an expert. What do you suggest we do with Miss Beatrice's hair? I shall rifle through my gowns and find something more ... appropriate to the evening I have in mind for us.'

It was only when Adelaide had overseen Beatrice dressed in a fashionable and modestly cut silk gown in palest pink adorned with tiny red roses that Adelaide was satisfied.

She was determined the evening would be one to remember for both of them. Adelaide certainly wanted to make the most of her first night out in public following her sensational debut. So with this in mind she made her entrance at the top of the stairs with all the dashing style at which she knew she excelled.

Even her mother's gimlet eye had not the power to dampen her spirits.

The smouldering desire she recognised in James's expression was some compensation for this but not for Tristan's absence. She wished James's kindling look was more obviously directed at Beatrice, who balanced awkwardly on the landing beside her, too shy to focus on the assembly downstairs.

James, a leering Mr Donegal, together with star-struck Mr Gilchrist, and Mrs Henley offered a mixed reception as Adelaide gripped Beatrice's hand, pulling her into a well-paced descent to the rapturous admiration of the young men while Mrs Henley's sniffed, 'There's no doubt, my girl, you're going to get yourself into deep trouble.'

'Do you know where I'd find Tristan this evening?' Adelaide spoke to James, ignoring her mother whom Beatrice seemed unable to address. Her embarrassment at appearing to advantage for the first time in her life – for that is how Adelaide regarded it – meant she was barely able to raise her eyes from studious contemplation of the blue and ocean-green silk dancing slippers which Adelaide had laced upon her. Beatrice's formerly lank tresses had become ringlets tumbling from a filigree of silver, creating a charming effect which Adelaide directly charged James to admire after ascertaining her husband was 'no doubt at his club following a debate in the House'.

'We shall send a message for him, but isn't Beatrice looking lovely? Mr Gilchrist will have to paint our future Baroness.'

'Lovely as ever,' James said in the bolstering tones he might have reserved for a favourite cousin, adding, 'Let's look in at Lady Pemble's later this evening. It'll be just the thing for Beatrice. Can't deny I'm mighty curious to ogle Lady Pemble's daughter and see if her handsome dowry can compensate for the fact she resembles Gentleman Jackson himself – or so I've been told.'

'Terrible man!' Adelaide admonished. 'Instead of saying such ugly things about others why not call upon your reserves of praise for your future wife?'

It was Donegal who answered with a backhanded compliment as he interjected, 'Your future wife, James, is wise to attach herself to a star like the incomparable Lady Leeson. Why, she's this season's newest sensation, just mark my words.'

He'd had a little to drink and, swaying on his feet, appealed to Mrs Henley. 'I crave your corroboration, Mrs Henley. The two ravishing young ladies are going to captivate London tonight and whither they goest,' he hiccupped, 'goest I. I shall look forward to reading about my exploits in tomorrow's news-sheets.'

'Stars have a habit of burning out and crashing to earth,' was Mrs Henley's blunt rejoinder as she inclined her head before signalling her intention to leave. 'Good night, everyone – and Adelaide, have a thought for poor Tristan who is working so hard. He doesn't want to see you with dark shadows under your eyes and bearing no resemblance to that apparently magnificent portrait executed by Mr Gilchrist.'

The lively group squeezed into one coach. Beatrice clung to Adelaide's arm, unable to look at James sitting across from her and regaling Adelaide with a litany of their afternoon revelry.

When finally the conversation turned, after Adelaide admonished, 'Hush, now, James, or your intended will think you live for nothing but pleasure,' he declared, 'We have but one life. Why, Beatrice, what would you rather do with yours to make it a worthwhile one?'

Challenged so directly, she managed bravely, 'I would like to go to my grave knowing I'd been a good person. I want to help people.'

'Help people?'

The horror with which James imbued the question startled them all. He went on quickly, patting her knee, 'That's good of you, Beatrice, but there are other people in the world who can do that much better than you. You're going to be my wife, remember?'

'And why should that preclude her from helping others?' Adelaide admonished as she put her arm around Beatrice. 'You, James, will be the celebrated poet,' she went on, 'and Beatrice can provide the balance in your partnership. Her gentle demeanour and charming looks will ensure the public's sympathies, no matter what wild and foolhardy course you embark upon.'

Donegal, who had regarded proceedings with a

lugubrious air, laughed softly. 'Lord Leeson takes the moral high ground against the excesses of our age while our venerable future baron here is likely to be the very manifestation of those excesses Leeson so deplores and against which he is no doubt speaking this very evening.'

James leant forward. 'I say, Donegal, what an odious statement. You are in your cups and I think it's you who are more inclined to take the moral high ground than our good friend Leeson.'

Donegal shrugged. 'Lord Leeson is known for his intolerance of vice and scandal. Who cannot recall his refusal to include Lady Barnstable in the Christmas festivities on account of her liaison with Lord Baverick?'

Adelaide looked out of the window. She didn't want to hear it.

'Perhaps society would have accepted her if the affair had not resulted in an illegitimate child,' he rambled on, clearly more drunk than Adelaide had realised.

'That's enough, Donegal.' James motioned with his eyes to Beatrice but Adelaide knew it wasn't Beatrice he was concerned about. She pretended not to notice his searching expression.

Mustering up her gaiety, Adelaide pushed back her shoulders and declared, 'Let us go to the play another night. I would rather lose myself in the Serpentine Walk and listen to a concert at Vauxhall.'

She did not seek consensus. Tonight was her evening and although she'd been primed for gaiety she felt a sudden desire for anonymity after Mr Gilchrist's speech.

Taking a supper room in the gardens, Adelaide was surprised by their popularity, for they were soon joined by three gentlemen and several ladies who seemed instantly to recognise them.

'Lady Leeson, why, I saw your portrait when it was

revealed to the world yesterday. You are even more exquisite in the flesh.' Light-hearted with liquor, they crowded into the supper room, ordering more refreshments, ensuring Adelaide's glass was never empty.

She was vaguely aware of Beatrice, separating herself from the company, stiff and unsmiling as she hunched on a chair in the corner while the revelry escalated. But tonight was the first Adelaide had properly stepped out of the careful shell she'd constructed about herself at her mother's behest to protect her from the world.

She mentally reoriented herself as her head reeled pleasantly.

To protect her from this? The gaiety and goodwill of people who saw nothing wrong with enjoying themselves? Why should she not enjoy herself? She was young, beautiful …

'More champagne, Lady Leeson?'

Another gentleman whose name she did not know refilled her glass. He was with a woman with jet black hair drawn back from a widow's peak who wore a red satin dress with a very low décolletage. His wife? It didn't matter. She heard the gentleman was somebody's heir so she was keeping respectable company. Tristan would know him. James was here to keep her safe. Mr Donegal, too, and she was doing nothing wrong beyond enjoying herself, though perhaps she ought not to finish the glass that had just been refilled since she was generally so restrained in her drinking habits and she rather suspected this was going to her head.

They left the supper box to listen to the orchestra and were recognised by others. She remembered acceding to a request to dance and enjoying the compliments that followed. It reminded her of her debut all those years ago; the truncated reception that had filled her young heart with pleasure before her mother had shoved an unflattering bonnet upon her head and bucket in her hand and demanded she accompany her and Hortense to the prison.

How like Hortense Beatrice sometimes seemed.

Beatrice!

Duty banished the woolly headed sensation that slowed Adelaide's wits and she cast around in panic. Beatrice was James's intended and Adelaide's duty of care.

She reflected a moment on James's intended. There was something about Beatrice that needled Adelaide's conscience. Beatrice needed just a little tweaking to engage James on all levels, she was sure – and Adelaide could help her achieve that.

No, Beatrice deserved James in a way Hortense never had. She was a saucer-eyed ingénue with a big heart. She wasn't a pinch-mouthed Puritan who wanted to mould James into something he'd never be.

Sudden realisation of her present obligations intruded once more.

'Beatrice!'

Miraculously the girl appeared. 'What have you been doing?' Adelaide set down her champagne, resolving to drink nothing more until she'd discharged her duty while hopefully appearing in control of the situation. The truth was, she couldn't remember the last half an hour at all, though she certainly had ventured no further than this riotous assembly in the midst of the gardens.

'Your aunt will be anxious if I don't see you home shortly. Say goodnight to James.' Frowning, Adelaide cast around for James, trying to remember if she had seen him since they'd left the supper box. Although … wasn't it he who'd requested that she dance for the gathering?

A chill ran through her at the wisp of memory. She looked around the tiny supper room, thronged with people. The same people who'd pressed up against the walls to make room so she could sway and twirl to the distant strains of the orchestra.

Oh God, best not think about that now. Where *was* James?

'James, there you are! Beatrice is exhausted. I must take her home if you won't.' Adelaide should go home, too. Immediately. She wasn't thinking clearly.

'Addy, are you alright?'

Adelaide shook off his arm, although his gesture stemmed from concern, which she heard in his voice. She'd closed her eyes as she rested briefly against the wall.

'Please take Beatrice home,' she repeated. 'It's only fair—'

'I'm taking you home, too.' He tucked Beatrice's hand into the crook of his arm and gripped Adelaide's shoulder. She seemed to need more steadying and she was mortified. 'Now, my fair maidens, bid your admirers good night ….'

'No,' Adelaide protested. 'I'll stay here.'

She'd expected mild resistance from James and was surprised when he said, firmly and with no evidence of the quantities he'd consumed, 'Tristan will never forgive me if I leave you like this.' He lowered his voice. 'Come, Addy. I know you don't want to be alone with me but you're really in no state to be responsible for your actions. I swear to you as a gentleman and … someone who cares deeply for your well-being, that I will do nothing more than discharge my duty of care and take you home.' He paused, then added, '*Before* I take Beatrice home.'

She realised it was the only sensible course of action. Smiling her farewells, she made it to the carriage and sank back against the squabs, welcoming the darkness as she closed her eyes. In the gloom of a passing street lamp she opened them to see Beatrice looking at her anxiously.

Ashamed, Adelaide made an effort. 'Goodness, I'm as bad as any snoring old dowager with one foot in the grave. Please don't take a leaf out of my book, Beatrice. You're young and lovely ... and sensible.'

James, facing them, patted Adelaide's wrist and said with a smile at Beatrice, 'Adelaide is as far from being a snoring dowager as can be imagined. Why, Adelaide, you shone! I only wish Tristan could have been here to see you dancing to such acclaim ... and that he could have escorted you home and told you what a sensation you were. Ah, here we are at your address, Addy, and Barking is opening the door for us. Come.'

Adelaide tiptoed into the house feeling as wayward a wife as was possible. The effects of too much champagne made her sway and she was sure Barking was not deceived when she passed a languid hand across her brow and declared she was 'drunk with exhaustion'.

'Very good, my lady,' he said, soberly, and with a discreet elbow positioned so he might assist her to navigate her way to the bannisters.

He was no doubt as pleased as she when he announced, 'His lordship'll be with you in a moment, m'lady.'

For there was Tristan, still fully dressed though Lord knew what hour it was, advancing towards her, thankfully with his limp not in evidence this evening, a smile on his face.

'I take it you've had a good evening, Addy,' he remarked after dismissing Barking for the night. 'I knew you'd be in safe hands if James were looking after you. I'm so sorry I couldn't have been there.'

Adelaide sank against his side with a faint hiccup and exhaled on a sigh as his arm went round her. He was just the sanctuary she needed. No, she would have no more nights like this unless Tristan were by her side. He'd keep her wayward spirits in check without reminding her that her wicked impulses would always be waiting in the wings to destroy her.

Well, her wicked impulses were gathering like screeching vultures at Tristan's proximity, and by the time he'd carried her to the bedroom she had determined that her wayward impulses were going to win the order of the day.

When he'd set her down, Adelaide reclined upon the counterpane and pointed her foot as she draped one arm across her brow. 'You're going to have to undress me, Tristan,' she whispered, 'since it appears Milly is not on hand. No need to sound so apologetic,' she added with a giggle when he told her he'd dismissed her maid for the night as it was nearly three in the morning. 'I'd much rather have you to attend to me. Here, the buttons are at the back.' She rolled over obligingly.

When she was dressed just in her chemise and stays, she proffered one ankle so he could remove her garters. Then, to be absolutely sure he could be under no illusions that the line had been crossed from practical necessity to outright seduction, she slanted her gaze across at him and waggled her foot.

'Oh yes,' she breathed. 'Take a step closer, Tristan.' For that took him to within easy reach of unbuttoning his breeches.

To her disappointment he stepped back. 'You've had a lot to drink, Addy, and it's been a taxing night for you. Here, let me help you.'

He untied the ribbons which secured her white silk stocking above the knee and rolled the flimsy article down her leg. Adelaide sighed and offered him the other, then indicated her stays. 'And my chemise, too,' she murmured.

He shook his head. 'It's too much, Addie. After last night you were unwell again—'

'I was *what*?' She sat up straight and glared at him. 'I slept like a baby and when I woke late, as is only to be expected, you'd gone.' She pouted. 'And you were gone all day. I wanted you to accompany me tonight so badly. What made you think I was unwell?'

He looked confused. 'Your mother told me over breakfast that you had had another of your turns in the night.'

Adelaide had had too much to drink to understand the implications of what he was saying. Waving a dismissive hand she dropped her head on his shoulder, breathing in the lovely familiar smell of him. 'My mother is not to be believed, clearly,' she whispered as she twined her fingers in the short hair at the nape of his neck and gave a wicked chuckle. 'In future you'll need to see for yourself what state I'm in.'

It was not too hard to get what she wanted.

She loved the weight of him on top of her. Loved the languorous escalation of feelings that grew from simply being held, until both were breathing heavily and clothing was being discarded with increasing speed before they lay wrapped in each other, naked, moving as one.

This was what marriage should be: the blissful union between two people of like mind, revelling in an intimacy that was sacrosanct and precious.

She never wanted anything else.

ADELAIDE WOKE in Tristan's arms for the first time. She snuggled closer, sighing with pleasure while the morning sun dappled the counterpane and dust motes danced above her sleeping husband.

With heart full to overflowing, she watched him. In repose he looked younger, the lines erased from his face giving it a boyish cast. There was an ascetic nobleness about him that made her heart clutch with pride. This serious, principled man had allied himself to *her*.

Tristan woke as she stirred, holding her closer before he opened his eyes, murmuring, 'How's my angel this morning?'

The truth was that Adelaide had a splitting headache, entirely self-induced, but she hooked her leg around her husband's and pressed her length against him, provocatively. 'Never better,' she murmured as she cupped his manhood.

'Not now, my love.' Gently he took her wrist and moved her hand away. The house was astir and she knew he had a meeting at his place of business.

Kissing her with lingering regret, he rose and put on his clothes. 'I feel like a thief in the night visiting my wife like this before slipping back to my own apartments.'

In response to Adelaide's wide-armed response, he lowered himself onto the bed and held her once more. 'Sleep a little longer, darling. You need it. I'll tell Milly not to disturb you.'

He pressed his lips to her brow, though she'd have preferred to have felt his lips upon hers and his warm body pressing her down. She felt on fire, as if last night's act had brought her back to life.

Closing her eyes as the door clicked shut behind him, she breathed out a sigh of pleasure.

It was all very well to be placed on a pedestal and to be cherished, but this was what she needed to feel complete. The earthy, sensual joining as one, of body, mind and soul.

At eleven o'clock Adelaide received her mother in the drawing room. One aspect of living together in London was the lack of privacy, occasioning such comments as her mother's thinly delivered: 'You were home very late, Adelaide.'

Adelaide smoothed her lilac skirts as she lowered herself into a chair and tried to temper the gleam in her eye and the self-satisfied expression which would only inflame her mother's curiosity if not her sensibilities.

It did not work.

'Three o'clock in the morning after obviously revelling in all this newfound adulation. I can't imagine what Tristan thought?'

Adelaide slanted a glance at her mother from beneath lowered lashes. Was she testing her? Did she know Tristan had taken her to her room and that he'd spent the night there?

Mrs Henley grunted. 'I hope he warned you against consorting with unsavoury types. Painters and poets, when your husband is such an important man. You certainly don't want to jeopardise his position by your behaviour.'

Adelaide sighed. 'Mama, my sole aim in life is to bring credit to my husband. If I can enjoy myself just a little along the way, is it such a bad thing to be feted for the only assets I have – and for just a few short years, too – my looks?'

'Your face will be your ruin – and has been once already.' Her mother's hand trembled as she put down her lorgnette. 'We'll talk no more about *that*, but my girl, a caution, if I may.'

Reluctantly, Adelaide waited for the inevitable.

'You can bring no credit to your husband if you yourself are not respected. And if your husband does not respect you, you have nothing. Just remember this, Adelaide, a husband has ungovernable impulses which he knows are too much of a burden for a wife he respects. That's why a good husband finds himself a mistress and leaves his wife in peace – once a nursery has been established.' Mrs Henley shook her head. 'You never could find the right balance in life, could you?'

CHAPTER 14

Adelaide drifted aimlessly from her room to the living room to the library after that.

The mindless revelry of the previous night felt like someone else's dream, though the memory of Tristan's touch remained as sweet as ever.

When luncheon was over, her mother snapped at her for failing to attend to anything properly and suggested she send a note round to Beatrice asking her to accompany them to Newgate prison 'to succour the inmates'.

Adelaide's patent horror was met by the sharp rejoinder, 'Beatrice was intrigued by the suggestion when I put it to her.'

'I've done my share of prisons, Mama, and no doubt Beatrice was only being polite. You know James forbade it, besides.'

'Perhaps, Adelaide, after last night, it's time to show a bit of gravitas to balance your feverish pleasure-seeking. Who knows how the gossip columns will choose to report your antics? At least you can appear to the world a beauty with a conscience. Wouldn't that be good for your husband's career? And for James's too, if Beatrice comes.'

For once Adelaide did concede there was value in her mother's words – if in fact she felt it necessary to atone in some way, or present a better front to the world on account of the previous night, which she did not.

To her surprise Beatrice was brimming with eagerness when they picked her up in the carriage an hour later. Her excited prattle as they wound their way through the streets to the prison was a contrast to the shy exterior she presented in social situations, though it stopped abruptly when they breached the prison defences. Her lively colour faded as she absorbed the reality of their mission: filth, squalor, screamed profanities.

Adelaide squeezed her hand. 'They're not screaming at you,' she reassured her. 'They scream at everyone.'

Wild eyes sunk in death skulls with matted hair seemed to leer at them wherever they went. It did not escape Adelaide's attention that she garnered the most interest. 'Come talk to me, pretty lady, and show me what's in your basket?' they'd call, dismissing Mrs Henley, and sometimes even Beatrice with a, 'Who wants a po-faced do-gooder what gives us a piece o' bread so long's we listen to a lecture?'

Beatrice had obviously donned what she considered garb appropriate to visiting a prison. Her drab brown walking dress with its lack of adornment seemed to leech all liveliness from her and as they trailed from cell to cell her spirits seemed to diminish even more.

After a while Adelaide felt the visit had not been such a bad idea. This was a fine way to reinforce to Beatrice that there were merits in making an effort to present as lively and comely a countenance as possible to the world.

While Mrs Henley dispensed food and good advice,

Adelaide received far more positive attention for smiling and looking beautiful. She touched Beatrice's shoulder. 'They're right. There's little enough loveliness in the world, Beatrice. While we are young and have our looks we must make the most of the opportunities these bring. Won't you accompany me to Madame Claudette's when Mama has released us? She has a bolt of the most divine Pomona green sarsenet which I think would complement your complexion far better than the colours your well-meaning aunt has chosen or that ghastly shade of sludge you're wearing. And you know how James appreciates beauty ... otherwise he'd never have chosen you.'

The corners of Beatrice's downturned mouth seemed to tauten even more. 'I don't know why he—'

'Chose you?' Adelaide put her head close to Beatrice's ear as they shadowed Mrs Henley down a stinking alley. 'James is an artist,' she whispered. 'He creates art from a blank page. That was his challenge when he met you.' She squeezed Beatrice's shoulder. 'He saw the beauty within you and the potential of your lovely exterior to match your good heart.'

Raising her head at the screeching of a vacant- eyed crone near them, she added, 'Now, I think we've done enough good work. Let's invite Mama to join us for an ice at Gunter's, shall we, unless she wants to spend her afternoon here alone?'

Mrs Henley chose not to accompany the girls, and it was clear the novelty of dispensing alms at the prison had worn thin as far as Beatrice was concerned. Adelaide was thrilled. Perhaps she was not going down Hortense's path, after all. The edge of jealous uncertainty in Beatrice's, 'Do you know where James is today?' despite the appearance of not caring, was another welcome sign. Hortense truly had not cared.

Adelaide shrugged as they strolled along Oxford St, seething with life in the afternoon sunshine. 'You should know better than I.'

Beatrice looked studiously at her feet beneath her muddied hem. 'You and he are such good friends. I think he'd tell you before he'd tell me.'

'Then it's up to you to change that.'

Hooking her arm into Beatrice's, Adelaide whisked her off the street and under a low door from which a steep staircase went up to the first floor. The unprepossessing exterior was belied by the familiar but ever-entrancing scene which greeted them as a young maid opened the door.

Bolts of fabric: delicate muslins, gold-flecked sarsenet and lustrous lustrings lay in haphazard disarray and half-sewn dresses were draped over chairs. In the centre of everything stood a young girl, very still, as a ballgown in the palest rose lustring was dropped over her head.

The small gathering that surrounded her gasped. One moment she had been a nondescript little thing with brown hair and a sallow complexion, the next she dazzled.

'A triumph!' Clapping, a middle-aged woman took several steps into the room. 'Miss Clarabelle will make a fine debut,' she pronounced, sending the girl off to change behind a screen before greeting Adelaide with respectful delight.

'But here comes the finest advertisement of my skills.' Rising from her curtsy to Adelaide, Madame Claudette flicked her wrist to her assistant who was soon back with the nearly finished gown Adelaide had ordered.

However Adelaide made it clear that it was Beatrice who was in need of her expertise on this occasion.

'Does the young lady wish to discuss her needs? A ballgown, is it?' She nodded as if she were running multiple possibilities for Beatrice through her head. 'And when will the young lady need the dress?' Madame Claudette gestured to her assistant to produce the various samples and bolts lying about.

Adelaide explained their need for haste. 'In five days'

time Miss Wells has an important political dinner and desires to make her husband proud.' She smiled at her friend's wide- eyed look. 'Yes, I know your good aunt intends for you to wear the jonquil and netting, and indeed it is a charming gown, but the shade is not as becoming as ... ah!' Adelaide clapped her hands together as the little assistant held up a bolt of coquelicot red and Miss Claudette declared, 'Once again Mme Sophie's expert eye has selected just the colour. Miss Wells requires a bold palette to enhance the darkness of her hair and the paleness of her skin.'

Beatrice blanched, her response immediate. 'I can't possibly wear such a colour.' She lowered her eyes at the questioning looks turned upon her.

Miss Claudette cleared her throat. 'Naturally, the gown will be in shades suitable to one in your unmarried state, but a sash and trimmings in this colour will provide the verve and dash you require. Miss Wells is, I believe, to be married to a man renowned for his passionate prose. All London is wondering who the muse is who inspired him. Surely, Miss Wells, you want the assumption to be that it is yourself.'

In the ensuing silence the noise of carriage wheels and whistles issued through the open windows mingled with the shouts of vendors and general bustle of busy Oxford St.

Adelaide curled her gloved hands tightly together and tried to block her mind to the modiste's words, so innocent yet so deadly.

It was inevitable that once they were alone, having ordered a fine gown with coquelicot red trimmings, Beatrice should ask in a low voice, 'Does *anyone* know the identity of the ... lady who inspired James?'

Now it was Adelaide who answered evasively, suggesting they return home via Green Park to Aunt Wells's townhouse so that Adelaide might help Beatrice with her toilette.

'Have you read *The Maid of Milan?*' Beatrice asked as Adelaide wielded the tongs.

'No, and nor do I think it's important.' She pretended the deepest concentration on her task while she went over what common gossip had disseminated.

So far, she gathered, there was little to specifically identify the woman who featured so prominently in so many of the poems. Early speculation had dismissed James's wife. Neither the fire-flashing emeralds nor the titian tresses, which were the only telling snippets of description Adelaide had gleaned, could have belonged to brown-eyed Hortense.

Steeling herself, she asked, 'Have you ventured your own opinion?'

'I still haven't read it.'

'Why Beatrice, you want to be able to discuss the work which is his lifeblood, else he will see your disinterest as a failure to honour him as he would want to be honoured in his wife's eyes.' Secretly, though, Adelaide was relieved.

Beatrice blushed. 'His poetry does not define him in my eyes,' she murmured. 'I fell in love with him on a dance floor in Vienna before I even knew he was a poet. Before his poetry was published to such acclaim.'

Beatrice rose and began to pace. Her normally pallid complexion was flushed, her agitation clear. 'James said you had not known Lord Leeson long when you accepted his marriage offer.' She turned and searched Adelaide's face. 'If you did not love him, did you ever wonder if there were another course open to you?'

Adelaide hesitated. Where was this leading? Was Beatrice questioning her own path? Could James have insinuated that Adelaide hadn't in fact loved Tristan when she married him and Beatrice was weighing up whether love could grow from tenuous beginnings?

'Do you not love James?' she asked slowly. 'Do you feel

trapped by the course you're on because you're concerned that to renege at this late date would be a scandal?'

Beatrice looked offended. 'I am not so lacking in pride that I would wed a man who had no feeling for me. If I believed James did not, and never could, love me as I would wish, then the scandal of reneging at the last minute would mean nothing to me.'

'But you do love James?' Adelaide's insides churned. 'Yes? I'm so glad.' She almost sagged with relief to hear the answer, adding hurriedly, 'Remember, so much has changed for James. His work … his passion … is suddenly receiving the recognition he's wanted his whole life.'

If she could rest easy in the knowledge that some flame would ignite relations between the couple then Adelaide need never again suffer the guilt of being singed by a smouldering look sent in her direction, or a seemingly innocent fleeting touch.

She went towards the young girl, her voice gaining strength as she said, 'People ask who is his muse? What does it matter? The time has come for *you* to be his muse. It's time to transform you, Beatrice, into what you could become only with long guiding, careful attention and sensitivity. I can help you reach that point sooner." She widened her eyes in enquiry, adding, "If you'll let me.'

ALTHOUGH TRISTAN HAD ASSURED Mrs Henley he'd not encourage Adelaide in yet another night of revelry, he was desperate to spend some time with his wife beyond the walls of Bruton Street.

When he presented himself in the drawing room that evening wearing the requisite knee breeches, white stockings with buckled shoes and coat of dark blue superfine, for Almack's, Adelaide's delight was ample reward.

'Darling Tristan, Mama said you weren't coming.' She danced before him, extending her arms so that he had no choice but to embrace her.

'And Tristan, you'll never guess it, but Mr Gilchrist is so enamoured of his skills as my portrait painter that he's asked me to sit for him again so he can sketch me for a series of drawings and paintings he plans for an exhibition in two weeks.'

'Why, that's marvellous, darling, if that pleases you. When does he intend to sleep?'

She didn't answer him directly, clearly too excited by the conversation she'd had with the painter. 'He discussed a range of attitudes of the kind which made Lady Hamilton famous, only he assures me these will be entirely original. But Tristan, they'll be slightly theatrical and since I always desired to go on the stage but of course could not since it's such a disreputable calling, perhaps this is one way to enjoy the same sort of expression but to do so respectably.'

'As long as it is respectable, my darling.' She looked so happy his heart clutched. Even if it wasn't respectable, he'd have sanctioned it if it delighted her this much.

'Lady Hawkins believes it is. She was in Mr Gilchrist's studio viewing his work and after much discussion it was decided that the ideas Mr Gilchrist has in mind are perfectly respectable.'

'Your mother might not—'

Adelaide's laugh was like a tonic. 'Mama will be delighted for I've negotiated with Mr Gilchrist a sizeable contribution that will go towards the poor unfortunate females with whom she is so concerned.'

❄

WITH TRISTAN BY HER SIDE, Adelaide had never been happier.

To augment her high spirits, when Tristan escorted her to the supper table at Almack's, loaded with its famously simple fare, she spotted Beatrice and James, who appeared on congenial terms with one another.

Beatrice had trimmed her evening gown with embroidered roses and threaded pearls through her hair. It showed how much she did want to please James.

And James appeared pleased.

Beatrice glanced up at Adelaide with a smile. 'James has just told me the manner in which he charmed Lady Cowper and ensured his receipt of a voucher'—her mouth turned up —'since I've heard he was told to leave on one famous occasion.'

James, sidling up to them, patted her shoulder. 'Beatrice will be the sobering tonic I need so I don't lose my place here or get blackballed at White's.'

Tristan helped himself to thinly buttered bread. 'Some things never change. Miss Wells is assuming the role I took upon myself when we schooled together, James.'

'I appear to be accused from all quarters of entirely lacking responsibility.' Grinning, James ran a hand through his tousled hair. Adelaide wondered how long it had taken him to achieve the effect or if he really had just got out of bed.

Beatrice sobered. 'Perhaps with a nature as creative and brilliant as yours it's necessary to have others to look out for you.'

Not long after their arrival at Almack's they were surrounded by a coterie of admirers.

'More lovely in the flesh ... I hear you're to sit for a vignette of attitudes ... My husband thought you the greatest beauty he'd laid eyes upon ...'

Snatches of praise drifted from all quarters.

James, raising his eyebrows as he caught Adelaide's look, suddenly declared that as there was only so much of the sickly sweet orgeat he could tolerate, would they not look in with him at Lady March's assembly ball.

When Tristan cited work commitments Adelaide said she'd return home with him.

He studied her a moment then said, when the others' attention was diverted, 'I shall be no good company to you tonight, dearest, when I can see your lively spirits are in need of more diversion than I can provide.'

'Let me help you with your speech,' Adelaide pleaded. 'I have a quick hand. You could dictate to me. I'd love to learn more about the reforms you believe in.'

'Yet you despise your mother for her reforming zeal? You're an odd mix, Adelaide, and while I am flattered you appreciate my reforming efforts, I have Mr Finch to carry out such work. No, I would rather you enjoy this evening amongst friends. I would be poor company by comparison.'

WHEN ADELAIDE ROSE JUST before noon after another late night, her mother was awaiting her in the drawing room with a large basket of tangled skeins.

'The cat has been playing with them and you need something to settle your mind,' she said, patting the seat beside her. 'Later, we might visit the prison.'

Adelaide wished she had the wit to tell her she was promised to Beatrice, but it was too late. She'd make her excuses as soon as she could and go and visit her friend.

She sighed. 'Will it ever improve, Mama? I mean, no matter what we do, the prisons will be bursting at the seams filled with people whose greatest crime is not being able to earn enough through their honest labours to feed themselves and their children. We need a revolution to change that. They did that across the channel and did it make anything better for the common people?'

'Have faith, Adelaide.' Her mother spoke calmly. 'If you make the effort and it rubs off on your friends who in turn make more of their kind – the decision makers – aware of the inequities, then it's people like your husband who can effect change through legislation. My dear girl, you've been given a great gift: a husband who will do anything you want him to do, go in any direction you lead him.'

'I didn't think you had much faith in my choosing the right direction.'

Her mother's look became more familiar as her mouth tightened. 'If you wish to be regarded as a shallow creature, go right ahead and continue on the path of mindless, endless frivolity in which you seem to be caught up. It is up to you to decide how you wish to be regarded.'

Adelaide concentrated her attention upon untangling a skein of sky-blue wool. The colour reminded her of the little jacket she had knitted once, all those years ago, for a child she never saw. A child who'd been born and died in sin. The memory was like a blunt instrument against a wound that refused to heal.

'Adelaide, your husband worships you.'

She jerked her head up. Her mother had *never* said such a thing before. Her mother never reflected kindly upon anything connected with Adelaide.

The words that followed made her realise she was a fool.

Of course she had misunderstood.

'You know why he married you. He recognised the wounded creature you were. He wanted to heal you and now he thinks he has by bringing you here to London. But you know what will happen? You will return to your old wanton ways. You will forever be a victim of your nature; you will destroy everything for which I have worked so hard … unless you can take stock, accept your newfound notoriety – yes – *notoriety*, with dignity and humility and try to temper your passionate impulses. Do you wish to disgust Tristan? Oh yes, he will enjoy the overtures to begin with, but when he starts to question from whence they came he will only question what you really are, Adelaide.'

'What I really am?' She repeated the words stupidly, the blunt instrument honing its point until she couldn't breathe from the pain.

Mrs Henley snatched the blue wool from her, inexpertly rolled and handed her a skein of red.

'You still are in a position to make that choice for yourself, Adelaide. To decide how you wish him to regard you.' Her look was piercing. Like the pain in Adelaide's heart. 'Think long and hard, my girl, because you need his high regard.'

Adelaide closed her eyes on the sense that her life was in perpetual rotation, with each moment of frivolity tempered by conversations like this one with her mother.

She wanted to scream.

TRISTAN GREETED Adelaide warmly when she met him in the hall on Thursday upon his return from parliament.

'Addy, you look well. Enjoying yourself, I hope?' He put his hands on her shoulders and regarded her closely. It clearly gave him great pleasure to remark upon her glowing complexion and bright eyes. 'Against your mother's expectations – and mine, I'll admit – London is proving good for you.'

'My natural giddiness is come to the fore,' Adelaide said, only half in jest.

He took her arm and led her up the stairs, holding her against his side as he declared with unusual vigour, 'Then I am the luckiest MP in all London town for I have a wife who will dazzle equally for her beauty as be respected for her good works. I look forward to observing the fine impression you will make upon our dinner guests.'

'I shall try to do you proud tonight, Tristan, and if it's deserved I shall enjoy your praise. But you know I absolutely loathe traipsing round after my saintly Mama so do not compliment me where it's not deserved.'

'I didn't need to be reminded of that, my dear,' he laughed, 'but thank you for your honesty. It's a refreshing contrast to the intrigue which festers in the circles I move in.'

BEATRICE WAS the youngest dinner guest by nearly a decade, but instead of allowing her to keep her views to herself, Adelaide sought to draw her out so that after her initial shyness the girl became an equal member of the party and even James seemed impressed.

During a lull in the conversation Sir Godfrey announced to the assembled party with great solemnity, 'Like everyone who's seen Lady Leeson's likeness, I agree, it doesn't do justice to her beauty.' He inclined his head. 'Fine painting but you're a finer looking woman.'

'You've seen it?' Adelaide felt the heat in her cheeks as she returned his smile. She'd never met this man or his wife until this evening and the painting had been finished only a few days earlier.

James leaned across the table and spoke directly to her for the first time. 'You're the toast of the town, don't you know, Addy? Surely Tristan's told you what the gossip sheets are saying?'

Everyone laughed at Adelaide's blush and Lady Runkle's eyes twinkled over the top of her wine glass. 'It's what I aspired to when I was your age.' She was a lively woman of middle age married to a fellow MP. 'The Prince Regent himself was heard to remark that he must see the painting.'

Adelaide's first impulse was to brush off the praise.

She glanced at her husband. 'I suppose I must enjoy this notoriety while I can. I have neither Lady Runkle's sparkling wit nor Beatrice's goodness to recommend me and *those* are attributes that will survive the passing of time.'

Lord Gantry laughed. 'Too modest, Lady Leeson. Yours is the kind of beauty that will survive age, and indeed you were remarked upon dispensing alms to the prisoners. In your finery, no less.'

Adelaide felt her husband's admiration like a glow from within. She smiled at him before turning to Beatrice. The girl looked radiant in her boldly coloured gown, and she felt relief as she transferred her glance to James, hoping to catch some similar emotion between the betrothed couple.

A relief short lived.

James was focusing his attention upon Adelaide, his shoulder to Beatrice, his body tense as if he would devour his hostess before the rest of them.

She turned away as she felt the fiery heat burn her face once more.

Lord Gantry took it for modesty. 'You *must* be new to town if you can blush like a country lass.'

Adelaide hoped this would not offend Lady Gantry so was relieved his wife was equally complimentary. 'It's as well to be able to charm the ladies as it is the men.'

'Adelaide charms everyone.' Tristan didn't seem like a man twice married, Adelaide thought with fondness. He looked like a man in love for the first time.

Suddenly she wanted everyone to be gone. She caught his

eye. Four couples either side separated them, but it was clear what he was thinking. And she was in complete accord.

The chinking of glass and babble of chatter faded into the background. She made the appropriate responses, she was fairly sure of it. Yet all the time it was as if the invisible chord separating her from Tristan pulled tighter.

She spoke to Lord Runkle, appearing to give him her full attention; but watching from the corner of her eye she was conscious of Tristan's furtive looks and her breath came fast and shallow as she envisaged what would happen between them, later. She sensed his desire. She shifted in her chair, restless from the need that pulsed through her.

The ladies retired to the drawing room to leave the gentlemen to their port and coffee. Beatrice, she was vaguely aware, acquitted herself commendably. Adelaide laughed and chatted, though she had no idea what she discussed.

Finally the party broke up just before midnight.

Carriages were called for; farewells were exchanged in the hallway while the servants cleared away the dishes.

Barking was told he was no longer required. The chatter of departing guests overlaid the clink of plates being removed from the dining room.

And then finally the last couple drove away and Adelaide turned back to a quiet and seemingly empty house.

Side by side, without speaking, they walked through the passageway, hesitating as one at the bottom of the staircase, ears attuned to the sound of a movement above. Mrs Henley?

Silently they continued their footsteps towards the dining room, throwing open the doors to be confronted by the now-empty room, a white linen cloth upon the table.

The blood was thrumming in Adelaide's veins. She sensed Tristan was equally enraptured at the possibilities.

Together they turned, stepping forward at the same time,

the touch an incendiary one, bringing mouths and bodies together in an explosive joining of need and lust.

Adelaide's lips parted, her tongue skimming the seam of Tristan's mouth, her womb turning to liquid need as her husband marched her back against the table, bending her over backwards to trail searing kisses down her neck. The bulge of his desire pressing into her belly ignited her hunger; her hands fumbled for the flap of his breeches as he grabbed fistfuls of her skirts, raising them as he parted her knees.

Her breath was rapid and shallow now, her excitement roaring in her ears, her vision coalescing into fiery flames of red and black, the colours of sin, the colours of need...

The colours of her lustful desire for her husband who made love to her on the table of their London townhouse in an act that joined two kindred spirits as one.

CHAPTER 15

The next morning Adelaide trailed through the house like a lost soul, wishing Tristan were at home. He'd been gone when she'd woken, and without his comforting morning caresses she felt bereft. He'd carried her to bed where he'd made love to her all over again. She stretched out her arms, savouring the memory.

London had reawakened the old energy that had fed her youthful impulses. But Tristan wasn't here and she wanted him. Desperately.

Passing the library she put her head round the door and saw Tristan's work spread out on his desk. He knew how to channel his energies into worthwhile pursuits, but what worthwhile pursuits were open to her other than attaching herself to her dreadful Mama?

Wandering over to his desk she saw the papers Mr Finch had delivered. It was his first draft of the speech Tristan had dictated to him, she'd been told. Once again she read his dry, unexciting prose with disgust.

How was such rhetoric supposed to appeal to hearts and minds? Seating herself, she dipped a quill into the inkpot and set about making a few judicious changes. An added phrase here and there, where there was room. Subtle, but effective. She'd done so in the past when James had been stuck for words in his poems. Adelaide was, after all, a born prattler; and, thank goodness, she thought, a born actress. At least finding the right words for the right occasion were, she hoped, amongst her attributes.

'This came for you, m'lady.' Adelaide looked up to see Barking hovering in the doorway holding out the silver salver upon which lay a pile of cream wafers.

She barely glanced them. More invitations, more charitable requests, another painter wanting her to sit to him.

She was tired of them all. She only wanted Tristan. 'Thank you, Barking.' She held out her hand.

It was only later, when she was changing out of her morning dress into something appropriate for the afternoon that she noticed the envelopes, unopened, on her bedside table.

She didn't recognise the handwriting of the first she picked up. She turned it over. The seal was plain red wax. Lowering herself onto her dressing table, Adelaide slid her fingernail underneath to break the seal and smoothed open the missive to scan the few words.

Breathing heavily, she dropped the paper. She blinked, wondering if her eyes were playing tricks on her, glancing up at the sun through the window, for a moment wondering if it could have distorted what she was seeing. Her hands began to sweat, her body to tremble. Very carefully, as if it would contaminate her, she picked up the paper and reread it.

No invitation, no request, no painter begging to execute her likeness. Just a few simple words which sucked the joy from her and filled her with a fear so terrible she thought she might turn to stone on the spot: *'I know your Secret. Stay away.'*

At the sound of footsteps in the passage she leapt to her feet, casting around the room for something, anything, to offer her salvation, rescue, an answer.

Oh God, what if it were Tristan? Or her mother? Anyone, really.

'Darling?'

When Tristan put his head round the door she was trembling uncontrollably. He took her in his arms and she eyed the charred remains of the awful missive over the top of his shoulder.

'Adelaide?'

What could she tell him? It was too late for the truth. She crumpled into his arms, her breath coming in short, frightened sobs.

'Dear Lord, Addy, what has happened?' Fear sharpened his voice as he carried her to the bed.

Still she couldn't stop shaking. 'I feel ill, Tristan,' she managed through chattering teeth. 'I'm engulfed with chills.' She tried to steady her breathing as he loosened her clothing at her throat, making her more comfortable.

'Darling, what's happened? Shall I call the doctor?'

Adelaide shook her head, her eyes clenched tight shut as she wrapped her arms around herself and began to rock, moaning with the torment she could not reveal.

It was all too much. Someone knew of the secret which had the power to destroy her and she didn't know what to do.

'No, I don't want the doctor,' she whimpered. 'I just need to rest here. In the dark. I'll be well again soon. I'm sorry, Tristan.'

'Sorry? Why are you sorry, my darling?' Tenderly he rocked her, his face buried in her neck. 'You have nothing for which to be sorry.'

The unsaid words swirled between them, engulfing

Adelaide with shame and misery as he whispered the inevitable: 'I should have realised it was too much excitement for you.'

She didn't argue, for what could she say? She let him believe it; let him believe that her mental torments had been brought on by their sexual intimacy as she let him organise warm possets, then call for Milly to fetch more blankets, before he sat down again to rub her fingers and her temples. He made her drink the soothing concoction that came up from the kitchen, murmuring his reassurances she'd soon be well, that he'd see to it, personally, though his expression was bleak.

Adelaide knew what he was thinking but right now she didn't care. Her future came in five minute increments. If she could only survive the next five minutes. She was an invalid again. Her wits were addled.

She covered her face with her hands and tossed beneath the covers, aware that he stood, watching her helplessly while she wished with all her heart for him to be gone. Or maybe that's what she was screaming though she had no idea whether the sounds in her head had any connection to what she uttered.

Poor Tristan, to be used so badly. Exhausted, she stopped fighting and soaked in the silence. She had no idea if she were alone in her room or not. Her mind was a black void, empty of all but the pain of her disloyalty. She – *Adelaide* – had sucked the pleasure from Tristan's life for the past three years. Her beloved husband who had tried so hard to do what he felt best for her had had almost no return for his care and concern. Now, when her heart was full to bursting its need to repay him for his loving generosity and her conscience was heavy with the desire to atone; when her body cried out for him; when she loved him so much, and finally *knew* it; there was someone else out there –some terrifying anonymous person who had guessed her guilty secret – waiting to destroy the happiness she'd found.

SEEKING the sanctuary of his study half an hour later, Tristan buried himself in his work.

Rubbing his eye sockets, he tried to concentrate on the blurred words before him. How could he concentrate on anything but his fears for Adelaide?

He had no idea how long he sat there but he felt Mrs Henley's presence before the woman spoke. It was like clammy fog wrapping its ghostly tentacles around him and he shivered as her voice reached him from the shadows.

'Tristan, a word if I may?'

Always the question was couched as a command. Always it echoed round his head like a clarion call to protect his vulnerable young wife. As if he hadn't done everything, at every step possible, that he could.

Even as he turned, his mind screamed self-reproach, just as he knew Mrs Henley would charge him with his culpability. Adelaide had taken a turn, and wasn't that an indication that Tristan had not listened to the mother's strictures? That he'd been remiss by forging his own path.

He'd lost track of time as he'd attended to Adelaide but now he saw that it was late afternoon, the long shadows casting their gloom over the house like a pall.

'Certainly, Mrs Henley.' He indicated a chair with a resigned wave of his hand and she rustled in, giving off a scent that reminded him of mouldering lilies.

Mrs Henley lowered herself onto an uncomfortable, little blue and silver upholstered chair and regarded him balefully.

'Tristan, you and I may have our differences but we are as one in two important regards.'

She spoke the truth, for this was not the first time she reminded him that Adelaide's welfare and that of the poor unfortunate souls whom society had relegated to the scrapheap were their primary interests.

She went on, 'You have, I gather, seen my daughter.'

'Of course!'

'No need to sound insulted. Naturally you have seen her but do you recognise in her the emotional, tormented creature who has taken to her bed as the Adelaide you married? Of course you do.'

He hated the way she spoke for him. She'd always done it, but he'd learned that to object merely prolonged the agony of the interview and delivered no real benefits. It was why he let her go on with merely an incline of his head. She knew Adelaide better than anyone. She'd been with her when Adelaide was vibrant and carefree. She had lived through her daughter's terrible ordeal. Hadn't he heard it a million times?

Tristan clenched his fists and strove for calm. God, but for those foul renegades who had raped his lovely Adelaide the two of them might be living in the kind of domestic felicity he dreamed about. With an effort he steadied his breathing as he wiped the back of his hand across his forehead.

'All this ridiculous gaiety and racing round London. Being feted and adored'—her nostrils flared—'is the worst possible thing that could have happened to her, and I blame you for not tightening the reins when you must surely have seen how it would end.'

'With due respect, Mrs Henley, I believed completely that gaiety was the restorative Adelaide needed. Two days ago – yesterday! – she was blooming.'

'Do you not understand that Adelaide's finely tuned emotions were slowly being wound up until the inevitable happened? I tried to warn you—'

'I believed my approach was kinder, Mrs Henley. Was it not natural to allow Adelaide a degree of freedom so she could enjoy what she missed as a young, unmarried woman? We both know the traumas she has been through. Is it not reasonable to expect that making the most of a London season would help compensate her for losses any normal, beautiful young woman must feel after living so very quietly recovering, in the country? I believed this would be just what she needed.'

'She needs a child.' Mrs Henley paused briefly before launching in. 'Most women her age are well and truly burdened by domesticity's heavy requirements. Adelaide is dancing around like someone just out of the schoolroom. Not only is it scandalous, it's clearly been detrimental to her.'

'Well, Adelaide and I have not yet been blessed,' he said coldly. 'In the meantime I shall ensure she has the rest and care needed to restore her health and spirits. She is laid low with nothing more than a bad megrim, such as she has had many times in the past. With time she will return to the lively, lovely creature she was yesterday.'

'You must rein her in, Tristan. It is not right.'

He stared her down. 'Are you telling me how to manage my wife? Her conduct is beyond reproach—'

'Overexcitement will be the death of her.'

'I did not know exuberance to be an official cause of death but I will bear your caution in mind,' he responded with heavy sarcasm. He rose, indicating the interview was at an end.

Mrs Henley flung her arms wide. 'Only you can be the calming influence you need, Tristan. Now her passions are released and it is affecting her mind. I implore you, Tristan, do what you can to keep her calm." Her nostrils quivered as she lowered her voice, adding, "Even you must see how injurious this pleasure-seeking is to her health.'

CHAPTER 16

Days passed. Light metamorphosed into dark. It was all the same to Adelaide. The fear that twisted so sharply in her mind when she'd first received the note became muted. Her senses grew fuzzy and her body heavy and unresponsive. Blessed relief it was to simply float away into a world where there were no consequences; where her happiness wasn't like a finely tuned object that could be regulated by the slightest turn of a screw.

One day consciousness returned when Milly drew the curtains to let in the morning light.

Except it wasn't Milly, and she saw that it must already be the afternoon.

'An excess of high spirits will inevitably lead one to crash to earth.'

Adelaide squinted at her mother who was just a dark shape against the bright light behind her. Her head felt heavy and her general disorientation made it difficult to make sense of the words.

She rose up on her elbows, struggling for clarity as her mother trained her accusing gaze upon her from the window embrasure. 'Enough of playing the invalid, Adelaide. The time has come for you to regulate your humours and become the wife Tristan needs. Here is something for you to drink.'

'Please say it's something stronger than warm milk?'

'Indeed, Adelaide. You've been abed for nearly a week and you've got work to do. This will help you recover your strength. Tristan needs you.'

'No, he doesn't.' She felt like crying.

With a snap of the curtains on the other bay window,

Mrs Henley turned her disapproving stare upon her daughter. 'Tristan needs you to support him, not to eclipse him as you've been hell-bent on doing these past weeks in London. Beatrice is waiting downstairs for you. She's concerned.'

'Has anyone else called?'

Ignoring this, her mother swept to the door, clapping her hands for Adelaide's maid who hurried into the room. 'Milly! Adelaide is ready to dress. Nothing too colourful, if you please. Sober colours for a sober temperament.'

Half an hour later Adelaide seated herself opposite her young friend and smiled a tentative greeting. She felt a little stronger but inside she quailed, her mind whirling with possible conspiracies. Could Beatrice have written the note? For days, in between horrible nightmares, her mind had gone round in circles trying to understand who would want to warn her off. Gentle, unassuming Beatrice had the greatest motive, but now that she was here in front of Adelaide and gazing at her with such concern, Adelaide found it hard to believe the girl capable of such malice. Besides, how could she have discovered such a thing? James would not have told her.

She rubbed a hand over her brow and Beatrice leaned forward to pat her shoulder. 'Poor Addy, you really are not well, are you?'

Adelaide studied her covertly. *Could* Beatrice have heard whispers about Adelaide and James and on a hunch penned those appalling four words? Four words which had the power, if acted upon, to completely destroy Adelaide's future happiness.

Oh God, as long as Tristan does not know, thought Adelaide with another lurch of fear. She'd been aware of him as he'd sat, worried and silent, at her bedside, during those days she'd drifted in and out of consciousness.

Poor Tristan.

Her mother simply thought Adelaide was indulging in vaporous ennui, as she termed it, endorsing the doctor's diagnosis of a nervous affliction brought on by overexcitement.

Now, apparently the remedy was for Adelaide to spend part of each day lying quietly in a darkened room as she was gradually revived by gentle stimulation. Strolls through nearby Green Park would be acceptable but no promenading in Hyde Park or parading on Rotten Row. And definitely no late nights at balls or assemblies or entertaining that included dancing, although the occasional musical entertainment was, apparently, acceptable.

'Everyone is terribly worried about you,' Beatrice said. 'James is in black despair that in some way he has triggered your …' She trailed off, embarrassed to give words to Adelaide's affliction.

Adelaide tried to keep her eyelids open as she managed a smile. What indeed was it being termed? She chose to let it go. But she didn't want to think about James. Her lip quivered; she was feeling extraordinarily emotional right now and could have done without having to account for herself to Beatrice. 'I've let down Mr Gilchrist, too. He wanted to begin the vignettes in order to display them next week.' Adelaide swallowed down a sob. 'And you heard that the Prince Regent himself showed interest in seeing them.'

'You mustn't concern yourself about that, Adelaide,' Beatrice reassured her. 'Miss Kitty Carew is modelling for Mr Gilchrist. She'll be your replacement until you are well again.'

Dismay, disappointment … Adelaide wasn't sure how to term the rush of feeling that swept through her at the news.

'Miss Kitty Carew?' she repeated, stupidly.

'The lead performer at the opera we saw—'

'Yes, yes I know.'

'James told me Lord Leeson organised it.' 'Tristan!'

Beatrice sent her an odd look. 'Yes, Mr Gilchrist was here when you were ill and most insistent about ascertaining your state of health. Quite ill-bred of him, really. Well, Lord Leeson said he knew someone just as beautiful who would sit to him while you were … indisposed.'

'*Just as beautiful?*' Had she said the words or just thought them? That Tristan could say such a thing made her want to cry. Could he really think that common little opera dancer was just as beautiful as Adelaide?

Beatrice fiddled with the silver-backed hairbrush she'd picked up from the dressing table then slanted a quick glance at her friend when she thought she wasn't looking. But Adelaide was all too aware of the scrutiny of others. Inwardly, she winced. What did Beatrice know? Was she speculating on the reasons for Adelaide's sudden decline? What about Miss Carew? Was Beatrice wondering if there were hidden reasons her husband had enlisted a common actress to model in Adelaide's stead?

Foolish fancies. Her mind was conjuring up all sorts of desperate scenarios and that's *all* they were, for Tristan was hardly the man to be unfaithful nor to discard his wife so peremptorily after they'd reached the pinnacle of their relationship only days before her lapse. She took a deep, steadying breath.

'What will you do, Addy? Are you *so* unwell?'

Adelaide looked up from her dismal contemplation of her friend's slippers and said in the tone of regretful admission, 'I fear I am paying for an excess of spirits, Beatrice. Take me as a warning and try and find some sensible midway point between your moral rectitude and my—'

'Adelaide!'

'It's true, Beatrice.' Adelaide knew she sounded as miserable as she felt. What must she do now? How would she dare to show her head in public again and risk another venomous warning?

Clearly Beatrice hadn't written the note. But who had?

And what did they want?

The question spun, unanswered, through her head every waking moment. Yet there'd been nothing further.

No demands, just the veiled threat that someone lurking in the shadows was only too happy to reveal all.

Adelaide stood up, her obvious determination causing Beatrice to cast a worried look at the door. 'You're not well enough for London revels yet, surely, Addy?'

'Not revels but reform or something along those lines,' she mumbled. 'Now, where is my writing paper? I need to compose a few lines to this apparently amazing woman whose praises Tristan sings: Mrs Fry.'

It was all she could think of: keep her head low, shun the limelight and concentrate her efforts on activities that were blameless. Entirely beyond reproach.

'I thought you said you hated traipsing around prisons.'

'I did and I do.' Adelaide began scratching a few lines. 'I live for gaiety and I deplore dirt and distress, but if I'm to be the wife my husband needs I must interest myself a little more in his concerns. I have an idea.' She looked up with a bright and energetic resolve, or so she hoped. At least she was still capable of pretending interest when her very soul felt like a dried up prune. 'If I can pretend concern for my husband's interests then you can pretend interest in your future husband's concerns.' She smiled at the juxtaposition. 'Inform yourself as to what will make your future husband happy while I reform myself into the model of propriety my husband will admire.'

Beatrice continued to look troubled. Adelaide ignored her, sprinkling sand upon the letter once it was finished, and saying, 'All perfectly reasonable if you'd only spend two seconds thinking about it, Beatrice. Now, you have seen me write my letter and can report to my mother when she quizzes you that her daughter has reformed. As you quite rightly remark, I am in no state to see anyone today. My mind is completely disordered. However, tomorrow we will see if my resolve to be good is just a passing fancy or if indeed I do have the gumption to become better than I am. Won't everyone be delighted at my transformation?'

TRISTAN LOOKED in on her later that morning to see how she did but Adelaide had retreated to her bed once more, her head still thick with the awful fug that made it hard to think clearly. She wished she could feign the energy she'd managed for Beatrice.

With the same tender care she remembered from the old days, he sat and stroked her arm.

What could she say? She was tormented by the fear of revelation but the silence forced upon her – for there *were* no words for what she wanted to say – was even worse.

'Darling,' he asked finally, as if he'd been thinking about it for some time and the words were reluctantly spoken, 'have you been taking laudanum again?'

She blinked, shocked at the charge, but he put his finger to her lips, his expression both stern and tender as he went on, 'I know how much you needed it in the early days of our marriage. You had good reason to dull your senses until I made you stop, and although you were angry with me, you were much improved afterwards.'

'No, I am not taking it!' Adelaide declared, sitting up in bed. Angry and ashamed, his suspicions brought back the moment of greatest discord in their marriage. She'd hated Tristan for keeping from her the blessed relief of the laudanum drops at the time, but how much better she'd felt when she found she no longer needed them.

'Hush.' He smiled, as if it were a relief, stroking her hand before he rose. 'I'm glad, Addy. I'd hate to think you,' he paused, meaningfully, 'had a reason for dulling reality.'

Through the cotton wool in her mind she realised he was referring to the explosive, blissful union that had occurred between them, and she gripped his hand to stop him from leaving.

'No, Tristan, what we had was wonderful! I'd never want to block that out.'

The gratification in his expression was some consolation, though his next words were small comfort. 'I love you, my darling. I want you to be well again, but we must take things slowly. Doctor's orders.'

When he'd gone she ordered Milly to lay out a walking dress in a subdued and not altogether flattering shade of primrose and then emerged for luncheon long after her husband and, thank goodness, her mother had finished theirs. This didn't mean, however, she escaped the house before her no-doubt well-meaning parent descended upon her in her bedchamber as she was putting on her gloves.

'So you have decided to cast off your malady and re-emerge, Adelaide. With reasonably becoming sobriety if your dress indicates the manner in which you intend to deport yourself.' The downwards tug of her mouth suggested Mrs Henley was reluctant to mutter something that wasn't criticism. An uncharitable reflection, thought Addy, who was determined now to be more charitable in both thought and action than her mother was at least in action.

She paused in the midst of tying the ribbons of her bonnet and managed a sweet smile. 'You're right, Mama, the endless gaiety of this town is corrupting. Now my head is clear and I can tell you that a saintly revelation intervened and persuaded me not to give my soul to the devil for all you've intimated he had it years ago. I'm off to do good works. Where is my work basket?'

'Don't you be saucy with me, girl.'

Adelaide fixed her with an injured look. 'Saucy, Mama? Perhaps I have been guilty of that in the past but I am reformed.' Quickly removing her gloves, she held out her hands, presenting her elegant, well-shaped nails and soft white skin. 'In a few weeks these will be calloused and ingrained with dirt: testament to my efforts at redemption.' She cocked her head. 'I thought you would look at me with delight, or at least affection, not as if I'd lost my mind. Will I never please you?' With a deep sigh, Adelaide brushed past her with her basket and made for the stairs, calling for Milly. Her plan was only half formulated, but at least, for the first time in her life, she had one. She was doubtful, though, that it would make a difference. All she knew was that she had to do something, for inaction was killing her. She was not a good person; she knew that very well. Always had.

For three years she'd been awaiting exposure; and now it was nearly upon her. If her secret was about to damn her in Tristan's eyes if not the eyes of all London, the more good works she could fit in first, the less dire her punishment, she hoped, as she swept out into the street in a sensible dress carrying a cane basket filled with victuals for the poor.

MRS FRY HAD RESPONDED with eagerness to Lady Leeson's request to meet her on short notice. Adelaide tried to match her enthusiasm as she trailed after her, dragging Milly along as her chaperone and hoping she sounded as if she were half as committed to the cause to which Elizabeth Fry was passionately devoted. Alas, when they parted two hours later Adelaide was exhausted and far more concerned with her aching feet than the conditions of the inmates.

Yet she wasn't quite ready for home.

'Where are we going, m'lady?' Milly asked when Adelaide turned her footsteps north.

'I thought we'd pay Mr Gilchrist a call and see how his vignettes are progressing?'

'You mean the ones wot Miss Carew's modelling for?'

'That's right.' Adelaide gritted her teeth in response to the girl's artless question. Kitty Carew might suffice as a model stand-in but it was Adelaide's face that would draw the crowds.

Surely?

Injured pride had spurred her on to make this journey, but as she neared the top of the stairs of the artist's studio, she was struck by uncertainty. Well, wasn't it only natural to enquire after Mr Gilchrist's progress?

Perhaps he'd beg her to sit to him without it being even necessary for her to open her mouth. Lord, she was pathetic, but right now she felt as forlorn as a ship's rat without a ship. There was no servant to show them in so when she put her head around the door she was startled to find Mr Gilchrist bent over Kitty Carew who was reclining on the day bed in a transparent gown of white.

Yes, all but transparent, Adelaide noted with shock, for it was clear she wore no petticoats or chemise or stays. Indeed, that was very clear. She heard Milly's intake of breath and gave the girl a light dig in the ribs to send her to admire the paintings at the far end of the room.

Mr Gilchrist leapt back to his easel, choking on his embarrassment while Miss Carew merely raised an eyebrow and said languidly but pointedly, 'Forgive me for not rising, Lady Leeson, but Mr Gilchrist asked me not to move while he rearranged my … limbs.' Her carefully painted mouth puckered. 'And I'm afraid we did not hear you knock.'

The remains of a half-eaten picnic of ham and plovers' eggs rested on a tray on the brocade chair near the window while Miss Carew's clothes were folded neatly on a chest nearby.

Mr Gilchrist bowed. 'My deepest apologies, Lady Leeson; indeed, we did not hear you knock.' His obsequious manner grated when not so recently Adelaide had been desperate for his fawning admiration. She should not have come. He was busy and clearly he'd transferred his interest. It was a desolate thought.

Hurt and anger welled inside her. Of course, a painting which would achieve notoriety because its subject appeared with so few clothes on would be in a different league from a painting of the society beauty, Lady Leeson. It had better not have *her* face.

'I wanted to see what progress you'd made on the series you are working on for unveiling next week, Mr Gilchrist. Now that I am quite well again I will be able to sit to you tomorrow.' She tried to sound imperious. 'That is, unless you have other priorities.'

'As ever, you are my first priority, Lady Leeson. You have

only to tell me what time is convenient.' His assurances could not soothe her ruffled feathers or ameliorate the aversion she felt to the woman on the chaise longue.

Adelaide was surprised when Kitty rose and began putting on her clothes with little respect for modesty, saying, 'I've done me three hours, Mr Gilchrist.' She wondered if they were lovers. Kitty Carew seemed so self-possessed and uncaring of the proprieties.

'Care to come along wiv me, m'lady, and see how the uvver 'alf lives since yer so interested in good works? I hear yous called the Prison Angel.' She put her foot on the chest to pull up her stocking, adding under her breath, 'amongst other things.'

Adelaide could only stare. Accompany a trollop from the gutter whose thick titian hair she'd like to hack off right at this moment? A woman once associated with her husband?

It was this which decided her.

'It ain't no palace like what yours is,' Kitty added, tying the ribbons beneath her bonnet, 'and you'll dirty your boots in the alley outside so p'raps it ain't a good idea, after all.'

'We shall go in my carriage.' Adelaide signalled to Milly then nodded at Mr Gilchrist though she was tense with suspicion as to Kitty's motivation in inviting her to her home.

To taunt her that she'd usurped the glamorous peeress in her husband's affections?

To flaunt her previous association with her husband?

It was a short journey during which they did not speak until the carriage turned into a narrow, overcrowded street and Kitty leaned out of the window to shout at a child squatting by the wall that he must come inside and 'mind his manners' when he did.

They entered via the apothecary's downstairs and

mounted the stairs to Kitty's dwelling on the first floor, the child trailing after them.

'How old are you, Thomas?' Adelaide enquired as the child stared at her through large, curious eyes after Adelaide took a seat on the only decent chair in the room while the boy knelt on the floor a few feet from her. On a sudden premonition that it might be best that Milly were not privy to whatever reason Kitty had for inviting Adelaide home, she produced a couple of coins from her reticule before sending the maid off to buy buns.

'Come now, Thomas, cat got yer tongue?' his mother demanded. 'This is kind Lady Leeson who's giving you a treat of some raisin buns so I want you to be polite to her. You're four, aren't yer? And tell her wot nice man gave yer them tin soldiers.'

Thomas's fist closed protectively over the tin soldier he was holding as if he feared Adelaide might take it away from him, but he remained silent.

'Come, Tom, wot were the gennelmun's name? You remember, don't yer?'

The boy regarded Adelaide warily. ''Twere Lord Leeson.'

Adelaide darted a look at Kitty and her mouth went dry. Was this her reason for inviting her here, after all? To gloat?

'I got a few treasures wot 'is lordship gave me. Ain't just the boy he tried to do good by.' Kitty pointed to a canary in a cage. 'That's right, m'lady, it was your husband wot bought me this, too. Just afore 'e left me.' She directed a pointed look at Thomas's fair head. 'Oh don't worry, it were afore he married you. 'E's a good man, Lord Leeson. You know that, as well as I.' She smiled. 'A canary cos I sing like a canary, understand?'

Adelaide was speechless.

Kitty reached into the cage and the little bird hopped onto her wrist. 'Not the same little feller, mind. There've been a couple since 'im, but what do you expect? No feller stays around for long, leastways not when they're given a chance, eh, Lady Leeson? Course, you're one o' them what has to get married to 'ave a feller, unlike me. Still'—she gave Adelaide an assessing look—'sometimes it gives one peace of mind knowing they's there o' their own free will, an' I's had a few o' those, too, so I ain't complainin'.'

She sent Adelaide a challenging look.

'An' 'is lordship gave me this, too.' Thomas produced a spinning top which he added to his cache of treasures. 'E got me four. For each birfday he's sorry he's missed.'

Adelaide fumbled for her handkerchief while she willed herself not to cry. 'What do you want of me?' she whispered. 'Want of you?' Kitty's look was artless. 'Why'd I want anyfink?' The actress was milking her role as she pretended indignation for her benefit. 'Just wanted to offer you a little of me 'ospitality, that's all. 'Cept you're the one payin' for the buns, which is mighty nice of yer, only yer maid is taking her time about it. I did send her a way to travel, though, so's we'd have time to talk about certain matters. Private, if yer knows wot I mean.'

'I don't know what you mean' Adelaide whispered, staring at the boy.

'I mean, 'ow we live when we can afford to pay our rent,' Kitty went on, ignoring her. 'Course, the only way to do that is regular work.' Kitty arched her body, trim and still beautiful, and raked her fingers through her lustrous red- gold hair. 'I's lucky the grey won't show. Not like that dark haired miss wots going to marry the poet chappy. That 'andsome Lord Dewhurst I met when you were sitting for your portrait.'

Adelaide narrowed her gaze as she looked at the pert, confident face in front of her.

It hardened as she interpreted the subtext behind the actress's seemingly innocent words.

Dear God, Kitty Carew had written that letter. She must have seen the signs or overheard something when James was being overly attentive the very first day Adelaide sat to Mr Gilchrist. But why 'stay away'? Of course! Kitty was threatening Adelaide with exposure unless she stayed away from the limelight and what Kitty now regarded as her turf since she'd usurped Adelaide's position as Mr Gilchrist's model.

Panic sent her thoughts into a spin. What if Kitty told Tristan? What if she told *anyone*? Her stomach turned to liquid. She thought she was going to be sick.

'Yer orright, m'lady? D'yer need sommat to calm yer nerves? Mr Mendelssohn's Apothecary is right down below.'

Adelaide rummaged frantically in her reticule but there was no more money. Her hands scrabbled at her neck, and she unclasped the jewelled cross she wore and thrust it at Kitty.

'Take this! What can it gain you to tell my husband what you know? There, I have paid for your silence. It is a valuable trinket. Now leave me alone.' Wiping away her tears, she leapt to her feet, while the cross dangled from Kitty's hands. The woman looked surprised for a second.

Then a wide grin split her face. 'You're too generous, m'lady,' she said, tracing the tiny diamonds that studded the piece of jewellery, the sun behind her making a halo of her lustrous hair.

Her words followed Adelaide out of the door. 'In future I shan't believe a word of what others have to say about you, m'lady.'

CHAPTER 17

When Tristan returned he found Adelaide weeping in her private sitting room, unable to tell him the reason, for she hadn't yet formulated the words she could use to reveal the fact she knew all about Kitty; that she knew her husband had had a child by his former mistress; that she knew he still visited and … oh God, that Kitty knew far worse secrets about Adelaide.

She wanted to ask whether Tristan felt cheated and sad that Adelaide had failed to give him the child he desperately wanted; that they both desperately wanted. She needed to know if he visited Kitty for reasons other than the child. Truly, she didn't believe he sought diversion elsewhere; not when he and Adelaide had been so close lately. She just needed his reassurances.

But the conversation went in such a wrong direction, with Tristan patting her back and ordering Milly to 'fetch your mistress Dr Stanhope's calming concoction, for she is overwrought' and then sitting by her side and insisting Adelaide drink it while Adelaide, spluttering through her tears, tried to object. She had already availed herself of something dangerously similar to Dr Stanhope's calming concoction from the apothecary after she'd fled Kitty's veiled threats. No, Adelaide needed kindness and understanding from her husband. She needed to feel confident enough of his love so that she might find the courage to tell him that, just as Tristan had had a child out of wedlock four years before, so had she. But she could not tell him when she was so uncertain of his response, for if Adelaide lost the last vestiges of Tristan's love, and his respect, then she had nothing.

So, she was the invalid once more, only this time she was the unwitting instigator of her own incarceration.

Sitting on her bed on the pink and blue counterpane under which she'd writhed with such earthy passion just last week, Adelaide chewed her thumbnail and considered her options.

But when Milly arrived to help her dress for dinner, Adelaide had thought of nothing she could do, other than submit.

She presented herself at dinner feeling sick at heart.

It was just as it had been in the old days. A little desultory conversation about the food and the weather.

Adelaide stared at Tristan for some sign that there was more behind the façade of tender concern; a smouldering desire, perhaps, that she might glimpse in an unguarded moment.

There was not. Briefly he mentioned parliamentary matters before moving on to mutual friends and all the while he spoke in the same steady, unemotional tone which made her want to jump up and shake some spark into him; tell him there was not a thing wrong with her and could he just forget the past week?

'James was asking after you.' He was busy carving the saddle of beef. Adelaide sent him a surreptitious glance as she fidgeted.

Relieved when she'd decided there was no subtext behind his innocuous words, she answered carefully.

'James seems to be making more of an effort. I was afraid the adulation that's been showered on him lately might have made him neglectful of Beatrice's needs.'

She was on safe territory now.

Tristan raised an eyebrow. 'I suspect James's vanity will always be stronger than his chivalry, though I shall always be in his debt.' His look softened as he turned to look at Adelaide. 'After giving me back my life, he then gave me you. You *will* get better again, Addy. Just give it time.'

Adelaide forced her mouth into a semblance of a smile.

The end of the meal signalled a moment of obvious awkwardness for both. It was a Thursday, after all, but their routine had been overturned.

'You are tired, Addy.' Tristan came round and placed his hands on her shoulders. 'Shall I take you up to your chamber?'

Ridiculously, it took an enormous amount of courage to reply, 'Only if you stay.' At least she could say it without her mother being in attendance, for blessedly Mrs Henley had been invited elsewhere that evening.

He chose to misinterpret her meaning. 'I shall read you a chapter and sit with you.'

She took the stairs slowly. Strange how being told she was an invalid and being treated as one actually made her feel as if her strength reserves were truly half what they had been a week ago.

Milly helped her undress and when she was in bed

Tristan came through with a book of verse. Adelaide gasped when she saw the title. 'Why, it's James's book.'

'The first few verses are quite lovely and perfectly suitable. Since the *ton* can speak of nothing else I thought we could share it. You haven't read it, have you, Addy?'

'I … I'm not sure I'd be brave enough.'

'James will be hurt if we're the only ones in all London not to have read *The Maid of Milan*.' After plumping up her pillows he sat down and opened to the first page.

Adelaide had no idea what to expect. What transpired was a collection of tales centred on a knight returning from the Crusades who embarks upon a torrid love affair with one of his wife's ladies-in-waiting. A reverse of the King Arthur and Guinevere love triangle. And the first two verses, Adelaide realised with shock, had been penned by her. When the shock wore off she became indignant, then finally she was filled with a strange power as her own words floated between them. It was as if, coming off the printed page, they endorsed her as better than she'd believed herself. Better than she was.

Tristan stopped halfway through the third tale and sent her an anxious glance. 'Perhaps we should stop now. No, just one more poem.' His tone was decisive. 'Then we'll have something we can discuss with James if the subject comes up again.'

Adelaide nodded, soon wishing she'd objected, since the tale progressed from the hero's first chaste encounter with his lady-love beneath the cherry tree to a rather amorous encounter on a bed of straw in the nearby castle dungeons. She closed her eyes, reliving her early youthful experiences through James's eyes. Lost innocence freely traded for forbidden passion. Oh but she'd been as culpable as he, eagerly losing her virginity to James on a bed of fresh straw which he'd laid upon the dungeon floor of the local castle ruins. They'd returned there many times for pre-arranged trysts, never questioning their actions which painted James an adulterer and Adelaide no better.

No. Far, far worse.

'Please stop.' Adelaide opened her eyes and slid them over to Tristan. He had no idea what courage it took to face him.

But she saw no arrested consciousness, no hint of anything other than natural concern for her sensibilities.

He looked embarrassed, and Adelaide saw he'd been more drawn in by James's lurid prose than he'd expected. 'I shouldn't have continued and exposed you to James's descent into vice and sin in Milan, I'm sorry. Especially not when you're in such a ... delicate condition.' He placed a hand upon her brow. 'You're hot, Addy. I'll take the book away and I shall strongly counsel Beatrice not to read it.'

'She will be James's wife.' Adelaide could barely look at him. 'I don't think you can tell her not to read her own husband's book.'

'It might upset Beatrice. Clearly *The Maid of Milan* is as much a testament to a husband's philandering as it is about the depths of depravity to which an immoral woman will stoop in order to gratify her wanton impulses. It's inappropriate reading for any woman of delicacy. Now, Addy, shall I fetch you something soothing to send you to sleep?' He touched her brow again. 'You don't look well at all.'

Adelaide seized his hand. 'Are you forgetting what day it is?'

Extricating himself from her clasp, his smile was regretful. 'You are still unwell, Addy, and I fear that overexcitement may have contributed to a return of your previous ... maladies.'

'I thought you said the doctor recommended a return to the old routines.' She heard the edge of panic in her voice. She wasn't going to let him wriggle out of his duty. James's lustful poems had filled her head with too much. And her body.

What if Tristan was affected like she was but his misplaced need to protect her led him to seek less worthy affections?

Striking a deliberately disinterested tone, she said, 'Let us chat a little longer, then.' She took a breath. 'I believe you are quite well acquainted with Miss Carew.'

She was not prepared for the evasive look on his face. Slowly Tristan turned to look at her. 'I hope you don't mind, but in view of the fact that she, too, is a redhead and an acclaimed beauty who needed funds, I suggested she take your place when you were not well enough to sit to Mr Gilchrist.'

'I wish you hadn't.'

'My darling, I didn't think you would mind. If Mr Gilchrist is to have his series ready for the Prince Regent's viewing he needs a model, though of course it will be your beautiful face that stares out from the canvas. My love, you said yourself you were not up to going out in public for a little while.'

'I never did!'

'Addy, please don't cry. You're overwrought. Of course you weren't in a position to sit to Mr Gilchrist and he needs to fulfil his obligations.'

But now the tears had finally come she couldn't stop them.

'Please, lie with me, Tristan,' she wept. 'I do so long for a child.' Urgency filled her and she clung to Tristan, pulling him down and kissing his mouth and eyes with a desperate fervour, needing to indicate that her body was on fire for him.

'No, Addy.'

He gripped her wrists and put her away from him. The

regret she saw in his dark eyes made her churn with confusion and embarrassment.

'What is it, Tristan? Do I ... disgust you?'

There, she'd said it. Opened the way for him to tell her exactly what he thought of her, if he had in fact learned something of the truth of what she was.

'The doctor says,' he spoke with difficulty, 'that overexcitement in the marital bed has been a direct contributor to your ... sudden decline.'

'When was the doctor here?' She cupped her face, trying to remember but unable to; trying to keep the panic at bay. 'When did he say that?'

Tristan looked at her oddly. 'He was here yesterday, darling. Granted, you were very disoriented.' He picked up the mug from the supper tray Milly had sent up while he was reading. 'Now drink your milk before it goes cold.'

She didn't want to but she would be obedient because it was one small thing that would please Tristan.

When she'd finished she handed back the empty mug. Quietly she lay back on the pillows as all feeling drained from her. Not even disappointment or dread replaced the burst of passion she'd felt earlier. She felt dead inside. Wearily, she ran the back of her hand across her brow and tried to focus on Tristan's face. 'There,' she said. 'Now I've done as you've asked it's time for you to return the favour. I want a child, Tristan.' Defeated, she stared at the ceiling, unable to look at him. 'It's my duty to provide you with one and I can't do it alone.'

But he just stood, staring down at her with a look of terrible sadness and shook his head.

'You are unwell, Adelaide, and I dare not risk your health again.' Slowly he went to the door, unwilling to leave if the look on his face was anything to go by. He sighed, then added, 'Not for some time, the doctor says.'

CHAPTER 18

Astroll through Green Park was sanctioned when James and Beatrice arrived the following day full of cheer and high spirits. Tristan had apparently enlisted their help to keep Adelaide amused 'but calm', Beatrice told her.

'You're as pale as milk,' James chided.

At first Adelaide felt as if she were walking through a thick fog, barely conscious of James and Beatrice as they trod the gravelled walkways. The clear-headed feeling she'd enjoyed briefly the previous day was gone and she felt confused. She was aware of responding with a vague nod, or a yes or no, though the moment the questions were asked she'd forgotten what they were.

Gradually the sense of having a head stuffed full of wool began to subside and she became conscious of her surroundings.

When Beatrice remarked upon the extraordinary bonnet of the woman ahead of them Adelaide was cognisant enough of the spectacle to gurgle with laughter. 'She's wearing a false hair piece which is about to drop. That's why it looks so odd.

Poor woman. Should someone tell her before she's terribly embarrassed?'

The expressions her companions turned on her made her raise her palms in mock surrender. 'What have I said?'

'Addy, you've been in a trance since we left Bruton Street.' James took her wrists but Adelaide snatched them away with a quick glance at Beatrice.

'James was concerned, that's all, Adelaide.' Beatrice looked worried as she sanctioned her betrothed's behaviour. 'We all are,' she added softly.

'Worried? About me?' Adelaide laughed. 'I've been feeling in low spirits, it's true.' As if conducting an experiment she cupped her cheeks, then pinched her arms, holding out her arms and flexing her fingers in their beautiful York tan gloves. 'But I'm getting better. This is the first time in I don't know how long that I've felt … alive.'

As quickly as feeling returned, so did memory, bringing with it the familiar terror.

It was only when Beatrice was waylaid by a group of friends who pulled her into their company for a few minutes that Adelaide could speak freely, but not before James said under his breath while his face assumed a neutral look, 'So what's the real reason for this air of melancholy which has Tristan believing you're fading away?'

Adelaide gripped his arm convulsively, then immediately dropped her hands. 'James, I don't know what's happening to me. I've felt so strange for days now. Ever since I received an anonymous letter.' She swayed and James steadied her. 'Someone,' she squeezed shut her eyes, 'knows about us. Then, as she saw Beatrice coming towards them with a smile, she added hurriedly, 'They wrote me a note. *I know your secret. Stay away.*' She swallowed convulsively. 'Ah, Beatrice, is that your friend calling you back? I think you dropped your handkerchief.'

'*I know your secret?*' James looked as horrified as Adelaide felt, his eyes on Beatrice who'd stepped back into the circle of her acquaintances. 'Good God, Addy, why didn't you tell me?'

'You know I've barely left my room except yesterday when … well, anyway, I've discovered who it was and I've put a stop to it.' She hoped she looked more confident than she felt.

James took a step away as if fearing suddenly he could contaminate her by his proximity. 'Oh, Addy.' He looked shaken. 'This is appalling. Tell me who it was.'

She closed her eyes and whispered, 'Kitty Carew.'

James's gaze raked the surrounding area, as if Kitty could be hiding in the shadows. 'Think no more about it,' he muttered. 'I'll make sure this goes no further.'

'James, no!' Adelaide tugged at his cuff. 'I've secured her silence. I don't want any interference from you that could make matters worse. Do you promise?'

'Oh, Addy,' he said again. Shaking his head, James touched her arm in a gesture of sympathy before quickly withdrawing it. His expression was stricken. 'You know I'd do anything to make you happy.'

'I know it,' she said with a weak smile. 'I'm getting my just desserts—'

A greeting rang out, interrupting Adelaide who turned to see Phineas Donegal striding towards them. A flash of scarlet revealed him despatching a brightly dressed woman from one arm before he disengaged Beatrice from her departing friends and brought her once more into their fold. 'Good God, Donegal,' hissed James, 'what were you doing with … *her*… in public? And with Beatrice and Adelaide here.'

'That was Kitty Carew, wasn't it?' Adelaide asked coldly as she watched the young woman sashay into the distance.

'Mr Gilchrist is painting her for the vignettes that will

bear your lovely face, but rest assured, she ain't a patch on you, Lady Leeson,' observed Mr Donegal, though the leer he sent over his shoulder belied his supposed disinterest.

James sent his fair-weather friend a warning look. 'As Addy is completely well again Miss Carew's services will no longer be required. Mr Gilchrist, I hope, understands that.'

Adelaide struggled to contain her agitation. No, Miss Carew would no longer be needed. The exquisitely worked, delicate necklace Kitty had paid for her silence ought to more than satisfy her.

Donegal inclined his head, responding with sarcasm, 'Will you inform him, or shall we leave it to his lordship? Ah, James, your betrothed grows comelier by the day. She was a little mouse when I first set eyes on her and now she's a veritable—'

'Swan,' supplied Adelaide.

'Peacock,' mocked James, adding at her hurt look, 'for Beatrice is dressed so exquisitely in green and blue that I wish I could admire her strutting across the lawns from afar. Alas, by her side I gain nothing but a crick in my neck from the lack of perspective my too-close proximity affords.'

'You are ridiculous,' said Beatrice, relenting with a laugh, and Adelaide let her breath out in a sigh that the situation was defused.

For the moment.

CLOTHES HAD ALWAYS BEEN a source of pleasure and confidence, but even wearing her most flattering London ensemble Adelaide felt far from confident as she stood on the landing near her husband's study, chewing her thumbnail and wondering whether she should disturb Tristan.

He was working so hard these days and he always seemed

tired and, well – she felt the tears sting her eyes and the fear churn in her gut – just a little distant.

Three days ago, when she'd returned from her walk with James and Beatrice, she'd spent a tedious afternoon stitching in the drawing room while she waited for him. She'd heard his brief exchange with Barking in the hallway and then his footsteps on the stairs as he went directly to his apartments. Expecting to see him a short while later, she'd been dismayed when told that the master had in fact already left the house for another engagement and wasn't expected home until after midnight.

The brief, loving note he'd written could not compensate for her unhappiness.

She'd wanted to rage and cry but feared that if it were reported back to him her husband would see her excess of emotion as manifesting her instability.

Clearly Tristan was weary. He looked tired all the time. Well, during the few times she'd seen him, at least. But weary of her? Of her delicacy? Sad they had no child? Overworked?

She wanted to ask him exactly what plagued him but the truth was, she feared she didn't have the courage to hear the answer. She tried to summon the courage to knock.

'Eavesdropping, Adelaide?' Her mother emerged from her private sitting room two doors along and looked at her. 'You know Mrs Fry was here, don't you? Your husband will no doubt be more than happy to discuss with you the fruitful conversation we've had.'

'He asked *you* to be present?' She felt bereft.

'He knew you found your visit with Mrs Fry … fatiguing. In fact, Mrs Fry indicated that as she understood you had little real interest in her vision she requested that I be present'—Mrs Henley smiled thinly—'knowing how much she and I are in accord.'

'If he's busy I won't disturb him.' Adelaide spoke proudly

now. So Tristan had not even told her of this meeting thinking she'd reveal her boredom and perhaps embarrass him?

'He'll be pleased you're neither reclining in a state of perpetual ennui, Adelaide, nor gallivanting around London with your fast friends. Granted, you're delicate, but you're all too capable of being a good helpmate to your husband if you only tried. Where are you going?'

Adelaide was at the top of the stairs and she turned at the sharpness of her mother's question. 'I've a sudden notion to seek out some of my fast London friends and do a bit of gallivanting.' She used hauteur to hide the pain and disappointment over Tristan's lack of inclusion.

FOR THE NEXT few days Tristan was absent a great deal.

To pass the time Adelaide trailed through Tristan's library and read the parliamentary reports he obviously chose to pore over late into the night instead of coming to visit her. If she hadn't felt such a disassociation from her usual passions she knew she would be more affected than she was by the inequities that outraged Tristan. However, she did believe she could craft a more artful appeal to public sympathies than the dry litany of social injustices that Tristan's parliamentary secretary had composed.

Her head still often felt woolly inside, and her limbs leaden, but today she was a little more herself so she set herself the task of improving Mr Finch's prose as an exercise to clear her mind. After that she felt much better.

So much so that when the following day she received an invitation to Lady Belton's ball in five days' time her heart leapt and she knew that she was well again.

'You will accompany me, won't you darling?' she begged,

rushing into the library to give Tristan the details. 'I'm in such need of diversion but I can't possibly enjoy myself if you're not there.'

He smiled up at her from the ream of paper upon which he'd been rapidly jotting down notes in his precise and tiny handwriting and reached across to stroke her cheek. 'You really think you're up to it?'

Adelaide laughed and twirled for him on the carpet. 'Do I look like I'm about to fade away from some terrible wasting disease of either mind or body? No, Tristan, I'm as hale and hearty as I ever was but only your attentions are going to fully restore me. So are you going to say yes and be my most handsome escort for the night?'

Laughingly he agreed and Adelaide enjoyed the very satisfying sensation of having her husband stand up, enfold her in his arms and kiss her tenderly on the brow.

It was not such a satisfying encounter with him later that evening as they sat together in the drawing room after dinner and Tristan murmured that perhaps attending Lady Belton's ball on Thursday was not such a good idea as surely this was yet another example of her trying to take on too much too soon.

Adelaide was outraged. 'You've been talking to my mother, haven't you?' she accused him. 'Or rather, she's been talking to *you*.'

He didn't deny it, merely said soothingly, 'Remember the last time you assured me you were entirely well? Oh, Addy, please don't be like this.'

'Like what?' she demanded, glaring at him. 'Don't you understand how much delight Mama takes in undermining me? She doesn't want me to enjoy myself, can't you see that? She's a dried up old prune who'd trade her soul with the devil if she could have had a daughter more like … like Hortense.'

'Hortense?'

'Yes, I'm talking about your cousin and James's wife. Mama and Hortense were as thick as thieves and pillars of do-gooding. I'm not good like Hortense was, Tristan, and I never pretended to be—'

'Hush, now.' He stood up and went to her, stopping her protest with a kiss, holding her against him so she only then realised how much she was trembling. 'You're overset, my darling. Let's have no more talk about your mother who, thank God, is as different from you as it's possible to be. However, you can't discount the fact that she knows you better than you know yourself and that she wants only the very best for you.'

'She has *no* concern for what's good for me.'

He laughed gently as if she were a child throwing a tantrum which he was trying to curb using fond cajolery as his weapon. It did nothing to improve her temper.

Pulling away from him she paced to the fire. 'So you're telling me I *can't* go to Lady Belton's ball?' She glanced up at his silence and felt a chill of fear at his deeply troubled expression. Gathering her wits, she nibbled her lip while her mind raced. She mustn't behave like an intransigent child who wanted her own way. That's what she'd been like as a headstrong eighteen-year-old when she had defied her mother to follow her heart.

With James. Wild, passionate, volatile and *married* James. Hadn't she paid the price? And had she learned nothing?

The fire that had fanned her sense of rediscovery suddenly went out. There was no place in her new life for her natural defiance, the headstrong impulses that rushed through her body and reminded her she was *alive*. Lord, she hadn't felt that too often during the past four long years. The brief ecstasy in Tristan's arms those few nights had been like the elixir a dying woman needed to keep her grounded in the reality that was her lot. His kisses, the energy of his love-making had proved that the charade she'd kept up her entire marriage had been worth it if it would only lead to more of the same.

But it had dried up with the knowledge she couldn't have it both ways. Her punishment was the charade she must maintain to protect her scandalous past – a crueller punishment now for having sampled how sweet life could have been without the lies.

Adelaide's body was like a weathervane, pulsing with vitality and restless energy when the winds were favourable and still and lifeless when ignored.

For surely Tristan could be accused of ignoring her when for, oh, such noble reasons he soothed her and patted her. He thought he was so kind and noble, obeying her mother and the doctor for the sake of Adelaide's precarious nervous condition, her delicate sensibilities.

Did he really not understand the kind of woman he'd married? Was it really possible to ignore the fiery impulses each had ignited in the other so recently? Or was Adelaide's sensuality simply dismissed as further evidence of her dangerous inconsistency?

Despair literally felled her. In a billow of Pomona green skirts she dropped to her knees, put her head in her hands and wept. It was no act. She was defeated. Tristan treated her like a child. Her mother treated her like a Bedlam prisoner all but chaining her to her bed post. She might as well have erected the cold, impermeable stone walls and the iron rungs through which she could glimpse what she could never have: freedom to be herself.

'My darling, once again I have ignored the signs. You are more overset than I realised!' Crouching beside her, Tristan whisked her into his arms, stood uncertainly in the centre of the room, then took a seat on the sofa where he gently pushed her head onto his shoulders where she cried all the harder.

'Hush, my darling,' he murmured.

He was kind and loving and for the moment truly hers. She didn't want the contact to end and made no attempt to cease the shudders that wracked her body. If gaining Tristan's attention through her neediness worked, who was she to demand that she was perfectly hale and hearty and that her desire for frivolity must be met?

He carried her to bed, to her disappointment calling Milly to help undress her and put on her nightrail while he attended to some other matter before returning. When she was tucked up in bed, the candle flickering beside her, and he was seated on a chair at her side, Adelaide looked up from toying with the ribbons of her nightcap and asked the question at the heart of her anguish.

'Do you still love me when I'm such a poor wife to you, Tristan?' Again she wanted to ask him about Kitty Carew but had not the courage. Instead, she whispered, 'You have affection for me, I know that, but you no longer,' she swallowed past the lump in her throat, 'love me with the same … intensity you showed me after we first came to London.'

His shock was sharp and real. 'Adelaide, you have bewitched me. I should feel foolish saying such a thing but it's true.' With more energy than he'd shown for a long time, he gripped her hands and brought them to his lips. 'I desperately hoped London would make you better, my darling and indeed it seemed to … at first. It seemed to make you come alive. I thought gaiety was the tonic you needed to banish all memories of the terrible'—he looked away, unable to put it into words—'ordeal you'd gone through, but the excitement proved to have the very opposite effect of healing you.'

Tenderly he stroked her forehead. 'I've tried to explain that my love for you is as strong as ever, but my darling, I dare not risk compromising your recovery with the demands I might place on you were I to give in to the kind of impulses we husbands must temper if our wives are prone to emotional disorders of the kind Dr Stanhope says afflicts you. Addy, please don't cry.'

'I don't want you to temper your impulses, Tristan,' she wept. 'If I can't be a wife you can love fully, you'll look elsewhere.'

'How can you say such a thing?'

Adelaide opened her eyes and saw he truly was horrified by her fears.

His mouth was set in a determined line. 'Other men may stray but you know my feelings on loyalty, fidelity ... honour. I would rather burn for my sins than contaminate you with —' He broke off for she was crying harder than ever now. 'Please, Addy, what is it? Surely I've reassured you of my devotion.'

'I just want to be *loved* by you, Tristan.'

'And you are.'

'How can you when I am an invalid both in mind and body, and it would seem ... unable to give you a child—'

'Stop it!' He cradled her head on his shoulder and stroked the fine muslin of her nightrail. Her hair spilled, unplaited, over the fine lace edge and when his hand caressed the fine rippling tresses which covered her back she lurched forward, twining her hands behind his neck and pressing her cheek to his. She felt him stiffen at the intimacy of the contact and caught her breath as she willed him to make a conscious move to comfort her with more than just words.

With his body.

Carefully he unclasped her fingers then gently pushed her back down on the pillow. With quiet conviction he said, 'My happiness does not depend upon a child.' He'd brought the crux of the matter back to practicality. Practicality with no sentimentality, no room for passion or even the hint of romance.

'What *does* it depend upon?' she whispered.

He smiled and traced the outline of a tear with his finger tip. As if he expected his words to bring comfort, he said softly, 'Knowing that I have done everything in my power to safeguard the health of my beautiful, virtuous wife.

HE WAS as tender as if she were a piece of Dresden china. He brought her flowers from the hothouse: her favourite irises with their heady perfume and languorous drooping heads, brilliant pinks, purples and yellows, then left, saddened she saw, that his offering brought no smile to her face.

The following day he tried to tempt her failing appetite with sweetmeats he'd had the cook prepare. Her favourites once again, with tiny violet-topped chocolates framing the plate, but she only smiled weakly then turned on her side and said she'd sleep some more, she was very tired. And it was true. She didn't know how many days she'd slept. She was simply always tired. Indescribably weary.

TRISTAN PREPARED his speech on prison legislation, delivered it to more acclaim than he'd expected, for indeed Mr Finch had once again prepared a particularly eloquent and concise summation of the issues, then went to his club to drink more brandy than was usual and to try and forget his sadness by burying his head in the news-sheets.

He felt a rush of pleasure to see James, who was at White's on a rare visit.

Tristan called him over to join him in a dim corner and demanded to know why he no longer called at the house.

'Addy is in sore need of someone to lift her spirits and, God knows, she's always lively when you and Beatrice are around.' The brandy was not conducive to his spirits and he was ashamed of himself for sounding an accusing note. More reasonably, he said, 'Beatrice was to be her special project. Addy is cleverer than you might suppose. She wants to see Beatrice blossom into the ideal wife for you, James, and she can do that.'

James shrugged. 'Really?' He seemed disinterested as he relaxed in the leather wing chair and studied his brandy. 'Tell me about Addy. What's wrong with her?'

'She'll be fine when we're back in the country. She needs rest and quiet to be really happy.'

'When do you plan to return? I thought you were ready to throw yourself into politics and planned on spending more time in the city. What will *you* do?'

'Accompany her back to Hampshire, of course.' Tristan looked surprised at the question. 'I'll do whatever is required to ensure that Adelaide is restored to her former self. I'd thought a London season would be a tonic.' He drained his glass, his spirits plummeting even further. 'I had no idea that gaiety was the very evil that would bring her ... to this.'

James scratched his head. 'I don't think it's the excitement that is the problem.' He seemed to be weighing his words. 'I remember Addy as a girl who enjoyed fun and laughter and ... excitement.'

Tristan stared gloomily into his glass. 'Perhaps, but such a terrible experience as Adelaide suffered will forever affect her relations with men. Even a husband she loves. God knows, she tries so hard to do her duty, but as the doctor says, the more excited she gets, the greater the decline afterwards. I'm sure you don't mind my speaking frankly, but you're hardly coy about such matters.'

He was surprised when James rose, suddenly. 'Sorry, Tristan, I've just remembered I have somewhere I have to be.' He tossed back the errant curl that flopped over his forehead, clearly agitated at having forgotten his appointment. 'I'm so sorry to hear about Addy. Please send her my regards.'

Watching James depart when Tristan needed a trusted friend to whom he could unburden his tortured soul, made him feel more bereft than he'd believed possible.

CHAPTER 19

A delaide put down her soup spoon and smiled across the dinner table at her mother and her husband in turn. The sense of befuddlement that often frightened her was absent. She felt renewed confidence and vitality in her clear headedness.

'I hear you have tickets to the theatre this evening, Tristan,' she said brightly. 'Perhaps after that we might go to Lady Belton's ball.'

Mrs Henley's soup spoon clattered onto her plate and her mouth dropped open. Tristan's look of perplexity changed to horror as he seemed to realise she wasn't in jest.

It was Mrs Henley who spoke first. 'You have been very unwell for two weeks now, Addy, and you are going nowhere tonight. I thought that had already been decided.'

'You may forbid it, Mama, however, I am Tristan's wife. What do you say, darling? Shall we at least look in at Lady Belton's for an hour or so? I've had the most deadly dull time for simply an age, but right now I feel marvellous. A *little* excitement will do me the world of good. Just a little? Please indulge me.'

'A little excitement will see you back in your bed,' her Mama cut in. 'Goodness, Adelaide, have you learned nothing about what is good for you and what is most certainly *not?*'

'Your mother is right, darling.' Tristan's voice was sympathetic but kind. 'If you want company, I'll read to you before your afternoon sleep.'

'James's poetry?' She was gratified by her mother's predictable gasp.

Tristan looked uncomfortable. 'I think James's poetry is a little unsuitable for the occasion,' he said mildly. 'How about Sir Walter Scott?'

Adelaide rose. 'By all means. Come when you're ready, Tristan, for I am in no mood for stitching with Mama who has been perfectly horrid and has always enjoyed refusing me everything that I enjoy. Isn't that right, Mama? For two weeks you've kept me locked up, insisting I'm an invalid when I'd have been only too capable of cantering in Rotten Row with James and Beatrice when they invited me on Tuesday or attending Tristan to the theatre.'

She didn't wait to do battle with her predictably combative mother or even send another ameliorating glance in her husband's direction. With fury simmering just below the surface she marched off to her apartments and was reclining on the chaise longue when Tristan appeared, book in hand.

'So you think a bit of Sir Walter Scott is more conducive to my recovery than a convivial evening with society and you by my side?'

'What is the matter with you, Adelaide?' He seemed less patient than usual as he seated himself on the chair by the bed. 'Your mother has done her very best to ensure you are comfortable and cared for. Overexcitement is the last thing you need.'

'It's what I *want*. Do my wishes count for nothing?' She

looked at her hands folded neatly on the bed cover. Despite her desire to stroke Tristan's disapproval away she remained self-contained, talking over his stammered reply. 'You may read now and I shall try and force myself to sleep, though you're very welcome to join me, Tristan.' She patted the bed covers and sent him a smile of entreaty, a half-hearted attempt at cajoling him into some kind of declaration, perhaps even of surprising himself into relenting and doing what she asked, but predictably, her overtures fell on infertile ground.

Hiding her disappointment, she smiled. 'Ah well, it would have been nice, but if Sir Walter proves not the tonic I need then I'll creep out of the window and sneak off to Lady Belton's ball like a naughty schoolroom miss, and when you search and find me there you'll realise how fun it all is and want to stay and then we'll both be the happier for it. You certainly aren't happy with the way things are between us now, are you?'

'I think you're speaking nonsense to me, now,' he said carefully, taking her wrist and kissing the back of her hand before placing it firmly away from him, 'because you want to draw a more robust response from me than you're getting but I will not be drawn. I will not rise to the bait, Addy and I will not lose my temper. Didn't I once warn you I was not the most exciting of husbands?'

'I never thought it till now.'

Still refusing to be drawn, Tristan picked up the book to read.

AT THE CHIME of eight on the landing clock he closed the tooled leather cover, kissed her brow and rose.

'Where will you go now, Tristan?' Adelaide murmured,

obviously surprising him, for she had pretended to be asleep. 'Will you go out? To your club and then on to the theatre?'

'No, Addy. I have no time for revelry these days. I have speeches to prepare and bills to help pass or block, though I might look in at my club. Perhaps I'll find James there. He was yesterday.'

'I didn't think he looked in much at White's. Not at all the sort of crowd he likes to run with. Well, enjoy yourself, my darling, and think of me. I really am not tired at all, you know, but the thought of spending my evening stitching with my mother is worse than being chained in a cell with only a drooling crone for company. Will you send Milly to me, please?'

He hesitated in the doorway. 'I wish you'd not say such things. You make me feel *I'm* imprisoning you when all I want is for you to be better. Would you like some sweetened warm milk? I'll arrange for it to be brought up.'

'No thank you. Just send Milly, please, so I might discuss what clothes to lay out for me.'

'Yes, of course darling.' Another hesitation but then he thought she meant for the morning. He could not accuse her of lying, later. She had made plain her intentions.

'OH MA'AM, you can't possibly dress yourself for the ball and go without the master. Without any chaperone.' Milly's distress was comic. She was torn between her loyalty to the woman she was employed to serve and his lordship who paid her wages.

Adelaide looked up from her little writing desk in the corner of her room. 'That is why I want you to send the kitchen boy around to Lord Dewhurst's house with a note. He and Miss Beatrice can come by with their carriage.'

Milly was reluctant to take the note Adelaide held out to her. 'But Lord Dewhurst won't be home, ma'am.'

'Very perceptive, Milly. That is why I am offering the lad a handsome reward to run him to ground. If he can locate Lord Dewhurst and deliver me an answer, the boy will get half a crown. No,' she checked herself. 'A whole crown. Riches! Of course I will need my answer within the hour which means you'd better hurry and help make me presentable. If the master steps in after he's been to his club and wants to know where I am, tell him to find me at Lady Belton's ball.'

She slid onto the seat at her dressing table and Milly, eyes wide with doubt and concern, helped her remove her fine lawn night cap and brush out her hair. Adelaide smiled. 'Don't look at me like that, Milly. I told him I intended to go, so I've not told a lie. Now quickly, take that note down to the kitchen.' She reached for her reticule and pulled out half a crown. 'Offer the boy this and tell him there'll be another when I receive word from Lord Dewhurst as to when he intends to come by.'

'Only if you drink the milk your Mama sent up, for she'll have me hide if I bring it back and you ain't touched it.'

'Warm milk might be the thing if I wanted to go to sleep. You'll have to drink it, Milly.'

By the time Adelaide was dressed in a gold-flecked ball-gown, tiny bodice and short puffed sleeves heavily embroidered with gold thread to match the embroidered rouleau at the hem, her hair threaded through with pearls, there were only five minutes to wait before James, as loyal a friend as she could want, pulled up in the cobbled laneway that ran down the side of their townhouse. She ran to the window at the sound of carriage wheels in the laneway, wishing he'd drawn up at the front so she could not be accused of 'cloak-and-dagger' antics since she justified her actions on the basis she was doing nothing she hadn't told Tristan she planned to do.

James and Beatrice, together with Beatrice's chaperone for the night, a quiet woman who looked to be in her mid-thirties, greeted her with muted enthusiasm as the coachman put down the steps and James leapt down to assist her.

'What are you are up to, Addy?' he asked once they were on their way. 'I could make neither head nor tail over the meaning of your note. At first I thought you were implying Tristan had locked you in the house while he was out indulging his fancies. However that's beyond the realm of credibility.'

He sounded accusing and not the lively evening companion for which Adelaide had hoped. Spirits dashed but not wanting to show it, Adelaide leaned over and patted Beatrice's knee. 'My dear, you look absolutely ravishing. I just adore your gown.'

Beatrice glanced at her companion then back to Adelaide, beaming at the compliment. 'Madame Claudette created it for me. I'd so wanted your advice but when your Mama said how ill you were I was fortunate that James decided to become my arbiter of fashion.' She sent him a loving smile which did not lose its lustre at James's unresponsive coun-tenance.

Adelaide was overcome by a curious emotion. How familiar she was with that look. James blew hot and cold.

She well remembered the few occasions he withdrew into himself when she'd tried to compensate by demanding espousals of affection. She'd been too young and overcome by their passion to understand that he was simply caught up in his own thoughts and no doubt consumed by some composition taking shape in his head.

One look at Beatrice assured Adelaide that James's intended understood what Adelaide had not at the same age.

She felt a pang of regret overlaid with quiet relief. Beatrice was going to be his ideal consort.

After dispensing with the services of Beatrice's now redundant chaperone who was only too glad to have an early night, they returned to Covent Garden to see the end of the play James and Beatrice had left in order to pick up Adelaide.

'Tristan isn't here, is he?' she asked in sudden panic, adding hastily, 'Not that I've anything to feel guilty about since I said I intended going out this evening.'

'You certainly *look* guilty,' said James, before reassuring her he'd last seen Tristan at his club and her husband had made no mention of attending the theatre or Lady Belton's ball.

Adelaide soon had reason to regret her impulsiveness in coming out when she realised Kitty Carew was the lead actress. Her performance was going down very well with the male contingent which, she supposed, was little wonder for the actress was more than passably attractive. It didn't endear her to Adelaide any further.

Under the stage lights the woman's hair shone like spun gold and her body was lithe – everyone could see that – since Kitty lifted her skirt frequently to display her shapely legs clad in rose coloured hose. James appeared just as intrigued as those who whistled and called out and Beatrice glanced at Adelaide, uncertainty written across her features.

Adelaide took up her opera glasses and peered more closely at the impish creature cavorting across the stage and enchanting the audience with her lilting voice, wishing she could see more obvious flaws in the woman who had taken her place on more than one occasion.

She was glad when the final trills of the chorus were drowned by the crashing cymbals of the orchestra, signalling the end. She hoped she'd never see Kitty Carew again.

AT LAST IT was time to proceed to Lady Belton's ball.

As they rose to leave she glanced over the balustrade and her heart leapt into her throat, for she was sure she'd caught a glimpse of Tristan. Craning her head to look more closely down upon the company in the stalls, she saw him standing near the exit. He was dressed in sober evening attire and had paused to speak to a member of the chorus.

'Are you coming, Addy?' James touched her shoulder to get her attention but she shrugged him off. Her heart was thundering now as she saw the chorus girl point behind the curtain.

And then, suddenly, there was the star of tonight's performance, tripping lithely towards her husband, her smile and manner suggesting a familiarity that made Adelaide want to collapse upon the spot.

Kitty's legs were still just as much in evidence. There was something gamine about her that set her apart from her fellow players, even those females who'd revealed their limbs. She reminded Adelaide of the notorious Lady Caroline Lamb who had pursued Byron so relentlessly after his brief interest had waned.

Foolish, Adelaide derided herself. Tristan was merely exchanging pleasantries. He had as much right to be at the theatre as Adelaide. Of course there was no longer anything between Tristan and Kitty. Only days ago he'd reaffirmed his constancy.

Yet what of the past? Kitty knew Adelaide's secret and the knowledge was like a corrosive poison eating away inside her.

Reassuring James and Beatrice that she was following them, Adelaide leaned once more over the balustrade.

Where was Tristan now? Out of the corner of her eye she

caught a flash of red, the colour of Miss Carew's dress, followed by her own husband's tall form disappearing into the shadows at the rear of the theatre.

'What is it, Addy?' James and Beatrice stood waiting for her by the curtain. 'You look as if you've seen a ghost or at least something very unpleasant. Someone in the stalls has leered at you? I'd have thought you'd be used to that by now.'

Adelaide shook her head, smiling past the lump in her throat. 'I thought I recognised someone.'

'Someone you did not wish to see, clearly.' James turned it into a joke. 'Who is there in your long wicked past might you not have wanted to see?'

'I hope the supper at Lady Belton's will be better than at Almack's,' Adelaide deflected him with false gaiety. 'I'm ravenous. Shall we go?'

Without waiting, she swept past them to the head of the stairs, her stomach churning.

On the one hand she wanted to delay her departure to ascertain that Tristan remained closeted no longer than seemly with Kitty; on the other, she knew how she would be diminished in his eyes if he caught his wife, not only out against his wishes, but keeping an eye on him.

CHAPTER 20

T ristan breathed in the familiar smell of the theatre and faced Kitty across her dressing room.

'Well, Kitty? Why did you summon me here? The lad who brought your message said it was urgent.' He felt irritation and, increasingly, mistrust in Kitty's company, despite acknowledging that he'd more than likely fathered Kitty's son, as borne up by the boy's physical characteristics. He tried to block his mind to the past, but Kitty's warm smile and the artless way she seemed to draw attention to her womanly assets without appearing in any conscious way to do so brought memory flooding back.

For six months she'd been everything he'd needed: passionate, responsive … and discreet. When she'd taken up with a foreign count whose black moustache and intensely passionate overtures had eclipsed Tristan's more traditional approach, Tristan had found himself surprisingly relieved. Kitty, he'd realised, was not the sweet ingénue she pretended. There was a sly underhandedness about her that had begun, increasingly, to disturb him, though he'd never caught her out in a falsehood. She'd certainly been transparent about switching allegiances, so Tristan had no cause to call her a liar.

Nevertheless, sly was the only way he could describe how she was looking at him now, as she waved from her dressing room the two remaining chorus girls. 'There's sommat you should know, m'lord.' Her tone was conversational as she began to unlace her front-fastening stays. She'd already discarded the white linen shirt and now wore only her chemise.

Tristan turned his head away, offended rather than aroused by her lack of modesty as she dropped the leather stays and wriggled out of her remaining undergarment. Naked, her breasts swung free as she reached up to unpin her hair, shaking out the rippling titian tresses.

'I am not in the market for your charms, Kitty.' He made for the door but Kitty's cheerful tones arrested him.

'It's about your wife.'

His hand was already on the door knob but he turned as Kitty rose from picking up the dropped stays. She gave him a saucy smile, cupping her breasts, as if in offering. 'You sure you don't want just a bit o' the fun we had before since it appears you're missing out in your marriage?' Her eyes danced in invitation.

'I have no idea what would make you believe that.' He hid his fury, itching to leave but realising he had no choice but to hear her out. If Kitty knew something he didn't, he needed to be forearmed to protect Adelaide. He suspected Kitty's portentous words might be motivated by jealousy. Perhaps Mr Gilchrist, in an unguarded moment, had compared Kitty unfavourably with Adelaide. There was a purity about his wife he'd never seen matched. Kitty, beautiful though she was, seemed like a tarnished copy.

"My marriage?" His tone would convey to Kitty that this was a protected area.

"That's right, m'lord. Your marriage." Kitty smiled artlessly at him as she confined her breasts in their revealing corsetry.

Tristan breathed carefully. How dare she insinuate a deficiency in Adelaide?

Yet the thought of his beautiful wife filled him with yearning.

Hope, too.

Making progress in their dealings with one another was like taking three steps forward then two steps back.

But they would get there.

Kitty's tawdry offerings shored up his determination. He would do right by Adelaide. Once he'd dismissed whatever Kitty was about to say, he'd return to his role as protector: nurturing Adelaide as needed, and bolstering her fragile confidence.

Perhaps only he knew the potential there was for his wife to be the shining star she obviously once was. And so wanted to be again.

All that was needed was patience.

On both their parts.

'Well, the list of potions she orders from the apothecary don't suggest she's a happy wife." Kitty had taken a seat at her dressing table and was rolling on a new pair of stockings. "I assumed if that were the case it might cut two ways and that you might not be a 'appy husband.' She sounded apologetic. 'Pardon me for offendin', m'lord.'

Tristan dropped his hand and shook his head in disbelief while Kitty, who was not looking as impish as she had been, fished in her reticule and thrust a piece of paper at him. 'There's a list of 'em all wot Mr Mendelssohn gave me.

Mostly laudanum, but a few others wot he says might have rather a different effect.' Perceiving his shock, a smug smile turned up the corners of her mouth as she fingered the

227

jewelled cross she wore. It was nestled in the valley between her breasts. 'Recognise this?' she asked, and he felt the prickles of cold dread creep up his hands to the back of his neck to see it was Adelaide's. 'Ah, so you do,' Kitty whispered, moving closer and holding it out so he could look more closely.

'Cover yourself!' he snapped, bending to retrieve her petticoat and thrusting it at her. Nevertheless, he waited, his stomach churning.

'Lady Leeson gave me this to keep her little secret, she did.' Kitty preened, rising and taking a couple of steps forward. She was so close he could smell her breath. He retreated, nausea almost overcoming him while Kitty continued in a lilting, conversational tone.

'First I didn't understand what little secret she were talking about when she come over all queer and gave it to me, begging me not to tell yer.'

Tristan's brain worked feverishly as he tried to make sense of such a transaction.

'You didn't ask her?'

'Didn't have time, for she were gone from me lodgings like a frightened rabbit with a fox sniffin' at her heels.'

Kitty held the jewelled cross up to the light and fingered it, smiling. 'I were so surprised she'd given it to me to keep me mouth shut; you can't imagine how me brain worked after that. *Keep me mouth shut about wot? What were 'er Lady-ship so concerned to keep from 'er 'usband an' wot did she think I knew?"*

Kitty gave a little laugh. Spiteful. Vengeful. Tristan wanted to believe she was lying, but how had she come by Adelaide's locket?

Tucking a red-gold curl behind one ear, Kitty went on, "But then I followed her out and saw 'er go into Mr Mendelssohn's Apothecary and so later I quizzed him. He said 'e were a regular supplier of the lady's efficacies. When I asked 'im exactly wot these efficacies were, he said it were the lady's business and she'd said specifically 'er 'usband didn't approve.' Kitty cocked her head. 'So, m'lord, wot yer goin' to do, then?'

Tristan regarded the half-naked woman before him dispassionately. 'You wouldn't lie to me, would you, Kitty?'

'I'm a lot o' things, m'lord, but I ain't no liar. You know that.' She raised her chin, pretending offence while she toyed with her neck chain.

Adelaide's golden neck chain.

Tristan averted his gaze. 'Obviously you hoped to profit from telling me this … and had no compunction in breaking my wife's trust.'

'Pah! She'd a done the same to me. She's jealous o' me cos Mr Gilchrist's paintin' me instead o' her and she thinks herself a cut above. Thinks she's the greater beauty, too, but it's only wot money can buy that sets us apart.'

Tristan regarded her over the top of the list and wondered how this woman had ever charmed him. He'd been lonely, of course. Loneliness motivated a person to act uncharacteristically. Tristan had never taken a mistress before Kitty. Or since.

Rolling his shoulders, he felt like an old man.

What had motivated Adelaide to return to her old crutch, laudanum? he wondered, not liking the answer.

Relations with her husband? She'd only have done so if she found her new situation difficult. Yet she'd appeared to relish the gaiety and admiration society had heaped upon her as well as the intimacy she and Tristan had forged.

He scanned the list, horrified as he calculated the number of times Adelaide must have returned for more laudanum. When he raised his eyes he found Kitty looking at him with feigned sympathy.

'Yer didn't know she were so unhappy, did yer? Not that she's a reason to be, wot wiv everyone calling her the Toast of the Town.' Kitty sighed and closed the distance between them to stroke his shoulder. 'Them bedroom antics ain't always so pleasing to the wife of breeding and delicacy, eh, m'lord.'

When Tristan shrugged off her hand, she grinned, thrusting out her bosom as she reiterated her previous offer. 'That's why a lusty, willing wench such as meself can be just the panacea. You know I'm discreet. 'Er ladyship'll never know and I'll be doin' 'er a favour if she don't have to suffer 'er bedroom duties so often.'

She'd followed him to the door by the end of this speech, but he'd heard enough.

'Sorry, Kitty.' He tapped the parchment. 'This only proves that my wife needs me more than ever.'

In Lady Belton's thronged ballroom, while James was away procuring them champagne, Adelaide's misgivings at venturing out were soon quashed. The gaiety was like a drug, making her feel alive. She'd been complimented by seemingly every person who crossed her path and she pulsed with vitality. She wished someone would whisk her onto the dance floor. Even James.

Beatrice was chattering away, equally happy, it would appear. 'I wish you could have been there. I felt I set just the right tone when James was honoured for his brilliance. Everyone was so complimentary of his work – except Mr Donegal, of course.' She touched Adelaide's wrist. 'I told Madame Claudette I needed a wardrobe that would reflect my position as the wife of a brilliant poet; that I needed to shine but not to outshine *him*. Your advice has helped me to understand James so much more. Thank you.'

Adelaide swallowed past the catch in her throat, smiling as she accepted the champagne James handed her when he returned a little later. She took a sip and closed her eyes, savouring the smooth fizz on the back of her tongue.

'You look like you've found Heaven,' James said with a laugh, raising his eyebrows when Adelaide said more contritely than was her wont, 'I'm sorry I dragged you away to fetch me.'

'We were concerned that Tristan had turned into Bluebeard himself.'

Adelaide hoped she looked as ashamed as she felt. She dropped her gaze and thought with longing of her husband, wishing he were with her instead of James and Beatrice.

'Tristan was simply showing his great concern and care for me, as ever.' She took a thoughtful sip and was surprised to discover she'd finished the last drop in her glass. 'I told him that if he wanted to raise my spirits then he should escort me here tonight, but Mama *will* have him believe I'm a complete invalid on the verge of a breakdown.' She shrugged. 'I certainly will be both those things if I am not allowed a bit of liberty.'

'Hear, hear, Addy!' James refilled her champagne coupe and they toasted one another, spirits instantly fuelled by the bubbles and the lively atmosphere.

This was clearly not Beatrice's first glass. She was more lively than Adelaide had ever seen her. 'James, take Addy onto the dance floor. You look so graceful together. And I shall talk to my friend Miss O'Dowd,' she added over her shoulder.

The 'Sir Richard de Coverly' was playing and Adelaide and James took their places in the line-up beside a sober couple whom James whispered were about to announce their betrothal.

'Marvellous match for him,' he said. 'She has ten thousand a year and he's a self-confessed fortune hunter, but the parents have been trying to get her off their hands the past three seasons.'

'She looks very serious,' remarked Adelaide, moving her gaze away as she caught the girl's eye. 'How mortifying it must be to know everyone is talking behind your back.'

'You seem to take it in your stride.'

She felt a guilty pang of pleasure as James linked elbows and led her down the centre of the line-up. The music and the movement, even the knowledge that she was admired, fuelled her spirits like nothing else could. She was young and healthy, alive and, for the moment, free. She felt she could soar to any heights this evening. She didn't care that her truancy would inevitably come to Tristan's and her mother's ears. She would prove it was all the tonic she needed.

Grinning like a schoolboy, James said breathlessly, 'Addy, you are marvellous. Tell me this means you've come out of retirement.'

'That all depends on my mother,' she responded, executing an elegant figure of eight and smiling up at him as they put their palms together for a moment, 'and Tristan, of course. Perhaps you can influence him. You and Beatrice.'

He sobered. Lowering his voice, he asked, 'What about the... note? Do not blame Tristan entirely for your self-imposed decline after you received it.'

Adelaide closed her eyes, briefly. 'It's not important any more. I've taken care of it.' She forced a brave smile for his benefit. 'Come, let us find Beatrice who, I must say, is transformed.'

Ensuring he could make no rejoinder before they'd located his betrothed, Adelaide was soon smiling to see the pleasure that kindled in the young girl's eyes as she gazed upon her husband-to-be.

'She loves you more than you deserve, James,' Adelaide whispered as they joined her. 'Just as I am blessed in my marriage to Tristan, you are indeed a lucky man.'

Beatrice beamed. 'Did I tell you that Aunt Wells was horrified at both my choice of ballgown and the bill, but James has charmed her – haven't you James? – just like he charms everyone. James is in demand at all the best salons where he reads his poems aloud to the swooning ladies.' She giggled. 'Everyone is so jealous of me'—she hesitated, adding with a touch of defiance—'though they're even more jealous of James's mystery muse. She feigned resentment. 'But James will tell no one who inspired *The Maid of Milan*.'

'A secret I shall take to my death,' declared James in a tone of contrived passion, 'for were it to be revealed that she was in fact my mother's washerwoman more than half my interested audience would fade away.'

Beatrice tapped him playfully on the chest with her fan. 'You told me it was the fishmonger's wife.'

A look of rapture glazed James's eye. 'Ah yes, Goodwife Betty Busking's vacant-eyed beauty as she staggered up the drive with her basket of plaice. I was nine, and never the same after that. Only now do I understand it was the drink rather than my effect on women that accounted for her lusty welcome kisses before the scullery maid took over negotiations.'

'You are terrible,' Beatrice giggled. 'Everyone thinks you are so passionate and mysterious. If they only knew the truth.'

'You will keep my secret, won't you, my love?' He clasped her waist, murmuring with only a touch of theatricality as he pulled her to him, 'As long as I have you, sweet Beatrice, by my side, I will survive.'

More champagne was procured and Adelaide was claimed by others, until she found herself waltzing with Phineas Donegal.

'You have been notable by your absence, Lady Leeson.

I'm glad to see the rumours were just that.'

'Rumours?' Adelaide hoped she looked merely enquiring. Any suggestion of rumours was guaranteed to put her on edge. She was also conscious of time slipping by while niggling guilt was starting to mar her evening. She'd hoped more champagne would assuage that.

'That you'd succumbed to a fever was probably the most prosaic one.'

'There was more than one?'

'You look incredulous. Why, a beautiful woman who makes her mark with all the fanfare you did will certainly invite interest when she disappears from society overnight. A calculating and designing beautiful woman might engineer it.'

'Sadly, however, it appears I was easily replaced. Certainly from Mr Gilchrist's point of view.'

He looked shocked. 'Miss Kitty Carew? My dear Lady Leeson, I wouldn't dream of discussing the *demimondaine* on the dance floor – or anywhere else – with a lady. Suffice to say that Miss Carew knows how to make the most of what she is blessed with, but you have nothing to fear. Did you see her treading the boards last week? Of course not for you have been unable to rise from your bed until tonight. Suffice to say she was a sensation and will be remembered as an actress, not as anyone's muse. Certainly not Mr Gilchrist's. No need to concern yourself over Miss Carew.'

But Adelaide did. On so many levels. She believed Tristan when he insinuated he would not take a mistress, but the fact remained that it seemed clear he'd fathered Kitty's son and that Kitty knew enough about Adelaide's past to destroy her.

She tried to dislodge her fears with a toss of her head. If she'd stayed alone in her room they had the power to eat away at her sanity. At least here she could enjoy diversion.

Provided nothing reminded her of Kitty.

Mr Donegal brought her another coupe of champagne after he'd escorted her from the dance floor. The bubbles helped diminish Adelaide's fears and her guilt at being where she should not.

Another banished her guilt altogether.

CHAPTER 22

'Lady Leeson, you look ravishing.'

'Lady Leeson, we were so concerned at news of your lapse in good health.'

'Lady Leeson, all London is mad to see you in person, especially those who've only gazed upon your portrait.'

The compliments came thick and fast, making Adelaide feel more alive than she had in weeks. She accepted other offers to dance, the spinning and twirling fuelling her body like a drug.

She caught a glimpse of herself in a large gilt mirror and could not believe the flushed beauty was herself. She *looked* as she'd felt as an eighteen-year-old. Surely Tristan would want her like this? Want her more than the lacklustre invalid he'd been saddled with?

'Lady Leeson, you are ravishing this evening,' James's voice heated her cheek as he passed with more champagne for Beatrice. Adelaide held out her hand for the glass but he brushed it away, a frown replacing his admiring smile. 'You've had enough champagne for one night.' His tone was serious. 'I think I should take you home.'

'I don't want to go.'

Home was a silent, forbidding place with people who didn't treat her like they did here in Lady Belton's warm and wonderful ballroom.

His hand twined round her waist for the briefest moment as he gave emphasis to his rejoinder. 'It's two o'clock in the morning, Addy. Tristan will be worried if he doesn't know where you are.'

She relaxed on a sigh and closed her eyes, longing for it to be Tristan by her side, holding her, whispering into her ear.

'As you wish, James.'

'Don't sound so resigned. I don't want to go either, but I must take Beatrice home and I'm not leaving you here alone. Come.'

She left the entertainment at Beatrice's side, her exuberance returned as they discussed poor Miss Medley's lack of countenance and pondered schemes whereby the chinless heiress might entice a husband.

The swaying of the carriage soon had Adelaide fast asleep with her head on a cushion that someone had pushed under her cheek. She awoke with a start not knowing where she was and James squeezing her shoulder.

'Hush, it's alright,' he whispered as she squinted through bleary eyes, and his face inches away took shape in the gloom of a street lamp. 'I've escorted Beatrice to her front door and now I'll see you returned safely to Tristan. But listen'—he took her hand—'we're outside Mr Gilchrist's and I see a light on in the attic. Since our esteemed artist friend is still hard at work perhaps you would like to see his progress on what will, to all intents and purposes, be presented to the world as yourself?'

Adelaide blinked heavy-lidded eyes and focused on him for a few seconds before fear worked its way through the cotton wool that seemed to stuff her head. 'No, if Kitty found out—'

'Kitty is hardly in a position to hold the moral high ground sufficiently to be believed over you, my dear.' He slipped his hand into hers and gave it a squeeze. 'Come, Addy. Since when did you lack spirit? I know you want to see how Mr Gilchrist has rendered the vignettes for which Kitty has sat.'

It was difficult to think coherently. Adelaide knew she'd drunk too much champagne, although did that account for the fevered workings of her brain, the chills that wracked her body and which James mistook for cold as he arranged the folds of her evening cloak warmly around her when he helped her out of the carriage?

They roused a gateman to let them in. He did not demur as he turned the key in the lock and led them to the ramshackle building which, though close to the fashionable quarter, was still in an area decidedly insalubrious.

In silence they took the three flights of stairs to the attic studio, Adelaide tripping once, giggling as James held her up and led her by the hand the rest of the way, though she felt more like sinking into a blissful slumber than visiting Mr Gilchrist.

Tentatively they knocked and when there was no answer it seemed natural to let themselves in as the door was ajar.

'Perhaps we shouldn't,' Adelaide protested half-heartedly as they stepped across the threshold, but when her eye caught sight of her life-sized portrait in pride of place near the window and beneath the skylight through which the moon shone down, she dropped James's hand and hurried forward.

A lamp burned in the far corner, casting a rosy glow over the canvases that lined the walls and those laid along the floor together with the sketches that cluttered all surfaces.

The strong smell of paint and turpentine was overlaid by the general dampness of the building, dissipated by the gentle breeze that stirred the curtains.

'Society's darling,' James drawled, coming to stand beside her. 'Half of London has seen it. But you are nearly frozen. Let me stoke up the fire.'

For Adelaide was beset by tremors that even James's warmth could not still as he held her from behind and rubbed her arms.

She barely noticed as she took in the elfin features of the woman reclining in her diaphanous robes. For it was her. Adelaide, rather than Kitty Carew, that Mr Gilchrist had rendered so faithfully upon the enormous canvas.

And she was….

Beautiful.

Through chattering teeth, she whispered, 'Tristan has agreed to let Mr Gilchrist show it until we return to the country where he plans to hang it in the Blue Saloon.'

'When do you return?'

'After your wedding.' She glanced across at the candle sconces above the fireplace. Soon the flickering flames would die, like the flame inside her. Returning to the country felt like a cruel punishment.

James's own spirits seemed to dissipate as he held her. 'Beatrice will miss you. You've been good for her.'

'I shall miss you both. You and she are a good match.' She swayed and closed her eyes, suddenly light-headed. 'But perhaps we should go, James, for Mr Gilchrist is not here.'

He ignored her as he stared at the painting and she felt him rest his chin lightly upon her head, but as she was too busy trying to retain her balance she made no objection. When he spoke his voice sounded very far away. 'We intend to spend most of our time in London. Beatrice loves it and I have my audience here. I'd hoped we'd see more of you and

Tristan. I'm sorry he's taking you back. He doesn't know what's good for you.'

The fire hissed gently but gave no warmth and she shivered even more. James twined his fingers in hers. Still gazing at the portrait, he whispered, 'He loves you but he doesn't know how to bring you to life, Addy.'

His breath stirred the tendrils of hair that curled about her ears and closed her eyes as she wilted against him. Oh, but he did. Tristan had brought her to life and she'd gloried in it. It seemed such a long time ago, now. She must tell James so; not let him labour under the misapprehension.

But James went on, his voice gaining conviction. 'He deserves you but he doesn't know what you need, how to stoke the flames within you to make you shine like the glorious creature you are.'

He caressed her palm with his thumb before turning her in his arms to face him, his tortured look finding an answer in the depths of her heart; for the flame within had indeed been stoked and it was a bitter pill to swallow that she must forever be consigned to a role she had no wish to play.

Unless she was prepared to offer the truth ...

She swayed dangerously and James caught her to him as her knees buckled.

'No, James,' she whispered as she ran a hand across her burning forehead, the blood pounding in her ears. 'I'm not well. I must lie down.'

Wearily she sank down upon the cushions he placed on the rug before the fire, sighing softly as he tucked a blanket around her shoulders. For once it was good to feel someone was looking after her.

Was it the champagne? It had been a long time since she'd dulled her wits with so blameless a stimulant.

Champagne.

Every victory in her life had been toasted with champagne.

Why, in Milan, when she and James—

She shook her head. She didn't want to think of James but it was impossible not to, for in Milan she'd been free.

Free — at least for a little while — to love as she wished. James had adored her until the end but how wrong he'd been for her.

Tristan, on the other hand…

Her mind was floating, her limbs so heavy… She wouldn't think of James. No, she'd think of Tristan.

He was the man whose arms she wished were around her right now. He was the man who adored her and, even if he wasn't going about it in the way Adelaide would like, loved her above all others.

She sighed and snuggled into the offered warmth. What great relief it was to relinquish the uncertainties of the present for the sweet oblivion of sleep.

To relinquish the fears of exposure for the pleasures of contemplating future happiness.

Happiness? What *was* happiness?

Why, it was the mutual love and regard of the man she'd married so dutifully but whom she now loved with a fiery passion she had to suppress.

…If he were to love her back.

Like a spirit departing from her body, Adelaide's thoughts rose above her.

She was dancing. She gloried in dancing and she gloried in the fact that it was Tristan who held her. With slight surprise she noticed he no longer limped. In fact he was the consummate dancer, lithe and light on his feet as he twirled her an inch from the ground.

And the way he gazed at her filled her heart with joy. She

was the centre of his universe. He caressed her cheek and she shivered, closing her eyes and savouring the sensation. His hand was warm and soft and she felt so very loved.

She moved into him, twining her hands behind his neck as she raised her face, parting her lips slightly to receive his kiss, tentative at first for they were still back in exploratory waters and his kisses were usually brief and chaste.

Tonight, though, he took possession of her mouth like a lover rather than the custodian of her virtue, kissing her with increasing urgency, one hand cupping the back of her head the other moulding her bottom, pulling her against him.

And she, feeling his instant arousal, a sign of her power to ignite, was lost.

Drawing in a shuddering breath, she clung to him, her body pulsing with renewed life and energy as they sank to their knees, mouths fused, their bodies entwined.

A tiny kernel of consciousness had expected hard wooden boards beneath, but instead she sank into softness, though the body above her was hard and unyielding.

Mindless to all but the intoxication of the moment, Adelaide gave herself up to the glorious sensation of being desired by her husband. Her body was her temple and after the long drought, it was, at last, being worshipped justly.

With her being a mass of exquisite sensation, she moaned her pleasure at the long-forgotten sensations that coursed through her as Tristan took her nipple in his hot mouth. Wrapping her legs around his waist, she moved her body beneath his, basking in the fires stoked by his exploring hands.

Finally her adored husband wanted more than to protect her as if she were a precious object. Primal desire had trumped his finer sensibilities, bringing him on par with her own desires.

'Oh, yes,' she murmured, her voice hitching somewhere

between hope and ecstasy as she positioned herself to receive him, parting her legs, arching her hips, holding him tightly as she prepared for their glorious coupling.

Every nerve ending was primed, her skin prickling with awareness, her heart pounding with expectation as his hands worked their magic like the skilful lover he was, seeking out her hidden, secret places.

How deeply she had missed this base, elemental, exquisite act which united hearts as much as bodies.

It made her feel like a woman, not an invalid. A goddess of desire, not an apology of a wife.

'Oh, my love!' she wept, as he entered her, and she shattered beneath him, darkness and blinding colour coalescing in her mind.

Spent, and satiated, Adelaide slept in his arms, his warmth all she needed as the fire died down.

The thick rug beneath them and the cushions were sufficient comfort when she had rediscovered what had been denied her so long: love.

Adelaide needed to be loved. Her body needed to feel it or she was only a husk. The husk for which her mother derided her. As if her carnal appetites branded her a monstrous aberration.

'What is it, my adored one?'

His soft murmur was filled with sympathy and she realised she must have sobbed her pain aloud, in the midst of sleep.

She nestled into his warmth and stretched her neck to receive his kisses, soft and feathery from her jawline to her collarbone, and continuing south.

Fluttering open sleep-laden eyelashes, Adelaide took in her surroundings, alien and confusing: the meagre fire, shabby furnishings, the large bed in the corner with its curtains drawn right round, which surely would have been more comfortable than … She blinked again, confused even further by the cold dankness overlaid with the smell of oils and turpentine.

Her hands came to rest on her lover's head as he continued his sweet torture of his mouth on her chest.

And felt, instead of the soft, springy curls of her husband, the fashionably long, oiled coiffure of someone completely different.

Someone once well known whose presence in her arms was completely unexpected.

'Dear God, James!'

Gasping, she pushed herself out of his embrace, staring wildly from his slightly puzzled expression to her own state of disarray, her skirts tangled up about her hips, one discarded slipper taunting her from beneath a distant chair. Horror surged through her, fuelling her rapid rise to her feet so that she stood swaying, poised on the verge of flight as she stared at the man she'd once loved with every fibre of her being and whose presence here, now, confirmed that she had lost the right to any happiness in the future.

Ever.

'Addy, what is it?'

She put her hands to her eyes to block out of the image of him: pleading, confused. A supplicant, not the arduous lover of her past and no, oh God no, not the husband whose love she desired beyond anything.

As self-preservation came to the fore, she threw herself to her knees to seize upon her lost slipper, pulling it onto her foot, rising to smooth the rumpled skirts of her gown, hurriedly securing the tendrils that had escaped from her modish coiffure.

James now rose hastily at the sound of footsteps

pounding up the stairs and a voice calling, 'Kitty? Is that you, Kitty?' before Gilchrist burst into the room.

He looked as shocked as James, and certainly as Adelaide felt.

A horrible silence was suddenly filled by James's laugh, forced, but easing the tension as he went on, 'Sorry to intrude like this, Gilchrist, but we saw the light on from the street and the door was half open.'

Gilchrist's brow was creased with confusion and a degree of wariness. 'Perhaps Kitty didn't close it properly.' He darted a look at the curtained bed in the corner.

'You see, we thought we heard someone inviting us in,' James went on, as if to suggest he and Adelaide had only just arrived.

Gilchrist seemed embarrassed. 'Kitty? Er, yes, she stays here sometimes if it's been a late night at the theatre.' He began to warm to his theme, as if he might justify his own position when right now Adelaide was only concerned with justifying theirs.

She let the painter go on. He was clearly agitated as he ran his fingers through his tousled curls in awkward defer-ence to his patron's wife. 'Theatre's just round the corner, you know. I can get an early start painting Kitty, if you know what I mean.'

Adelaide felt as if she'd been turned to stone until James grasped her wrist. 'We really should return to Beatrice who is waiting in the carriage.'

How smoothly the lie tripped off his tongue.

Adelaide could only follow him meekly, offering not a word as Mr Gilchrist bade them goodnight and the door closed mercifully behind the scene of her greatest betrayal.

CHAPTER 23

The coachman was on hand to open the carriage door once they'd drawn up in front of Tristan's London townhouse but James waved him away.

"A few moments!" he barked.

This was not a time for softness. He seemed as shocked by what had happened as she.

Adelaide began to cry, covering her face with her hands, her shoulders shuddering.

'I'm sorry,' was all he could manage as he stared out at the starlit night, cold and bitter with a million twinkling, taunting witnesses to their crime. He felt as Adelaide did, she could tell. Ashamed, horrified.

Afraid.

'What must I do?' she whispered.

'Go back to Tristan.'

She took a shuddering breath. 'I … I must confess.'

'God, no!' James leaned forwards, gripping her arms before dropping his hands as if realising she was out of bounds. 'Not if you want to keep him, which I gather you do. Tristan will never forgive something like this. No, Addy, you will not confess—' His pupils were dilated in the gloom, indicating his horror until the softening of his stare revealed the intrusion of a different line of thought.

He held her shoulders again, his voice suddenly harsh with desire. '—unless you want to come away with me. You can do that, you know, Addy.'

He drew her against him, urgency radiating from him as the idea clearly gained force in his mind. His breath rasped. 'You came alive for me, Addy. Surely you have never done so like this with Tristan.' He spoke faster, as if the force of his desire could overcome whatever objection she might have. 'Yes, yes, I know you love him,' he cut short her protest, 'but I love you more. Now I have money to support us both and a reputation for wildness that will withstand the scandal. Come away with me, Addy. We'll escape abroad where we'll bask in the love we've never been able to find here.' He brought her hands to his lips while his eyes smouldered from above them. 'I swear you'll not regret it.'

Shock stopped her soft weeping but as his words sank in she began to sob even harder, great wrenching sobs that rocked her body until he pulled her across his knees; kissing her face, her neck, her hair.

'I want to go home,' she protested as she tried to push him away, but though he drew back so he could look at her, he would not release her.

'With *me*, Addy? Your home has always been with me. You know that's the truth.'

She felt the restless movement of the horses; the coachman's retort, followed by a gentle snort and a whinny.

'No, James!' Terror choked her as she tore out of his grip, her fingers fumbling to open the door, but James dragged her back inside before she fell to the cobbles.

'Addy, you don't know what you're doing. Stop! Please!'

Ignoring him, she wrenched herself free, stumbling down

the steps just as the coachman arrived to assist her, putting her hands up to her burning mouth, her mind churning its despair as she focused on the one thing she was bound to do:

Confess.

Not just for tonight but for everything.

Every past sin which made her what she was: the lying jade whose body had inspired a famous book, the scarlet temptress who had enticed another man from his far worthier wife; the seductress , invalid, charlatan, whose pretence and omissions had made everything between Tristan and herself a three-year charade.

In her bedchamber she threw herself onto the counterpane, neatly turned down in anticipation of a much earlier arrival home. She'd entered the house by the kitchen door, having arranged with Milly to ensure it was left unbolted.

The servants were sleeping; there was still a chance no one knew she'd been out, that no one but Milly knew of her truancy. James was certainly not about to reveal it.

Heart pounding she lay upon her bed, staring through her tangle of hair at the wall faintly illuminated by the lamp Milly had lit.

What had she done? Like gargoyles taunting her from the murky depths of her mind, like serpents roiling through her cankerous soul, the same sharp-edged question chased through her mind until she felt she must shriek her release.

She struggled into a sitting position and tore off her cloak. Her dress beneath was damp with sin. She tore that off too, plunging it into the copper basin of water on her dressing table. Shivering naked, she attacked herself with its sodden folds, scrubbing away her treason. Scrubbing vigorously in a vain attempt to excoriate her guilt.

The only result she felt for her pains was the red, rawness of her skin; a pain which did nothing to ease her mind. And as she stared at the raised wheals caused by the sharp embroidery that adorned her evening gown, she felt as if her very soul were burning to cinders and she longed, too, for an oblivion that would stop the dawn from ever breaking.

Tomorrow she would confess.

As God was her witness, she was determined to face what she must and take her punishment.

Crumpling to the floor she sobbed.

What had she done?

The litany chased itself round her brain.

What had she done? Why, she'd only fulfilled every doomed prophesy of her mother's. Only upheld Tristan's tremulous fears for the shaky foundations of her sanity.

After a few minutes she rose to her knees then crawled under the bedclothes until the demons in her mind forced her out of bed again.

Shivering in the centre of her room, she realised she could not wait until morning. Tristan must know, before she lost courage, the truth of what she was: a woman whose life was a lie; a wife he did not deserve.

He may cast her out but that was a risk she had to take. More than anything she needed to unburden herself. So that she could at least beg his forgiveness.

Her mind worked quickly.

If she appeared wearing her nightrail he may jump to the conclusion she'd had a nightmare and his first words would be of comfort before he held her to him. She didn't know if she had the fortitude to continue with her confession if that happened.

If she were dressed in a way that showed she'd been out for the evening he'd be shocked. He would question her and then it would be easier to say what she must.

The coquelicot sarsenet was the gown which called most attention to her natural assets. The scarlet, flecked with gold, made her feel as she had when she was a carefree seventeen-year-old, revelling in the limelight.

She struggled to put on the gown without Milly to help her but she managed. On the way to the door she glanced at her reflection. Her hair was wild. Pausing in front of the mirror she released it from the last few pins that secured it in its former style then raked her hands through it. There was no time for further finishing touches.

That would only be delaying the inevitable: Tristan's horror at the jezebel he thought so pure.

CHAPTER 24

Adelaide checked the study first. Though it was the early hours of the morning Tristan often worked late. Instead, she found him in his bedchamber, a candle flickering on the side table as he rested against the pillows, reading some government paper.

His face lit up when she entered and he tapped the parchment which had clearly occasioned some great excitement. Adelaide recognised it as one of his speeches. Another appeal to the emotions on which Mr Finch had again done such a poor job.

Well, Adelaide knew how to appeal to the emotions. She felt everything from the heart, and James had taught her how to express it—

If only her mother had allowed it, though there had been catharsis in tweaking the vessel by which Tristan might mine the desired outcome of his strongly-held convictions. Adelaide didn't always understand what was at stake but she knew how to express more artfully than Mr Finch what Tristan clearly wanted to say.

'I had no idea Mr Finch was capable of such compelling

and expressive argument,' Tristan burst out, seeming not to notice her gown, her tense mood. He straightened, his eyes glowing as he recounted his meeting with the esteemed Mrs Fry. 'While the woman drew to my attention many serious reform issues, the discussion I had with Finch was in only general terms.' Again he tapped the parchment. 'Why, my secretary has exceeded himself and, my darling, with such capable help, I believe I can look forward to spending more time with you in London than I'd believed possible. If my future appeals to those yet to be won over are as successful as tonight's, my parliamentary career is in the ascendant.'

He stopped, realising perhaps that it was odd to see his wife dressed for an evening out, in his room at such an hour. 'Addy?'

'I'm very glad your speech went well, Tristan.' Her voice sounded shaky to her own ears. 'I'm proud of you, but there's something you should know.' She closed her eyes and when she opened them it was to see Tristan out of bed and coming towards her.

'No.' She held him at bay, her mouth tight. She'd crumple into a pool of weak neediness if he touched her.

She heard the wind sigh in the trees outside and wished she could simply float away. Too long, though, she'd evaded this important duty and now the time had come. She heaved in a breath for courage and clenched her fists.

'I've been out tonight, Tristan.' Her voice trembled even more. 'I told you and Mama that I would, but my act of defiance ... and what happened after that ... cannot be exonerated by pretending that I simply followed through on what I said I'd do. No, it can't excuse me.' She heard the self-disgust as her tone hardened and hoped it would prompt Tristan to demand to know more. It would be easier than finding the words she needed to explain from the beginning.

He did not close the distance and she was glad. Obviously

he realised the matter was grave. Tristan was, as ever, sensitive to her needs. He responded with care. 'You went out, *alone*, Addy? Surely not?'

She tried to read his expression. Could he suspect?

'I am guilty of so many sins, Tristan. I've only just begun.'

He walked slowly back to the bed and lowered himself onto the mattress, a thoughtful frown creasing his brow. Solemnly he said, 'I'm glad you've chosen to confess to me of your own accord.'

Adelaide swallowed in the face of his sudden gravity and her whole world seemed suddenly to explode about her ears. *He knew?* Oh dear Lord, this was the moment, then. The moment when all her hopes and dreams came crashing down, like a house of cards.

Searing pain blinded her and with an anguished moan she threw herself at his feet. If she were incinerated into a pile of ashes that disappeared between the cracks of the floorboards it would be too kind a fate.

'Oh God, Tristan, I'm so sorry! My behaviour has been unforgivable and yet I'd do anything to turn back time … anything if you would only forgive me!'

She found little relief in the rasping sobs that wracked her body, but suddenly she was in Tristan's arms and he had her across his lap, rocking her, pressing her face gently against his shoulder as he kissed her neck.

'Hush, my angel,' he whispered, 'don't torture yourself like this. I know everything and I forgive you. I'll always forgive you.'

Gasping, she stiffened, her sobs subsiding as she drew back and stared, shocked, into his face.

He stroked her cheek, his smile one of unbelievable fondness as he soothed her. 'Kitty told me.' He kissed her forehead. 'I admit I was upset at first, but now you've come to me of your own accord and I can't tell you how much I admire you for your bravery.'

Her mouth dropped open as she dragged in a breath. 'Admire me?' she repeated.

He looked deeply into her eyes, his expression kind but determined. 'We can see this through together, my darling, and I'll be with you all the way.' Gently he kissed the tip of her nose. 'The first step is admitting that you've strayed. The next step is devising ways to ensure it won't happen again.'

She blinked rapidly, her brain in turmoil as she tried to make sense of his words, trying, but failing, to formulate her own.

He was silent a moment, clearly choosing his words carefully. 'I realise that I am obviously partly to blame—'

'You are in *no* way to blame.' She was trembling so hard she nearly fell out of his arms, but she had to pour out the truth. Her words tumbled out as she rose and began to pace. She swallowed as she wiped her sweating hands on her skirts, turning to face him from the centre of the plush Aubusson carpet.

Soon she would be cast out, as she deserved. She'd have to make her own way on a meagre allowance, and beautiful objects and comfort would be but memories. Could she survive without them? Did she have the fortitude to go ahead with her confession?

She pushed back her shoulders with renewed resolved.

She did. The price of deception was too high. Only the catharsis of confession would free her from the lies that bound her. She was a prisoner of her own making until she could confess. 'First I deceived you, then I went out with James and Beatrice. I drank too much champagne —'

He closed the distance to hold her, his finger upon her lips staying her words. His gentle voice, soft as it caressed her ear, was so very understanding. 'I think it more pertinent to address the reasons *why* you went out? May I offer my own suggestion?"

He kissed her brow and she felt a slight softening of some of the ghastly tenseness that held her captive.

"It was because the mood for gaiety was suddenly upon you and I was not on hand to cater to your need for diversion, just as I have not been for much of this season.'

He caressed her shoulders as he held her away from him, his look solemn. 'When these moods descend upon you I understand your desperation and your desire to resort to that upon which you relied so heavily in the early years of our marriage. Kitty told me what any good husband should have suspected and I deeply regret that I have not been more by your side. I thought gaiety would be the panacea you needed but I realise it was all too much, too soon. Gaiety is all very well when you're in the mood for it, but you're still fragile, I realise that now. And when blackness descended upon you and I was not there, you had no one to turn to except your old crutch: laudanum.'

She didn't know what to say. Opening her mouth to refute it, she found she couldn't get the words out. Where could she begin?

He cupped her face in his hands and stared earnestly at her. 'Yes, Kitty told me everything.' He raised an eyebrow. 'She's certainly no friend of yours, but the truth is, she's done us both a favour. Now that I know the full extent of your crimes we can, *together*, strengthen you and make you well.'

She could only mumble, 'I don't deserve this, Tristan.'

'Then look at it from my perspective.' He cocked his head, his smile wry. 'I've loved you to distraction, Addy, from the moment I laid eyes on you. What better way for you to repay that love than to strive to do everything you can to become the vibrant, *responsive* wife *I* want? The wife I know you're capable of becoming with the right care and nurturing? You weaned yourself off laudanum before. You can do it again. I promise I won't leave you alone so much because I can now be confident of Mr Finch's abilities.' He took her hands in his and brought them to his lips. 'I can escort you to those events you feel up to attending, but if one of your black moods descend upon you, I will remain with you until you defeat it.'

Stricken, she bit her lip. He was offering her too much. Yet how could she throw away this chance for the happiness they *both* desired?

'H-how—'

'For a start, we'll completely ignore any stricture your mother deems to be in your best interests.'

She managed a smile. 'That's a good start.' Haltingly, she added, 'Mama has her own singular ideas on how a good wife should behave.'

At Tristan's enquiring look Adelaide brought her hands up to her face. Turning away from him she squeezed her knuckles into her eye sockets, finding no relief from the blackness that briefly removed her from her surroundings. His silence gave her the opportunity to speak. It was her final moment to unburden herself, correct his misapprehension and reveal herself as the faithless, blackhearted jade he didn't deserve.

Yet it was also the moment she could take her greatest risk and perhaps forge a more fulfilling future for both of them.

Trembling, she turned, still not knowing what course she would choose as she opened her mouth.

'Tristan, I need to tell you …' Dear Lord, a true and good wife would have no compunction in choosing the right path. She licked dry lips and tried to force out the words as her eyelids stung with unshed tears. 'Oh God, this is so hard to say ...' She half turned away. Tears might blind her but the truth would not hobble her. She had to tell him.

'Then perhaps I might venture my own suggestion?'

'But Tristan, I want to confess—'

He smiled and put his forefinger to her lips. 'Your mother taught you that a good wife does not show her true feelings to her husband.'

His finger remained in place to stop her from speaking while his brow furrowed with concentration as if he were trying to find the right words. 'Since you've come to London you've blossomed, Addy. I can't tell you what a pleasure it's been to see you transformed into the joyful, vibrant woman I've always believed was hiding inside you. But with your newfound vibrancy came highs and lows. I battled with myself – and your mother – as to how to best respond. Your mother insisted you be kept calm at all times but that's *not* what you wanted, or needed, was it, Addy?'

She dared not answer him. Her tremulous smile of approbation must have satisfied him for he was doing too fine a job of teasing out the real reason behind her greatest unhappiness. If she'd sacrificed her opportunity to offer him the truth of her infidelity then she'd not stand in the way of him finding his way towards that other great truth. The truth that would set her free to love him as she wanted.

'James once made reference to something about you intimating an aversion to bedroom matters. I presumed he was discreetly passing on something you'd inadvertently mentioned, perhaps to Beatrice.' He shrugged. 'I forget the details but I do remember my shock, for at the time I remember thinking that such a short time earlier we'd never been happier. Only, fast on the heels of that great high, you were again bedridden. Why, Addy? I've asked myself this time and again? What causes these violent swings in mood?

Do you resort to laudanum to dull the guilt you feel at the pleasure to which you cannot admit?'

He moved his head forward to look deeply into her eyes. Only the greatest compassion radiated from his soulful look. He had the eyes of a man who had seen much and who knew how to forgive.

The eyes of the only man Adelaide knew she'd ever love.

He touched her cheek. 'I think that is the reason, but you're unable to say, or perhaps even admit it to yourself because that's what your mother has made you believe. Well, let me suggest this, Addy.' He tightened his grip on her shoulders. 'You be true to your heart and I will be by your side all the way. I will try to give you everything you need so that you never again resort to the little blue bottle. In return, you will be by my side as I embrace my new political fortunes and I shall revel in the support of the dazzling, vibrant woman I love above all others and whose love and constancy will see me forge ahead to realise my ambitions.' His voice, which had become impassioned, dropped to a whisper as he drove home his hopes for the future.

For their shared future.

'The great, lofty ambitions that I believe I can only realise with *you* by my side.'

What could she do but nod her head, mutely corroborate all he said, then offer her own whispered avowals as Tristan made her stand so he could undress her, kissing her earlobe, nuzzling her neck as her gown pooled around her ankles? She wanted to do exactly as Tristan proposed: put the past behind them. She wanted to be the wife a respected politician needed.

Any hint of scandal might destroy his political career, yet with the threat Kitty posed neutralised by the fact Kitty traded on supposition, not facts, surely Adelaide could relax and let love lead them to a brighter future?

And if Kitty had made more than was warranted of Adelaide's single visit to Mr Mendelssohn's which Tristan had then built upon, did it matter that Tristan misinterpreted her supposed mood swings? He'd certainly hit upon a solution that promised greater happiness for them both.

And wasn't that what they both wanted?

Happiness?

With each other?

She swayed against him, her mind churning once more with so much that was too confusing to understand.

Nearly drowning with feeling, she opened her mouth to say, she knew not what.

'Tristan, you must know—'

'That you love me?' He cupped her face and she sank against him, murmuring against his lips as she finally cast her last shred of honour to the wind.

'And that I want you.' Yes, that would do, she thought in final surrender as his hands strayed over her curves and warmed her naked flesh. 'As a husband,' she added against his lips.

His grip on her tightened as his tongue breached the seam of her lips in the gentlest of kisses. He drew back, his mouth quirked in a crooked smile as he murmured, 'As a lover, Addy? Not as a kind and considerate protector?'

'As a lover,' she responded, smiling as he scooped her up and deposited her on the bed.

He joined her, raising himself on one elbow to look at her. Tracing a line from her collarbone, over one breast, he rested his hand lightly upon her belly. 'Now you're back in my bed again, darling, shall we risk what your mother considers overexcitement?'

She felt her mouth stretch wide as she cast from her mind all the demons of guilt and remorse that threatened to mar her happiness. She'd forged her path so what use was guilt?

She'd not entertain it now, at any rate. Not when her beloved husband had opened up to her the future she'd always wanted.

The future he made clear *he* wanted.

If she was to grant him happiness, she knew how to do it.

By being the wife and lover he'd always dreamed of.

CHAPTER 25

Her gift to him was her body and her heart.

He could do to her as he wished and she'd respond to his gentleness, and his growing ardour, like a creature brought to life.

When he lay naked by her side, starting slowly and nuzzling her shoulder, she trembled as if no man had ever wielded such power.

And nor had they.

She let him stroke her into trembling expectancy; then thrilling awareness.

When he angled himself over her, caging her with his lithe, sinewy length, she made no secret of her awe and admiration; toying with his nipple as if she'd never seen something so novel.

And she hadn't.

When he nibbled her earlobe, she squeaked and cleaved to him, pressing her breasts against his hard chest, delighting that his response was so immediate.

He loved her.

It was all that mattered.

He believed she could assist the future for which he'd worked so hard; and this she knew she could only do if he was untouched by scandal.

Her love — untainted by her mother's strictures; untainted by her continual sublimation of her desire for him — would be her gift.

Her atonement.

Her path towards a future that promised them both happiness.

SHE WOKE as if in a dream and floated into consciousness through a haze of sensual rediscovery as her husband made love to her once again. He was no longer the caring but distant man whose heart she owned at the cost of all else that constituted a life bearable.

Under his tender ministrations she would think of only their gilded future as he stroked her into wakefulness the following morning. It did not take much to stoke her fires.

Before the dawn parade of housemaids tiptoed down the passage with their clanking buckets and ewers of water, Tristan and Adelaide had celebrated their union once more, and with a regret like that of newly discovered lovers, tore themselves apart, Tristan to attend to business in the Lords and Adelaide to sleep some more in her large empty bed in her own chamber.

She lay undisturbed until mid-afternoon. When she awoke her mind was clearer and she stared at the beautifully decorated ceiling and contemplated the events of the night before with a mixture of self-disgust, remorse, and finally hope. Tristan's misinterpretation of the reason for her unexplained changes in mood suggested something she'd begun to suspect: that her mother had taken Adelaide's medication into her own hands, doctoring her milk with laudanum when she perceived Adelaide was enjoying too much physical intimacy with her husband. Perhaps her mother had told the apothecary or his apprentice that the laudanum was for Lady Leeson.

If Tristan had once hinted to Kitty that Adelaide had had too great a reliance on the drug in the early days of their marriage, Kitty, being the sly, sharp opportunist she was, might then have used this against her.

Now that Adelaide had unravelled the more than likely reason behind Kitty's note and Tristan's interpretation of events, Adelaide drifted back into sleep.

She even slept through her mother's imperious knock and then emerged for dinner, resplendent in a daring gown of gold netting with jet trimmings, an ensemble her mother regarded with a beady eye which only grew beadier as Tristan stood behind Adelaide and, placing his hands upon her shoulders, declared her the finest woman ever to grace London.

'Adelaide must not tax her strength,' Mrs Henley protested when Adelaide declared that she and Tristan would be attending a masquerade at Vauxhall Gardens.

But Tristan declared roundly that he'd never seen Adelaide in more robust health and that a masquerade sounded just the thing.

It was, for Adelaide spent the evening either on her husband's arm or in his embrace as they walked, danced or made a point of avoiding anyone they suspected they knew.

When Tristan looked like approaching James, who looked very piratical and was the subject of a great deal of feminine interest that did not include Beatrice, Adelaide declared she wanted this evening to be hers and Tristan's alone. 'We said we'd look in for a few hours then have an early night, my darling.'

When Milly brought up a mug of warm milk to Adelaide's bed chamber after she and Tristan had returned, Adelaide roundly ordered her to take it back to the kitchen. Her mother was never going to interfere in her life again.

They made love again that night. Twice and twice the next night, never speaking of the past but only of what the future held.

No, Adelaide had drawn a line behind the moment Tristan had forgiven her.

He'd stumbled upon a reason to release her from having to live a lie; the lie, at least, that masked her true nature. It might be the wrong reason, but he'd set her free, nevertheless.

Now Adelaide intended to repay him for the second chance he'd given her. He would never have reason to regret the decision he'd made in marrying her three long years before. She would see out the remainder of the season quietly and then revel in her country solitude with Tristan by her

side.

Next year's London season would herald a new start.

CHAPTER 26

The days grew warmer. A hot July became a steamy August. With no masquerades to ensure her anonymity, Adelaide kept to her room and Tristan slipped away from the quiet, endless evenings when he was working to visit her like a secret lover.

She wanted the company of no one else, she said, and he did not question her but instead became complicit in her game of deception. Adelaide was happy to play the invalid for the benefit of her mother, who stitched away with gloomy contentment; the mother who thought Adelaide's spirit was broken, that Adelaide could cause no trouble. Tristan saw how it was.

He did not see Adelaide's guilt, though. Tristan had wiped the slate clean for her but the guilt was still there. How could she ever look James in the eye again? Or Beatrice? No, Adelaide wanted to remain a prisoner in her own house as penance. And as Tristan's prisoner, because his love, she now believed, was all she needed to sustain her.

Three weeks passed and an invitation Tristan had accepted many weeks before became the sticking point for whether the charade be maintained or a new reality established.

Adelaide, in undress, wearing a loose, floating gown, the folds and flounces of which Tristan had just plumbed for the delicious bounty of his wife's curvaceous form, paced the room, wringing her hands.

'Accompany you, Tristan? Can I not be allowed to enjoy the solitude and sanctuary of our home a little longer?'

'I shall be by your side, Addy.' He began to chafe her hands, his look both bolstering and pleading. 'What of your brave words when you said you were ready to shine as a great politician's wife?' His voice dropped. 'I'm counting on you, Addy, for you will do me proud, I know it.'

She sank upon the bed and buried her face in her hands. 'I fear I am wanting when it comes to being the focus of attention for all I once believed it milk and honey to me.'

He lowered himself onto the mattress beside her and stroked her hair. 'You were magnificent when we first came to London and you found your confidence, but you soared too high. You want to return to society, you say? You want to organise my dinner parties, converse with my associates and you are so very able to do all these things. We shall take it gently, Addy. Starting now.'

She closed her eyes. The rhythmic stroking of his palm was once again creating those dangerous, familiar sensations within her she was so often unable to resist. She didn't want to go to the Duke and Duchess of Ridgeway's ball. The prospect was terrifying, though for reasons Tristan could never know, and it tore her apart. Being loved by Tristan was everything. She wanted nothing else in life.

And she told him so.

He kissed her brow and held her tightly. 'I'll do nothing to jeopardise what we have at last found between us, Addy. Nothing. But we have been living a fairy tale. A fairy tale I have as little desire of ending as you. The fact remains, however, that life is about to intrude on our lovers' idyll, whether we like it or not. Rather you take small steps with me by your side than that you are thrust into the glare of public interest where I cannot protect you. And as you know, that can happen anywhere. You are a well-known face thanks to Mr Gilchrist's portrait. You can create a stir merely by promenading in Hyde Park. No, Adelaide, unless you stamp your foot and beg otherwise, you will accompany me tonight.'

She didn't mind that he spoke so forcefully. Tristan had always tiptoed around her desires, fearful of seeing her slide into deeper invalidism. She admired him all the more for brooking no argument and her reward was his utter stupefaction when she appeared in shining glory, adorned in a gown of gossamer silver netting over a petticoat of palest pink sarsenet with a filet of pearls through her hair.

'Addy, darling ...' He crossed the room, arms outstretched as his admiring gaze raked the length of her magnificent ensemble. 'All London will be in raptures tonight over the breathtaking beauty of the incomparable Lady Leeson.'

She was drunk with love for him. His words were, as ever, balm for her hungry soul.

Nevertheless, she shrank from the idea of venturing forth as the sick memory of a night half shrouded in obscurity pulsed through her. She swayed on her feet and Tristan caught her.

'Addy, are you unwell?'

She opened her eyes in his embrace and rested her head not so willingly against his shoulder; he was comforting her for something for which she deserved no comfort. But no, the time for confession had passed and she had not availed herself of the opportunity. There was no point in further torturing herself. She only needed to confront James and

Beatrice in some normal exchange to break the ice and put aside her fears.

Before she could answer her husband, her mother emerged from the corridor, beady-eyed gaze taking in the scene.

'You look like you're about to brand your mark on London once more, my girl.'

This could have been regarded as bolstering talk for a daughter so long confined to the proverbial sick bed, but Addy knew her mother better than that and her skin crawled as she registered the critical glance that swept her from head to toe.

Resisting the temptation to turn away, she met her mother's hard look, struggling against the crippling ennui that threatened to sap the marrow from her bones whenever her parent's powerful will asserted herself.

Was it not unreasonable to want a normal life with Tristan? Surely it was a small enough desire for a wife? Especially one in love? Regardless of her past?

Tristan, who had been eyeing her with concern, cupped her elbow, a gesture which seemed to charge her with the necessary bravado to say proudly, 'I'm glad you like my gown, mother. Lady Halpern was with me when I selected the silk at Madame Claudette's. Tristan, shall we go?'

THE MUSIC, the smell of beeswax candles, the gaiety and excess of spirits that greeted her was overwhelming in a way it had never been before. What was wrong with her? This was what fed her desire for life; at least it had before. Now, she clung to Tristan's arm and had to force the light into her eyes as well-wishers accosted them and others appeared from nowhere to congratulate Tristan on his lovely wife's return to health.

Caught up in the centre of the room Tristan had no shortage of company in the form of politicians anxious to speak to him, for he had been absent a great deal these past weeks through his need to be with Adelaide.

They were a welcome barrier to the company Adelaide was more wary of courting.

When she saw James disengage himself from Beatrice, who was surrounded by a cluster of artistic-looking gentlemen, and come towards her, she feared she was about to faint.

Once again the sins of her past rose up to meet her. James steadied her discreetly as the blood rushed from her head and she gasped in a breath.

'Surely you expected to see me here?' His mouth quirked. 'Ah, good evening, Tristan? Yes, it *has* been a while. What? Of course I shall take Addy onto the dance floor, if that is your wish. And hers?'

For Tristan was surrounded by sober politicians and Adelaide needed gaiety, she thought bitterly. Was she not the lovely, shallow wife he loved nonetheless and whom he thought he was doing the right thing by in releasing her into the arms of his friend? Their friend?

Of course she did not resist but, oh, how her body revolted as James took her hand and held her around the waist for the first waltz of the evening. How her heart became a large stone dragging down her spirits, her joy in what she had managed to achieve with Tristan ... at such cost with this man?

'You are pale, Addy.'

She turned away from the quiet intensity of his scrutiny. 'You are holding me too tightly.'

'Why did you not reply to my letter?'

'Why did you write? It was dangerous. I threw it in the fire before I read it. Fortunately you understood me and did not persist.'

She was regal in her rebuke. The letter had come the day after … their sin, delivered to her amongst a pile of well-wishes and invitations. She'd opened it in error, tossing it upon the flames without reading beyond the first impassioned paragraph.

She heard what it cost him to force out the words, 'Would you treat me so shabbily? I forced you to do nothing you did not do willingly, Addy.'

Unable to control her trembling, Adelaide focused her gaze over his shoulder, aware he spoke the truth and hating herself as much as he in that moment. If she allowed them, her torments would consume her. For weeks she'd been looking to inhabit some plane that enabled her conscience to cohabit with reality. James's words must not find their mark. Tristan loved her as he never had. She had to salvage something from the tragic irony.

'What happened was … unfortunate,' she whispered as she clung to her dignity and managed to maintain a semblance of a pleasant smile upon her face for the benefit of observers. 'Something I deeply regret.'

'Do you?'

She refused to be deflected by the pain that clearly choked him and was reflected in his look. 'Yes,' she whispered. 'And you and Beatrice are to marry in two weeks.'

For some reason he seemed to read hope into her words. He gripped her more tightly. 'Is it on Beatrice's account – and Tristan's – that you would choose to override your happiness?'

'Override my happiness?' She brought her head round to stare at him, truly aghast at his lack of comprehension. 'Do you understand what you're saying, James? Have I not been entirely clear in my desire to forget *everything* that happened between us?' She was trembling so much she could barely force the words out. Lowering her head so that she was staring directly at his lapel, for *by God* she could not look him in the eye with the intensity that might be her undoing, she hissed, 'Because, James, Tristan is the *only* thing important to me.'

'And you only realised this five minutes after offering yourself to *me*?' Disgust dripped from his tone.

'Stop it, James. We cannot speak of it here. We can *never* speak of it, do you hear?' She swallowed painfully. 'And if you have even the smallest respect for my wishes, please make your excuses to Lady Ridgeway. The thought of encountering you again fills me with the deepest dread. Go back to Beatrice and never trouble me again.'

Pale and shaking Adelaide left the dance floor, still trembling as she was delivered into her husband's care.

'I feel faint and nauseous, Tristan,' she responded to her husband's concern. 'Please, darling, take me away from here. I need air.'

Immediately he acceded to her request and in the morning the doctor voiced the suspicions which had been niggling Adelaide for the past couple of days.

Tristan was overjoyed as he gazed at her, lying on her bed. 'It's too early to say for certain, my darling'—he knelt at her bedside and took her hands which had been resting on the turned-back coverlet, kissing her brow after the doctor's examination. His eyes shone and he could barely contain his excitement—'but it would appear that after all these years you may be *enceinte*.'

Tenderly he held her to him while Adelaide, caught between joy and trepidation, forced a smile and returned his kiss, saying in heartfelt tones she did not need to feign, 'You will be the best father this child – if it's true – could have.'

She had never seen him so transformed. He cupped her face, his look suggesting he gazed upon a vision. 'At last you shall get what you deserve, Addy. A child to bring you the joy you might never otherwise have known. The joy I'd come to fear you'd never know.' Placing his cheek against hers, he added in a whisper, 'You are too good and worthy to be denied that.'

A PREGNANCY WAS CONFIRMED and a regime of rest combined with an earlier return to the country was settled upon.

The gaiety of London would soon be but a memory; a flare of danger and excitement in an otherwise contented life, Adelaide hoped as she directed Milly which gowns needed packing for a short visit to Honeyfield, the Duke and Duchess of Veal's country seat; perhaps signalling the last events on their social calendar, together with James and Beatrice's wedding, before Adelaide's official retirement to the country.

Three days of whist before the fire, quiet evenings with a little music and Tristan by her side would, she was quite sure, be the tonic she needed. Adelaide was all too ready to shun the glare of beeswax candles and admiration and interest of her earlier life.

WITH RELIEF that the most demanding days were behind her, Adelaide settled into their comfortable apartments at Honeyfield. Ten guests had been invited, including Beatrice's Aunt Wells who was bringing Beatrice for some rest and calm before her nuptials. Adelaide, dismayed at first to learn of their inclusion, now saw this as an opportunity to forge a new understanding with the young girl she'd once hoped to shape into James's ideal.

Her last contact with James had given her little to be optimistic about. He was as much in love with Adelaide as ever so what hope did he and Beatrice have of being happy together?

Guiltily Adelaide returned the young girl's greeting as they encountered one another in the vast lobby. Adelaide had come downstairs to find Beatrice and her aunt had just arrived and were being greeted by the duchess who was a particular friend of Mrs Wells.

The younger girl drew Adelaide aside as the older women talked and servants carried their trunks upstairs.

'I'm so sorry that you've been indisposed, Addy, but I'm glad to see you're better.' The overhanging fronds of an enormous potted fern seemed to envelop Beatrice, and Adelaide was transported back to the day she'd met the young woman and talked to her by the river that ran through Deer Park.

As ever, Beatrice had been serious and self-contained, but hope had radiated from her. Now she regarded Adelaide steadily. 'James has been distracted with worry about your uncertain health, but your colour is back. You look well and you're as beautiful as ever.'

Beatrice was neatly dressed in a pale pink carriage dress with a floral festooned bonnet. She looked prettier than Adelaide had ever seen her, and confidently in control as she called after one of the servants to be mindful of her trunk which contained something valuable.

Adelaide managed the right responses while she tried to detect any suggestion of either hostility or a subtext beneath Beatrice's words.

Hiding her unease, she smiled. 'As hale and hearty as I ever was. How nice of James to be concerned. And fortunate it was not *you* to suffer ill health or he'd have been distracted with worry. We both know how passionate James can be.'

'Certainly where you are concerned, Addy.'

Beatrice looked at her with quiet intensity. Raising her chin she said, 'Let's not tiptoe around the truth. James has always been in love with you.' Her voice was very low, and with the older women only a few feet away, Adelaide felt trapped. She didn't know what to say.

Beatrice went on. 'Don't tell me you've never been aware of it because it must always have been as plain to you as it has become to me. I'm certainly not suggesting you ever encouraged James, but the fact is, I'm glad the season is coming to an end and he won't see you again until next year.'

The older women broke apart and Aunt Wells moved forward to reclaim the attention of her niece.

'I'm so glad to see you're well again, Lady Leeson,' she said. 'Come now, Beatrice. Perhaps you could pursue your conversation with Lady Leeson later this afternoon.'

But Adelaide, who had no desire to further this line of discussion, claimed that as her strength was only just returning, she needed to rest. She hoped she'd not have to encounter Beatrice alone for the rest of her visit.

SHE WAS LYING on the chaise longue a little later when, after a light knock, her husband entered the room.

Tristan smiled when he saw the thick tome she was reading. 'Mrs Elizabeth Fry?' He raised his eyebrows as he glanced at the name of the author. 'Surely you have something a little lighter? Sir Walter Scott, perhaps? Jane Austen?'

Adelaide flipped through a few more pages. 'Mama has joined Mrs Fry's Association for the Improvement of Female Prisoners and tells me Mrs Fry's brother-in-law was recently elected to parliament. In view of your similar views I am trying to educate myself.' She smiled up at him. He need not know that she'd altered the proposed speech Mr Finch had delivered the previous week. However, when they were back at Deer Park she would ensure she was given the role of unofficial secretary. 'Of course Mama derided me, saying I did it merely to impress you and I shan't understand a word of it.' She smiled and, despite her unsettling encounter with Beatrice, real happiness fluttered in her stomach as she registered his regard. 'At last I feel I am becoming transformed into the wife you deserve.'

Tristan took the report from her and to her surprise deposited it on a side table.

It was four o'clock in the afternoon and soon she'd need to dress for dinner. Their hosts were old fashioned and kept country hours, which suited Adelaide in view of the extreme weariness she now experienced at the end of each day. She was with child and determined to be both careful and joyful. She would entertain no doubts as to the rightness in maintaining that certain events in her past would be forever under lock and key.

'You always have been the wife I deserved, Addy,' he whispered, kissing her behind the ear. 'Deserved and loved more than I believed possible.'

The gentle heat of his breath ignited her need to be in his arms. They'd not made love for days, Tristan fearful of her fragile health, Addy fearful of everything else. Now she twined her arms around his neck and nibbled his earlobe.

He groaned, held her to him, then with obvious regret put her away. 'You don't know what you're doing to me,' he whispered, but she only laughed softly, pushed him gently down upon the bed and straddled him.

'Yes, I do,' she replied, hiking up her skirts which were hampering her, and placing his hand upon her naked thigh.

'We have an hour before I must dress, my darling. Your challenge is to show me just *how* much you love me.'

'Too much to do what you think I want to do.'

'Too much to do what *I* want to do?'

He did not protest, only chuckled with pleasure as she fumbled with his breeches, and set their course for a frenzied hour of insatiable passion.

CHAPTER 27

Tristan should have been working but his mind was on other things.

Besides, the keening wind which whipped the tree branches against the window panes and rustled under the door was disconcerting. Like a harbinger of doom it wailed across the rooftops, making its presence impossible to dismiss. The wind had sounded like this the day he'd married Adelaide. Perhaps it was just a foolish fancy, but he was suddenly afraid for her.

Setting down his pen, the ink dried unused on the nib, he rose and made his way to Adelaide's room, dismayed to come upon Mrs Henley obviously returning from a visit to her daughter.

'She's sleeping at last.' Clearly Mrs Henley did not wish Tristan to intrude.

'Then she will not even know that I've looked in on her.' He was not about to be deflected.

'Adelaide is a light sleeper, you know that.'

'Something's troubling her and I'm concerned. If she wakes she may want to unburden herself.' He held his temper. 'She holds great fears for this child after believing herself barren for so long.'

'As you wish.' Mrs Henley gave a curt nod as she passed on.

When Tristan cautiously opened Adelaide's bedroom door he was not surprised to find Adelaide wide awake and reading on the window seat. She looked up with a smile.

'Poetry?' He nodded at the book, adding when she nodded, 'James's?'

'Oh, no!' she exclaimed.

'Too louche for you, my darling?'

'I … I just prefer gentler poetry.' She blushed. 'He's very talented but his words are very—'

'Passionate,' Tristan supplied, seating himself beside her.

'So now you're off to attend Mrs Waring's soiree. You're looking very handsome. But then, you always do.'

He stroked her shoulders, his overwhelming fondness vying with his concern. 'You haven't always thought so.' Hurrying on, not wishing to discompose her further, he said, 'I hoped you'd accompany me. Your mother told me you were sleeping.'

'Did she? But I'm afraid I can't accompany you, darling.' Adelaide shook her head without considering it. 'I'm really not up to it.'

'You've been very quiet. It's not like you to forgo so many events in one week and it's very early days with the baby.'

It was hard to take his eyes off her face, she looked so serene and beautiful. The prospect of having their own child seemed to have imbued her with a quiet peace, the antithesis of the placid listlessness he'd become used to during the first years of their marriage. He stroked her forearm, unable to hold at bay his longing to touch her. 'I'd thought with the nausea and fatigue gone, and the fact you're not yet show-ing'—he traced the outline of her lower lip, restraining the urge to kiss her—'you might consider being the consort I'm so proud to show off tonight.'

When she dipped her head, colouring charmingly, he added, cajolingly, 'James and Beatrice will be there. As will Mr Donegal. You haven't seen your friends for some time, now.'

He felt her stiffen and he dropped his hand.

'I'm very tired today. When did you say we leave for the country?'

'Next week, immediately after James and Beatrice are wed. I know how much you're looking forward to that.'

Adelaide flicked over some of the pages in her book, seemingly absorbed in the words. 'I hope I'll be well enough to attend the wedding,' she mumbled.

Tristan sighed. 'If you desire it sufficiently, I'm sure you will be,' he said, aware that an edge had crept into his voice. Immediately he regretted his lack of care as she jerked a wary face up at him.

Despite that, he pressed his point. 'I think it would be good for both of us if we were to show a united face to society during our last few days in London.' Maybe there were occasions when she needed a firmer hand. 'I would be grateful if you could bring yourself to just look in with me, and to meet some of my parliamentary colleagues.'

For a long moment she searched his face, before she nodded. 'Of course, Tristan. I shall always put my duty towards you before my own desires.'

'Good Lord, Addy, if you put it like that—'

'No, no, it came out wrongly, Tristan!' She put out her hands. 'I meant that I would do anything for you because I *love* you.'

MRS WARING WAS a keen patron of the arts so a mixed crowd was in attendance. Poets and artists rubbed shoulders with the *ton* and Tristan smiled to see a well-known society matron ostentatiously parading her daughter before Mr Gilchrist, clearly hoping he'd paint her portrait.

Out of the corner of his eye he noticed Phineas Donegal lounging on a sofa beneath a luxuriant pot plant, talking to a group of men of letters, but James was not amongst them.

He noticed Adelaide scan the room while she clung to his arm.

A clear lovely voice floated over the crowd which Tristan recognised as the dulcet tones of Kitty Carew. He hoped he'd not come face to face with her this evening.

An aged scion of the nobility was propped up on cushions by the wall in conversation with a showy creature Tristan was certain came from theatrical ranks. Mrs Waring had indeed invited an eclectic gathering and it was odd Adelaide seemed so ill at ease. Something had been troubling her for days and he wished she would confide in him. She said it was her fears for her unborn child, but refused to cite anything specific.

Soon they would return to Deer Park and he was looking forward to it as much as Adelaide. In the country they could rusticate for the next nine months, the baby would be born and Adelaide's depressed spirits would be a thing of the past as they basked in the tenderness – no, passion – they'd unexpectedly discovered in London.

'Tristan! I hoped you'd be here.'

It was James, looking well and jaunty though a little flushed of face. Tristan was not surprised when he added that he'd just come from The Cocoa Tree.

Adelaide nodded at James before unclasping her hand, indicating that she'd been hailed by someone across the room.

'How is Adelaide?' James enquired.

'She was feeling unwell earlier but I induced her to come along, though I think it will be an early night.'

'Ah, too bad. Still, you're here and that's the main thing. Come! Champagne! Just what's needed as you tell me what you've been about. It's been an age since we last spoke.'

They procured drinks from a passing waiter and James led Tristan out of the melee to a quiet corner.

'I hope Adelaide will be well enough to attend your nuptials,' Tristan said when James made mention of them. He was surprised at the casual response of his friend. 'She's having the child she's longed for all these years. Lord knows, I'm well acquainted with the moods and strange fancies of women when they're breeding.' He gave a wry laugh. 'Hortense even had time for me.' His tone changed. 'So of course all Addy wants to do is return to the country and concentrate on you and the baby. Please don't make her stay in town on my account.'

'You really wouldn't mind?'

'The sooner you go, the better, I believe.' James clapped him on the back. 'You're a lucky man, Tristan. Adelaide is lucky, too. You deserve each other. Excuse me but I must go.' He inclined his head and took a step into the crowd, turning to say with careless abandon, 'Do what you must, dear friend.'

'James!' Tristan called him back. He hesitated when James turned, his look enquiring. 'James, I can't tell you how delighted I am that at last you're receiving the recognition you deserve.' He felt his congratulatory smile falter as he was gripped by some strange emotion he didn't recognise. James had saved his life and given him Adelaide. He owed his old friend so much and now James was at last realising his life's ambitions, yet for some reason Tristan felt fearful for him. As if, somehow, James were at greater risk than ever of the demons that had plagued him as a youth. There was something odd – something he couldn't put his finger on – about James's cavalier attitude lately that discomfited Tristan.

But perhaps Tristan was imagining it. James was no longer the wayward adolescent he'd known all those years ago. James could look after himself. At least, Tristan hoped so.

'You mean the recognition I've always craved?'

Tristan thought a shadow crossed his face, but then James was laughing his usual devil-may-care laugh. 'Thank you, Tristan, but I sometimes wish I'd been blessed with half your common sense rather than a head full of passionate nonsense.'

Tristan watched his friend weave his way through the crowd and turned to see Adelaide back by his side. She curled her hand discreetly around his before smiling up at him and his heart clutched with love. She looked so beautiful; clear-eyed and brimming with health.

If she wanted to go back to Deer Park tomorrow, he'd indulge her. If she wanted to dance each night away for the next four weeks, he'd indulge that too. The truth was, he knew he could deny her nothing.

They turned as the orchestra began to play and once again Kitty's clear, high voice floated across the room from the dais upon which she stood. She looked lovely tonight, he thought dispassionately as they moved closer to the music. Her thick red-gold hair was caught up in tiara, a style which accentuated her cheek bones. A diaphanous rose-coloured gown adorned with bugle beads hugged her shapely form.

'Do you think she's beautiful?'

'Undeniably so, but she'll never hold a candle to you, my darling.' He was surprised Adelaide had asked the question and was about to say so when he observed Mr Donegal join the tableau near the dais and whisper something in James's ear. He knew the men were fair-weather friends; that they called themselves rivals, and sometimes enemies, but that their dealings in public were always civil. Tonight, though, they were in discord and the surprise Tristan had felt at Adelaide's question turned to concern when he observed James's face contort in sudden anger as he swung round to respond to Donegal. Tristan was prevented from seeing more when a stout woman wearing a feathered headdress obscured the pair.

Kitty's voice rose in a final high note and Tristan's eyes were again drawn to her. Who funded her lavish wardrobe? he wondered as he moved Adelaide out of the way of a couple towards the dais.

Surely Kitty would not use the money Tristan paid for Tom's upkeep on herself, though he knew a woman in her profession needed fashionable, colourful clothes for her work; just as he knew a woman, alone, had not the means to support a family.

A full-time wage was often insufficient to provide the necessities of life for the working poor, now that the price of bread had soared. The injustice angered him. He'd taken up his seat for this very reason. If the season had been a success in launching Adelaide as a noted beauty, it had been equally successful for him. His arguments and concerns had been heeded, it seemed, by those in government who counted. He was disappointed he was leaving London early, but he'd continue his written contribution, with Mr Finch's help, and he'd return next year. Adelaide's well-being was his greatest priority.

Several fellow parliamentarians joined him to discuss the previous day's sitting and he introduced them to Adelaide, conscious of their admiration and even more proud of his wife when she engaged them in conversation, proving she could be lively and entertaining but that she was fully cognisant of the issues underpinning her husband's crusade. He even recognised some of the lines from Mr Finch's speech which Tristan had built upon.

He was about to whisk Addy away to the supper table when he heard raised voices in the vicinity of Miss Carew, who was now bowing to her audience. A collective murmur rippled through the crowd before Mrs Waring's shrill voice rang out: 'Artistic rivalry is so much more rewarding than the clash of swords. Come, gentlemen! Let our two resident poets take the stage and enthral us as Miss Carew has just done.'

'Tristan, I'd like to go now.' Adelaide gripped his hand tighter but Tristan resisted, drawing her closer to the stage, intrigued.

'The fun is just beginning. Don't you want to hear James recite his poetry? He'll be disappointed if you leave just as he embraces his moment of glory. You know how he likes attention.'

However, when Tristan looked closer, he saw that James didn't appear to be enjoying it right now. Mrs Waring and two eager minions had shepherded onto the stage the slender, grim-looking poets who had clearly been caught out in the midst of a private, angry altercation.

'Gentlemen, the ladies of all England are swooning over the poems of our two most illustrious poets, Lord Dewhurst and Mr Donegal.' Her shrill declaration brought a hush to the room. A couple beside Tristan jostled to get a better view.

Tristan felt Adelaide's hand convulse in his but even if he acceded to her mute signal that she wanted to leave they were hemmed in on all sides. Besides, Tristan was curious to see how James acquitted himself.

'For the entire season society has been speculating over the identity of Lord Dewhurst's mystery muse.' Mrs Waring's frog-like eyes bulged with prurient excitement. The large sapphire in the centre of her purple toque winked like another eye as she moved to the centre of the dais and began to wave James's book in the air. The crowd murmured their approval, though there was some tutting, Tristan noticed. Nevertheless, Mrs Waring held her audience captive. Or, at least, her apparently reluctant poets did.

'Who, we ask, *is* the Maid of Milan? Indeed, as the book is devoured in every salon, every drawing room, the question of identity becomes more pressing. Now Mr Donegal's new *Ode to a Comely Wench*, published only three days ago, is creating its own delicious intrigue. Come, gentlemen, indulge the assembly as they pose their questions and try to guess the identity of your mystery muses.'

Adelaide's grip strengthened as she tried to pull Tristan away. 'Please, Tristan, I'd rather not stay.'

'Darling, it's too difficult. We'll go as soon as James has said his piece.'

Coyly, Miss Carew drew Phineas Donegal, who clearly was only pretending resistance, forward, but James, who usually embraced the spotlight, was determinedly trying to leave.

It was only when the stout and flamboyant Mrs Waring reached for his wrist and drew him over to Kitty's side that he stood, staring grimly across the crowd, refusing to catch the eye of the now smirking Donegal who rubbed shoulders with him.

Tristan lowered his face to Adelaide's ear. 'Poor James. Professional rivalry has come to a head but Donegal doesn't hold a candle to him, I'm told.'

They were near the front and crushed on all sides by the rapt audience. Even Tristan felt a thrill for he was certain James was putting on an act and soon would entrance everyone in the room with his eloquence and theatrical style.

Fluttering her painted ivory fan, Mrs Waring sashayed

past the artists, head tilted coyly as she asked, loudly enough so her audience could hear, 'Mr Donegal, pray tell, who is the alluring creature who inspired your new book? Or will you make us work for the answer?'

Grinning, Donegal cleared his throat before executing a flourishing bow to his audience. He stepped forwards. 'Perhaps a stanza will make plain the goddess who inhabits its pages'—he raised an eyebrow, adding—'and my heart.'

It was clear the simpering Kitty Carew by his side was the chief inspiration for Donegal's poetic impulses as he proceeded to read a revealing description from his epic poem.

A middle-aged woman on Tristan's right whispered loudly to her husband that she couldn't wait to hear Lord Dewhurst give an account of himself and she'd yet to meet a young lady unable to resist his charms.

He glanced at Adelaide and was surprised by her lack of expression. He squeezed her hand. Perhaps she was afraid for James.

'Don't worry, he will amaze us all,' he reassured her.

Not that James looked like he wanted to amaze anyone. He appeared in a black humour; very different from when he'd greeted Tristan earlier.

Tristan leant across to attend to something Adelaide said, then glanced up at a gasp from the crowd. Kitty fluttered to the edge of the stage like an exotic plumed bird, on the heels of Donegal, who grasped at James's sleeve. But James elbowed him roughly so that the other man nearly fell backwards over Kitty, who shrieked loudly.

'I daresay there's more to this than just a few poems,' Tristan heard the red-bearded gentlemen on his left tell his wife as Tristan pushed forward, alarmed. He'd known James to overstep the mark only once or twice in his life and he didn't want to see it happen again.

Mrs Waring looked goggle-eyed as she helped Kitty onto her feet, but when she returned her attention to the audience a smug smile twisted her mouth. This was sport she clearly hadn't anticipated.

'Gentlemen, gentlemen!' she cried, clapping her hands for calm as she approached James, whose path had been blocked by several gentlemen at the bottom of the steps to the dais. 'This is not a competition as to who is the more accomplished poet. Indeed, there is nothing more than the public's desire to know—'

But James was having none of it. Shaking off restraining hands, his expression black as thunder, he strode towards the double doors, cutting a swathe through the crowd before him.

Tristan, turning to go after him, looked down as a mauve gloved hand was laid on his forearm.

'James has left me?' Beatrice's large brown eyes mirrored Tristan's shock.

He'd not known his friend's betrothed was here this evening. But to think that James had abandoned Beatrice was as incomprehensible to him as it must have been to her. 'James begs your pardon and has entrusted your wellbeing to me,' Tristan lied.

Beatrice chewed her knuckles as she stared at the door through which James had just departed. Mr Donegal was speaking on stage and the attention of the audience was divided. Tristan lowered his head so he could hear her.

'Please, Lord Leeson,' she begged, 'I must go after him.'

'Your chaperone—'

'It's Adelaide. Did she not tell you? Aunt Wells felt unwell and left me in her care.' She touched his wrist briefly in entreaty. 'Please, Lord Leeson?'

Tristan looked over his shoulder for Adelaide. She was

right behind him but her face was blank. Perhaps she'd not heard Beatrice's question, or understood the situation.

'Beatrice, James is in a wild mood. It would not be appropriate.'

'If I'm to be his wife in three days, my lord'—she gripped his wrist and her face contorted with sudden anger—'I *will* go after him. Adelaide? Will you come?'

CHAPTER 28

Tristan stepped into the chill night air in time to see James leap into a passing hackney, shouting directions. The moon hung low in the sky, burnishing the streets with a waxy yellow glow.

Something had upset James deeply and although it was dramatic behaviour for a public event, Tristan had seen him in similar black moods. Whatever James's reasons for rushing off, it was not right to subject Beatrice to them.

He swung round, about to go back inside to tell the ladies that he was unable to arrest James's departure, but nearly knocked into Beatrice who'd come up just behind him and was speaking rapidly to the butler.

'Here's James's carriage now! Bunting has just brought it round!' she cried, pointing to the coachman who was climbing down from the box of the commodious equipage James had bought as a wedding present to his wife.

Drawing Adelaide with him, Tristan hurried after Beatrice, who was giving orders for Bunting to follow James. He'd leapt into a passing hackney which was now just disappearing around the corner. Guests were milling nearby, senses no doubt attuned to any hint of scandal. Tristan couldn't let Beatrice travel alone.

He called after her and she looked up as Bunting held the door. Taking in her mutinous expression, he decided there'd be less of a scandal if he tried to persuade her to go home once they were in the carriage rather than risk a public scene, here.

'I will not be abandoned without learning why,' Beatrice muttered under her breath once he and Adelaide climbed inside the vehicle before it lurched forward. There was no trace of the shy submission that had concerned Adelaide when she spoke of James needing a wife with the strength to keep James in check. Adelaide, by contrast, was silent and withdrawn, her eyes closed as she leaned back against the squabs across from him.

'Addy, should we take you home first?'

She shook her head, her eyelids fluttering open, her expression one he couldn't read. 'No, Tristan. Beatrice needs to know what has upset James. It would be wrong to put myself first.'

The glow of the moon lit up the carriage interior. As Tristan reached to clasp his wife's hand, the carriage careened around a corner, throwing them upon each other. He realised it was madness to be racing hell for leather after a disgruntled James. That was Tristan's job for later – when he was alone.

'Addy, we must go home. Think about the baby—'

Adelaide cut in before he had a chance to push his point. 'Both the baby and I will be fine. It's Beatrice we must worry about.'

She sounded grim and Tristan noticed the hesitant look Beatrice sent his wife. But she said nothing and the carriage continued its course for what seemed an eternity until it eventually ground to a halt, well beyond the metropolis.

Through the window Tristan saw they were by a large expanse of open land bordered by hedgerows, the full moon making long shadows of James now fleeing across the marshy turf.

Dear God, and there was Donegal in hot pursuit. He'd not seen the other man leave the assembly.

It was an incongruous sight, both men in evening clothes, labouring over the uneven ground as they raced towards the distant woodland, like the devil was snapping at their heels. Beatrice was halfway out of the carriage before Tristan could stop her. He caught a snatch of discussion between the two coachmen, the hackney driver being of the opinion the men were up to nefarious activities and that the silver-topped cane left in his hackney would cover his costs.

Before Bunting could respond, the man had cracked his whip and set his horses on a course for town.

Adelaide already had one foot upon the top step and was following Beatrice outside when Tristan gripped her wrist. 'No, Addy. I can't subject you to whatever it is going on between James and Donegal. It has nothing to do with you.' Over her shoulder he called to Beatrice, 'Please come back, Beatrice. This is no place for a lady. I'm taking you home.'

He reached for Beatrice's arm but she pulled away from him, starting in the direction of the men, an unlikely figure in a delicate pale green ballgown and flimsy slippers that sank into the mud.

'Adelaide—'

Adelaide stared up at him, acquiescent for the moment, but determined. So unlike the Adelaide he knew. Her lip trembled but her voice was firm. 'Beatrice needs my support. You have no choice but to go with her ... and I'm coming too.' She swung away from him, hurrying after Beatrice who was now running to keep up with the men. The black-clad figures were small shapes in the distance and clearly unaware of their pursuers.

Tristan snatched off his low-crowned beaver and tossed it onto the seat as confusion and indecision warred within him. It was a completely ludicrous situation. Both women were throwing caution to the wind, risking reputations and ruining ballgowns, to get to the heart of what lay between the obvious but unexplained antipathy between James and Donegal.

Clearly more was at play than Tristan had first believed; but what did Beatrice and Adelaide know or suspect that he didn't?

A brisk wind whipped his face and, drawing level with the ladies about one hundred yards across the field, Tristan drew them into the shelter of a copse of trees a short distance away from James and Donegal. The men's angry exchange which had been borne indistinctly upon the wind became clearer now. Tristan put his arm about Adelaide's shoulders but she took a step forward, taking up a position of solidarity with Beatrice.

Alone, he watched them cling to one another as James turned suddenly to face Donegal, a self-satisfied sneer on his lips, dark eyes glinting in the moonlight.

The men faced each other with clear loathing, sizing each other up in the middle of a small clearing.

Donegal's voiced came in puffs of frosted air as he derided his rival, circling James like a predator, while James turned in increments to keep eye contact, hatred curling his lip. He tossed back his head.

'I'd have called you an inferior poet before I called you a coward, Dewhurst, but tonight you've proved yourself both.' Donegal's gait was unsteady but his grin confident.

An owl hooted, the sudden flapping of its wings in the tree above startling them.

Donegal and James were about to resort to fisticuffs and Tristan had to get the women away.

'Their quarrel has nothing to do with you ladies,' Tristan muttered. 'You mustn't be exposed to this. Beatrice, you must come home now.'

'It has everything to do with us, Tristan.' Adelaide turned to look at him over her shoulder. He felt her distance, her coldness, and a strange emotion, almost like fear, gripped him.

A feeling he had no time to dwell on as James's angry shout punctuated the air. 'I called you my friend, Donegal!'

He turned to see Donegal shrug. 'Friendly rivals. Isn't that what we've always been?' He raised his hands, palm outwards. 'But a woman changes everything.'

'Enough!' Moonlight flashed off the steel blade of the knife James now waved menacingly in front of him. 'I paid you for your silence not once, not twice, but three times, Donegal. When will it end?'

Donegal laughed a bluff, confident laugh. He'd been drinking. It was too much. James was courting grave danger. Tristan moved forward. He needed to break this up before it got ugly. He was a few yards away, downwind and as-yet unobserved but about to declare himself when Donegal's words drew him up short.

'You'd pay to the grave to protect the precious reputation of the woman you love, Dewhurst, so why would I stop?'

'For God's sake, *shut up*!' James lunged, waving the knife, and Donegal did a parody of a few dance steps, throwing his head back as he let out a cackle. 'Too amusing, Dewhurst. First you try to bamboozle society by claiming credit for your fine poems, and now you think you can frighten me off with your fierce fighting abilities.'

'By God, I'll use it!' James threatened.

Donegal continued to taunt him. 'You claim to have written *The Maid of Milan* but it was actually the Maid herself who wrote those poems, wasn't it?' Donegal chuckled. 'Not that she'd claim credit, would she? Hardly in a position to. A politician's wife must conduct herself with more decorum than most.'

The small hairs prickled the back of Tristan's neck. He listened, his mouth dry. This was more than simple professional jealousy. He needed to hear James defend himself. James surely would not have palmed off someone else's work as his own. And the woman Donegal referred to was not Beatrice, clearly.

'Three poems. That's all she wrote. And I would defend her to the death, so just be warned, Donegal.' James sounded strangled.

'A fine way to repay the woman you love, eh? Claiming her work as your own then seducing her in Gilchrist's studio? Oh, yes, Kitty told me all about it. She was there, don't you know? Listening to it all from the curtained bed. Gilchrist proved too much the gentleman to come after you for a little something to keep his mouth shut, and the lady's reputation safe. Or was he too cowardly? Not something of which I could be accused. I could ruin you both, Dewhurst, so you'll have to keep paying, won't you?'

'Don't come any closer, Donegal. I'm warning you—'

Tristan was torn. Should he intervene or should he get the ladies away? What if James really did harm Donegal, rather than just threaten him? He could never forgive himself if he'd made the wrong call.

For the moment they were safely sheltered within the copse of trees which hid them from James and Donegal.

But no sooner had Tristan decided to lead Beatrice and his wife back to the carriage and leave the men to fight their own battle when he heard James hiss, 'Addy thought you her friend yet you would ruin her with no qualms?'

Adelaide? Confused, he looked back at his wife, who stood several yards away. Her expression was inscrutable. She did not meet his gaze. He saw she was too busy staring at the two men. He saw his horror reflected on Beatrice's face as she pushed away from Adelaide in the same moment James shouted, 'Well, Donegal, what of it? Yes, I would give up my life for hers, and you know it, but this has gone far enough.'

'Then pay me what I ask.'

'I've paid you more than enough.' James's face was dark with anger. 'I told you, three times I've come up with the blunt to satisfy your grubby blackmail demands and I won't do it any more.'

Blackmail? Adelaide and James? Across the small distance that separated them, Tristan finally met his wife's gaze before she looked away. Her eyes were dull, her features marred by defeat and misery. Her radiance had deserted her. Even the mantle of beauty that clothed her in her moments of vulnerability had fallen away.

He dropped the hand he'd extended towards her, and in the void where once his heart had beat with determined energy to be her one true saviour, a new cognisance took up a painful tenancy.

Snatches of James's poems darted through his mind, wisps of memory tugging at him, coalescing into blinding realisation.

Adelaide was the Maid of Milan.

He doubled over, a searing pain in his chest cavity as the words chased themselves round and round his brain, mocking him, taunting him for the fool he was.

Adelaide was James's Maid of Milan.

Adelaide was the woman over whom James was being

blackmailed; Adelaide was the woman Donegal claimed Kitty had seen in Gilchrist's studio … in James's arms.

Adelaide was – dear God, no! – the woman to whom James had been making love?

Bile rose up his throat while disbelief warred with a slow burning rage. Straightening, he returned his focus to Adelaide's face and saw the guilt that branded it like a malignant birthmark, distorting her beauty, while Beatrice, ashen-faced, swayed at her side.

'Adelaide—?' He could barely say her name.

She did not defend herself, merely clutched at her tattered pride, pushing back her shoulders as she sent them both a cold stare.

Beatrice made a small movement and Tristan's shock turned to something more murderous. They'd both been fooled: Beatrice and himself.

And then a blood curdling cry rang out and they all swung round to see James and Donegal wrestling on the muddy ground.

Adelaide was the first to respond, Tristan following. Despite her betrayal, his first instinct was to protect her. She might throw herself into the fray to shield the man she loved and he couldn't allow her to risk harm, regardless of where her loyalties lay.

The pain in his chest grew in proportion to the void he sensed would soon consume him, but action would be his salvation.

Catching up with her, Tristan threw out his arm to deflect Adelaide as they drew level with the wrestling men. There was no question that his first priority was to get the knife away from James before someone was hurt. It was up to him to defuse the situation, to remove all weapons and the capacity to kill. James was no fighter and Tristan owed James his life.

Yes, regardless of what James had done, he had saved Tristan from certain death and Tristan would never forget it, even in the midst of his murderous rage towards the friend he'd loved above all others.

The friend who had betrayed Tristan with his own wife.

CHAPTER 29

The throbbing pain was a blessed relief.

Adelaide crawled up from the mud where she'd been flung by the force of Tristan's side swipe. An irony, considering all the tender care he'd expended their whole marriage to keep her safe.

But isn't this where she deserved to be? In the mud, begging his forgiveness?

Except that she would not beg. And Tristan would not forgive. Her husband had learned enough of the sordid facts to be resistant to the begging of a woman he could only consider beyond redemption. She knew that.

So she stayed where she was, on her knees, watching the scuffle with a strange detachment. Vaguely she wondered where she'd go after this was all over. Tristan might despise her but he had too much honour to force destitution upon her. Not just because he had his position to maintain but because he was a good man.

Much too good for her.

She put her hands up to her face and began to rock, back-

wards and forwards, her mind journeying from the awful-
ness of the present through various possibilities.

She was sorry she'd ruined Beatrice's happiness. One
glance from the girl made it plain that Beatrice would never
forgive her. She dropped her hands to see that Beatrice was
safe, though tense with fear, her gaze fixed on the men who
tussled in the mud and grass.

It occurred to Adelaide that the scene she was witnessing
was a parody of her life. Lust and treachery were fighting
against honour but no one would be a victor. If it would help
she'd happily have broken up the fight by offering up herself
in whatever capacity was deemed an appropriate ransom.
She would accept the penalty handed down, exit quietly to
serve out her sentence. Hadn't she always known she'd not
yet paid her dues? It wasn't only her mother who'd rammed
the point home whenever the opportunity presented itself.

Another anguished cry brought her sharply back to the
present.

Tristan! Her heart clutched as she saw her husband hurl
himself upon Donegal and then the glint of steel as Donegal
spun round, grabbed Tristan in a headlock and positioned
his own knife at Tristan's neck.

Springing to her feet, Adelaide expelled a lungful of cold
air in a panicked scream. Dear God, if it were only possible
she'd hurl herself into the fray and take the blade in place of
her husband.

James lurched forward, obscuring her view; the owl,
whose tree harboured them, screeched once again amidst a
wild flapping of wings and Adelaide ran towards the men as
Tristan's voice rang out. 'No, James! You fool!" And, then in
more strangled tones, 'Oh God, what have you done?'

Ignoring the slipper she'd lost in her haste, Adelaide cast
herself onto her knees beside Donegal who lay writhing on
the grass.

Beside him, James and Tristan faced each other, both on their feet, eyes locked, hardened with an enmity more savage than Adelaide could have imagined.

James held up his knife. It seemed to take on a ghastly, mystical quality in the moonlight before he dropped it at Tristan's feet. 'I've evened the score, Tristan. He was going to kill you.'

He opened his mouth again, but the words he might have said were truncated in a howl of pain as Tristan's fist connected with his face.

James doubled up, holding his bleeding nose, and Beatrice ran forward, screaming.

Adelaide watched the tableau, frozen to the spot.

Tristan's expression was black. She'd never seen him look like this and it terrified her. He breathed heavily, his mouth working as he forced out the words, 'You think saving my life – twice – evens the score after you betrayed me with my wife? No, James, nothing you do will *ever* even the score.' He hauled his friend up so that James stood before him, swaying on his feet as blood streamed from his nose.

A groan from Donegal brought Adelaide's attention back to him and galvanised her into action.

'I think he's dying!' she cried. Donegal lay on his back, a look of surprise upon his face. His own knife lay discarded, nearby.

'We must get him to a doctor.' Tristan bent over Donegal and put his head to the man's chest. Adelaide could hear Donegal's rasping breaths from where she stood. 'Help me carry him to the carriage. Addy, Beatrice, are you all right?' There was no tenderness in her husband's enquiry.

Mute, she nodded, following them to James's carriage.

Fortunately it was a commodious vehicle and with difficulty they squeezed in. Adelaide was vaguely aware of her husband giving directions, then her mind went blank to all but the dull acceptance that she was a prisoner within the equipage being conveyed towards her fate, a nebulous state that stretched long into the future and over which she had no control.

She was brought back to the present when the carriage lurched to a halt. Tristan's bulk pressed her against her the squabs in the confined space but nothing in his manner suggested he was even aware of her as he leaned out of the window to shout orders to an ostler who was passing with an armload of hay. She looked past the servant and noticed they were in the courtyard of an inn.

'It's close and we want to avoid gossip,' Tristan muttered in answer to her enquiring look. He stepped out, helping first Beatrice, then herself, onto the damp cobblestones before leading them inside.

The publican, a squat man with unkempt and over-long grey hair, issued out of the tap room, his eyes widening as he took in the mud-spattered ladies. Adelaide and Beatrice said nothing as Tristan asked for a doctor. 'The best you know of,' he added. 'He'll be well paid. In the meantime, do you have a private parlour where the ladies can wait?'

Too agitated to sit once they were led to a room along the passage, Adelaide went to the window and stared into the moonlit night. She heard Tristan and James enlist the publican's help to carry Donegal to a room upstairs, and then the dull, muffled noises of the wounded man being moved. At least Donegal could shout from the pain. He wasn't dead yet. Adelaide shuddered, forcing herself not to think about it, though clearly that's exactly where Beatrice's thoughts were.

The girl's tearful words drove home Adelaide's self-loathing. 'If Mr Donegal dies James will be tried for murder and I will never forgive you.'

Adelaide turned to meet her former friend's look of hatred.

'I'm sorry, Beatrice,' she whispered. And she was. It was difficult to believe matters had come to this. She wondered what Tristan would say to her when he came downstairs. Was James at this moment revealing every sordid, dirty detail of their affair?

Tristan had heard enough on the common to discard her if he chose, but was James driving the sword in deeper ... so Adelaide would have no choice but to go to him?

'James loves you, Beatrice.' Her voice broke. 'What happened was a terrible mistake. We both realised it. I ... I don't know how it happened.'

'Don't spout virtuous nonsense to me,' the other girl spat. 'You can have any man you want, clearly. You were so confident of your beauty you knew James would not be able to resist if you offered a lure. So you did.'

'It's not that simple.'

But Beatrice didn't respond and Adelaide wasn't in the mood for offering either lame excuses or trying to defend herself. She concentrated on sending up prayers that Donegal would pull through. Then her thoughts turned to where she would spend the following night.

And the rest of her life.

She'd have made any sacrifice to still have Tristan's high regard.

IN THE LOW ceilinged bed chamber in the attic, Tristan had removed Donegal's white linen shirt which he was using to stanch the blood.

'Do you love her?' He couldn't bring himself to look at James. Rather, he focused on the wad of linen that was slowly turning crimson. Outside, a pair of tom cats screeched over territorial rights. Or perhaps they were fighting over a female.

James did not waver in his answer. 'I've always loved her.' He went to the window, silent for a moment as he stared out. The tom cats were hissing at each other in the courtyard below, but other than that the night was silent. 'I wanted her to run away with me but she wouldn't.' His voice hitched and his shoulders slumped. 'Addy loves you, Tristan. What happened between us was … an aberration.'

Donegal made a noise of disgust from the bed, the old wooden frame protesting as he thrashed with the pain. 'All very well … to say sorry … when the deed is done.' He pushed out each word with difficulty, punctuated with moans of pain.

James ignored him, turning to rest his back against the window frame. 'It was more than lust, Tristan. Addy needed something you couldn't give her.'

Tristan clenched his hands as he watched the play of emotions upon James's face. The double betrayal scored more deeply than Donegal's injury; it was perhaps fatal, too.

'My fault, then, eh?' He couldn't help his bitterness. The wife he'd thought so fragile had betrayed him with his best friend. The pain of it was almost more than he could bear. It was hard to breathe through it but he ground out, 'I wish to God you'd not tried to save my life back there. I wouldn't be dead and I wouldn't owe you anything.'

'It didn't help, did it?' James agreed ruefully, studying his nails. He hesitated then raised his face to Tristan's, his look bleaker than Tristan had seen it. 'If it's any consolation, Addy hated me when she realised what she'd done.'

'Unfortunate accident?' Tristan snorted. 'It's one thing to be cuckolded, but spare me the exaggeration. I'm not the complete fool you and she have obviously thought me since …' His mind went back to the moment James had burst into his studio at Deer Park all those months ago; he needed to assimilate the past.

He recalled Adelaide had been discomposed – unusually so – at the time. Tristan closed his eyes and tried to order his thoughts. He needed to understand how it could have happened; how his perfect, virtuous, seemingly loving wife could have fooled him so completely 'How long have you and Addy …?' He couldn't bring himself to say it.

Donegal groaned again and Tristan saw his linen needed changing. He cast around for something else to stanch the blood, striding to the door to shout for fresh linen when he could find none.

'Doctor's on 'is way,' said the maidservant who briefly attended him.

'Do you think he'll pull through?' James looked fearfully at the man on the bed then began to pace before the window, running his hands through his disordered dark locks. 'By God, if he dies I'll pay the price, but it was he who brought it upon himself.'

'Perhaps if there'd been nothing over which to blackmail you we'd not be in this situation.'

'Perhaps if you'd just paid up … it would've been better for all of us,' Donegal contributed with difficulty. His black, shadowed eyes blazed from his pallid face which was streaked with mud and blood.

James turned on him, flexing his fingers as if he'd like to put them round Donegal's neck and squeeze out what life remained. 'You tried to frighten Addy too, didn't you, Donegal?' he charged. 'Weeks ago you wrote Adelaide the note that set this course: *"I know your secret. Stay away"*. You were planning to blackmail Lady Leeson even before the events in Gilchrist's studio, weren't you? It's all because of your threatening letter to Addy that we're here.'

Donegal's thin lips curved in a grimace as his eyes flickered, trying to maintain their focus. He gave a hollow laugh. 'I don't know what you're talking about,' he defended himself, wincing with the pain of speaking, 'though it's amusing ... to think I'm not the only one who knew about you and Addy.'

Tristan swallowed, a bitter taste burning the back of his throat. It seemed he was the only one to have known nothing. 'How long were you and Addy laughing behind my credulous back?' He had to force the words out through a barrier of pain and blinding anger. 'Did it amuse you? Or did you pity me for being such a fool?'

'It wasn't like that.' James had the grace to look miserable. Unless it was an act. One never could tell with James. Just as, clearly, he'd not been able to tell with Addy.

James gripped his hands, perhaps to stop them shaking, as he hung his head. 'The only time Addy was ever ... unfaithful was in Gilchrist's studio. She didn't love me. But that night she'd sent a message to me to say you wouldn't let her go out, and I was all too happy to be seen as her rescuer. She drank too much champagne, and after some dancing she wanted to go home to you, Tristan, but I persuaded her to go to Gillchrist's studio. She nearly fell asleep standing, and I couldn't resist lying down beside her as she slept before the fire. She must have had a dream, for suddenly ... she was in my arms. I should've realised she didn't know it was me, but I thought my own dreams had come true. If it's any consolation, she hated me afterwards.' He trailed off and Tristan was silent as he sought for answers, reasons, in the bleak scenario James had just painted.

'But Adelaide loved me once.' James spoke into the silence, his voice heavy with longing.

Tristan jerked forward. It was like a light had flicked on inside his brain. 'In Milan? Oh my God, you and Addy were lovers in Milan when—'

'When I was married to Hortense. That's right.' James swung round, his mouth working. 'Your cousin, Tristan. Your dismissive, disinterested, *unloving* cousin. You and I both married young women who were the best of friends when we were such a happy foursome at Deer Park all those years ago. No point telling you we didn't both have joy of our unions. I certainly didn't.'

Tristan felt his face heat. 'Hortense was single-minded and difficult but that's no excuse to defile an innocent ... child. That's what you did to Addy, didn't you, James?' He was clutching at something to lessen the pain. Deflecting it for the moment, anyway.

'Addy loved me.' James rubbed his eyes. 'When I realised I was in so deep but that we had no future unless I publicly ruined her into the bargain, I left Vienna for Milan, but she followed me.' His eyes were black with entreaty. 'Do not cheapen it, Tristan, for she *loved* me.'

The words were like a sharp weapon chipping away at his long, confidently held perceptions: that damaged Addy had relied single-mindedly on Tristan to return her to the happy, confident creature he knew she'd once been.

'And the ... attack on Adelaide during her return?' He lowered his voice so Donegal couldn't hear.

James shook his head, and Tristan dropped his eyes to his muddy feet. So the past was *all* a lie. His head hurt as his brain churned over everything he'd ever believed, while the new information took shape. 'So, Adelaide is your Maid of Milan,' he muttered, assaulted again by images from James's poems of love and passion, of writhing white limbs and rippling titian tresses.

Donegal's rasp from the bed made them turn. 'Adelaide wrote half the poems James palmed off as his own.'

'Untrue!' James leapt forward as if he would attack Donegal once more. Checking himself, he hovered by the injured man's side, his hands clenched, his expression help-less and pleading. 'Addy wrote three poems. Three of the loveliest poems, granted. Poems that have been well received. How could I claim they were hers without destroying her reputation? I had no idea the book would succeed as it has. And I won't have you point the finger, Tristan, when Adelaide's been the one writing your speeches.'

'What a preposterous allegation!'

'It's true. You know she hates traipsing through prisons, but she has a keen intellect and she believed words are more effective. She rewrote Mr Finch's speeches when you were away. She enjoyed it, she said. It passed the time.'

The pounding in Tristan's head redoubled. He remem-bered seeing the crossings out, the inserted paragraphs, the altered phrases. Had he not noticed they were in a different hand?

'Why didn't she tell me?' *She'd shared this with James, and not himself?* He took a painful breath. 'Did she not feel she could talk to me? Tell me she was interested in ... more than I was offering her.?

'She was afraid you'd disapprove of her poking her nose into men's matters.'

A sharp rapping on the door heralded the doctor. Grey haired and stooped, he shook his head when he saw the patient and the blood-soaked linen. As he lowered himself onto a stool at Donegal's side, Tristan saw the hem of his black cloak was caked with mud. Pale blue, shrewd eyes twinkled from his wizened, wrinkled face. 'Mind, I still expect my money, for I can tell you now, I'm not a miracle-worker,' he informed them as he unscrewed his jar of leeches.

'But he'll live?' James sounded panicked and the doctor raised an eyebrow as a toothless grin split his face. 'Not likely and if you're the perpetrator of this heinous crime I suggest you make hasty preparations to flee to the continent.' He chuckled as he spooned out the leeches and Tristan wasn't sure if it was at Donegal's cry of pain when the doctor prodded his open wound, or the prospect of the dire situation facing the prospective murderer. The doctor shook out the last of the leeches and set them round the wound. 'Justice is swift and the noose rarely frays.'

The flare of fear in James's eyes touched Tristan, even as he struggled to understand.

Ignoring the doctor, he asked, 'How long have you been carrying on behind my back? I need to know.'

James evaded his look as he stepped back to the window. 'Don't torture yourself like this, Tristan. I've already told you, Addy loves you. But if you have to know, our affair ended when she was torn from my arms at the Villa Cosi four years ago.' He stared at the window, then traced his fingertip down the frosted glass. 'I'd gone to Milan with Hortense, who thought the warm air might help her carry her pregnancy to term. It was torture to leave Addy in Vienna, but I knew I had nothing to offer her. I was a married man.'

'So noble,' Donegal contributed with a gurgle of pain, followed by another shriek as the doctor put his fingers on his wound.

'Noble? I hoped I was. I visited you at Deer Park all those months ago as much to seek confirmation of Addy's happiness as to suggest a solution to Beatrice's need for a chaperone.'

Tristan grunted. He thought James's pain was genuine, but it was nothing compared with his. James and Adelaide. All the time he'd been throwing them together they'd been trying to deny the passion that had been their undoing four years before.

James raised his face to the ceiling. 'Then Hortense died suddenly. Before she was even cold in the ground I wrote begging Addy to marry me.' He transferred his pained gaze to Tristan's face. 'Do you remember that day the four of us walked by the river? When Beatrice and I were staying with you at Deer Park? I asked Adelaide why she'd not replied to my letter. Do you know what she told me?' He gave a short laugh before answering his own question. 'She said because there was now no point since my letter arrived the day after she wed you. *She* was now the married one.'

Tristan grappled with the implications. The kernel of dread and disgust in his gut grew larger. Dear God, Adelaide had been in love with James when she'd arrived at Deer Park with her mother four years ago. Her listlessness and ... repugnance stemmed from her grief at having been *parted from James*. He closed his eyes and concentrated on his breathing. Why had he not seen it? Considered the possibility? Had he been a blind fool?

He forced himself to look at James, to see beyond the mud spattered clothes and the sweat-streaked face, haggard in the moonlight that spilled into the room. His dearest friend ... his wife's lover ... from long before she'd known Tristan. 'Tell me about the rape? The French renegades?'

'A fabrication. Mrs Henley concocted the fiction to explain Adelaide's lack of ... enthusiasm and purity.'

How much more could he absorb? His whole body throbbed with the pain of her deception, but still it got worse. 'So she's been lying to me since the day I met her.'

'Come now, what could Addy do? Her mother told you those lies to explain Addy's past. When could she have told you that everything you believed about her was a lie? She was in too deep, Tristan. It tortured her.' He tapped the window in agitation. 'Because she was now in love with *you*, Tristan. Has been this past year or more and she was terrified of losing your regard.'

'Not too terrified of losing it to sleep with you, though,' Tristan muttered. 'Did she tell you she loved you?'

James shook his head. 'She said she never wanted to see me again. She was furious with me … as if I'd somehow coerced her. She said the past was the past and she loved only you.'

Tristan watched the doctor work on Donegal. Donegal's breathing was now more a gurgle. It wouldn't be long now. Dully, he said, 'But that's not where it ended, because Donegal was blackmailing you over what Kitty had seen in Gilchrist's studio when the two of you …' He tried not to conjure up the image of Adelaide with James. He'd be ill.

Donegal's hacking cough dragged their attention back to him while Tristan fought to contain the emotions which he could not allow to get the better of him. Adelaide and James four years ago? It made their entire marriage a lie. And yet, it was in the past, he told himself. If Addy still loved him … After all, there was the baby to think of. At last he had a child he could claim.

Shock sucked the air from his lungs. His head reeled and his hands turned clammy. When had Addy fallen pregnant? His brain spun with the calculations. God, it was impossible to know.

James was still talking in his wretched monotone, as if he truly might be able to exonerate the pair of them. 'You insisted I squire Addy around London when you had not the time, though you cannot believe how reluctant she was.' His look was accusing. 'At first she tried to invent illness, but she'd promised to chaperone Beatrice. She said Beatrice was everything I could want in a wife. That I needed someone calm and wise. Not passionate and wilful like herself. Addy said she was no longer the girl she'd been at seventeen who'd thrown herself into love with me and paid the price, ripped from my arms before her child was ripped from hers.'

Tristan swung round. 'There was a child?' Still it got

worse. He clenched his fists as he sought to contain his rage, until he could ask quietly, 'And what became of the child?'

James exhaled deeply. He began to pace again, first in front of the fire, then back to the window where he pressed his cheek against the pane. 'When Mrs Henley discovered Addy was pregnant, she sent her to a couple in the Black Forest. From all accounts they were not kind to her, though they looked after her until her confinement. Shortly after the birth Mrs Henley took Addy to England'—he glanced at Tristan—'where she met you.'

'I asked you,' Tristan repeated crisply, 'what became of the child.'

'Mrs Henley told Adelaide it had died.'

Tristan strode forwards and gripped James's shoulders. 'Yet it did not?'

James shook his head, unable to meet his eye. 'Hortense arranged for Charlotte to be brought to live with us after Addy returned with her mother to England.'

'No!' Tristan closed his eyes as the pain in his head scored deeper. '*Your* Charlotte is that child? Taken from Adelaide and brought up as your own?'

James looked ashen as he conceded this with a nod.

'Hortense was desperate for a child. She'd lost five, the last just before Addy gave birth. She was insistent we claim Charlotte as our own after Mrs Henley took Addy away, and why would I refuse? After all, the child was mine and would have been brought up in a foundling home, likely not to have made its fifth birthday. But Addy couldn't know. It would torment her. Mrs Henley insisted Addy be told it had breathed its last within the hour of its birth.'

Something inside Tristan – perhaps a small seed of hope that had survived everything else up to this point – seemed to die another death. All these years that Adelaide had longed for a child and a husband to love she was in fact mourning James and their child, both lost to her forever.

Carefully he asked, 'You told her the truth? When you came back to England? To Deer Park?' He realised the little seed of hope deep within him hadn't quite died. In fact, it was relying on the answer to this question. 'You told Addy that her child was with you yet *still* she declined to run away with you?'

'I've never told her.' James stared at Donegal whose ragged breathing was now a death rattle. 'I loved you too much, Tristan, to press the advantage to that extent. Besides, she had to want to be with *me*. It wasn't about the child.' Wretchedly he added, 'But she would have none of it. She claimed she'd fallen in love with you and that I must go. She said she never wanted to see me again.' He sent Tristan an accusing look. 'But Tristan, it wasn't all her fault for it was you who forced us together.'

CHAPTER 30

When Tristan went downstairs later that night Adelaide was standing by the window, staring into the night. Beatrice was asleep in a chair, an untouched tray of food on the table.

He registered the fear in his wife's expression when he came close, so as not to wake Beatrice.

'Donegal is dead.'

She gasped and moved forward, as if to seek comfort in his arms, but then she held her hand to her breast, instead, and closed her eyes briefly.

Tristan went on, 'I must make arrangements for James to flee to the Continent tonight. The risk of the hangman's noose is too great if he remains in England.'

'You would help him escape justice?' Her eyes widened. 'You who are such a vigilant upholder of the law? After all he and I have done to you, Tristan, you would still aid him?'

Tristan shrugged. 'I owe James my life. The only reason James put his knife into Donegal was to prevent him stabbing me in the throat.'

She nodded. 'I knew sentiment would not be clouding such a decision.'

'You must stay here with Beatrice and I will organise papers for you and James.'

'What?' She threw up her head, horror luminescent in her gaze. 'I don't want to go with James. I don't love James.' She drew back her shoulders and faced him squarely. 'I can understand your reasons for no longer wishing me for a wife, but you cannot make the decision to send me away with James. I've had enough of other people deciding who I'm to spend my life with.'

'I take it you refer to your mother deciding you were to spend it with me.' He hid his pain with irony.

'Yes.' She fixed him with a level look then gazed over his shoulder, into the darkness beyond the courtyard. Her voice was steady. 'I hated her for it at the time. When I received a letter from James telling me Hortense was dead and asking me to marry him, the day after I wed you, I wanted to kill myself. Mama, naturally, said I must make the best of it. The doctor prescribed laudanum which she said would dull the pain of having to give myself to you when my heart belonged to James.'

Tristan tried not to wince, visibly, from the sharp sting he felt at her admission.

Something changed in her face, though, as she went on, fixing her sad eyes on him. She raised a hand as if she might touch his arm and he found himself disappointed when she dropped it. But he did not try to touch her.

'After a year, however, I found myself no longer consumed with pain and regret at what I'd lost. I began to see you for the kind and good man you are, and to embrace what you offered me, Tristan. You were so patient and loving. Your decisions were always in my best interest, I realised, whereas James acted on impulse. He was too like me. Instant gratification fuelled him, as it did me, but time with you had tempered my worst impulses. First I admired you. Then I loved you. I realised James and I would have come to hate one another had we married.' She smiled sadly and this time touched his cheek, and Tristan thought he should have been relieved when she drew back her hand. But he was not. Still, he could not allow Addy's confession to weaken his resolve. Addy must go with James now, and learn the full truth. Lies, deception and half-truths belonged to the past.

She went on, 'So when James returned all those months ago I told him I never wanted to see him again.' She gave a short laugh. 'Ironic that you kept throwing us together, though I don't excuse myself for one moment. I betrayed you with James. I truly do not know what happened, Tristan, for it was not done consciously, but it was done. And now,' she patted her belly, not yet showing the contour of the baby within, 'I can see why you would send me away. Though it is just as likely yours, you will always question who was the father and that is no way to live.' She swallowed and a tear gathered in the corner of her eye. 'I love you, Tristan, and I don't want to leave you. Do you believe me?'

He turned away. Her pleading would be too much for him when he knew there was no choice about it. Adelaide had to go with James in order to learn what she had truly sacrificed: the child she had borne James. Perhaps a full blood sibling to the child she carried now. In a few months it may be possible to believe he had fathered it, but could he really live with the doubt and the constant reminder it would be of his wife's deception?

So Tristan knew everything, including the fact she loved him. Yet he was still sending her away, and who could blame him?

Grief clutched at her as she rested her cheek against the tavern's foggy window pane. She didn't want to go with James yet Tristan claimed James had to leave that night, that he was injured; that he could not go alone in case he took a turn for the worse.

She knew it was not true. James had suffered no injury, though it served as an excuse, of course. He was sending Adelaide away because he believed she would find herself, yet again, unable to resist the man she'd ceased loving years before.

But it was her punishment. Tristan would retreat to the country where everything would be hushed up until it emerged that the wayward Toast of London for a season had betrayed the noble politician. Adelaide could never return to society. That was another price she had to pay. Strange that she didn't care about that. She cared about Beatrice, though.

Mostly, she cared about Tristan.

Tristan had gone upstairs to make arrangements for Donegal's body to be attended to, and then he was leaving to organise for James to leave the country. With Adelaide.

A log exploded in the fireplace and Beatrice stirred, her eyelids fluttering open. Adelaide went to the girl, crouching on the worn rug beside Beatrice's chair. She looked up into Beatrice's dark accusing eyes and wished she could find the right words.

'You're going with James, aren't you?' Beatrice straightened, her expression hardening. 'Has anyone thought to ask my feelings on the matter? James has not yet formally withdrawn his offer. We are to be wed in three – no, two – days' time. Perhaps James should be allowed to make his own decision, though I've no doubt if you put yourself forward as a candidate the answer is plain.'

While the men had been upstairs Adelaide had explained the past as best she could to Beatrice. Her shame had been laid bare but she was glad. It was better Beatrice knew what had been between her and James.

'Tristan wants me to assist James to leave. I'm sorry, Beatrice.' She put out her hand but Beatrice batted it away, rubbing her eyes and blinking. She looked very young. Especially when she bit her lips and said in such a hurt tone, 'I hate you, Addy, but if Tristan wants you to go with James, I can't stop you. James will want it, too. I do have one request, though.' She drew herself up proudly. 'Will you at least allow me to speak to my intended, alone?' Her tone was heavy with sarcasm.

'Of course,' Adelaide replied, but then Tristan appeared, James looking tousled and anguished by his side, and before Adelaide could petition him on Beatrice's behalf Tristan was ushering Adelaide and James out of the room.

'I'll take you home, Beatrice.' Tristan spoke briskly over his shoulder. Beatrice had risen and was standing, lost, in the centre of the room. 'I'm sorry, Beatrice. It's late and your aunt will be worried.'

'I'm going with James.' The girl looked mutinous, glaring at them, wraith-like and shivering in her thin, ruined green ballgown. 'No one has thought to ask how I feel about what's happened. James, have you discounted me completely?'

He had the grace to look ashamed. 'Beatrice, I'm sorry—'

She cut him off. 'Sorry for what, James? I'm coming in the carriage with you so I can hear from own lips what you are sorry for.'

'It's too dangerous, Beatrice. Think of your reputation,' Tristan began, but Adelaide rounded on him. 'Following one's heart is sometimes more important than one's reputation, Tristan. Do not dictate to Beatrice.'

He raised an eyebrow. 'As I am dictating to you?'

'You have every reason to dictate to me after what I have done. Beatrice, however, is blameless and yet she is as much affected as the rest of us. Come, Beatrice.'

As James helped Beatrice into the carriage Adelaide turned to her husband.

'Goodbye, Tristan.' She touched his cheek, her fingertips seared by the contact, her mouth trembling so much it was difficult to push out the words. 'I shall take care of Beatrice. I shall do what's right by her, and I will tend to James if it's needed, but I will go no further than is necessary to ensure his safety. I will find somewhere to live quietly, away from you, if that is your wish, but I will not go with James.'

To her surprise he gripped her hand in an impulsive gesture that gave her hope. His sensitive mouth, though pressed thinly with contempt, tremble. So he still had some feeling for her that was not complete disgust?

She waited for him to speak as his eyes bored into hers, the flame of feeling within growing stronger as he maintained his hold her on. So, he didn't want to let her go? Perhaps, indeed, there was still hope?

His words, however, were the opposite of what she'd desperately anticipated. 'James can be very persuasive,' he said softly. 'I think you know that.'

Two hours later dawn was breaking and the letters of recommendation Tristan had written on James's behalf were on their way to the docks. Tristan trusted they'd reach his former friend before the packet departed. Now all that remained was for him to acquaint Mrs Henley with matters.

He'd hoped for a few hours to digest all that had happened, but as he was leaving his study he was confronted by Adelaide's mother in the passage, a shawl over her night-gown, her small eyes assessing him beneath her night cap.

'Where is Adelaide?'

He might have said she'd gone to bed, but Mrs Henley seemed to sense something was wrong. 'With James,' he replied. He was in no mood to pander to anyone right now. 'She's gone with James to France. I shall make arrangements as to how we proceed once I hear back from them. A great deal has happened tonight.'

'It would seem,' she said dryly. She watched him rearrange some papers on his desk while he tried to ignore her. In the lengthening silence, she muttered, 'Clearly then, you know everything.' She took a few steps forward and rested her bony frame against the back of the sofa as she regarded him.

He straightened as he prepared to hear what she might have to contribute. She looked much smaller in her night attire, her little black eyes blazing with self-righteousness from her wizened face, her voice a nasal whine.

'I might have known it would come to this.' Mrs Henley sniffed. 'Adelaide was destined to throw her life away, a slave to her wanton impulses. Her mother was an actress, you know.'

Tristan jerked his head up at her words, delivered almost conversationally. Mrs Henley had wrapped her shawl tightly around her and her mouth was a thin line of disapproval. 'My husband's whore, though you're the only one to know it aside from me. You might as well since it explains a great deal.'

Anger welled up inside him as his mind churned with what this might have meant for Adelaide. 'What does it explain, exactly, Mrs Henley?' he asked crisply.

'Her behaviour. Adelaide was always seeking the limelight from the time she came to us as a babe. I did my best to curb her attention-seeking but she was impossible. Tainted by her mother's blood.'

She brushed past him to seek the warmth of the small fire still glowing in his study, as if she intended to regale him with a litany of Adelaide's misdemeanours. Tristan followed reluctantly, though part of him wanted to learn more of the wife he did not expect to see again.

Perhaps, instead of dwelling on the pain in his chest and the shock of learning their entire marriage had been a sham, it would be a tonic to turn his attention to his mother-in- law.

'Clarabelle Mountjoy was Adelaide's mother's name and I'd have scratched her eyes out had I got the chance, so for once, Tristan, I believe our feelings are in accord.'

He stared at her. No, their feelings were not in accord, even now, for vengeance would not make him feel better.

He'd often wondered how Adelaide, so vibrant, so beautiful, could have been related to joyless, prune-faced Mrs Henley. If he hadn't been so astonished he'd probably rejoice. 'You took in your husband's child, Mrs Henley?' he clarified.

She nodded. 'Mr Henley was about to take up his posting in Vienna when our only child died.' The first suggestion of real sorrow crossed her features. 'I knew my husband had a mistress but did not know the child existed until he brought Adelaide home the night we were due to set sail for the Continent. He told me the mother had been killed in an accident and his child had no one. That we would bring it up and pass it off as our own dead Adelaide.'

The hissing fire and the rumble of carriage wheels from the road outside were the only sounds to break the expectant silence.

'You cannot have embraced such an idea, Mrs Henley.

She shook her head. 'I loathed the child, but my husband was insistent. Adelaide went away to school as soon as she was old enough. Her father doted on her when she was home, and indulged her wicked excesses, but when Mr Henley died, I was determined to ensure Adelaide's soul would not go to the devil.' She gave a bitter laugh. 'I was not in the least successful for the moment her schooldays were behind her and she came to live with me she met James.'

Tristan's mind worked quickly to assimilate this new information. He thought of everything he'd learned tonight about Adelaide and James. So many shocking revelations. Had he been blind to what was right before him? Mrs Henley claimed Adelaide had wished to be an actress yet Mrs Henley was clearly well versed in maintaining a life-long charade, herself. He decided to challenge her. Adelaide was gone and, though it would be too late, it would be some comfort to learn Mrs Henley's version of the truth.

'You concocted the lie that Adelaide had been attacked by French soldiers. You needed to give me a reason for why she was so withdrawn when I first met her.'

'And to excuse her impurity,' Mrs Henley added. 'I knew she was damned after what she'd done, but I needed to hide from you the truth of her wickedness. I hoped you would offer her some kind of future. You were clearly not immune to her charms.' Mrs Henley's lip curled. 'But Adelaide was too steeped in sin to make the most of the opportunity you offered her. It was inevitable you'd one day have discovered her true nature, Tristan.'

He rose suddenly. Like a wave breaking he remembered what Adelaide had said about Mrs Henley's methods for calming her. '*You* insisted Adelaide take laudanum to quell what you saw as dangerous impulses, didn't you? It was more than medicinal.'

She shrugged as if what she'd done were of no account.

'You'd have been disgusted if you'd known the passions that corrupted that girl's wicked nature. I did everything I could to prevent Adelaide revealing what she really was. So I monitored her moods through varying amounts of laudanum. For a long time it worked.'

His brain did some rapid calculations as he dwelled on what she'd left unsaid. 'But when it stopped working you had to come up with some other method to ... control her.'

Mrs Henley smiled. 'Do you mean the letter?'

He tensed. 'What letter?'

'The one I sent to Adelaide just after the political dinner you hosted? Her smile broadened and she chuckled, as if proud. *"I know your secret. Stay away."* That frightened her terribly. She wanted nothing to do with anyone and locked herself up in her room for days.'

Tristan recalled those few days, remembering what James and Donegal had said tonight about the threatening letter. Yet again Tristan had seen Adelaide's withdrawal as symptoms of a weak mind. He'd thought plenty of rest and lack of excitement were the answer at the time.

If he'd only known the truth.

Yet how would he have felt had he known of Adelaide's past affair? Of her intimacy with James? He ran his hands through his hair, wincing.

Adelaide's affair had ended before she'd met him. And Tristan had to acknowledge he'd been so in love with her he'd have forgiven her anything just to have her promise to be his bride.

The truth might not have been palatable but if he'd got past that point he'd have also learned the truth of her vibrant nature with time. He'd have managed Adelaide and their marriage so differently. *Managed?* That's what Mrs Henley had done.

He cut off the thought.

'I had not known about the letter, Mrs Henley, though James mentioned it tonight. He was being blackmailed and thought the letter you wrote was from the man blackmailing him: Phineas Donegal. He and Donegal fought over the allegation and Donegal died from his wounds a short while ago.'

She'd hear about it in the news-sheets sooner or later. He breathed deeply then began the litany of events in a toneless voice. 'I have just come from Donegal's bedside. Adelaide and Beatrice witnessed the fight after James accused Donegal of writing that letter. The letter *you* wrote, Mrs Henley. When we carried him to the inn and waited for the doctor, that's when I learned everything. Everything you've spent years trying to hide regarding Adelaide's affair with James. So I have sent Adelaide away with James, knowing now how much she'd loved him while she'd been coerced to wed me. They're waiting for the next boat to France. James had no choice but to leave the country, otherwise he would face trial for murder here in England. I couldn't see that happen when he'd just saved my life.'

Mrs Henley no satisfaction, for after all, that put her in a tenuous position. 'You know Adelaide does not love James?'

'That may change when she realises his child, Charlotte, is in fact the child she bore him and which you spirited away, Mrs Henley.'

She sniffed. 'Adelaide could hardly have claimed Charlotte. But you're wrong if you think she'll stay with James when she loves you. I tried to temper Adelaide's growing feelings for you. I was afraid you would be disgusted by her … enthusiasm.' She shrugged. 'Of course, she's ruined now, and she cannot stain the good name you are only just making as a politician. She'll just have to make her own way, as I daresay you'll expect me to make mine. I trust I won't be left completely destitute.'

'You were well provided by your late husband.' He spoke

dryly though his thoughts had returned to Adelaide. What was she doing now? How would she manage? *Did* she really love him? Yet how could she when she had deliberately slept with James; not only her past lover and the father of her child, but her husband's best friend? Could she have done anything more calculated to extirpate any charitable feeling Tristan might have for her?

A blinding flash of cognisance tore through him. Mrs Henley was already turning but he cut her off at the door. 'It wasn't Adelaide who ordered the medications at Mendelssohn's Apothecary, was it? Laudanum, mostly, but you gave her something different the night she went to Lady Belton's ball a month ago – didn't you?'

He recalled the list Kitty had given him. There'd been some latin name at the bottom which meant nothing to him. He waited tensely. Perhaps it was some hallucinogen Mrs Henley had supposed might temper Adelaide's waywardness but which in fact had exacerbated it. James had said something about Adelaide believing herself in a dream.

He held his breath, waiting. Tristan could forgive her if she'd not been responsible for her actions. And if she did not in fact love James, she would come home to him. To Tristan.

Mrs Henley creased her brow as she recalled. 'I was at my wits' end. Adelaide didn't always drink the soothing concoctions I sent up for her. On the night of the ball she was extremely agitated. She wanted to go out and I was determined she must remain calmly in her bed, especially as you were unable to escort her to the ball. The doctor was unhelpful so I consulted the apothecary. Mr Mendelssohn gave me a different powder to put in Adelaide's milk that he said would be pleasing to the palate and offer a sedative effect.'

Tristan's scalp prickled as he waited for the answer he

prayed would exonerate Adelaide. For if she had not been responsible for her actions—

'Adelaide refused to drink it.' Mrs Henley clicked her tongue. 'Milly brought back the milk, untouched, saying Adelaide refused to take whatever calming concoction I had decided she needed. I knew, then, that I had lost an important means of curbing her excesses.' She fixed him with a gimlet eye. 'And I was right.'

Disappointment knifed him. 'Please make arrangements to leave in the morning, Mrs Henley.' He didn't trust himself to say more.

She looked outraged as she snapped the ends of her paisley shawl. 'You blame me for Adelaide's lapse after everything I have done to limit the damage her unstable nature might cause?'

'Not for Adelaide's lapse.' He shook his head, a dull, fearful sensation burning him within. He waved his hand in dismissal as he added, 'For creating the demons that have plagued her since she left Milan.'

CHAPTER 31

S he had no option but to do as her husband requested.
Leave him.

Leave him to accompany James, though to what
purpose, Adelaide did not know.

As the carriage jolted over cobbled streets, then through
the ruts of rain-gouged dirt roads, Adelaide remembered her
many clandestine meetings with James. They'd ignited her
senses and sparked life into her. As a thoughtless seventeen-
year-old she could not see past her own gratuitous pleasure,
never questioning the pain she'd cause Hortense or the fact
that her behaviour would send her to hell.

Her mother had told her so many times she was destined
for hell that the threat had lost its ability to cow her.

All that had mattered was James. He was like a drug and
Adelaide would have sacrificed anything to have been
with him.

How differently she felt now. Tristan had sent her away
with James and she felt her life was ending.

A boat would be leaving on the morning's tide. If
Adelaide travelled on it, her fate would be sealed. The

whole world would know she'd run away with her husband's best friend. She could never recover from the scandal.

But could she recover from her broken heart?

'You shouldn't have come, Beatrice.' James sounded surly and ungrateful as he faced them across the small space, the rhythmic clip-clop of the horses' hooves and the rattle of harness punctuating the tense atmosphere. 'It's four o'clock in the morning. You'll be ruined if we don't get you home before dawn.'

Beatrice squared her chin. 'Do you think I'd allow others to seal my fate when I've danced at Vauxhall later than this? If I return home what is to become of me, James?'

She seemed to be gaining a little spirit. Adelaide admired her. But what did Beatrice know of the world and did she know enough of the sordid truth to make a considered decision?

James threw up his hands and turned to her angrily. 'I've killed a man, Beatrice. I cannot marry you.'

She did not flinch. 'Well, I'm not leaving until we've had this conversation. Are you running away with Adelaide, then? Because you've always loved her? Well, I knew that from the start. I just thought that as you couldn't be with her you might, over time, form some real affection for me. Just as Adelaide has for Tristan.'

The frightened whinny of a horse pounding towards them spurred Adelaide into a more robust response.

'Yes, James, Beatrice is right. I love *Tristan*. I am here in this carriage with you *only* because Tristan requested it.' She raised an eyebrow at the single blood stain on his shirt point. 'Apparently he had grave fears for your health and wellbeing so entrusted me as your nurse. Nonsense, of course! The real reason is that he expects I will succumb to your persuasive charm yet again.' Before James could reply she turned to

Beatrice. 'As I told you, Beatrice, when the men were upstairs earlier, I love my *husband*.'

'Tristan lives by high ideals, Addy.' James looked hesitantly at Beatrice before he continued with a pointed look at Adelaide's belly. 'You cannot go back to him and he will not take you ... knowing you carry another man's child in your womb.'

'No!'

The pain of Beatrice's cry lanced Adelaide with guilt, exacerbated by the blazing hatred in the young girl's eyes. 'Surely not—' Beatrice stopped as she battled for breath. 'You did not tell me *everything* when the men were upstairs. And all this time you pretended you were my friend.'

Adelaide forced herself to hold her look. It was the least she could do. 'It was a terrible mistake.' She wished her voice were stronger. 'If I could change everything that's happened since I fell in love with my husband, I would. Instead, I continued the terrible charade my mother imposed upon me which she used to explain my childish love affair with James.' She placed her hands over her belly, saying firmly, 'Nevertheless, it is just as likely that it is Tristan's child.'

James leaned forwards to grip Adelaide's wrists. 'Tristan has not fathered a child in two marriages. The coincidence is too great. You are carrying *my* child, Addy. I know it, you know it and now Tristan knows it. You'd be living yet another lie if you ignored the truth of it.'

Adelaide snatched her hands away. 'For the first time I'm actually grateful to Kitty Carew since I can confirm that she's borne Tristan a child.' She turned to Beatrice. 'Yes, my husband's mistress before he met me. A pity I wasn't allowed similar licence before my marriage. The fact, though, James, is that you cannot use this as a weapon to entice me to go to France with you. Not that I would go in any case. I am merely here to discharge my husband's wish that I see you safely out of the country. I shall be glad to see you go! And then I shall take Beatrice home, if that's what she wishes.'

Beatrice drew in a shuddering breath. 'I shall do whatever James wishes.'

They travelled the rest of the journey in unhappy silence, arriving at the inn to be met by the publican who'd been informed of their arrival by a horseman Tristan had dispatched earlier, together with letters.

Adelaide was nearly crippled by another surge of longing for her husband. How competent he was. He'd thought of everything.

But he would not take her back. She knew that.

In the small private parlour, as they waited for the dawn to break and the tide to turn so that the next packet to France could return, James paced restlessly in front of the fire.

The two women could not sit, either. Adelaide leaned against the back of the sofa and Beatrice stared out of the window.

'You cannot stay here all night, Beatrice,' James muttered. 'I can't ruin you, too.'

'You won't ruin me if you take me with you. There's nothing for me if I remain in London. I won't get a respectable offer, now. Adelaide's told you she's not accompanying you to France. If she can learn to love Tristan for his quiet calm and strength, you might do the same.'

Though she spoke in a measured, level tone, Adelaide saw the hope in the young girl's eyes and her heart clutched.

If only *she* had hope.

The pain was getting harder, not easier, to bear. It was pointless to stay when she'd made up her mind. James had his letters of recommendation from Tristan and a boat to board. He had Beatrice and that, really, was the only reason she was delaying her departure. Perhaps there was some chance of happiness for Beatrice, once the pain of all that had happened had somehow been diluted by time.

She took a couple of steps towards the door and turned. 'Goodbye James. I'm sorry it ended like this.'

'No!' In two strides he was at her side, dragging her to him. The nervous energy that had always reminded her of a caged lion now seemed nothing more than restless dissatisfaction. James was used to getting his way. But he'd not get it now, she thought as he growled, 'It'll never end, Addy. You and I were destined to be together. Are you so cruel that you'd give yourself to me, only to throw it back in my face and leave at the first opportunity?'

'That's not the way it happened and you know it!' Adelaide flung back, the remorse and pain surging back up and swamping her once more. She opened her mouth to say more but then the sobs came. Pulling away, she covered her face with her hands. 'You're killing me, James! I never sought your attentions when you came back. You said you wanted to ensure I was happy with Tristan. And I was. But you ruined everything, James. Just as you ruined me before.' She began to cry harder as the realisation dug deeper of what she'd lost. The floor was cold and hard and she welcomed the discomfort as she sank to her knees. She wished she could sink right through it, into eternal oblivion. Instead, she felt James's arms enfold her as he pulled her against his chest.

She fought herself out of his embrace, rising shakily then began to pace, but he moved in front of her. 'Come away with me, Addy,' he begged, gripping her arm. 'Tristan won't take you back. Not after everything that's happened.'

'How can you saw speak like that with Beatrice in the same room?' Adelaide demanded. 'You are cruel, James, you've always been cruel and self-obsessed with never a thought for anything but your own pleasure.'

'Addy, don't you see, we deserve each other. We're cut from the same cloth: passionate, restless … immoral.'

She turned her blazing eyes upon him. 'James, I've singed my wings at your flame once already. No! I'm not coming back to incinerate my soul.'

The flare of hope that had animated his features dissipated. He looked ashen, his mouth turning downwards as his hands hung at his sides. 'How can you say such things,' he muttered, 'when we both know how much we are to one another?'

'*Were*, James.' *Dear God, would he not understand her?* 'I fell in love with my husband a year ago and that love has sustained me … given me a strength I did not believe I possessed; a passion for life I'd not felt before. Tristan's goodness is what I crave. I'm no longer the girl I was when I loved you. I'm someone completely different. I've moved beyond that and so must you, James, if you are to survive.'

Adelaide knew from his clenched jaw and the tic at the corner of his temple that James was trying to rein in his emotions. She knew so much about James.

She didn't know if she could survive much more.

She made to move towards the door again, but the bleakness of his voice stopped her. 'You'd just leave me?'

He sounded as if he could not believe it.

'James, I don't know what I'm going to do, but I can't stay with you.' She was desperate for him to understand.

'You're willing to take a gamble on the unknown when you know how good we are together?'

The pain in his voice lanced her but she stood firm. 'James, I realise your future is endangered on account of me. God knows, I'd repay you any way I could, but not with my love. I can't do that.'

Her hand was on the door knob now. She *was* leaving.

Soon she'd be free.

'Addy, there's something you don't know.' Something in the meaningful resonance of his words hit their mark. She turned and met his blazing gaze. He took a step forward, slowing, extending his hands as if afraid of frightening her. Her breath caught. There was something more? How could there be? Everything that had been between them had been laid bare.

'It's the real reason Tristan sent you to me.' He swallowed. 'It's the reason he believed would make you want to return to me.'

He was relentless. Over his shoulder she saw Beatrice leaning against the window, wide-eyed as her fiancé moved slowly towards Adelaide. She shook her head, shrinking from his open arms.

Undaunted, breathing heavily, he went on, 'It's about our child, Addy. The child you bore me; the child your mother said died. It's not true, Addy. The child lives.'

She heard the shrill cry of a seagull outside the window and the heavy flap of sails and rigging as sailors prepared the packet in the harbour ready for departure; the boat on which James would have Adelaide travel with him.

With growing dread she steeled herself to hear her greatest joy subsumed by her greatest sorrow, and she had to grip the door knob to stop herself falling as his voice, merciless, went on, 'It's my child, Charlotte. The child Hortense and I claimed as our own."

CHAPTER 32

This was not happening to her. Surely it was a lie? More lies. She wanted to scream to block out the sound of his voice but he would not desist.

Covering her face with her hands, she had no choice but to listen; try to stop herself from crumbling while the torture continued.

'Hortense lost the child she was carrying when you last saw her. Afterwards she took it into her mind to adopt Charlotte. Our child, Addy. I made no objection in the face of her determination. Why would I when it was mine and I believed we might one day be together, you and I?' His tone was pleading but she could hardly bear to look at him. 'Addy, Charlotte has been living with my sister in the north. She's the most winsome child you could meet. Adorable. Like you, she has titian curls and a smile that would melt an iceberg. All you need do is say the word, come away with me, and we will be a family again. The family we were meant to be.'

He was speaking as if she would be overjoyed to hear it.

Instead the rage and pain inside her grew in proportion to her helplessness. No, it couldn't be true. This wasn't how it was meant to be. Not with James dangling this carrot of hope and happiness before her.

It was getting harder to breathe. He swam before her eyes, blurred at the edges while she tried to suck in air, but her lungs could not expand. Blackness enveloped her. Swaying, she found herself in James's arms, his breath warm against her cheek as he begged again, 'Come away with me, Addy. Please!'

Finally she found the breath to shriek, 'Get away from me!' With all her energy she pushed out of his embrace and fell, shaking against the mantelpiece while the import of his words screamed in her head. *Her child lived? The child her mother told her had died? A child that had in fact been claimed by James ... and he had never told her?*

She brought her hand back and struck him hard across the cheek, screaming while the tears ran down her cheeks. 'You lied to me! You're just like my mother! You want to control me and you think you can do it with your lies, revealing the truth like some great magician ... thinking I will just dissolve into love and gratitude before you.'

'You cannot return to Tristan, Addy. I have Charlotte in my care. *Our* child. You're carrying *our* child. You have no choice but to go with me.' The anguish in his voice only made her more desperate to escape.

But to what? What future did she have if she didn't go with James and return to the child she'd thought dead? What future was there for the child she carried?

Despairingly she pressed herself against the wall, covering her face with her hands and weeping. 'I don't love you anymore, James. I can't go with you.'

'Tristan *sent* you. He *wanted* you to go with me, Addy—'

'I don't know why he sent me. He had no right. You don't need me, James. Neither as your nurse or as your lover because we would make each other miserable.'

She dropped her hands and looked at Beatrice, suddenly calm. Weariness and pain coursed through her, but she had some understanding of her responsibilities. Quietly she said, 'I can understand why you hate me, Beatrice, but please come with me now so I can deliver you home.'

'I'm going with James.'

'What?' She and James uttered the word in unison.

Beatrice met their shock with defiance. 'Perhaps it's as my Aunt Wells says, I will always be a martyr to hopeless causes, but unless James forbids it, I will travel to France with him.' She shrugged. 'If I go with you, Adelaide, I will still suffer the stain of James's crime. My reputation will be damaged regardless and I will be the subject of whispers and speculation. I would rather take my chances and go with James. Forge a different future and perhaps even find love, as you did, Addy, for it came when you least expected it.'

Adelaide stepped towards her, halting at the coldness of her reception. Still, she tried. 'You forget that I have lost everything, Beatrice. You risk the same if you do not come with me. What kind of future is that?'

Beatrice ignored her. 'James, Addy will not go with you. I know you don't love me like you love Adelaide, but will you marry me if I go to France with you?'

His laugh was a cold, bitter sound. 'God knows why you'd want that after all you've learned and heard tonight.' He contemplated her as if seeing her for the first time and Adelaide watched his chocolate brown eyes darken with some indefinable emotion. Perhaps because Beatrice was braver than he'd thought? She was certainly braver than Adelaide.

He shrugged. 'Yes, I'll still marry you. I do have some shred of honour.'

CHAPTER 33

Tristan paced his study, like the wild beasts he'd seen incarcerated in the Tower. Slowly the pieces had come together, the truth constructed like a jigsaw puzzle, painting him not as the caring husband but as his wife's unwitting jailer – at Mrs Henley's pleasure.

He winced at the irony. Had Addy paced like this when she'd been confined to her bedchamber, her strong will forced into submission by Mrs Henley's threats?

The idea sickened him, as did the knowledge he was already too late to stop Addy leaving on the packet to France. It was like a lead necklace, weighing him down, for it had been four hours since he'd despatched his wife in the care of his best friend – or was it the other way round? – to the docks.

Added to the sick knowledge of the truth his own culpability.

Yet despite that, Addy had claimed she loved him; had begged to stay, whether or not he forgave her. And *still* he'd sent her away, compounding his mistakes of the past: unable to see what was right before his nose.

He tossed down his whisky. What was he doing still at home if he considered himself a man of action?

He'd remained because some tiny piece of hope had lodged in his mind that if Addy truly loved Tristan, she would return to him. That in a few minutes she would be framed in that doorway, her red-gold hair cascading down her shoulders, haloed in the morning sunlight, her lovely face angled towards him wearing an expression of heartfelt entreaty as she begged that he take her back.

God, he'd take her back in a flash, but he'd sent her away with not the slightest suggestion he understood or forgave her for anything.

The boat had sailed and Addy had left for her new life with James.

What other choice had he given her?

Cursing himself, he slammed down his glass and stared into the pale morning sky and then at the half finished bottle.

Whisky at this hour?

The fact he'd been up all night was no excuse. Tristan was a man of moderation. It was why he believed his measured, steady approach to be just what Adelaide needed.

Thanks to Mrs Henley, it was the opposite of what Adelaide needed.

What if Tristan had revealed the natural passion that lurked beneath the surface, ready to undermine his best efforts at calm? In his own way he, also, had been living a lie, subduing his instincts to accommodate his lovely wife.

But all the time she'd pretended otherwise, she'd wanted passion.

Admiration. Gaiety. She admitted this freely, as if it tainted her.

Addy's image of herself had been tainted by her mother – the woman she believed to be her mother – and the poison had seeped deep. She'd hated herself for what she'd been given to believe were wicked traits. She'd been told so many times she'd been born to sin, it was inevitable she'd fulfil the prophecies.

The clanking of buckets as the housemaids began their work heralded the start of a new day.

Mrs Henley would be packing her bags. She would likely never see Adelaide again. No doubt she had no wish to when she'd made it clear how much she despised the girl she'd been forced to acknowledge as her own.

Her revenge had been malignant.

A tweeny bringing in the coal squeaked with shock when Tristan swung round from the fireplace at her entrance. His expression must have been as black as his thoughts.

'Sorry to disturb you, m'lord. I'll come back later.'

'That won't be necessary. I'm going out.'

He knew now what he had to do. He scribbled a note that he would be out for some hours which he thrust into the butler's hand. Barking had arrived at his summons, smoothing his sleep-tousled hair as he took in Tristan's instructions to order his lordship's carriage.

Fifteen minutes later Tristan was urging the coachman not to spare the horses, although in his heart he knew his mission to be a futile one.

And that he had no one but himself to blame.

He slept in the carriage. It was some hours' travel but he would stop only to change the horses and to refresh himself. The weather was fair and no mishap delayed him but although he made good time he arrived to find the docks deserted.

Of course the boat had departed long since and he was a fool to imagine he'd find Adelaide waiting for him.

It was only when confronted with the bleak, empty wharf and not a soul in sight that Tristan realised how much he'd hoped against hope for the happy ending; the reconciliation.

Nevertheless, he went through the motions, scanning the shoreline then trailing through nearby taverns and coffee houses in the vain hope of finding Adelaide, the wife he'd loved and had sent away.

Once again he cursed himself for a fool to think he'd given her no choice but to go with James. James offered her everything Tristan could not, or would not: love, passion … and her child. And hadn't Tristan reinforced that in those dreadful last moments?

Yet Adelaide had claimed she didn't want to go away with James. That she loved *Tristan*.

Returning to the most respectable inn, he bespoke a bed and lay down his weary body. He was heartsore and his conscience smote him as much as thoughts of Adelaide's crimes – those she'd committed and those committed against her.

When he awoke it was dark. He ordered food and a maid-servant brought him pigeon pie and a bottle of claret.

She was friendly and when she commented that there'd not been enough room on the boat for all the passengers his heart leapt. Perhaps Adelaide was still in England after all.

'The handsome dark-haired, poetic gentlemen and his wife? Oh yes, they left, m'lord,' she confirmed in answer to his enquiry. 'Goin' back to their child, they said. Course I remember 'em. I remember all the passengers.'

He'd not expected to be disappointed to such a degree by what he knew to expect – in fact had demanded. There'd been no talk of forgiveness or understanding on his part. He'd offered nothing to Adelaide that suggested he'd take her back.

He drank his claret in a mood of quiet reflection, wondering why he'd acted contrary to his character and sent her away with James in the heat of the moment rather than consider her desires once he'd heard her side of the story.

Allowing her to stay under the circumstances hadn't seemed possible at the time; but he should have known better.

He began to pace, the boards squeaking beneath his feet. If Tristan had been a more caring husband, he'd have taken Adelaide home with him to pack a trunk. Mrs Henley's confession, which had put an entirely new complexion on matters as they pertained to Adelaide, would have mitigated Adelaide's guilt, even if the fact remained that Charlotte was the child she'd borne James.

The truth twisted painfully in his gut. Adelaide had been a victim her entire life and Tristan had only compounded her suffering.

WHEN TRISTAN RETURNED to Bruton Street some hours later he received another shock. One that, had he been thinking more clearly, he might have considered.

Beatrice's venerable aunt was waiting in his drawing room. Declining his offer of refreshments, her stout, purple-clad form trembling with emotion like the peacock feather in her toque, Mrs Wells announced that Beatrice had eloped.

With James.

CHAPTER 34

One year later

Dusk was Tristan's favourite time of day.

He liked to savour a whisky and watch the long evening shadows from a wingback armchair positioned to take in the peaceful view from his study window.

He would imagine Addy was sitting opposite him, quietly stitching, or chatting with him about local matters. Occasionally, when a matter of more immediate interest roused the local community he'd wonder what her views might be, were she still with him, and able to offer them. The speeches and pamphlets he wrote lacked the style and flair that engaged the public's interest and he'd come to realise how great Adelaide's contribution had been to his political aspirations.

Another silent reproach from fate that the man who'd prided himself on his moderation his whole life should have been the architect of his own unhappiness through his hasty, immoderate actions.

He expected he'd continue to pay for the rest of his life, for his wife's image haunted him, day and night.

He realised he'd only begun to understand and appreciate the real Addy in the last weeks he'd known her when excited by her flashes of her vibrancy, and intrigued by the depth of her thinking.

At the time he'd imagined himself responsible for nurturing her growth.

He'd believed French renegades had marred the future he and Adelaide might have shared.

Now he realised Mrs Henley had done that, though, he acknowledged with painful clarity, he was more culpable than anyone for sealing her unhappiness.

He'd been blind to so much that was happening in front of his nose and when the obvious could no longer be ignored he'd withheld exactly what Addy had needed her whole life: the reassurance that she was better than she believed. Better than the trollop Mrs Henley painted her.

Tristan's directive that she leave in the dead of night with James had given her absolutely no choice in her future except to run away.

To simply disappear without trace.

ONE PARTICULARLY BEAUTIFUL evening Tristan dispensed with routine and instead focussed his attention on the dispatches he'd received regarding the growing unrest amongst mill workers of a factory two hours north of where he lived. Generally he'd not rush off on a whim but it was the first anniversary of the night he'd sent Addy away and he was desperate for something to distract him.

He felt he should investigate the matter for himself and hear the workers' grievances as it was just another example of the sort of agitation that was becoming endemic.

Barking looked at him with mild disapproval but said

nothing as Tristan arranged for his trunk to be strapped to the carriage. No doubt his butler would confess his grave misgivings about the master when he convened in the servants' hall that evening. Tristan knew the servants gossiped; that they said he'd not been the same since his wife had left him.

For a long time he'd held out hope, living on a precipice of expectation that he'd turn and find Addy on the threshold, perhaps watching him with a quiet fearfulness that he'd put to rest by the unequivocal joy of his welcome.

Indeed, when he'd learned that Addy had not gone with James, he'd experienced hope and joy to a degree unprecedented in his measured life.

When she did not return, Tristan still held out hope.

Regardless of Addy's feelings for him, he assumed financial necessity would force her back. After all, how was a woman with a new child going to support herself?

But there had been no communication.

He'd located James and quizzed him but James, apparently, was as in the dark as Tristan, though he conveyed nothing of his true feelings regarding Adelaide.

He was now living in Spain with Beatrice whom he'd married shortly after their arrival on the continent, and who had just had their first child, a son.

James reported being content and proud of his son and heir. As if it might be some consolation, his letter had included details of Adelaide's refusal to accompany James; of her declaration that her heart belonged to Tristan and nothing would induce her to go with James.

But where she *had* gone remained a mystery.

Weeks had turned into months and now, on this, the first anniversary, Tristan had to accept Addy wasn't coming back.

And that it was his fault.

THE JOURNEY that was supposed to take three hours was only half complete when the carriage axle snapped while traversing a deep rut in the road.

While his coachman Tom went for the wheelwright in the closest town, Tristan went for a walk. It was a picturesque part of the world. A pleasant wooded area drew him from across the common and he found a flat rock where he sat and ran his hand through the clear waters of the little stream that burbled past.

He'd expended so much energy on his search for Adelaide he was exhausted. Emotionally and physically drained. Advertisements in the local news-sheets had yielded nothing but a spate of bogus claims, clearly in the hopes of a reward. He'd had Adelaide's portrait reproduced in a small, transportable version which he took with him everywhere and showed at any opportunity in the hopes it might flush out someone who recognised her. This, however, had resulted in nothing but desperate anticipation followed by crushing disappointment on multiple occasions.

Lord but he missed her. His heart felt as raw as it did when the full extent of her betrayal had sunk it. Worse was learning the full set of circumstances, though this had only become clear, in snatches, as time passed.

Addy had loved James long before she'd met Tristan. Her mother had concocted the lie that had forced Adelaide into years of pretending to be an invalid when the truth was so different.

Mrs Henley had regulated Adelaide's moods and humours with varying amounts of laudanum. Tristan had taken the list Kitty had given him of the concoctions Mr Mendelssohn had supplied and discovered that the apothecary had seen Adelaide only once. Mrs Henley had been the customer and her questions regarding quantities and doses had specifically outlined a patient she wished to sedate for various lengths of time and to varying degrees.

Adelaide had begged Tristan not to send her away with James, and even when she'd learned being with James would reunite her with the child she'd thought dead, she'd still resisted going with the man she'd once loved. The father of her first child. Perhaps of her second, also, a child that would now be nearly four months old.

Was it a girl or a boy? Did it have James's chocolate-brown hair and dark eyes, or Tristan's pale colouring?

The need to know ate away at him, yet whatever it looked like, Tristan would take Adelaide back – and claim the child as his – in a heartbeat if he only had the chance.

So why hadn't she come back?

Tristan had to face the unpalatable truth: he had made it abundantly clear that he was not a man to forgive those guilty of morally reprehensible acts and Adelaide was not prepared to endure a marriage poisoned by low regard.

Removing his hand from the water, Tristan rose and headed back to check on progress. As he topped the small hill by the road he saw the wheelwright rising to his feet, his work done.

'So you's brought the picture wot the squire's son had painted, eh?' the man said after they'd exchanged greetings. At Tristan's look of enquiry the wheelwright stabbed his thumb in the direction of the trunk and Tristan saw the portrait of Adelaide was propped against it.

Tom must have mistaken the shock on Tristan's face for anger as he quickly explained they'd had to unload the carriage in order to work on the wheel, which accounted for why the picture was outside, on the grass.

'The squire's son?' Tristan frowned.

'Aye, that picture. It's for the squire's son. He's taken a right fancy to the young widow in town. Said he was going to get a likeness done.' He stepped towards the painting and bent down, resting his hands on his knees to peer more closely at it. 'A fair likeness, in't it?' He whistled through his teeth.

Quelling the inevitable hope that always resulted in trails that went cold, Tristan nevertheless quizzed him. 'You say the squire's son has been courting this widow?' It was not a pleasant thought, even if Addy *was* in a position to marry anyone.

'Won't have none o' him, though, m'lord, for all that the ladies have swooned over Master Orlando since he were out of swaddling clothes. That's why I were surprised she must 'ave agreed to get her picture painted, after all.'

'Where does the widow live?'

'With her infant and old Biddy Biddolph. She teaches sewing and reading to the lasses wot have parents that can afford such fancies, and she looks out sometimes for the wretches at the poor house with Master Orlando's saintly Mama.'

'Very admirable pursuits.'

The wheelwright smiled, a glint in his eye. 'She's an admirable woman. Came to the village in the middle of a storm just after she lost her husband. Wanted to find work straight away for he'd left her nothing, and then suddenly there was a young 'un to take care of. Some might ha' wondered at her story but no one thinks to wonder now. Always there to help. Ain't a better woman, most of the villagers agree.'

Tristan was breathing hard as he climbed into the carriage. Still, he managed to keep his voice steady as he ordered Tom to stop by the village square.

It wasn't much. More a hamlet with a few streets that

took some higgledy piggledy turns into the hills and woods that bordered it.

The largest building was the grey, forbidding structure of the poorhouse on the outskirts, its Elizabethan tower outlined against the grey sky.

It was here that he made his way, following the path pointed out to him by the wheelwright.

His hands were clammy and his chest tight when he arrived a little while later at a tiny cottage, its door festooned with dog roses, its shutters open to let in the fragrant afternoon breeze.

An old woman answered his knock and invited him into the parlour, grumbling as she led him through that she hoped he wasn't one of Master Orlando's cohorts.

'Then 'oo are ye, if I might ask?' she asked when Tristan assured he did not know Master Orlando.

'A friend of the widow's husband,' Tristan replied after some thought, jumping at the sound of a loud wail. He felt as if he'd been stabbed by a needle and his heart began to hammer. 'May I see the child?'

The old woman looked as if he'd gone queer in the attic. But she led him through to what Tristan instantly recognised by the familiar scent of orange flower water must be Addy's bed chamber, then over to a small crib in one corner.

Tristan took a cautious step, then halted. 'Is it a girl or a boy?'

The old woman screwed up her face. 'It ain't that hard to see for yerself.'

Tristan nodded, but still he could not bring himself to gaze upon the child.

Though what would it matter? He'd claim it as his, regardless of whether it had dark, brooding eyes and a mop of inky curls.

That is, if Addy would allow it.

The child stirred and Tristan clenched his hands, the sound of his rapid heartbeat loud in his ears.

Finally, he looked over the top.

'It's a girl!' *A daughter*, he nearly said, as he worked to contain the feeling that coursed through him.

Staring up at him was a child with a pink and white cherubic face, blue eyes and a mop of fair curls. Not brown eyes, or inky black curls, but the white blonde curls that had crowned all the infants in Tristan's family.

His first smile of a year took him by surprise, stretching unused muscles around his mouth, instantly quelling the child's grizzling. The angry little face creased into a gummy smile in response and it raised two clenched fists.

'Hello, little lass.' Emotion choked his greeting. Heart hammering, he turned and asked the old woman where he'd find the child's mother.

'At the workhouse, sir.' She, too, was smiling her first concessionary smile as she picked up the baby, adding, 'I think little Victoria likes you.'

HE TOOK the shortest route possible. Over the stile he leapt, hurrying down a steep, narrow street that stank of the refuse that ran down the middle.

By a stand of giant elms he found himself confronted by the huge wooden gates of the forbidding workhouse, which must have served as a garrison in earlier days. He gave his name, invented a plausible reason for being there, and gained access.

Stepping into the building that represented to its inhabitants the forfeiture of all hope, a terrible chill permeated his bones. The damp, dark walls seemed to close in on him, like a prison, and he shuddered to think of those who lived out their days in such an environment for no other reason than that they could not earn an honest living.

He'd written speeches that decried such inhumanity yet he'd never visited such a place.

Guilt needled him once more as he recalled Adelaide's gift for imbuing the dry language of his nevertheless sincere concerns with a heartfelt poignancy that had touched the hearts of those who'd received it.

What a jewel she was, yet he'd failed to realise it. Intelligent as she was beautiful, she'd hidden her true nature beneath a mantle of studied control.

His throat was dry but his hands clammy as he began to walk the lonely corridor. Was he any closer to finding her? And if indeed she were here, would she come back with him?

The fear she would refuse was like a physical pain he was only just able to endure, yet while there was hope, he would keep walking.

Still, he wasn't sure he'd survive it if she said her love had died with his inability to acknowledge the trials she'd endured and the love she maintained in the face of them.

Tristan turned into another cold, damp passage. Human misery was manifest everywhere he looked, from the malnourished faces that peered furtively at him from beneath ugly, grubby bonnets to the sound of stones being crushed and the distant wails that reverberated throughout the corridors.

The setting could not have been a greater contrast from the dazzling surroundings where Adelaide had glittered, always appearing to such advantage.

He tried to breathe evenly. He was so close. She was here, he was sure of it; could feel it.

Yet what if she no longer loved him?

'Can I help you, sir?' A tall, bony servant holding two pails of dirty water appeared around a corner.

'I'm looking for someone.' He tried to keep his tone level. This was a place where hope would rarely be repaid. 'A red-haired woman. A very beautiful woman.'

The servant gave him a strange look but beckoned him to follow her. Beauty must stand out in a place like this.

She led him down a series of corridors, all equally dark, the faces of the wretches he passed equally bleak, until she opened the door to a large, sun-filled room, its walls decorated with various childish attempts at decoration.

Before leaving him, she jerked her thumb in the direction of a cluster of young children seated on the cold stone floor in the far corner of the cavernous room. On a chair, facing them with her back to him, sat a woman, reading aloud. He couldn't see her hair for it was covered by a grey bonnet, but the way she carried herself, proud and erect, and the sweep of her neck, left him in no doubt.

Tristan stepped forwards and the children raised their heads to look at him though their storyteller didn't falter. Her voice made Tristan's heart sing. Clear and lovely, it was Addy at her most vibrant, bringing joy and adventure into the grey existence of these children through her tale of courage and hope.

It took a moment before she realised she'd lost the attention of her young pupils. Lowering her book, she rose, slowly. As always, with grace. Then, as if sensing his presence, she stilled for a moment.

Carefully, she turned to face him.

Tristan swallowed, too afraid to speak until he could read something of what was written on her face. God, he wanted her to want him still.

Needed her to forgive him.

The blank expression she perhaps cultivated for a demanding workhouse matron flickered for a moment before recognition transformed her features. He heard her sharp intake of breath as she took a step forward, faltering as uncertainty replaced her moment's elation.

So much was contained in the depths of her moss-green eyes. So much pain and endurance.

But most of all, hope. He could see it reflected there; the hope that he'd come to find her, not just to see her.

But it was Tristan who had to bridge the final distance. To show her what was truly in his heart.

To embrace the happiness the future promised as he embraced his wife.

'Why did you not return to me, Addy?' he whispered into her hair. Her warm, soft body fitted perfectly against his, pulsing with life and vitality, imbuing him with hope anew as she clung to him.

'You sent me away, Tristan.' Her voice was thick with pain. 'You had every reason to do so. I betrayed you, so how could I remain? How could I come back to you, after what I'd done?'

'That's not why I sent you away.' He forced the words out, though the guilt remained. 'You were in no position to make decisions if you didn't know about Charlotte.'

She stiffened, stepping out of his embrace; facing him with wary caution. 'You gave me no choice, Tristan. Yet I couldn't go with James, no, not even after he told me about Charlotte.' She drew in a shuddering breath and closed her eyes. 'Not when I didn't love him.'

Tristan cursed his wrong- footedness; the high handed-ness that had cheated him of the past year of his life. Of both their lives.

Once again, he'd claimed the moral high ground when he had no right. 'Come home with me, Addy.' He heard the pleading in his voice and didn't care. Just as he didn't care that more than a dozen small faces watched them with curiosity. 'Please, Addy. We'll fetch little Victoria—'

'You've seen Victoria?' she cut in sharply.

He nodded. 'I have, and she's the spitting image of my niece when she was a baby.'

He hoped this might soften some of her tenseness, just as a wave of fear washed over him that a year was a long time; and certainly long enough for a beautiful, supposedly abandoned widow, to have formed other affections.

Dear Lord — he exhorted the heavens, silently — *let me be in time for a second chance.*

Adelaide glanced about her, at the room of expectant little faces trained upon them, then back at Tristan.

'Why do you want me to come back?'

He could barely hear her, though he hoped that he'd not misinterpreted the pain in her tone; as if she hung upon his answer.

He lowered his voice to a whisper, glancing from the children to the face of the woman he loved above all else, as he replied, 'Because my life is worthless without you.'

Still the tense, fearfulness did not leave her. 'What about the scandal? The wife who abandoned you? A new baby?'

His heart expanded; for her willingness to consider his reputation before her … happiness? But mostly on account of the hope he heard in her voice, despite her uncertainty.

He shrugged. 'There is nothing that cannot be overcome, Addy, my love.' Slowly he put out his hand, gently clasping her wrist and drawing her to him. "I don't care how much you protest, I'm taking you home, Addy, where we can discuss this in warmth and comfort. Home, where Mrs Henley no longer lives and where you are owed more explanations than anyone.'

Her gentle shudder reverberated through him and he heard the children's collective gasp as Tristan cupped the back of her head and brought her close until his mouth gently covered hers in the briefest of kisses.

'You don't know how much I've longed for this moment,' she whispered against his lips as she rested her hands lightly on his chest. 'When I dared to dream.'

She drew back, and Tristan saw his own longing reflected in her beautiful, wide-set green eyes.

Renewed urgency fired him as he squeezed both her hands before letting them go.

'Come, Adelaide. Say your farewells to the children and let us fetch our daughter. Come home with me so we can talk of the future, and reconcile the past.'

'I am forgiven?'

'Can you forgive *me*? is the question I would have answered.' He smiled at the flare in her eyes, then waited as she directed her pupils to recite their alphabet for the dark-haired woman who'd entered the room and taken over at Adelaide's behest.

'Forgive you? For sending me away with —' she began as they traversed the cold, damp corridor.

But Tristan shook his head, putting his finger to her lips and pointing to the carriage waiting outside the front door.

'You have another daughter and I would not have denied you the happiness of knowing her. Hush,' he whispered, wiping away the tears that spilled from her eyes. 'You chose me over James and, in doing so, granted me more joy than I deserve.'

The coachman had leapt from the box and was now putting down the step.

Tristan took his wife's small hand in his and helped her into the comfortable interior. She seemed overcome, and the tense hope that radiated through her was exactly what he felt.

'There is so much to tell you, Addy, and so much for you to forgive, now that I understand the extent of your suffering.'

She gave a little gasp as he settled himself beside her; and as she leaned her head against his shoulder and closed her eyes, the weight of the past months seemed suddenly to slip from his shoulders as he murmured, 'Let us return home to Deer Park, Addy, where you and I can begin again…'

He wasn't certain how to go on, until she supplied, upon a soft sigh, 'To love each other as we would wish and without interference.'

THE END

ALSO BY BEVERLEY OAKLEY

The Daughters of Sin series follows the intertwining lives and sibling rivalry of Lord Partington's two nobly born - and two illegitimate - daughters as they compete for love during several London Seasons.

With Hetty and Araminta both falling for men on opposing sides of a dastardly plot that is being investigated by Stephen Cranbourne, now a secret agent in the Foreign Office, there's lashings of skullduggery and intrigue bound up in the central romance.

What Readers are Saying About the Series which is now available as a complete Box Set.

"...lies, misdeeds, treachery, and romance. What an impressive story! Ms. Oakley has a unique way of telling her stories, bringing unknown heroes/ heroines into the spotlight, as they navigate a world of espionage, and intrigue, all while trying to survive and find their HEA. Magnificent and mesmerizing!" ~ **Amazon reader**

"Full of secrets, murders, intrigues and you feel you know the characters and want to strangle some of them, especially Araminta!!! I have since read all in the series and can't wait for Book 5... This is a series I will read again and again." ~ **Amazon reader**

Below is the order of the books:

Book 1: Her Gilded Prison
Book 2: Dangerous Gentlemen
Book 3: The Mysterious Governess
Book 4: Beyond Rubies
Book 5: Lady Unveiled: The Cuckold's Conspiracy

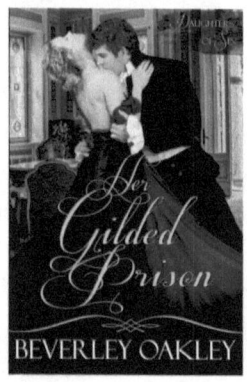

She was determined to secure the succession, he was in it for the pleasure. Falling in love was not part of the arrangement.
*** When dashing twenty-five-year-old Stephen Cranbourne arrives at the estate he will one day inherit, it's expected he will make a match with his beautiful second cousin, Araminta. But while proud, fiery Araminta and her shy, plain sister, Hetty, parade their very different charms before him, it's their mother, Sybil, a lonely and discarded wife, who evokes first his sympathy and then stokes his lustful fires.

Shy, plain Hetty was the wallflower beneath his notice...until a terrible mistake has one dangerous, delicious rake believing she's the "fair Cyprian" ordered for his pleasure. *** Shy, self-effacing Henrietta knows her place—in her dazzling older sister's shadow. She's a little brown peahen to Araminta's bird of paradise. But when Hetty mistakenly becomes embroiled in the Regency underworld, the innocent debutante finds herself shockingly compromised by the dashing, dangerous Sir Aubrey, the very gentleman her heart desires. And the man Araminta has in her cold, calculating sights. Branded an enemy of the Crown, bitter over the loss of his wife, Sir Aubrey wants only to lose himself in the warm, willing body of the young "prostitute" Hetty. As he tutors her in the art of lovemaking, Aubrey is pleased to find Hetty not only an ardent student, but a bright, witty and charming companion. Despite a spoiled Araminta plotting for a marriage offer and a powerful political enemy damaging his reputation, Aubrey may suffer the greatest betrayal at the hands of the little "concubine" who's managed to breach the stony exterior of his heart.

*Two beautiful sisters – one illegitimate, the other nobly born –
compete for love amidst the scandal and intrigue of a Regency
London Season. Lissa Hazlett lives life in the shadows. The
beautiful, illegitimate daughter of Viscount Partington earns
her living as an overworked governess while her vain and
spoiled half sister, Araminta, enjoys London's social whirl as its
most feted debutante. When Lissa's rare talent as a portraitist
brings her unexpectedly into the bosom of society – and into the
midst of a scandal involving Araminta and suspected English
traitor Lord Debenham – she finds an unlikely ally: charming
and besotted Ralph Tunley, Lord Debenham's underpaid,
enterprising secretary. Ralph can't afford to leave the employ of
the villainous viscount much less keep a wife but he can help
Lissa cleverly navigate a perilous web of lies that will ensure
everyone gets what they deserve. THE MYSTERIOUS
GOVERNESS is Book 3 in the Daughters of Sin series but can
be read as a stand-alone as it features the sibling rivalry
between Viscount Partington's two nobly-born and three
illegitimate daughters from a completely different perspective.
Heat rating: sensual. The Daughters of Sin series has been
described as a Regency-set 'Dynasty'.*

Fame. Fortune. And finally a marriage proposal! Book 4 of the Daughters of Sin series introduces Miss Kitty La Bijou, celebrated London actress, mistress to handsome Lord Nash and the unacknowledged illegitimate daughter of Viscount Partington. Having escaped her humble beginnings, Kitty has found fame, fortune and love, but the respectability she craves eludes her. When she stumbles across Araminta, her legitimate half-sister, on the verge of giving birth just seven months after marrying dangerous Viscount Debenham, Kitty realises respectability is no guarantee of character or happiness. But helping Araminta has unwittingly embroiled Kitty in a scandalous deception involving a ruthless brothel madam, a priceless ruby necklace and the future heir to a dazzling fortune. And when Kitty finally receives an offer of marriage she must choose. Respectability or love?

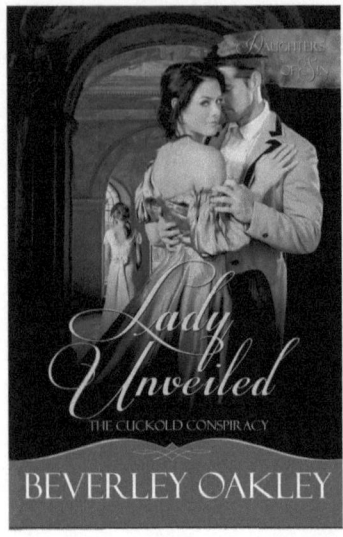

Kitty has the love of the man of her dreams but as London's most acclaimed actress and a member of the demimondaine, she accepts she can never be kind and handsome Lord Silverton's lawful wedded wife. When Kitty comes to the aid of shy, accident-prone and kind-hearted Octavia Mandelton, her sense of justice leads to her making the most difficult decision of her life: Give up the man she loves for the sake of honour. For Octavia is still betrothed to Lord Silverton who'd rescued Kitty in dramatic circumstances only weeks before. Cast adrift, Kitty joins forces with her sister, Lissa, a talented artist posing as a governess in order to bring to justice a dangerous spy, villainous Lord Debenham. Complicating matters is the fact Debenham is married to their half-sister, vain and beautiful Araminta. However, Araminta has a dark secret which only Kitty knows and which she realizes she is duty-bound to expose if she's to achieve justice and win happiness for deserving Lissa and Lissa's enterprising sweetheart, Ralph Tunley, long-suffering secretary to Lord Debenham. All seems set for a happy ending when Kitty tumbles into mortal danger. A danger from which only a truly honorable man can save her. A man like Silverton who must now make the hardest choice of his life if he's to live with his conscience.

Daughters of Sin Box set

Daughters of Sin series
Her Gilded Prison
Dangerous Gentlemen
The Mysterious Governess
Beyond Rubies
Lady Unveiled: The Cuckold Conspiracy

Hearts in Hiding series
The Duchess and the Highwayman
The Bluestocking and the Rake
Duchess of Seduction
The Countess and the Cavalier

Scandalous Miss Brightwells series
Rake's Honour
Rogue's Kiss
The Wedding Wager
The Accidental Elopement
The Honourable Fortune Hunter
The Courtship Caper
The Wilful Widow

Fair Cyprians of London
Saving Grace
Forsaking Hope
Keeping Faith

Wedding Violet
Christmas Charity
Loving Lily

Georgian Mystery/Romance series
Wicked Wager
Her Valentine's Secret

Scandalous: Three Daring Charades
Lady Olivia's Butterfly
Lady Sarah's Redemption
Lady Rose's Secret

Africa novella
Okavango Angel